18.17 Alll

D0428948

GALE
CENGAGE Learning®

LIBRARY OF CONGRESS CATALOGING-IN-PUBLICATION DATA

Names: Mulligan, Gina L., author.
Title: Remember the ladies / by Gina L. Mulligan.
Description: First edition. | Waterville, Maine : Five Star, 2016.
Identifiers: LCCN 2015046114 (print) | LCCN 2016006935 (ebook) | ISBN 9781432831769 (hardcover) | ISBN 1432831763 (hardcover) | ISBN 9781432831714 (ebook) | ISBN 1432831712 (ebook)
Subjects: LCSH: Women in politics—Fiction. | Lobbyists—Washington (D.C.)—Fiction. | Women—United States—History—19th century—Fiction. | Women—Suffrage—Fiction. | Women's rights—Fiction. | Political fiction. | GSAFD: Historical fiction.
Classification: LCC PS3613.U453 R46 2016 (print) | LCC PS3613.U453 (ebook) | DDC 813/.6—dc23
LC record available at http://lccn.loc.gov/2015046114

First Edition. First Printing: May 2016
Find us on Facebook– https://www.facebook.com/FiveStarCengage
Visit our website– http://www.gale.cengage.com/fivestar/
Contact Five Star™ Publishing at FiveStar@cengage.com

Printed in the United States of America
1 2 3 4 5 6 7 20 19 18 17 16

REMEMBER THE LADIES

REMEMBER THE LADI

GINA L. MULLIGAN

FIVE STAR

A part of Gale, Cengage Learning

GALE
CENGAGE Learning·

Farmington Hills, Mich • San Francisco • New York • Waterville, Maine
Meriden, Conn • Mason, Ohio • Chicago

ACKNOWLEDGMENTS

My appreciation to editors Hazel Rumney and Tiffany Schofield at Five Star Publishing for their confidence in my work. Thanks also to my enthusiastic agent, Holly Lorincz, for taking on all of my projects with a smile. To Mary Strobel, I can't thank you enough for believing in me, for pushing me, for holding my hand, and making me a better writer. You're truly special to me. I must also give a shout-out to my talented writers group for your honesty and heart, and to the dedicated Girls Love Mail volunteers who keep my charity running while I'm writing. I wouldn't be here today without encouragement and love from my family and friends. And to Grant, my wonderful husband, sounding board, proofreader, quipster, dedicated fan, and the most excellent person I know, I couldn't do this without you. My gratitude runs deep.

"Remember the Ladies"
Abigail Adams to John Adams while he was drafting the
Declaration of Independence

★ ★ ★ ★ ★

PART ONE:
1861

★ ★ ★ ★ ★

CHAPTER ONE

Amelia opened her eyes and found herself on a riverbank; smears of mud ruined the new skirt Mother had bought her for the big family trip. Staying clean during the carriage ride meant a molasses square when they reached home. Now she wouldn't get a treat. Tears slid down her cheeks as she saw the empty road above and, below, the carriage wheels spinning midair like windmills. Amelia pushed herself upright until she sat with her legs stretched out in front of her and blinked against the moonlight. "A bright night with a full moon—good for traveling," Mother had said, but Amelia didn't see her parents. The top of the carriage sank into the edge of the black jagged water, glare from the whitecaps like eyes watching her. She didn't see her mother and scrambled to her feet. Pain seared through her ankle and she cried out a shrill harmony to the Montana wind, the kind of gusts her father called "widow makers."

Amelia shouted for her father that she didn't want to play hide and seek. She wasn't supposed to go near the water because river currents carried away small children. A thud made her jump and she turned to find a log lodged against a massive rock. Amelia rubbed her eyes. Not a rock. Her narrow body trembled before her mind settled on what she already knew. Amelia slapped her hands over her face and shook her head. She wanted to tuck herself under her mother's arms and feel her father's dry kiss on her forehead. Amelia bit her bottom lip and pulled her hands from her eyes. Daisy rested on her side, still tethered to the front of the carriage, motionless like the rattlers Father hit with his shovel. Dead. Amelia screamed for her mother and ran toward the water.

"For the last time, hold your tongue, child." The woman wore a black cape over her head and wouldn't say where Amelia's parents had gone. A man in work pants had carried Amelia up the riverbank, wrapped her in a thick, wool blanket, and set her in the back of a hay wagon. Then the caped woman appeared and wrapped bandages around her wet, swollen ankle with calloused, gnarled hands, the backs a web of blue veins. Amelia imagined her mother's soft, gentle hands and asked again.

"We're taking you to your parents. Stop your blubbering," the lady said. The man patted Amelia's shoulder.

Amelia hadn't meant to fall asleep but awoke with a start when the wagon stopped. In the dim moonlight she saw a flat, pale building that glowed at the edges and watched fallen leaves swirl around bare trees, then huddle together at the base of a short stairway. She wished to see purple flowers like the ones she had at home.

"Hurry up, child."

The lady dragged her by the elbow to a wooden door with strips of pitted metal pressed across the front. She knocked, careful not to touch the dirty metal, and while they waited the lady licked her fingers and ran her moist hand across Amelia's wavy hairline. Amelia flinched, repulsed by the stranger's touch on her face. Then the door opened and Amelia smiled.

A fairy in white stood in the doorway, the features of her face blurred to a serene mask by the glow from a slim candle in her hand. The fairy motioned for them to come forward, then knelt down so Amelia saw her wide-set, pale eyes. "I'm Mistress Lucy," she said. "How old are you?"

Amelia held up four fingers just as her mother taught her.

Then the fairy nodded and stood. Amelia couldn't wait to tell her mother how well she'd done. Mother always kissed her on both cheeks when she acted like a proper lady.

The caped woman left and the fairy closed the door. "You must come with me now," she said.

Amelia followed the halo of light through the night corridor. Darkness circled around them and she felt puny and isolated against the pleading moans and a rhythmic thump that leaked through the walls. Amelia shuddered and stopped, but the fairy nudged her to keep her moving.

"I want my mother," Amelia said, tears spilling onto the bare cement floors.

"Tomorrow."

The fairy lifted the light and pointed to where Amelia could sleep for the night. She had never seen a bed with a roof.

"Can you change yourself?"

Amelia nodded.

"Then do so. A gown is there." She hovered the candle over the foot of the bed. "We will go over the rules in the morning."

The fairy turned to walk away but Amelia grabbed her knees and held tight. "Aren't you going to read me a story?"

Amelia felt her pause as her mother did when considering a request for an extra cookie or more time to play with her dolls. "We don't do that here," the woman said. She removed Amelia's hands with gentle force and left.

The room went dim and pulsed with the sounds of coughing and squeaking metal. Amelia sensed there were many others, felt the moist air from each of their deep exhales, and then, when she bumped her sore ankle on the frame and cried out, someone shouted for her to be quiet. Amelia scooted into the bed, the nightgown forgotten. Metal coils pressed through the pad, and the blanket, not any thicker than the rags her mother used to dry dishes, felt coarse and smelled of mildew.

13

Amelia closed her eyes to wish herself home, imagined the field behind their house where Mother hummed as she hung clothes on the line. She couldn't picture her mother or her house; Daisy's body lay in the water, her jaw agape in permanent disobedience against the metal bit. Amelia pressed her forearm against her mouth to muffle her sobs. She didn't want the people of the darkness to yell at her again and pulled the blanket over her head. The caped lady hadn't taken her to her mother and the woman in white, Mistress Lucy, had no magical powers. Real fairies read stories and rocked little girls to sleep when they were frightened. Amelia ached for her mother, a pain seared against her heart far worse than the sting in her ankle. If she stayed quiet and out of trouble, then her parents would find her. Tomorrow, the woman said. Tomorrow she'd see her parents and they'd take her home.

From the corner of the rectangular dining hall, Amelia sat alone at the end of a long row of tables and watched the other children while practicing her knots. Her father taught her how to tie granny knots each night after dinner while she sat on his lap and nuzzled her head under his chin. She'd found the scrap of rope lying in the hallway by the boy's workroom just a few days after Mistress Lucy told her that her parents were gone. That was four years earlier and the Mistress still used the word *gone* instead of *dead*, citing that no one had ever found the bodies of her parents. Amelia once tried the term "washed away," but she preferred to say her parents were dead. Death felt final and simple in a way she understood.

"She thinks she's a boy," Tom, eldest of the three Lathrop boys, said again.

Amelia kept her eyes down but heard the rolling laughter pass from boy to boy, could feel them pointing at her when Tom called her a ninny critter. Boys delighted in calling her names and she held back stinging tears by sheer will and the fact that crying made everything worse. Tears beckoned the persecutors as efficiently as the dinner bell. After four years of practice, she knew when to hold herself together and no longer responded when the older girls stole her meager portion of bread or yanked her braid so hard and often that she hid a small bald spot under a thick ribbon. As the boys poked Amelia's shoulder, she held tight to her rope, now frayed and dingy, and kept her eyes on the ground.

Clacking footsteps meant Mistress Lucy approached and the boys fled with a final round of cackling. Amelia raised her gaze and watched Mistress Lucy in her regulation long black skirt, stiff white blouse, and cameo pinned at her throat. Most of the other children had left to step outside before afternoon classes and the unadorned ashen walls closed in tight around them. The plain hall built to serve plain meals to one hundred children in fact fed two hundred souls so pressed together that the head lice passed back and forth as easily as the salt shakers. Children ate three meals a day in the windowless room, two during the ration years, and in the winter when the Montana gales shook the uneven metal beds of anxious little girls as if wanting to destroy every last unclaimed mongrel, Amelia appreciated the inner sanctum away from the haunting gusts. She dreamed of someday living far away from the evil wind that carried away her parents and carefree childhood.

"Haven't you worn out that rope yet?" the Mistress asked.

Amelia held Mistress Lucy's stare, not looking at her own hands as she looped the rope and pulled the ends through.

"You're getting quite good," Mistress Lucy said as she sat down across from Amelia. "Do you feel like speaking today?"

Amelia didn't have much to say so she shook her head and the Mistress smiled, the grin that tried to show concern while still maintaining a cool distance. Older girls, the ones who slept

15

at the top of the bunks stacked three high, explained that the secret rules were far more important than teeth brushing and plate clearing. "The Mistresses never get too close to us. Too dangerous," Rachel said as Amelia crawled into her bottom bed the first week of her arrival. Rachel slept on the highest, above Miranda, who called herself the meat in the bunk bed sandwich. Dormitory life focused on order: a pecking order, an order of conduct, and a schedule of when to rise, dress, eat, and sleep. The bells, bed checks, class assignments, and straight lines kept the simmering external chaos at bay. Tying knots kept Amelia's inner turmoil in check.

"I have a new knot to show you," Mistress Lucy said. She pulled out her own length of rope and tugged so the rope went taut. "You don't have to talk, just watch."

The Mistress looped the rope to form a figure eight, then pulled so each end stuck out in opposite directions. "It's called a Becket knot. Pretty fancy. Want me to show you again?"

Amelia shook her head, then tied the new knot.

"You learn everything so quickly. Very impressive."

Amelia appreciated the compliment but kept her expression guarded, private. The sound of Matron Chamberlain's forced cough drew both of their attention and they looked up at the matron standing over them with her cool expression. "Mistress Lucy," the matron said, "I've been looking for you. Hello, Amelia. How are you today?"

Matron Chamberlain, dressed to match Mistress Lucy minus the brooch, spent much of her day in long, purposeful strides through the hallways to straighten collars and pick stray threads from skirts. Gray strands, which Amelia wondered why she didn't pluck like the errant threads, ran through the thick, dark hair she kept in a tight knot at the base of her head. Rumors circulated about what dangerous creatures the matron kept trapped in her hair to torment rowdy children.

"Why isn't she with . . . ?" The matron sighed, then seized the rope from Amelia's grasp, leaving a long scratch on her palm. "Enough of this," the matron said. "You will not get more rope or tie any more knots. You are to focus on your studies and spend time with the other girls. If you do not obey, you will clean the stalls for a month. Are we clear?"

Amelia's stomach tensed with rage beneath her polite nod. The matron knew her horrific fear of the horse stalls, or at least the images they evoked.

The matron swept away with Mistress Lucy on her heels. Amelia waited until they neared the door, then followed them through the empty hall and stopped when she heard the women in the corridor.

"Why were you so harsh with Amelia about the rope? Why now?" Mistress Lucy's voice shuddered as if she fought back tears of her own.

"I know I seem insensitive, Lucy, but we have to teach them to be self-sufficient. Once they leave here, they're on their own. The best we can do is to help them prepare. Amelia is an intelligent girl, but we must force her to untie herself, quite literally, from her past. She needs to move on, study, and make friends. This is for the best. We'll not discuss it again."

The echo of the conversation surrounded Amelia. She couldn't remember the cadence or pitch of her mother's voice, and she'd long forgotten her touch other than a lingering sensation of warmth down her back as she drifted to sleep. Mistress Lucy had no children of her own, and the matron's two boys had grown and left the area. Amelia couldn't see the matron as anyone's mother, but then Amelia had no reference, only random fragments like the bright spots that lingered after glancing at the sun. Without her knots, Amelia knew her father would slip away, too, and she'd lose the only male figure in her life. She balled her hands into fists, pressing her thin, sharp nails into where her palm stung from the matron's scratch. The physical pain helped push away the deeper wounds that brought the tears. She wouldn't cry. Tears always made everything worse.

Amelia rolled over and flopped her arm over her ears. She heard the faint crying again, like a sick cat, and she didn't want to wake from the fun of her dream where bright characters led interesting lives. The cries faded as Amelia ran down a rolling green hillside toward a group of people who danced in circles and sang a familiar melody. Another cry, louder, and Amelia looked about the meadow for the cat. None of the others noticed the noise; they continued with their merriment undisturbed and happy. No longer a cat, Amelia thought; the cry came from an infant. A starving baby. Amelia woke with a start; newborn season had begun again.

In the fall months, the nursery flooded with unwanted new cargo that needed constant and delicate attention. Starting at age ten, all of the girls took turns caring for the newborns, which meant missing class time, and Amelia didn't care much for the smells or distraction from her studies. "You're not as naturally maternal as the other girls," the matron once said as Amelia struggled to swaddle a flailing little boy. Amelia nodded, careful to keep her head lowered. She didn't care about motherhood; the notion felt distant and impractical. But how many times did the matron or teachers point out her differences from the other girls—smarter, taller, quieter, even prettier—when no one could hear? She wanted to be like the appropriate girls who enjoyed sewing and rarely asked a question in class. Life seemed easier within the pack instead of circling the edge for scraps.

Candlelight bobbed down the hallway as the teachers on watch gathered to take in another wayward soul. Several of the girls muttered with excitement as Amelia slipped deeper into her bed and tried to conjure the green meadow of her dreams.

If she lacked a natural maternal instinct, then let those with such gifts do their best. And if the girls had to learn to care for infants, why didn't the boys? Everyone ignored the simple notion that children, the lucky ones, have both mothers and fathers.

Needlepoint and knitting required that the girls sit on short stools with their full, long skirts arranged to hide their legs as they practiced running stitches and buttonholes. Colorful yarns and threads draped across laps and onto the floor, and some of the girls made yarn flowers to put in their hair. Amelia wore a crude, green rose tucked behind her ear and sat perched like a hawk just before the evening hunt. She'd already finished embroidering a blue jay on her decorative bib collar for Sunday church with a steady, competent stitch and waited for Mrs. Pramble, the home economics teacher, to check her work. Fifty teenage girls clamored for attention so Mrs. Pramble had little time for each student.

"Fine," Mrs. Pramble said to what Amelia held up for inspection. Amelia nodded, then asked to be excused. "I have the feminine curse," Amelia said.

Mrs. Pramble tapped her thin walking stick on the floor. "Young ladies, how many times must I tell you not to use the word 'curse'? You are 'taking care of lady business' or some equally ladylike phrase."

Amelia cringed from the lack of privacy and her own mistake in using the wrong excuse to slip unseen from class. All of the girls looked up and several laughed and pointed.

After a quick apology to Mrs. Pramble for her language, Amelia ducked out of the classroom, pulled the green yarn from her hair, and tossed the flower over her shoulder as she trotted down the hallway toward the boys' classroom. Boys and girls learned the basics of reading and arithmetic together as one class until the more advanced curriculums and pressure for modern decorum forced the separation of the sexes until emancipation at age eighteen. The girls read poetry and literature, studied basic bookkeeping to run a household, learned to make clothing, and practiced cooking skills. Boys studied mathematics, science, philosophy, literature, and economics. Where the girls played with colorful yarn, the boys swirled vibrant liquids in glass beakers and slid specimens under microscopes. Harold, one of the boys who gave Amelia the required penny to sit next to her at dinner, showed her his textbooks. In stark contrast to the orthodox rhetoric peddled in the yearly almanacs and home journals in the girl's rooms, Harold's thick, leather-bound volumes brimmed with ingenuity.

During good weather, boys spent an hour each day outside with balls and kites. They walked through the yard on crude stilts and ran about shouting as the girls watched through the windows from their perches. Frolic caused injuries, which left unsightly scars and prospective husbands wanted pristine skin. With all of the boys outside in the fresh air, Amelia slipped into the boys' classroom to the bookshelf. Though it teemed with bound books, Amelia surprised herself by finding just what she wanted within a few moments. She felt luck on her side as she tucked *Eddleburg's Basics of Law* between her petticoat and skirt, then held the book against her thigh. She listened at the door. When she didn't hear anything, she opened the door and stepped into the hall.

"With me, right now," Matron Chamberlain said. "And give me what you've taken, Amelia."

Amelia removed the book with care; she didn't want to damage the edges. "I was just going to borrow it for the night," Amelia said.

The matron's long, thin fingers, the color of chalk, motioned for Amelia to follow her and Amelia knew where they were headed. She knew where the miniature statue of Saint Christopher sat on the shelf under the window and could draw the disproportionate silhouette of the cowboy looking out at the barren plains in the amateur painting over the small stone fireplace. Matron called the painting a gift for her office but she never explained the patron saint of travel, an odd choice in deity given that the matron never left the orphanage grounds.

"You're starting a life of crime, it seems. How many books have you taken now?" the matron asked from behind her desk.

Amelia picked at the small hole in the cracked leather below the curl of the chair's arm. "I wasn't stealing. As I said, I had every intention of returning the book before anyone missed it."

"I remind you again that such material isn't appropriate for young ladies."

"Who says it's inappropriate?"

"Myself, the other teachers, the school's board of trustees. In just a year you leave us and I want you to understand that the world outside these protective walls has even more rules for you to follow. Rules are in place for a reason."

"Matron, if the rules are in place for a reason, is it fair to say that the reason is to keep girls ignorant? Why else do you and the trustees keep us from learning mathematics or science? Or do they believe we're incapable of understanding the material?"

The matron leaned back and laced her fingers under her chin. "That depends on what you believe makes a woman intelligent. Do you think that a woman who runs a good home is stupid? Must a woman know physics or chemistry to earn respect?"

Amelia often watched the fathers tour the infant room looking for a prodigy to carry on the family name. The men in their straw boaters and pressed waistcoats never wanted to see the girls even if their wives, always a step or two behind, repeatedly mentioned they should check the girls' nursery, just in case. *A little girl might be nice, too, darling.*

"What I think doesn't matter. Society sets the rules," Amelia said.

"But who makes up society?" the matron asked.

"Men."

"And women, Amelia. A society needs both genders to continue and thrive. No matter what your role in society, your responsibility is vital to the community as a whole. Without all of the parts, society can't function."

"Bull," Amelia blurted, then slapped her hand over her mouth. "Forgive me," she mumbled through her fingers.

The matron shook her head. "Soon enough we'll release you on the world. Until then, you are to watch your language and not steal any more books."

Amelia nodded. She had a stash that she could re-read to fill the time. She'd all but memorized the volume on medieval warfare. When Amelia rose, the matron came around her desk and stood in front of her.

"You will do well in this world, Miss Amelia Cooke, if you remember that finding a place doesn't necessarily mean making a place. Do you understand the difference?"

Instead of returning to class, Amelia went to the empty dorm room and sat on her bed. If she understood the matron's parting words, then she disagreed. She knew better than the matron, a woman who lived a small life in the confinement of her own making more to manage her fear of the world than help anyone. Amelia had no real place, not since the night her parents died. If she'd ever have a place where she fit, Amelia knew without question she'd have to make one for herself, by herself.

"We're going to miss you." Mistress Lucy handed Amelia her diploma and emancipation papers.

The mistress, matron, and a classroom of young children

exploring plant life with their teacher filled the front lawn of the orphanage.

"Good luck, Amelia. I wish you well," the matron said after she'd finished her mandatory speech about a bright future if Amelia worked hard and stayed out of the proverbial trouble.

Two boys fighting over who got to blow the wisps from a dandelion drew the matron's attention and she marched off yelling, "That's enough of that, the both of you."

"You won't soon forget her shouting," Mistress Lucy said. The mistress wore a light-blue skirt and white blouse for the special day. Delicate stray hairs fell loose from her chignon and she'd placed a white gardenia behind her ear. Amelia took a deep breath of the sweet scent.

"I don't suspect I'll forget much about this place," Amelia said.

The state required that all emancipated adults leave the orphanage within two weeks of turning eighteen. Amelia had counted down the days but now felt lost in her confused grief.

"It's normal to feel sad and scared," Mistress Lucy said.

"Who said I feel . . ."

Amelia saw the tears before the mistress could wipe them away with the back of her hand and then realized she'd never seen the mistress cry. The rims of her pale eyes turned red and she chewed her bottom lip like a small child waiting for punishment. The mistress's tears seemed fitting, foreign in the same way as Amelia's leaving what she knew. She had never traveled anywhere on her own, had never left the grounds without knowing she'd return at the end of the day. With only the name of her destination and a small idea of the work to come, Amelia felt nerves twitch in her gut. She'd told the other girls of her excitement, bragged about her foreseeable, even inevitable, grand adventures. In the light of the day with a coach rattling down the long drive, Amelia wanted to run back inside.

"Ignore me. I always blubber when one of mine leaves. I'm just so excited for you, Amelia, and all that you're going to accomplish." The mistress straightened and grinned. "Now, do you have all of the information?"

Mistress Lucy had found Amelia a job at a cotton mill and had arranged the travel and accommodations. "I have everything, mistress. Thank you again."

The children looked up from their plants to watch the driver stop the coach and load Amelia's lone trunk. All of her possessions, all of her memories, fit in one average-size travel trunk.

"This it, miss?" the driver asked Amelia as he would any adult. Amelia knew she looked the part of a grown woman, with a tall, shapely form commented on by the boys for years.

"Here," the mistress said. "I have something for you."

Amelia accepted a small box from Mistress Lucy and then lifted the lid. "I don't know what to say. I can't believe you kept this all these years," Amelia said.

Mistress Lucy seized Amelia, squeezed her around the shoulders, then set her upright. "Good luck, Amelia." The mistress patted Amelia's hands, then dashed inside and closed the door without looking back. The children had gone back to their work and Amelia stood beside the carriage that waited to take her on, take her away.

"Are you ready?" the driver asked.

Amelia didn't know but nodded and stepped into the carriage. Through the back window she saw fluffs of drifting dandelion seeds and watched the orphanage shrink until she saw only the dirt path and flatlands. On her lap she held Mistress Lucy's gift and felt the same surprise and delight when she opened it again. The knots she'd last tied were still in the rope, plus she saw a new knot like crossed fingers. The mistress had tied one last knot just for her.

Amelia closed her eyes and did nothing to stop her tears. No

one could see her now. She had nothing, no more help in a terrifying world shaped by the sort of attachments she'd never
had. A job at least meant she had a destination for the day, and
Amelia said a prayer for Mistress Lucy's good health. The carriage bumped and she flashed to the night the wind took her
parents and left her alone. Once again she'd have to start over
and, even in the bright sunshine of midday, Amelia saw the
cruel void of the deep, black waters. No longer a mere child,
and yet she feared what might sweep her away or perhaps cast
her adrift like the fragile dandelion florets carried by the wind,
never to be seen again, never to be missed by anyone.

CHAPTER TWO

After a year of sweeping up fiber dust, rat droppings, and the occasional dead rat, Amelia knew just what sort of grime hid in every corner of the Mabelvale Cotton Mill, including the sort who drank whiskey shots in the loading dock between shifts. The women without support, financial or otherwise, worked twelve-hour days alongside men who left the worst jobs for the ladies, like gleanings on the edge of a field. All female employees started pushing brooms, then moved up to either operate overgrown mechanical beasts with sharp teeth or haul enormous tubs filled with seed cotton across the factory floor, their floor-length black skirts scattering the piles of Amelia's menial work. Unmarried women also had the additional requirement of living in the factory's onsite dormitory. Most of the women complained about the cold water, meager meals, and rampant thieving that led to slapping fights after curfew. At first, Amelia felt right at home and the routine gave her a bit of comfort. Then boredom set in and she felt isolated by the monotony of the work and uneducated, small-minded co-workers with narrow perspectives on life. That the factory hid in the remoteness of Arkansas's backwoods did nothing to help Amelia's growing restlessness.

Opened in 1870, Mabelvale Cotton Mill had the first steam-powered loom in central Arkansas and was the hometown of the Mabelvale clan for two generations. The permanent residents of Mabelvale, all 95 of them, lived in small shacks along dirt roads more than four miles from Alexander, the nearest town with a general store, saloon, train stop, and Baptist church, whose preacher doubled as the barber. Little Rock, the largest nearby city, required a three-hour buggy ride, longer if the driver had a full jug of tarantula juice riding alongside on the box seat. *A buggy in the bog means a driver on the grog.* Those with some means and fortunate timing preferred the train to Little Rock, which ran much faster but only every other week.

The factory itself consisted of three tall square buildings: main plant, delivery bay, and storage. Constructed entirely of wood with pitched, barn-like roofs, the structures often caught fire during the scorching summer months so male workers doubled as the fire crew. To keep those living on the grounds safe, the matriarch of the family, Grandma Mabelvale, insisted on lath and plaster walls for the dormitory and paid for the exorbitant building costs out of her own personal funds. Amelia admired her intelligent forethought that created a protective barrier for the women and the townsfolk.

In the tepid spring weather of April, flowering trumpet weeds sprouted out of the corners of the buildings like an old man's ear hair. Along with the benefit of more pleasant co-workers, Amelia found relief in the gentle Arkansas breeze and so took her dinner tray outside to picnic with the ladies beneath the shortleaf pine trees, then dipped her feet in the small creek behind the loading bay. The scene reminded Amelia of a colorful prairie painting she'd seen on a postcard, the colors muted by a carefree brushstroke. The hint that life was not as relaxed as an artist's rendering came when the whistle sounded and the women shuffled back to their narrow existence easily contained within the dormitory walls.

Unlike at the orphanage, the factory dorm felt grand, almost luxurious, with just ten women in a large room and iron bunks only two high. With more space and fewer bodies, the inherent frenzy felt distant and Amelia could breathe, though she'd grown to hate the smell of tobacco. The middle-aged loader in the next bed, Baty, snuck out during the night to smoke cigarettes and by the morning whistle at four A.M., the whole area reeked.

The ritual of groans and cursing in the wee hours comforted Amelia as she tied up her boots. She always dressed before the others, then sat on the edge of her bunk watching the delicate shadows before dawn. The darkness created the illusion of solitude, and she found a calm she didn't have the rest of the day, especially with having to spend so much time with her assigned bunk mate, Vivian.

"I hate the dang whistles," Vivian said in a dry voice as she swung her legs over the edge of the top rail and dangled her feet so Amelia saw the holes in her stained, knee-high stockings.

Amelia thought the whistles a refreshing change from the orphanage's cowbell, which somehow rang in a dissonant chord. Like many of the women, Vivian began each morning listing her grievances like a prosecutor in front of a judge. The food tasted rancid, possibly even lethal; she'd had to patch her flimsy work blouse at least a dozen times; and the permanent mold in the bathing area had grown eyes like potatoes. During work time, Amelia did her best to steer her broom clear of Vivian's prattling, but after a dinner of tasteless boiled meat and potatoes, Vivian went on about the day's gossip until the evening whistle and lights out. Amelia responded with little more than a polite nod, for which Vivian seemed content, likely because Vivian chattered enough for the both of them.

"Dang whistles," Vivian said again as she hopped down from her bunk and landed in front of Amelia.

Amelia stood. Her sleek auburn hair, delicate features, and tall, womanly stature created a stunning contrast to Vivian's puny, boyish frame and mess of black curls, which bounced as

28

she walked. Even though Amelia stood five inches taller than Vivian, taller than most of the ladies, when Amelia shook her head at Vivian, the feisty girl lifted her chin, put her hands on her hips, and said, "What? You like it here?"

Liking had little to do with tolerating, a fact Amelia thought time Vivian should learn.

"You've been here six months already and you still don't understand. In a place like this, you need to know a few tricks," Amelia said. She looked around, then leaned forward and motioned with her index finger for Vivian to move closer. Vivian's breath mixed with the tobacco fumes. "So I'm going to do you a favor. You get me some toothpaste powder, and some for yourself while you're at it, and I'll teach you a couple tricks."

One week later, Amelia returned after her shift and found a small package wrapped in brown paper on her pillow. Being so far from town made getting simple supplies an annoyance but even so, she most enjoyed the delightful rush of adrenaline from getting others to do her bidding. She'd mastered how to gain a scrap of control by watching the boys lord toys and snacks over each other. Since Vivian fulfilled her end of the bargain, Amelia agreed to teach Vivian a few perks about living with a surplus of women.

Amelia and Vivian began by trading plump peppermint drops for small chunks of lye soap. For weeks, dorm mates called them *suckers* for their foolish dealings, and, while Amelia ignored the criticism, Vivian asked constant questions, unsure of the plan even after repeated explanations. When at last the final Saturday of the month arrived with paychecks and time off for escorted evenings into town, most of the ladies had used up their soap. Lest their burly companion find them offensive after a week of hard labor, soap became a rare, and expensive, commodity.

"How do you know all this?" Vivian asked, holding a

hollowed-out copy of *War and Peace* that served as Amelia's personal safe.

They sat together on Amelia's bunk, Vivian's short legs tucked beneath her like a newborn giraffe. Most of the women had left to cavort with the men; the ones who'd outgrown the novelty or fantasy of romance had gone to sleep early or snacked on sour-milk cakes and tea in the dining hall.

In the echo of the empty room, the concept of knowing felt fragile and Amelia wanted to tell Vivian she really didn't know much other than her desire to flee, which felt like a constant tremble in the pit of her stomach. Amelia just wished she had somewhere else to go.

"Never mind how, what else can you show me?" Vivian asked and pulled Amelia from her thoughts.

Amelia knew lots of tricks and when she needed something else, she'd show Vivian how to dip stale bread into salted water and the best places to find lost change. Didn't the mistresses teach self-sufficiency above all else? Amelia watched Vivian tuck her valuables into Amelia's book and then open and close the cover, checking to be sure the contents hadn't disappeared like in a magic trick. With Vivian's paws still on her belongings, Amelia wondered why she'd trusted Vivian enough to show her where she kept her money. A girl's mistake. Amelia seized the book from Vivian.

"By end of week, you keep your own money," Amelia said and then waited until Vivian crawled up to her bunk before she tucked the money under her mattress and set out her clothing and toiletries for the next day's work.

One of the most difficult jobs at the factory required loading the seed cotton into mechanical strippers, which removed the plant. Women used their hands to quickly stuff the contraption before a metal blade crushed down on them. For a year as Amelia pushed her broom past the loaders, she grimaced as she

...ut the opulence felt like a cozy blanket after years ...
in the cold. Instead of going back to her place, Ameli...
lone empty seat beside a man holding up a news...
hen the man didn't stir, Amelia decided to stay just ...
...tes. She felt more relaxed, more at home than she had...
...g time, maybe ever. Until the ticket taker made his...
...and dragged her back to working class, Amelia wanted...
...every moment.

...man beside her snapped his newspaper, causing Amelia...
...p. She turned and heard the man grunt from behind the...
...per raised in front of his face. Dimples of colored light...
...d on the seatback and window, and for a moment she...
...ned mesmerized by the display. Then she realized what...
...d the colorful light and her eyes widened.

...elia had never seen a ring on a man, especially one with...
...any diamonds surrounding an enormous blue sapphire, no...
...than five carats by her estimation. She'd learned about...
...ious stones in a geology book she'd taken from the boys'...
...sroom. The thick gold band and complement of gems made...
...man's pudgy hand look elegant and refined, not unlike the...
...t bit of rouge on a lady's cheek. Amelia wanted to compli-...
...nt the man but held her tongue. She didn't belong and...
...ought best to stay quiet.

..."Tickets please," Amelia heard before she had time to take...
...en one more inhale of the lovely clean aroma. She didn't look...
...p but felt the conductor looming over her as she fumbled in...
...her satchel and then handed him her second-class ticket. She...
...raised her head and grinned like an innocent, ignorant of her...
...situation. The conductor didn't flinch. He wore a stiff, black...
...coat buttoned to the top and a pillar box hat with "Conductor"...
...embroidered in gold thread. Amelia waited for her scolding, but...
...then the conductor looked from her to the man seated beside...
...her and then back again. She followed the conductor's surprised...

watched the women risk their limbs to the dangerous practice and wondered why anyone with sense wanted to work their way up to such a dangerous job, even for more pay. There seemed an obvious solution, and over evening meal Amelia finally asked several seasoned workers.

"Management don't give a hoot about us. We're dispendable," Baty said.

"Expendable, you ninny. Land sakes, read a book once in a while," a thick older woman named Ruth said.

The women moved brittle rice, burnt lentils, and wilted collard greens around their dinner plates as they spoke. Amelia had already eaten every bite and couldn't understand why the women wasted so much food.

"What about the union?" Amelia asked. "I thought unions were put in place to help with safety issues."

Baty huffed. "You sound like one of those rubbish books. You're just a young pup. What do you know? You think life turns out as you expect? Well, it don't and them union b'hoys don't think much of us."

Amelia held her tongue at Baty's remark about the expectations of life for fear a biting retort could reveal her own dark thoughts. She wondered if the years of fending off and fighting for had led to an instinctual self-preservation that also left little room for charity, or even simple kindness.

"Okay, so no one cares. Still, why don't you just use some sort of tool instead of your hands to load the cotton?" Amelia asked, still dumbfounded by their flat, indifferent stares. "One of you must have thought of this already."

The women didn't hear her because they had already moved on to complaining about the unions, which plummeted to a rant about the fallacies and idiocies of men in general. Amelia slipped away when the language grew coarse. The women could be just as lewd as the men.

Work continued, and with the summer humidity as thick as well-fed chiggers came an erupting disquiet among the workers. In the midday heat, tempers flared and loaders passed out from dehydration. Management called a meeting and crammed all 150 employees together in the thin shadow of the loading dock, their mass body heat far worse than the stagnant air in the factory.

"We'll not discuss shorter sleeves or thinner skirts for the women," the supervisor replied to a shouted comment about the men with rolled-up sleeves. "As I said already, you are to drink more water to stay hydrated. And for those of you with good sense and savings, I have a special announcement."

The P. T. Barnum's Museum, Menagerie & Circus had ventured to Little Rock and those who worked enough extra hours could take two days off to travel to the city, at their own expense, of course. A round of groans did nothing to sour Amelia's mood. As one of the few who worked extra to pass the time and spent a lifetime stashing her money, Amelia couldn't wait to get away for a few days to go anywhere, for anything. She smiled. She'd never been to the circus.

A few days later, Amelia stood on the platform of the Alexander train station, a lone room with a few cracked wooden benches where an elderly man sold tickets and took naps. She traveled alone because few of the other ladies could go and management forbade her to travel with any of the men for fear of gossip. Arrangements at the Little Rock YWCA included a shared room and light breakfast, plus she had time for a bit of sightseeing with the implicit instructions to dine only in restaurants where she saw other ladies. Amelia didn't care that she had rules even when away from her job. She felt giddy and enthralled to do something new.

The whistle sounded and Amelia turned, aware for the first time of an approaching wagon headed toward the tracks. She

watched the driver whip the reins
meant to beat the train. Three shor
lowed by squealing brakes. Just befo
platform, the wagon cleared the trac
whooping. A group of young people,
grand time risking their lives and the l

Amelia unclenched her fists and let o
Death seemed like a droning backgroun
it grew louder and became unnerving
parents and the jostling wagon made her
leather in the sun that would someday
Youth, in fact, seemed frivolous and Amel
prancing and strutting with nowhere to g
hooting just to draw attention. The darede
same age as her and yet she felt no connecti
ness.

The train stopped only long enough for pas
so within a few moments the conductor yelled
Amelia scrambled to pick up her shoulder bag
into the nearest door as the train began to move

On the train from Montana, Amelia's seco
consisted of a hard wooden chair beside a lat
smeared with dirt and flanked on either side by a
grimy green cloth that served, with little success,
Amelia moved into the depths of the car and i
noticed the smell. Instead of the stench of body
with sour food and moods, Amelia sniffed linseed oil
lilac. She stepped further into the train, her feet cus
plush carpet, and saw red brocade fabric over padd
Small glass fixtures lit the first-class car with a soft glow
wide rows gave each passenger plenty of room to stre
without draping legs over neighboring seats.

Amelia knew she should walk through the breezeway b

stare until she saw that the stranger held out five dollars from behind his newspaper. The conductor snatched the money and Amelia's benefactor waved the man away as if swatting a fly.

"I . . . uh, thank you, sir. But I can't repay you," Amelia said.

"You already have," he said as he lowered his paper shield.

Amelia smiled at a gentleman in his early sixties, stocky, a fringe of white hair around a bald center with a thick, white mustache and trimmed Van Dyke beard. He looked wise, like a modern age wizard in a well-groomed linen suit with pearl buttons and a red rose in his buttonhole. The dazzling ring flashed each time the man moved his hand.

"Sitting beside a beautiful young woman is payment enough. I enjoy the jealous looks from the others on board."

Amelia glanced around the car and saw a few men sneaking peeks at her. She hadn't noticed them and found repugnant the idea of being thought of as a decoration.

"So a lady is nothing more than an accessory?" Amelia asked.

The gent chuckled, the sound light yet deep and sturdy like the cello music she'd once heard at a charity concert at the orphanage. Then he nodded and smirked in a way that made him look both clever and sincere at the same time.

"Can you think of a better description for yourself? You're too young to have accomplished much yet, so you must use what nature has given you. Be grateful, my dear; not every lass is as lovely as you. If you were a homely girl, you might be sitting on those hard benches in the back."

"That's . . ." Amelia had never heard anyone speak with such candor while at the same time making her feel respected. He hadn't mocked her as so many she'd met, and, though she didn't fully agree with him, she liked the idea of the influence she commanded and looked again at the men who continued to watch her.

"Are you suggesting that I'm treated differently because of

my . . ." Amelia felt arrogant saying any more.

"Of course. We're all judged at least some by our appearance. That's just human nature, my dear, and nothing more. True, there are some who take the whole physical appearance, vanity, too far, but those are true dullards. Intelligence is knowing your strengths and using them to the advantage of yourself and the world. Are we not here on God's green earth but to serve others?" he asked. The man then lifted the newspaper back in front of his face.

"But—"

Amelia stopped when the gentleman wiggled his index finger at her. "Read physical cues, my dear, and you will go far in this world."

She waited but he didn't say anything more. He continued with his newspaper and Amelia sat silent, unsure what to do but watch the passing trees through the spotless windows.

As the train slowed to exchange passengers in Sweet Home, Amelia sat up and straightened her ruffled blouse. She wanted to ask him what else she could do to go far in the world, but as soon as the train stopped, the man stood.

"I leave you here, my dear. Your passage is paid to the end of the line. Good luck in your endeavors, whatever they may be. And if you use your lovely appearance to the betterment of society, then indeed you've made good use of your special fortune."

He gave Amelia a slight bow, placed a sloped Homburg hat on his head, then handed her his newspaper. She watched him leave with a vague hollowness that reminded her of waking in the middle of the night to the empty sound of muffled cries, and then she looked down at the newspaper on her lap. With nothing else to do, Amelia snapped open the day's *Washington Post,* just like the white-haired stranger.

Two days in Little Rock melted into a blur of excitement

coated with too much cotton candy and lemon taffy. She sat amazed when a magician sawed a woman in half; followed the crowd into the sideshow tent to see the bearded lady; and rode a pony so small that her feet walked along to help the poor little nag. Several young men, and more than a few far too old, asked Amelia to accompany them around the circus or dinner, but she declined and kept her distance. The men were dirty and cheap in a way that made her want to take a bath. Plus she'd heard the lusty women at the plant returning from their evenings out, complaining that the men made crude remarks and touched them with rough, cracked hands.

Amelia enjoyed her few hours exploring the city even more than the circus. The rush of buggies and people created a contagious, spirited energy and she'd never felt so enthralled. The elation and newness of her experiences made returning to the factory feel like going back to the gallows after a pardon. Amelia shared her fun with Vivian and sold taffy to the ladies. Her enterprise paid for her entire trip. Still, the air felt more stagnant, more repressed in the shadows of the bright city lights. Nothing had changed during her absence except, Amelia knew, herself.

The general attitude of the mill darkened with the shorter days of fall, and Amelia kept more and more to herself.

"Why do you bother reading the newspaper? Ever since your big trip over the summer you're like those men, all noses in the paper, arguing over stuff they read. Next you'll want to join them and share your opinion," Vivian said from her bunk, confident in sharing her own opinion in the safety of the darkness.

Amelia let the question drift through the open windows and land in the crusts of ice by the loading bay. The mystery man on the train had given her a gift she didn't know she needed, and she could never explain to Vivian that a whole big world existed beyond Mabelvale, beyond Arkansas, where people did wonderful and courageous work, enjoyed music and art, discussed politics and economics with intelligent thought. Being stuck in the wasteland felt like punishment for the missteps of her youth. Amelia prayed for change, for a new life and renewed spirit. In hindsight, she later decided she should have made her wish more specific.

The accident happened on a cold Tuesday afternoon, just after the workers had eaten. Amelia had finished cleaning Baty's area when she heard what sounded like a coyote's howl with the timbre and depth of a human voice. Hairs stood on Amelia's neck and she knew what she'd see even before she turned around. Blood spurted in the rhythm of a heartbeat from the gaping space above Baty's right wrist as she held up her arm, transfixed by her missing hand. Blood trailed into the mechanical stripper and Amelia imagined Baty's hand ground to the same meaty pulp as the cotton. Amelia vomited on her own shoes as a man tore his pant leg for a tourniquet and an older woman—Ruth, Amelia later thought—coaxed Baty to sit down before she fainted. When those with medical training took Baty away, one of the shift leaders told everyone to get back to work.

"That includes you, Red." The man shoved Amelia's broom in her hand and added, "Clean this up. Mops are in the back."

That night Amelia dreamed of Daisy, black and dead, and the Montana wind plunging Amelia in the river. She awoke covered in sweat. The following morning, muttering workers, some clutching their hands or crossing themselves, gathered on the plant floor. The shift supervisor stood with a brass megaphone on the metal stairwell leading to the offices of upper management.

"Your attention. You are to return to work just as if this unfortunate incident didn't happen. The woman," the supervisor paused to look at his notes, "Miss Baty, has survived the night and should make a full recovery. Of course, once she's able, she'll have a job in the office. We take care of our own."

"Are you joking?" Amelia shouted.

Vivian grabbed her arm. "Shut up."

The supervisor saw Amelia, glared, and then mouthed "ignorant girl" before he set down the megaphone and stomped upstairs. Amelia thought of all the boys and men who called her stupid, laughed at her, and made disgusting thrusting gestures with their hips that management didn't condone, though didn't stop either. She'd been a useless girl, now a useless woman, and the idea of continuing to hide in the back of the classroom infuriated Amelia. She'd read more and had a sharper mind than the foul man who liked to twirl his mustache with his grubby hands while he stared at her breasts.

Amelia snapped off the bristles from the end of her broom, strode to the stairwell, and seized the brass megaphone left on the bench.

"For goodness sake, you just need this." She held up the broom handle like a sword. "You have to agree that a pole, a stick, anything is safer than using your hands."

After a few shrugs, the workers went back to their stations. The only enthusiasm for her public appeal came from the shift supervisor, who seized the megaphone and dragged her back to his office by her forearm.

Amelia hadn't known of a job lower than sweeper until demoted to pest removal using the "wheel of death." Rats caused extensive damage so traps were set nightly. The contraption engineered by a local farmer consisted of a bucket of water, a can coated in butter and suspended by wire so it spun over the water, and two wooden ramps balanced against the bucket. Rats went up the ramps to get to the butter then jumped onto the can and slipped off into the water where they drowned. Each day, Amelia had to empty the buckets of dead rats into the incinerator. Their swollen bodies shifted in a mass of putrid brown, and sometimes a few near the top struggled to climb over their fallen brothers to safety, piercing eyes and chewing off tails in their panic. The routine of the job couldn't overcome her daily repulsion, so she felt thankful she didn't have to endure the disgusting job for long.

Pride clouded Amelia when she thought having to report to the plant manager's office meant a promotion for suffering in silence. Mistress Lucy liked to say, "Ego makes the fool."

The plant manager watched over the entire factory through an impressive window, though Amelia first noticed the pristine quiet. In the office stood two men in pressed suits and a thick woman in a clean white blouse. Amelia greeted the plant manager with a nod, then waited introduction to a union representative and payroll clerk. Instead of a promotion, Amelia needed to make a public apology for her unacceptable outburst. In exchange, she'd receive one week's pay and a hushed dismissal. If she refused, a policeman waited outside to forcibly remove her from the premises.

Amelia wanted to know what she'd done and the union man rattled off statutes and bylaws that she didn't understand. Then the manager grumbled about the difficulty of splinters in the cotton, which Amelia recognized as farce. They removed all kinds of foreign particles, including splinters from wagons and farming tools. As he spoke he kept looking to the right corner of the office. Amelia glanced to the right and saw a cardboard box.

Bristles stuck out in all directions so she couldn't count how many broom heads had been pulled from their handle. Amelia grinned and the manager called her willful, but she felt empowered in a way she'd never experienced. She'd motivated the others to action, and they had in fact listened and believed a lowly sweeper had something worthwhile to say. Then Amelia

at else she could improve upon and in hindsight
ement must have had the same thought.

ghtened her collar. "My suggestion will keep
afe. What's wrong with that?" she asked.

Her answer came in the form of a policeman's firm grip. The women averted their eyes as Amelia left under force, and she felt their betrayal and self preservation with the same sting as if they'd cast stones.

Losing her job meant parting from her temporary home. Not sure where to go, Amelia lingered over her small travel trunk with her face down to hide her fear. She didn't hear anyone approach and jumped when Vivian tapped her on the shoulder.

"Here," Vivian said. "We thought you might need this." Vivian handed Amelia an envelope. Behind her stood a group of at least twenty ladies.

Amelia opened the flap and found much more than one week's pay inside.

"I don't know what to say. Thank you." Amelia looked at the women, surprised to see several who'd been particularly upset by needing soap.

"No one has ever stood up for us before," Ruth said.

Amelia wanted to tell them she'd never stood up for anyone before nor had she ever received such kindness, but a catch in her throat prevented speaking. Each woman hugged her in turn and wished her well, and then when the ladies left, Vivian grabbed Amelia's shoulders and kissed each of her cheeks.

"I thought you were a tough nut, but now I think you have what Ma calls grit. You know, hard on the outside but softer in the middle. Anyway, I gotta get back to my broom; she might miss me. But here." Vivian shoved a torn piece of paper in Amelia's hand. "My pop almost sent me to this factory instead of here. Not sure what changed his mind, but he said it's honest work."

Amelia thanked Vivian, then slid the paper into her s
pocket.

"I think I'm going to miss you," Vivian said before she scooted
from the dormitory.

Amelia asked herself if she'd miss Vivian. So many faces came
and went over the years, and with the passing of time she let
herself forget. But she'd never forget the power of hearing her
own voice, loud and strong through the megaphone, or the honest appreciation from the ladies for her doing what they couldn't
do for themselves.

"Life only moves forward," Mistress Lucy often said. Amelia
thought of the mistress as she sat on the firm, second-class seat
on the train to Little Rock. Vivian had meant well, but she had
poor writing skills and Amelia couldn't make out a word of the
note. Even if she had deciphered the scrawl, Amelia didn't want
to work in a factory. She wanted a city job where life moved fast
and in many directions.

Amelia opened the evening's *Washington Post* and read a
chauvinistic article about the Women's Christian Temperance
Union and their *futile, nay childish* march on the Capitol to
prohibit liquor sales. Then she turned to the second page and
gasped. Beneath the caption *Sam Ward Entertains Polish Countess
During Goodwill Tour,* Amelia saw a drawing of her white-haired
benefactor from the first-class compartment. He stood beside a
lovely woman in a full skirt that looked as if woven from peacock
feathers.

The columnist, a Clancy Doyle, dubbed Sam Ward "King of
the Lobbyists," and reported a lavish gathering at the home of
Mr. Ward. Along with seven dinner courses and chamber
orchestra, the satirist suggested that the party also created a
diversion from a scandal involving Mr. Ward and The Pacific
Mail Steamship Company. Wealthy organizations hired lobbyists
to persuade legislators to vote in their favor, though Amelia

couldn't imagine the kindly gent involved in anything disreputable. She thought of the power of a lobbyist and how she'd persuaded her coworkers to action. A slight surge of excitement made her smile. She needed to find out more about Sam Ward.

The conductor approached and Amelia stopped him. "Sir, can I transfer to another rail line in Little Rock? I'm making a change of plans."

Chapter Three

Amelia's first impression of Washington, D.C., in the late winter of 1877 left her worried she'd made a huge mistake. The glamour and influence she'd read about included only what went on behind and inside. She'd had to stay in Little Rock for a few days due to inclement weather and track work, so Amelia scoured the Little Rock library for articles on Sam Ward and had a bird's eye view of his grand and exciting occupation. Down at street level, the average citizen rarely went to formal galas hosted by the influential and wealthy. Day to day life seemed far more dirty.

Mud from the bare roads oozed through the slats on the walkways and stuck to the bases of buildings and bottoms of shoes, leaving dried chunks in the foyers of shops and apartment houses. Clearing the roads behind the horses appeared and smelled arbitrary rather than routine, and the cold air felt thick from the profusion of plaster dust. Everywhere around the city one could see the grand vision of French engineer and architect Pierre L'Enfant and his quest to transform a backwater company town into a thriving metropolitan hub of government. Construction of elaborate central fountains, a new Library of Congress, a Supreme Court building, and the final tiers of the impressive monument to President Washington himself gave the city a regal purposefulness unlike other cities. However, with advancement came snarled traffic and annoyed masons who shouted at pedestrians and flung buckets. Amelia found the confusion and animosity alarming at first; then after a few hours lost, circling the same pinwheel of blocks, she marched with purpose and stepped over the rogue hammers lying on the sidewalks like a local.

One of the most notable city attractions focused not on the buildings but a population so dark and numerous that Amelia wondered if she'd ever fit in with her pallid complexion and auburn hair. Newly emancipated slaves walked with their heads lowered as a matter of training and routine, whereas the northern Negros showed no hesitation around the policemen and weaved through the knot of buggies to cross the road just as the white pedestrians. Raised alongside so many colors and creeds, Amelia rarely noticed the differences and felt ashamed for her observation.

On the train to D.C., Amelia had found an advertisement in the *Post* for inexpensive rooms in the low-rent area of Canal. Tall, narrow houses stood in a long queue and owners shoveled the snow only wide enough for a footpath. The Locke Boarding-house on M Street consisted of a plain white box with black shutters and cleared porch. The house next door looked like a poor distant cousin. Bits of gray peeped through the large chips in the white facade as a petticoat from the bottom of a skirt, and a large clay pot shaped like a blue goose sat as sentry on the top step. Women in long coats slouched against porch railings to watch Amelia drag her trunk up the front steps of the boardinghouse. The ladies appeared as ornaments, languishing on the porch because someone told them they needed an airing.

The available room on the second floor had a single bed without a head or foot board; a yellowed washbasin with matching water pitcher that the landlady, Mrs. Stockett, knew had a crack so she wouldn't charge Amelia for the damage; an unpainted, three-drawer wooden dresser; and several wall hooks for clothing. For six dollars a week, the room also included a window that opened to the street; coffee and a roll for breakfast; a modest dinner of basic but hearty food; and use of the bathtub three times a week with hot water, provided Amelia rose early. Amelia chuckled but Mrs. Stockett glared at her and said a full-length dressing mirror required an extra fifty cents a week.

Mrs. Stockett stood with her arms folded over her ample chest and shook her head when Amelia asked to have the dressing mirror included. Her tight frown and the way she tapped her thick foot reminded Amelia of the matron, and Amelia almost turned and left to find other accommodations.

"My terms are firm, as are the house rules and the curfew even if you're my only tenant at the moment. Is that clear?" Mrs. Stockett asked.

Amelia nodded. "I'll take the room with the added mirror charge if you allow me to use the sewing machine I saw downstairs. I assume it works properly."

Mrs. Stockett agreed to the terms and took the first week's rent before leaving Amelia to unpack. She washed her face and neck, changed into a fresh white blouse, and then locked her trunk and headed downstairs. When Amelia reached for the front door, Mrs. Stockett stood in the kitchen doorway and shouted, "You always go out to the right, Miss Cooke. Don't you go near the Blue Goose. You don't need to know about that. They won't bother you if you don't bother them. You go right, you hear me?"

Sam Ward lived at 258 F Street in what one journalist called "an oddly modest domicile for the lavish dinners enjoyed within." In fact, the Ward homestead looked no more resplendent than the adjacent homes, where Amelia guessed doctors and attorneys ate trouble-free meals with docile wives. The quiet neighborhood with freshly cleared walks and painted black wrought-iron entrances gave no hint of what went on behind the lush damask curtains.

46

A bright sun added to Amelia's zealousness and kept away the raw bite of the cool air. She'd been so excited to locate Mr. Ward that now, standing on the street corner like the working girls of M Street, she didn't know if she should knock on his door or wait till he emerged and greet him as if by happenstance. He might not even be at home. As Amelia stood vacillating, the front door opened and Mr. Ward filled the threshold.

He held a carved walking stick and wore a charcoal-gray, cashmere overcoat that looked silken even from Amelia's distance down the street. She'd seen him stand up on the train but as she had remained seated, she hadn't realized that his average height meant she could see him eye to eye; she might even be a little taller. He paused in the door to set a bowler hat on his bald head, then started down the steps in a purposeful manner, his stick placed with care even as he kept his eyes stationed forward and a smile tugged up the ends of his long mustache. The enthusiastic tap of his stick matched Amelia's heartbeat.

She grinned and thought to wave; then she felt silly, knowing he hadn't seen her and likely wouldn't recognize her without an elaborate introduction and full inspection. Nerves twisted her stomach and her palms felt damp in her gloves. The stranger who had inspired her rash move to Washington to seek out a new life stepped onto the sidewalk and headed down the street in the opposite direction. Unsure what else to do, Amelia followed.

Few men had a presence as discernable as the man with the legendary ring, so Amelia followed Mr. Ward with ease. She felt like an urchin or nefarious hound and wondered what she could possibly say in defense of her actions if he spotted her. Mr. Ward stopped at a corner bakery and stayed for a few minutes to chat with the cashier, then he walked to the middle of a square community park with a few small benches. Amelia stayed pressed against the entrance gate.

Mr. Ward removed a bright white handkerchief and dusted the seat before he replaced the square and sat down. He propped his walking stick against the bench, set his bakery bag beside him, and then removed a flaky pastry. Amelia's memory of eating outdoors included fending off ants and flies, yet somehow Mr. Ward looked as if indulging in a charming soiree.

Men and ladies passed, and Mr. Ward bid a greeting to each with good humor and a wide smile. His jovial manner gave Amelia courage and she decided after ten minutes of gnawing her bottom lip to unlatch herself from the park gate and introduce herself. She fluffed her plain black skirt and made sure her bonnet hadn't slid off center from her twitching nerves.

Mr. Ward finished his breakfast and gazed at a tall building across the street as Amelia approached. She felt just as nervous as the first time the matron had dragged her to her office. Each step felt weighted by an imaginary string pulling her back, taunting the foolishness of her own creation. Only momentum and the embarrassment of having to stop and turn around kept her moving, and she thought to just keep walking past Mr. Ward as any pedestrian out for a stroll. Then she heard Mr. Ward's voice and her heart flopped.

"What are the odds?" Mr. Ward said. "You're the young lady from the train."

"You remember me?" Amelia sounded too wistful and cursed her nervousness.

"I remember everyone, my dear. Never forget a face, certainly not one as lovely as yours. Is there something I can do for you?"

Amelia planned to tell the brilliant Mr. Ward that she'd read all about his trade and saw the need for real female lobbyists, not the washerwomen begging for local rations on behalf of starving children. With her, he had the opportunity to shepherd

white chenille bedspread and replayed the conversation as an actor rehearsing lines. She'd made a complete and utter idiot of herself, and worse, Mr. Ward's comments hit the bull's-eye. How had she thought she could waltz into a new town and demand a job knowing as little as she did, about anything, really; about anyone?

Shadows from the tree outside swayed across the dresser like a hand reaching for the knobs and the sounds of false, high-pitched laughter drifted through the walls from the house next door, the house of ill repute. Amelia knew of such places; she'd heard the older boys brag about sneaking off in the night to some ranch. She felt sorry for the women condemned to a demeaning role no one deserved. Mr. Ward hadn't said the words outright, but he'd called her decoration on the train and insinuated she couldn't do much, not so unlike the working girls next door. True, she didn't know much about politics or the workings of government, but she knew something far more valuable.

Mr. Ward gave her a challenge, and Amelia meant to meet the call like the brave soldiers who fought to free their Negro countrymen. She knew how to read and learn, so in the morning she'd find a library and get to work. Amelia slipped beneath the covers, pulled the blanket to her chin, and closed her eyes thinking of how quickly she needed to learn so much. In the same instant, her eyes popped open and she sat up and looked around her simple room.

Her day of firsts pressed in around her: Washington D.C., brothels, approaching a stranger to ask such a grand request, and most of all, her very own room. Tears burned in her eyes and she thought of the rows of bunks and all the hours spent with a pillow pressed to her ears to shut out the audible pain. In twenty years, Amelia had never slept alone in a room of her own. She closed her eyes to let the solitude sink in like the water of a hot bath. Her eyes still closed, Amelia interlaced her hands and made a vow to herself. She'd never sleep alongside gaggles again and she'd leave her childhood in the past where it belonged. Mr. Ward wouldn't help a pitiful orphan. Like all of the new monuments rising from the dust, she, too, could create herself into anything she desired. She'd no longer think of herself as Amelia Cooke, the girl with the broken past, but Miss Cooke, the forthright woman with a bright future. "I am what I believe I am," Amelia said to herself without fear of someone yelling for her to be quiet. She'd create her own place in the world just as she'd always knew she'd have to, and her grand new future began the following morning.

Over the next two months, Amelia lived on her savings while she spent every Monday through Thursday at the main library reading news clippings, government books, law journals, and pamphlets. Sam Ward used his natural charisma to not only gain votes, but also raise money for almshouse charities. Amelia even found a rendering of Sam ladling soup at a local wayward shelter. Although often called King of the Lobbyists, Everybody's Friend, and a Man-About-Washington, not everyone agreed on such favorable titles for Mr. Ward. "Sam Ward's nothing but a wicked lobbyist riding through the city buying and selling votes with trunks full of cash," one editorialist wrote. Self-righteous politicians blamed the downfall of the democratic process and the loosening of American values on men like Sam Ward, and Mr. Ward himself spoke of the innate problems that accompanied a lobbying system, namely greed. Exonerated of any wrongdoing with the steamship company, everyone in the courtroom during Mr. Ward's testimony spoke of nothing but his forthright manner and honest charm. Mr. Ward appeared the model of decency, which made Amelia wonder about his methods. She hoped to find out the truth about the great man first hand, but until then, she checked her pocket watch.

The library closed in ten minutes. She closed her book on filibustering and made her way to the librarian's desk.

"Thank you for your help tonight, Patricia. I guess I won't see you next week. Are you excited about your trip to Delaware? I'm sure your in-laws will be glad to see you," Amelia said.

"Well, I don't know about that but I'm happy to get out of this bog," Patricia said. She leaned forward and slipped a reference copy of Standing Congressional Committees into Amelia's tote. "These aren't supposed to leave the library but I know you need it. Just bring it back when I see you next."

Amelia had smiled at the research librarian during the first week she stayed until closing every night, but not until Amelia asked her name and chatted about daily life did Patricia go out of her way to help. A lesson learned, just not the one she expected.

"To become a constitutional amendment, a bill requires a two-thirds majority vote in each house of Congress and then must be ratified by three-fourths of the state legislatures," Amelia muttered to herself as she paced the confines of her room noting that expanding the mind seemed paired with the need for more space. Late into the evening, long after Mrs. Stockett's curfew, Amelia wore a path in the thin rug. She had the reference book open on the dresser to the Budget Committee to memorize key facts she thought Mr. Ward might ask. Tomorrow, Friday, she'd see how much she remembered in a more practical way.

Amelia reserved Fridays for touring landmarks and public government buildings. She positioned herself beside the docent so she could hear every word about government printing and the story of building the White House. The history of her country had a pulse she couldn't feel from the pages. To touch the books Thomas Jefferson donated to Congress or stand within the walls where Lincoln signed emancipation papers became a raw and enthralling realization of tangible power.

On Saturdays, Amelia worked as a stock clerk in a family-owned fabric shop just a few blocks from her rented room. The shop needed a girl but only for a scant few hours one day a week, so Amelia negotiated an extra allowance of fabric and patterns to offset the minimal salary. If Mr. Ward agreed to her tutelage, she needed to look the part of a respectable, business-minded lady of some means. To that end, Amelia rinsed her hair with Macassar oil to add shine and spent all day every Sunday at Mrs. Stockett's rickety machine sewing, then re-sewing, three essential pieces for her wardrobe according to the "Women at Home" column in *Tribune and Farmer*. According to Louisa Knapp Curtis, every young lass needed a functional day dress, a sophisticated evening gown, and a moderate dress for cocktail hour.

Part of her education, as valuable as knowing the names of all of the sitting senators, came under what Amelia considered clever learning. Each day she grew more and more fascinated by the human nature that governed the true workings of D.C. in more ways than any committee meeting or bond initiative. Like Patricia at the library, shop clerks enjoyed hearing their names and talking about their children and grandchildren, and Amelia's fabulous memory amazed them. The skill of learning names came from a lifetime of having to learn so many. When flattery didn't work, Amelia bartered for what she needed by offering to clean a backroom or alter a skirt for free, and often just the promise of returning with a plate of warm cookies meant borrowing what she needed. In her trading, Amelia found an instinct for building relationships, the hidden force turning the wheels of the city.

Amelia also found the workings of government fascinating and enjoyed the unexpected ease with which she memorized the material. Her newfound passion encouraged her to work hard, and as she finished a buttonhole on a smart carriage cloak, she recognized not only her aptitude for the Washington game, but also how much she liked playing.

"Come on, girly, I got the book," Mrs. Stockett said to Amelia as she hurried past the sewing room. Amelia finished her stitch, then unwrapped herself from the sewing machine to sit with Mrs. Stockett in the kitchen.

When Amelia started pacing in her room and rummaging the kitchen in the middle of the night for a wedge of cheese or heel of bread, Mrs. Stockett sat her down at the scrubbed kitchen table and wagged her index finger.

"I told you not to get mixed up with those girls next door. Are you working for that bad egg now?" Mrs. Stockett had asked.

Amelia explained her efforts, then waited for Mrs. Stockett to scoff at her schoolgirl silliness and tell her she had no place working at a man's occupation. Mrs. Stockett smiled so wide that Amelia saw her missing molar. "About damn time I met a young lady with some real pluck. I want to help."

Mrs. Stockett's help came in the form of quizzes over pot roast and potatoes.

"You're ready, girly," Mrs. Stockett said waving around a rare stock of broccoli speared on her fork. "Tomorrow you go up to this fancy Mr. Ward and tell him all that you know. He's bound to take you 'under his wing,' as Mr. Stockett used to say."

She'd never mentioned her husband. "Where is Mr. Stockett?"

"Drunk somewhere, dead. Don't know, don't care. Only kindness he ever showed me was putting this house in my name after his brother died from the bottle. Thought he'd be next. Then one day he just left and never came back. Good riddance, I say. Men ain't nothing but a waste of good time and money."

"Do you have any children?" Amelia asked.

"Two boys, wouldn't you know. Both moved on. Young men have no need for an old woman."

Amelia watched as Mrs. Stockett cleared their plates. Once the dish powder came out, the evening dinner conversation ended.

In her room after supper, Amelia counted her remaining savings. Skipping lunches had helped, but she couldn't last much longer without fulltime employment. For a week she'd felt equipped to speak intelligently to Mr. Ward, even had two of her three costumes pressed and ready. Fear felt like stones piled on her feet. Every time she thought about talking to Mr. Ward her stomach turned and she heard his laughter.

Like most men, Mr. Ward hadn't made grand statements against the role of women in general, citing adherence to societal rhetoric taught to innocent boys by the generations before them. His laughter proved all too clearly that Mr. Ward didn't believe in her specifically; that he didn't think she had the intelligence or abilities beyond her fine appearance. Tucked away in her own room with Mrs. Stockett shuffling about the kitchen, Amelia feared Mr. Ward had good reason for his doubt.

The following morning Amelia found Mrs. Stockett pounding an innocent lump of dough on the cutting board. Mrs. Stockett never baked bread because she said she hated the work.

"I'm making this special to celebrate tonight. You're ready, Amelia. Just take a deep breath and jump in. That's what my ma used to say. 'You gotta jump in.' "

Mr. Ward's house looked the same as a month earlier, as did the neighborhood and Mr. Ward himself. He wore a double-breasted, mid-length jacket and had his walking stick as before, but he'd donned a different hat, a sleek crown hat with wide brim that Amelia thought better suited his round face. His routine started unchanged, too—a stop at the bakery for a roll and quick chat with the salesgirl—but then he walked through the park without stopping. Amelia dropped back behind two men in helpful tall bowlers. After months of sightseeing, she knew her way around the city like a native so she wasn't surprised when Sam Ward turned down 7th Street. His direction meant he had business at the Capitol, and she grinned. She hadn't yet seen the Capitol building up close, had avoided glimpses of the impressive dome like a child saving the precious raisins to eat last. Amelia looked up as she rounded the corner on to Maryland Avenue and stopped square in the middle of the crowded walk; a woman ran right into her. Amelia stood with her mouth agape as the woman pushed around her and snarled.

A sketch in a book gave an outline, a two dimensional impression meant to depict or perhaps pique the interest of a reader. Amelia knew the curves of the dome and the heights of the columns, but drawings hadn't conveyed the building's true place of authority and dignity. She felt pride in her country and the brave men who defended its borders; pride in a people who had and could embrace change. Amelia's fears and doubt fell away. Her future stood before her, solid and unrestricted but by the bounds of her own making. *One could only fail if they gave up,* the matron said. Amelia shook her head to push the matron away; that foundling child no longer existed. Miss Cooke hustled up the long dirt walk toward where Mr. Ward stood at the top of the long staircase talking to an enthusiastic, round man. She paused at the base of the wide flat stairs to view the Capitol from a new angle, then Amelia took a deep breath, smiled, and hustled up the steps, two at a time.

CHAPTER FOUR

A patch of clouds shaded Amelia as she stood back a few feet and waited until Mr. Ward and the unknown man shook hands and the stranger walked away.

"Yes, I see you, Miss Cooke," Mr. Ward said. He tugged down the base of his jacket with both hands.

"I wasn't hiding. I was waiting, Mr. Ward."

He raised his thick eyebrows, which looked like little jumping caterpillars, and then ran his hand over his whiskers.

"If you'll excuse me, Miss Cooke. I have a very busy schedule. Good day."

"Please, if I can have just a minute of your time," Amelia said.

Mr. Ward tilted his head and paused. Amelia's heart raced. Then he tapped his walking stick on the Capitol steps and walked away. "Do not follow me," he called out.

Amelia took a few steps to follow, then changed her mind. He'd only listen when he wanted to listen and that moment had passed. She'd find another moment.

Mr. Ward's schedule varied each day, as Amelia discovered after following him from his house every morning. But whether at the War Department or in front of the National Cathedral, the scenario played out the same as on the Capitol steps. Then, at the end of two weeks, Mr. Ward seemed exhausted by Amelia's persistence and at last spoke to her. They stood on the sidewalk in front of a bistro on Second Avenue, where Amelia had waited outside until he'd finished his breakfast.

"If you can tell me why you want to be a lobbyist, Miss Cooke, then I might consider training you," Mr. Ward said.

Determination had supplanted fear, so Amelia recounted her study and newfound passion for government with ease. When she went on to say she desired to prove that a woman could serve in the role of a proper lobbyist, Mr. Ward huffed and tried to shoo her away with a flick of his cane. Amelia smiled to hide her doubts. If she couldn't convince him of her sincerity then she had no chance, whether male or female, of being a lobbyist.

She started to say more but Mr. Ward interrupted. "You're not being honest about your motivations, Miss Cooke. At the core of everything I do, I'm honest about who I am and what I stand for. That's why I'm successful." He paused then added, "You got that lesson for free."

Mrs. Stockett sat with Amelia in the parlor as Amelia shared what Mr. Ward had said. The plain room had two burgundy winged-backed chairs, a matching loveseat, and a fireplace blackened from years of soot.

"He has a point," Mrs. Stockett said over the chip in her teacup.

"How can you say that?" Amelia had finished her tea and sat with her back to the fire.

"Girly, when you saw Mr. Ward's picture in the newspaper, what really made you want to come to this swamp? And don't go on about a job and a new life. That's the kind of malarkey them politicians are always spewing all over. If you ask me, all that caterwauling is what really makes everything so muddy."

Amelia didn't have an answer so she excused herself and went to her room. In the middle of the night she dreamed that hands surrounded her face and neck, trying to crush the life out of her, and she awoke with the answer to Mrs. Stockett's question. By morning, when Amelia opened the newspaper and saw an announcement for a dinner hosted by the "Lobbyist King" at the Old Ebbitt Grill, she knew just what she had to do.

The Old Ebbitt promised mahogany wood, velvet booths, and beveled glass. Amelia stood in the hallway outside the banquet room that served ten-dollar plates of gourmet fare and looked down again at her ensemble. She felt foolish but Mrs. Stockett had said she looked perfect and had even enlisted help of sorts from Mr. Stockett. " 'Bout time the no-good louse did something to help somebody," Mrs. Stockett had said. Amelia adjusted her hat one last time before she opened the door and marched uninvited into the party and right up to Sam Ward.

At first Mr. Ward didn't recognize her, which she understood, given her unique presentation. Then he chuckled and said, "My friends, come look at this young lady. Is she not fetching even in a man's tuxedo and top hat?"

The roomful of men and women overfed on food, wine, and their own success huddled around Amelia and fussed as Mr. Ward attributed her costume to part of the evening's festivities. When, after a few minutes, the guests grew bored and moved away, Mr. Ward pulled her into an empty side room and demanded she explain herself or be arrested for disorderly conduct.

"You asked me to be honest about my goals, so here I am. I don't want to be a man, but I want a place in this world like one. I want others to listen to me, and I want to do as I please. I want to prove women are capable of handling complex jobs, of throwing a stupid ball and learning science. And I admit that I also want a fine lifestyle and having a room full of people pay attention to me and my opinions."

"No one will ever listen to your opinions, Miss Cooke."

Amelia yanked off her bowtie and threw it on the floor. "They will if you teach me how to make them listen. For weeks you let me follow you and stopped every time I tried to talk to you.

Why? Why didn't you send for the police then? I'm not that pretty."

Sam Ward stroked his white beard. "You make a good point, Miss Cooke. I'm not sure why I listened to you. Perhaps you have a natural gift I've overlooked. But that doesn't tell me anything about your ability to do the job."

"Ask me anything."

Amelia's heart fluttered with excitement as she watched him study her manly attire. "All right, I have just one question to ask. Follow me."

Mr. Ward led her back into the party and introduced her to twenty dinner guests. When the polite nodding concluded, he took her back to the parlor.

"Now tell me all of the names of the people you just met." Mr. Ward folded his arms and rocked back on his heels.

Amelia recited all twenty first and last names and their titles as if reading from a list. When she finished, she enjoyed seeing his astonishment. His eyes couldn't open any wider.

"Impressive, Miss Cooke. You may have something I can work with after all." He straightened his face as he ran his hand down the lapel of his coat. "Why don't you come to my home tomorrow morning at ten o'clock? And this time, knock on my door."

"Thank you, Mr. Ward. I won't disappoint you."

"No, you won't. Only expectations lead to disappointment, Miss . . . May I call you Amelia?" he asked.

"If I may call you Sam," Amelia replied.

His whiskers fluttered above his surprised smile, and he patted her once on the back as she'd seen gentlemen do. "You may call me Sam if you promise never to wear a man's suit again. Most impressive, Miss Cooke, I mean Amelia. See you tomorrow, then."

"Yes, Sam, see you then," Amelia said, bolstered, she

surmised, by wearing pants for the first time. She watched Sam leave, then glanced down at the trousers and smiled. She'd overcome the first test. How many more she'd have to pass remained a mystery.

Whereas the outside of Mr. Ward's house looked identical to the neighbors, Amelia doubted the doctors and lawyers had an interior as staged as Mr. Ward's.

Parties at the home of Sam Ward gained fame and success for the eclectic guest lists, exotic foods, stimulating conversation, and a generous, gregarious host who entertained former slave-owning Democrats as well as patriotic, abolitionist Republicans. The foyer had a coat rack with a brass umbrella stand the size one finds in a hotel, and delicate etched glass panels on the walls created the illusion of starlight. Square gaming tables and several service carts filled the front receiving parlor, and Amelia could picture the guests with cigars and cards, spilling drinks and secrets.

Sam directed her into a second, smaller parlor more on par with the neighbors except for the solid-gold fireplace poker and trinket box made from elephant tusk.

"Do you know why I asked you the names?" Sam asked.

"Because relationships build trust. Knowing someone's name is the first step to a relationship."

"I see you keep up with the news. I believe you just quoted me word for word."

"Yes, but does that make the sentiment any less true?"

"Touché. You have a quick mind, my dear, and we shall see if we can use that to our advantage. But first we must talk terms."

Sam rattled on about percentages and cuts from her work. His conditions sounded like gibberish, so when Sam finished, Amelia just nodded. She required only one concession, one grand, necessary condition.

"I accept whatever you just said as long as you can pay me something or give me room and board until I can work on my own." Her savings almost gone, she had to ask.

"You want a stipend?"

Amelia learned a new word. "Yes, or a place to live."

"Living under my roof as a tenant is ludicrous. Your first lesson is about gossip and the proper image you must maintain at all times."

"So a stipend then. I don't need much but if I am to be your apprentice, then I'm limited in other employment."

Sam considered her request, then agreed to two meals a day and a small advance on her future earnings as his employee. If unable to learn the job to his satisfaction, she then owed him for money rendered plus the cost of the meals. Amelia held out her hand and they shook on the deal. Then they got to work.

Amelia thought he'd test her new knowledge of how government worked and use terms and phrases without explanation. Instead, he ushered her into the dining room and placed her in front of a properly set dinner table with four forks, two spoons, two knives, and four wine glasses of different sizes.

"Note that the full complement of silverware means this is a dinner with six courses. Do you see how the dessert spoons are set? Now tell me why you should care about dessert spoons."

She thought for just a moment. "Six courses is a long meal, which gives you lots of time to talk to your guests. And if I saw there were two desserts, I wouldn't dream of leaving early even if I had to endure the most dull conversation known to man. The idea of a second dessert is exciting."

He pursed his lips. "A long meal doesn't give me time to talk to my guests, Amelia; it allows the guests time to talk to each other and to me. The more a person speaks about *themselves*, the more interesting *you* are. And as for your reasoning about two desserts . . . ," he stroked his beard. "Well, you have a sharp mind indeed."

When pleased, Sam rubbed his beard or lowered his head to scratch his ear to hide his smile. If Sam disliked the way Amelia folded napkins or that she didn't know the full responsibility for the job of tax assessor, he tapped his foot or cane, impatient that she hadn't remembered every word he uttered.

"Why do I need five different smiles? For Crocket's sake, I only have one face," Amelia asked as Sam stood beside her while she again practiced grinning in the mirror Sam had moved into the parlor from one of the guest bedrooms.

Amelia's training advanced over the next three months. Each morning they worked together for four hours, and then, in the afternoons, Sam left her with stacks of historical congressional vote records and bills that he'd lobbied into practice. Piles of papers covered the floor, dining table, and every chair.

"I don't understand why you took on that nickel mine project in Mexico. You didn't make much money and had to travel so far," Amelia said when Sam asked her what she'd learned from the previous day's review.

"This job isn't just about brokering the deals right in front of us. Advance preparation is key. I did a great service to a gentleman in Mexico and my absence gave the Washington crowd time to miss me. I returned to quite a nice homecoming.

"You must remember that my methods are discreet, even if that means travel abroad. I never talk directly about a project. I just ask the right questions. This work takes knowledge and planning."

"Planning or scheming? It sounds a little like you're saying the ends justify the means." Amelia had heard that phrase too many times over the years.

"Not at all. There are many ways to reach an end. Our job is to find a way that needs no justification."

She smiled at his use of "our job." If Sam noticed, he

continued his lesson unfettered.

"I don't threaten or bribe as some in our field. I p
must plan and anticipate. And, yes, I have many frier
friends, whom I help and ask to help me when ne
introduce people, ask them about their life, and get then
about the weighty matters of running our country over du
dressed in orange marmalade. People must be able t
municate for this country to function. There are many s
any debate so we help each side reach at least a co
understanding, if not agreement."

He sounded sincere and Amelia nodded. She'd se
enormous bouquet of flowers he sent for the death of a
aide's child and when she asked the reason for a packa
seemed keen to get in the mail, he looked honestly perp
He had no agenda and loved giving gifts. He often sei
friend, Henry Longfellow, a bushel of Chesapeake oy
because he knew how much he liked them.

His lecture concluded so he could prepare for his ever
Sam rubbed his hand over his round belly. "All these wor
dinners have a downside. But unlike me, my dear, you can'
ford to lose your fine figure. You must watch what you eat."

"Why do you always segregate me by my gender?" Sh
argued this point many times. As before, he waited until
finished going on about the intelligence and competence
women before he spoke in a soft, clear voice.

"If I had black hair, scarred skin, and dark beady eyes, wo
you think of me differently than you do now?" he asked.

Sam made friends in part because of his gregarious person
ity and soft, kindly features that gave him the look of a doti
grandfather. Amelia nodded her answer.

"The first time we met I told you we are all judged on ou
appearance. For you, that includes your gender, which I say i
an asset if used properly, and I mean that in every good sense o

hat word." He looked at her then as a well-meaning guardian worried for her virtue. Then he chuckled at his own thoughts and said, "Just be glad you aren't old like me. People judge by age, too."

She hadn't thought much about her own age and Sam's comment made her grin.

"Today's actually my birthday," Amelia said, not adding *or at least the date selected for me to celebrate.*

"Well, my dear, why didn't you say something sooner? Splendid. I was going to have you come with me tonight to observe. We shall make it a birthday celebration. I should have guessed you were a Taurus."

Amelia thought about herself as the sign of the bull during the carriage ride to the evening's agenda. Sam looked dapper in his tail tuxedo and commented several times on her dress.

"You look quite dazzling, Amelia. You should always wear green. Your eyes look like emeralds. Dazzling."

Upon arrival, Sam instructed Amelia to walk behind him and speak only if spoken to. He'd introduce her as his apprentice to the small gathering and then continue with his work as if she weren't there. Her job required only that she pay attention and stay out of the way, preferably in the corner.

"We can celebrate your birthday later. Our host doesn't like attention diverted from himself. But I ordered a small cake in honor of your big day."

Had Amelia heeded any of his commands, she might have avoided exile to Ohio and had her first-ever piece of birthday cake.

The home on Lafayette Square housed a diplomat from Paraguay in the lush manner Amelia expected. Dinner included delicacies shipped in from the countryman's homeland and she overheard rumors of a course of oysters garnished with a real black pearl.

"Mr. Doyle, this is Miss Amelia Cooke, my apprentice. Mr. Doyle is with the *Post.*" Sam introduced a bony man with a narrow chin and crooked bowtie.

"Are you Clancy Doyle?" Amelia said.

"One and the same. I take it you read my column. Well, of course you do, everyone reads my column. I'm great."

Sam didn't much like reporters, whom he said printed sensational lies and unfounded theories rather than news. Still, he invited the likes of Doyle to his gatherings whenever appropriate. "A comment in the newspaper is free advertising," Sam told her.

"Miss Cooke, perhaps you'd like a crab cake from the appetizer buffet. You'll find them over there, out of the way," Sam said.

Amelia nodded as Sam moved on, but she didn't leave Mr. Doyle as instructed. She'd read much of Clancy Doyle's work and asked about his sensational editorials.

Mr. Doyle stuttered in a loud, raspy voice, and Amelia realized he held the edge of the table to steady himself. Several times she tried to back away only to have him lean farther forward. She worried he might fall over.

Sam stood across the room with two senators and Amelia saw him check on her several times before he narrowed his eyes. He didn't want her talking to the reporter any longer. She must go to her safe corner immediately.

"Mr. Doyle, I'm very sorry but I—"

The reporter put his hand on her waist. His breath smelled of gin and crab cakes and his grip felt tight even through the boning in the bodice of her dress.

"Let go of me," Amelia said in a forced whisper. She didn't want anyone to see them.

"Why? You like it. I know your type. You work like a man and play like a woman. Isn't that right?"

Amelia reacted without thinking first. She slipped her arm around the base of Mr. Doyle's collar and pinched the thin skin.

"Ouch. You little Jezebel," Doyle said too loudly and then grabbed her arm.

Sam and the other guests turned to the commotion just in time to see Amelia punch Doyle in the gut. He folded over and shouted a string of vulgarity as she dashed from the room.

Amelia hid in the carriage and waited for Sam to finish his evening. When he at last emerged, she tried to explain that she'd been protecting herself.

"You had one task, Miss Cooke. To stay quiet," Sam said as the carriage moved forward.

Amelia felt unsettled by his using her surname and liked the dark carriage because she couldn't see his disappointment.

"Maybe I've misjudged you, but I don't have any more time to coddle you. And I don't want to watch you fail," he said. His voice caught before he cleared his throat. For a moment he sounded like a papa bird pushing a baby from the nest.

"I've been thinking about this for a while and now I've decided," Sam continued. "I'm sending you to a conference in Ohio."

Amelia hid her surprise in the darkness.

"You're going to the American Medical Association conference in Cincinnati for two weeks. I want you to meet the doctors and find out their thoughts on the Department of Agriculture adding prescription-drug regulations."

"You want to send me away because of that dolt reporter?"

"There are several important bills on the horizon and we need information on how the AMA is going to react so I can make appropriate plans. Plus, this gives us the opportunity to see how you do on your own. But don't get too confident. This is a test. One that I hope you pass."

Amelia bristled again about the reporter and not wanting to leave D.C. In truth, she didn't feel ready to be on her own and didn't want to disappoint Sam again.

"I don't care what Mr. Doyle did. They will all do something like that, Amelia. Put yourself in the piranha tank and what do you expect? But you must learn how to handle the men without causing a scene. Whatever you did to Clancy I'm sure he deserved. One of the real tests for you in this job is to put those hooligans in their place without them knowing you've done it. Do you understand?"

"How can I—?"

"You'll figure that out in Ohio. You'll be in a room full of men without me watching to make you nervous. My dear, as I've said before, men are drawn to you. Even beyond your fine appearance, you have an unassuming way of enticing men that I can't quite describe and won't train out of you even if I could. You just haven't learned to fully use your feminine gifts yet, but you will, and on your own. I can't teach you how. I was never very handsome."

Amelia smiled. "I'm sure that isn't true."

"You see that, the playful tone in your voice just now. Mesmerizing. Natural."

She shrugged, not sure Sam wasn't exaggerating in the same charismatic way he embellished stories about dinner with royals, and then asked when she had to leave.

"As soon as you have some proper clothes. In the morning you're going to see Estelle for a full complement of dresses. You look exquisite tonight but you can't wear the same gown every night. Plus, I'm extremely tired of seeing such a lovely young lady in such homemade frocks."

The carriage stopped to let Sam out. "One caution," Sam said, his hand on the open coach door. "Not all men are as harmless as Mr. Doyle. His kind is easy to identify and handle once you get the hang of it. The ones to beware of are the charmers, good-looking young men who'd like to seduce you, make you fall in love with them. You must remember your purpose and keep your wits about you. There's already enough gossip about you. Some even insinuate you and I are in a tawdry affair."

"Who says that?"

"It doesn't matter. I've taken care of what needs attention. My point is that you work in an industry run by and for men. For all that you've learned—and you are a highly intelligent person, my dear—I fear there will come a moment when you'll have to define yourself as either a lobbyist or a woman. I'm truly not sure you can be both."

Sam waved as the coached pulled away. His warning felt protective and Amelia recognized how much she cared for Sam as she would an uncle or even perhaps a father. But he had no grounds to worry. She'd go to Ohio and do just as he instructed. When she returned with the information he needed, Sam would realize just how well she could do the same job as a man. She'd worked too hard to jeopardize her success for a ridiculous entanglement of any sort, especially the complexity of falling in love. How could she ever fall in love when she really had no idea what the word meant? As the carriage rattled over the cobblestones in front of the White House, Amelia considered her situation and realized that, for once, never having experienced love gave her the upper hand.

CHAPTER FIVE

Cincinnati sparkled. Amelia had forgotten what city streets looked like without a thick layer of cement powder and mud. Just the same, her light mood changed the instant Amelia saw the room Sam let for her at the Beechmont Lodging House. Rather than unpack, Amelia wanted to send Sam a telegram with a few choice, unladylike words. He made clear that her accommodations came out of her future earnings, but, even so, she had listened to him go on and on about how much he enjoyed a suite at the Palace Hotel whenever he visited. His luxury suite didn't have stained rugs or wallpaper coated in years of grime.

Per Sam's instructions, Amelia had one day before the conference began to orient herself. His parting words included, "A well-trained lobbyist always knows the best in town and gives suggestions when asked," which Amelia found ironic. He also said, "Never expect anything and you're never disappointed." As Amelia picked flecks of porcelain from the stained wash basin in her room, she realized her first test. She pushed aside her bitterness and focused on how to hang her enchanting new wardrobe on two rusty hooks.

Before leaving for Ohio, Sam had spared little of Amelia's prospective income on a full complement of day wear, party dresses, and cocktail attire. Hats, gloves, and bags matched for style as well as function, as Sam understood how ladies used such accessories to acquire a glass of wine or seat in a crowded room.

"I've picked up many a handkerchief and helped remove a glove in the name of chivalry and sneaking a peek," Sam had admitted.

After liberating a length of rope from the desk clerk, Amelia engineered a clothesline from the hooks to the window hinge using simple overhand knots every few inches to hold the hangers in place. She fluffed her garments, careful to keep anything from touching the walls, then stacked hat boxes on the small desk with chipped paint and two stuck drawers.

With half a day still left to investigate, Amelia changed and stood in front of the scratched cheval glass with the thought of how much the added "luxury" cost her. Guided by her reflection, she tipped the broad brim of her hat to peer from beneath without drawing suspicion. She'd already practiced with her wares as a magician with cards, being sure she kept her handbag on her left arm so her right stayed free for a champagne glass or handshake. Amelia felt ready to make an impression, though to what ends she still wasn't quite sure.

After strolling through the city proper with a map, Amelia knew well enough how to get from her room to the Palace Hotel hosting the conference. She ate lunch at the hotel's elegant bistro overlooking the lobby to watch for arriving doctors as a sort of preview. Sam wanted her to find out all she could about how doctors and the American Medical Association felt about prescription-drug reform to help plan for several upcoming bills. From a safe distance she watched bellmen haul trunks for aging gents in custom-made, Italian shoes. The doctors seemed harmless enough until one of the herd, a lithe man with round, gold spectacles perched on a long nose, walked right up and sat down at her table.

"Can I help you?" Amelia asked. She heard her own anger

and thought of the reporter and her need to perform. "I apologize if I sounded a bit harsh. You just startled me Dr. . . ."

"Graham." The doctor scratched his ear. "How did you know I'm a doctor?"

Amelia grinned. "A man of your stature can't be anything but something so grand. My guess was either a doctor or statesman." She wished Sam could overhear her now.

The doctor popped a blue pill in his mouth, seized her water glass, and took a long swallow. "I have to take my medication on time and there wasn't any water around. Sorry to bother you."

"No bother, Dr. Graham, I assure you. Please take care of yourself," Amelia said.

Amelia felt she could handle the men with finesse given time for practice. As she gazed out at the crowded lobby, she knew she'd have lots of opportunity to improve.

The conference began with a luncheon, so Amelia skipped breakfast and spent the next morning preparing. She chose a fitted, short-sleeved, chiffon dress; pinned her hair up in the front but left a curled cascade from beneath her hat; and wore long white day gloves of light cotton that stopped several inches shy of her capped sleeve to highlight her skin. Sam told her never to underestimate the power of a woman's soft skin no matter where the location.

Men crowded the hotel lobby to shake hands and slap backs as they waited to register and get their entrance tags, a square paper with their names written in calligraphy that they pinned to their breast pocket. Since Sam hadn't changed the invitation from his own name to hers, getting into the conference became her second challenge. He forbade her to use his name to persuade anyone; he wanted her to stand alone and see if she landed right side up, or on her head, as she thought Sam sometimes imagined.

Amelia got into line behind the doctors and took an inventory of the filling lobby. She noted just one other woman, who stood close enough so Amelia overheard when one of the men addressed the woman as Dr. Stevenson. Amelia nodded to the woman in the unadorned day dress with her hair pulled into a tight bun, and the woman seemed to understand Amelia's approval and nodded back. Amelia wanted to ask her about her experiences in medical school, but Sam cautioned against diversions of any kind so she turned away and refocused her attention on the task at hand.

After five minutes spent in line concocting a story, getting a name tag required just asking with a big smile. A young medical resident smiled back and within moments Amelia pinned her own paper square to her chest.

Eli Lilly, owner of an emerging pharmaceutical company, hosted the elaborate luncheon due to the company's interest in prescription-drug reform. Sam had explained their holdings as purely financial and so of little interest. With the doctors in her sights, Amelia stepped into the hotel's outdoor rose garden, straightened her shoulders, and mingled.

A string quartet played as Amelia wove through the crowd behind waiters with trays of appetizers and glasses of wine and listened to snippets of conversation.

"Can I interest you in a glass of champagne?"

Amelia turned to find a man, no more than twenty-five, with light hair and an enthusiastic grin, holding up a wine glass with delicate, soft hands.

"Are you a surgeon?" Amelia asked as she took the glass and nodded her thanks.

The man seemed eager to tell her all about his attendance at Harvard Medical School. Amelia thought the young man friendly and a waste of her time. She began plotting her escape when another man, in his early thirties, stepped in front of his inexperienced junior.

"Edward Stillman. And you are?" he said to Amelia.

She'd seen the man turn and watch her when she'd first entered the luncheon. From across the lawn, her admirer looked like all the others wearing their summer suits and confident smirks as a uniform. Up close, Amelia couldn't help but notice that his appearance, in fact, looked nothing like the others.

Amelia introduced herself and held out her hand. Edward Stillman shook her hand with a gentle touch, then caressed her fingers as he let go of her hand.

"And what do you do, Miss Cooke? Please don't tell me you're the wife of one of these sawbones."

"I take it you're not a doctor then, Mr. Stillman?" Amelia hid her disappointment with a shy head tilt.

"Afraid I'm just a lowly state senator."

Arrogance and candor seemed fixed as part of his personality and Amelia found the combination oddly attractive, like the right balance of bold color in a muted painting. The young doctor excused himself, though Amelia had forgotten his presence, and she allowed the senator to escort her to a table for luncheon service.

"A lobbyist? Can that be so?" the senator asked.

They sat at a table for two, Amelia aware of failing Sam and his directive with every bite.

"Indeed. I'm working with Sam Ward. Perhaps you've heard of him?" Amelia hadn't meant to sound so coy but her manner met with the senator's approval.

"*The* Sam Ward? Yes, I believe I've run across his name a time or two. A protégé, then? I'm impressed, Amelia. I assume I may call you Amelia. In my five years as a state senator, I've never called any lobbyist by his, or her, last name. Political suicide, I assure you."

Amelia saw his statement as bait and let the game continue.

"You may call me Amelia if you explain such a dramatic declaration. 'Political suicide' seems a little extreme."

He spoke about the role of state government in a burst that sounded rehearsed and yet genuine. He believed his job required he keep those outside government, like lobbyists, in their proper place.

"And what place is that, Senator . . . Edward?"

Amelia nodded when appropriate but she hardly listened as he spoke about upholding the prestige and bipartisanship of his office. He had broad shoulders that hinted at a college athletic career and a strong, handsome face. She liked the way he brushed her forearm as if accidental and yet didn't apologize, and she could see that people trusted him because of his receptive blue eyes that created a startling, inviting contrast to his thick dark hair. Over the years, several boys sent her love poems and one of the swine at the cotton mill proclaimed his love daily, but Amelia had never sat across from what she felt justified in calling a true man.

A waiter cleared away Amelia's untouched chocolate cake and then the senator stood and reached out his hand. "Come with me. Let me introduce you to some of the doctors. I can only assume that with your job title, you're here to socialize and gather information about prescription drugs."

Amelia found his perceptiveness and intelligence reason enough to take his arm and allow him to lead her to where men stood in groups around a champagne fountain. Good to his word, the senator introduced her to several experienced physicians, a dean of admissions, and two journalists covering the event for the *Journal of the American Medical Association*. The men varied in ages but not in the surprised, dismissive look when the senator told them of her occupation. Two of the doctors chuckled, citing the senator's proclivity for pranks.

"I assure you, the senator is quite serious," Amelia said.

One of the doctors gave a sheepish apology but the other, a pompous cardiologist from Boston, shrugged and walked away. Amelia looked for Dr. Stevenson in the hopes of finding strength in female camaraderie, but she didn't see any other women. Just as Sam foretold, she stood the lone doe in a pack of wolves.

The luncheon over, just a few men lingered about as the senator walked Amelia to the hotel lobby.

"Why didn't you laugh when I told you I was a lobbyist?" Amelia asked.

"Why would I laugh? A man in my position can't afford to make an enemy of half the population. Some men forget how many of your fair kind influence their husband's vote. Of course, few are as fair as you." He paused as if shy, but she didn't sense any embarrassment in his flirtatious comment. "You have the presence of an angel, Miss Cooke."

Amelia rarely blushed, which she held up as a badge of honor given her fair complexion. She laughed to avert attention from her burning cheeks. Never had anyone given her a compliment that felt like a gift.

"A lobbyist who blushes. Now that's something you don't see every day."

"I should hope not. I like to think of myself as an original," she blurted, annoyed with herself for again sounding so playful.

"You are that, Miss Cooke. You are that."

Back in her hotel room, Amelia reflected on her first day at the conference with relief. She'd survived and met many potential sources and one possible distraction. The senator had left with the warning of his future attendance at the conference. Then he again shook her hand and let his fingers linger too long on hers. Amelia couldn't stop thinking about his touch and how her heart fluttered when he smiled at her, his eyes so receptive and interested in her every word, and she didn't know what to think of her desire to feel his special handshake without her gloves.

Over the next few lunches, Amelia joined a rotation of doctors and did her best to make pleasant conversation. Though Sam felt confident in her training, the doctors didn't want to talk to her about work. Most had too many glasses of whiskey and were more interested in cricket and the never ending hassles of wives. *No offense.* She diverted a few doctors who made inappropriate advances with a question about the horrendous disfigurement of leprosy patients; the mention of a missing nose seemed to chill any libido.

When Amelia next saw Edward, he had stopped at her table to taunt the doctors with his good humor. He had a straightforward, charismatic style that Amelia admired. Then when one of the physicians attacked Amelia for her work, Edward defended her career with outlandish statistics. When Edward winked at Amelia, she stuffed a cracker in her mouth to keep from beaming at him.

In between the educational sessions and committee meetings, Amelia loitered in the lobby but few doctors had time or wanted to stop. She contemplated seeking out their company at dinner, but couldn't figure out how to join the men without the appearance of a tawdry proposition. She stood perplexed in the lobby on what to do next when Edward approached. "Frustrating day?" he asked.

That he could read her emotions meant she needed more time with the mirror. Amelia smiled but said nothing because Edward looked like he had something more to say. He, in fact, had a question, and Amelia hid her excitement with her handy hat.

"And before you say what I know you're going to say, the opera is a perfectly respectable evening out with an unmarried man," Edward said. "Tonight then?"

Against the nagging she heard as clearly as if Sam stood right beside her, Amelia agreed to accompany the senator, provided they meet at the opera house. Edward conceded, and then she watched him walk through the lobby in a manner that reminded her of Sam. People gravitated toward Edward, and he shook hands and chatted with an easy confidence as if everyone were a long lost friend. Amelia turned away lest he look back and find her staring. She would see him again in a few hours.

Newly built, the Cincinnati Music Hall reminded Amelia of a scene in an Oscar Wilde story, with elegant arched windows and red-brick facade. Amelia spotted Edward by the plaza's fountain in full black tail tuxedo and top hat. His eyes brightened as she approached and she knew she'd selected the right dress.

"You look . . ." he shook her hand and paused to admire her. He looked at her yet he didn't leer like men on the street. Amelia felt like a prize and not a possession.

"You also look nice," she said to break the awkward silence.

Edward straightened his bowtie. "Yes, well as handsome a couple as we are, we'd better hurry. Showing up after the curtain will get us tarred and feathered."

Amelia had never been to an opera and liked the music of *Die Fledermaus* very well, more than she expected. Edward sat beside her, his hand in his lap, but every so often he'd lean close and whisper something about an important aria or the soprano's high note. She enjoyed the closeness every time she felt his breath on her neck.

During the intermission, the senator introduced her to an envoy of politicians and their wives, though, unlike at the conference, he avoided any mention of her occupation. Before Amelia had time to correct Edward's oversight, the wives hustled her from the men to find out more about Edward.

"He's so handsome. If I were younger . . ."

"So, how long have you known Edward? Do we see a future?"

Amelia touched the woman's arm. "What a lovely brooch you're wearing, Mrs. Huffington. Did you get that abroad?"

She'd diverted the conversation, but Amelia wanted to get back to where the discussion might include something she could report back to Sam. The pleasantness of the ladies did nothing for her career, and she feared they might want to talk about Edward again. Edward kept glancing at her and each time he smiled, Amelia felt a wave of tingling in her chest. If the ladies pressed, she didn't think she could veil her growing infatuation for long.

After the fat lady sang, during which Amelia bit her lip to keep from laughing, Edward took her hand and led her through the crowds toward the exit. Once outside, he didn't let go of her hand.

"Where can I take you now? To your hotel?" He sounded harmless and pleasant in the warm spring air even as mischief played in his grin.

"You can hail me a hackney and let me thank you for a lovely evening," she said, aware of his disappointment even as he continued to smile.

Once in the cab, Amelia peered through the open window. "Why didn't you tell your colleagues that I'm training with Sam?"

She watched his face twist into a sideways grin, then he touched her cheek. His hand felt warm and smooth, and for a moment she considered letting him escort her home. Then he removed his hand and she felt cool air on her cheek.

"My darling Amelia, as much as I understand what you're doing, I'm not so sure you'll get such a progressive response from everyone, especially the wives. Privileged ladies of the sort tonight frown upon women in the workforce. I can't imagine what they'd say to a job such as yours."

"But that makes no sense. Why should they care if I work?"

"Why indeed? A mystery to me, I assure you," h
Amelia saw knowing in his glance. He understood mo
let on and likely felt ashamed of her.

"I should think a man of your position could handle
criticism, even value the attention given that you have y
set on Washington. You do have your feet directed to
Senate seat, a real one, I mean."

Amelia's anger surprised her, and she felt foolish and th
Edward might lash out in response. Instead, Edward le
forward and kissed her. She felt his lips against hers for ju
moment before he pulled away.

"I'm sorry . . . I shouldn't have . . . it's just that you'
magnificent. So fresh but so clever at the same time. You don
know how intoxicating you are. At least you don't yet."

Edward slapped the side of the hackney and then Amelia sat
alone in the carriage all too aware of her first kiss. Romance
seemed impractical and she didn't have sappy daydreams about
the man she'd marry like so many of the girls her age. Still, she
didn't expect the heat down her back. Amelia licked her lips
and closed her eyes; she'd felt something beyond his touch and
liked the feeling a little too much. Amelia opened her eyes and
thought of Sam's warning.

The following morning Edward sent a bouquet of wildflow-
ers and a note asking her to join him for an intimate dinner at
the city's best French restaurant. After a day spent trying to
speak with doctors who wouldn't make eye contact with her,
Amelia met Edward at the restaurant and over s*alade niçoise*
they chatted about state funding for a new bridge. She appreciated that, not only did he look at her, he also used government
jargon and answered all of her questions in detail.

"So, tell me more about Sam. Is he really as debonair as they
ay? I read he sprinkles gold flakes on his breakfast," Edward
id.

"Not true. Though he believes a gold-rimmed glass makes ine taste sweeter. And he enjoys the occasional quail eggs with ɔast."

Edward tilted his head. "You really admire him, don't you? You light up even a little more when you speak about him."

"Do I?" Amelia thought of Sam and all he'd done to help her. She considered Sam the first person to form an opinion of her based on her mind and talents, and not just her pitiful circumstances.

A waiter appeared and refilled Edward's glass of wine. Amelia had taken just a few sips.

"So, you know I'm from this fair city, but you probably don't know that my father was a congressional representative and his father, Grandpa Benjamin Stillman, was once attorney general. Family business, I guess. Dad got me into politics. Pushed me, really, but it's a good career path. He's a good man."

"And do you see him much?"

Edward nodded. "He stays involved in politics while Mother's busy with her charity work. And what about you? Is your mother as beautiful as you?"

Though she'd said the word more times than she liked to admit, Amelia didn't want to tell Edward that her parents were dead. In the dim, romantic lighting, she felt too vulnerable, exposed in a way that made her question how much she might say. She didn't know how to share the details of her pain, and yet Edward's honest interest and caring made her nervous that she might try to explain her feelings. When she delayed answering, Edward reached across the table and squeezed her hand.

"You don't have to talk about anything you don't want to. Wⁱ all have a history, but that doesn't mean our past has to be of our present or future. Right?" He grinned and tar table. "I say we order dessert. And you have to eat ⸱ nibble."

Bolstered by a lemon tart and glass of cognac, Edward's manner changed over dessert and he put his hand on Amelia's knee. When she removed his hand, he said, "No one can see. It's hidden under the tablecloth."

"Not the point, I assure you," Amelia said, annoyed by his presumptions and something more. When they spoke as equals, she felt empowerment. With his altered demeanor and hand on her knee, Amelia didn't like the way she felt about herself. She saw herself through his eyes; a cheap girl he wanted to bed and toss away like the prostitutes she thought of as neighbors back in D.C. Amelia hated that Mrs. Stockett called them jezebels rather than consider them sisters in need of help.

After dinner they couldn't find a hackney, so Amelia allowed Edward to escort her through the dark streets back to the Beechmont.

"Sam picked this place as a learning tool," Amelia said in front of the building's unlabeled front door.

"I like it. It's rustic."

"That's certainly one word for it."

"So, I don't see any witnesses. Perhaps I can come up for a few minutes," Edward said.

He'd guzzled two cups of coffee after the wine and seemed more himself than earlier. Even so, Amelia had her refusal ready when Edward slipped his hand around her waist, pulled her to him, and covered her lips with his before she could say anything at all. She thought to push him away but she'd never been held in a man's arms, in anyone's arms before. The newness of being so close to someone whispered through her whole body and she realized what she'd missed her whole life. Within his arms she at last felt safe and shielded from the darkness. She fought the tears by closing her eyes then pressed herself against him as he kissed her neck. When Edward asked again about seeing her inside, Amelia let her new raw emotions take over.

The hotel room felt even smaller with two people pressed together and Amelia grew more and more conscious that her knee rested against the bed.

"Edward, I don't think—"

"I know I should go," he said, his hand curled around the small of her back. "But I don't want to. I . . ." he paused and leaned back so Amelia saw his full gaze.

The distasteful room fell away and she saw only his gentle eyes looking at her with true admiration. Amelia knew logically that her parents loved her but she couldn't remember them well enough to know what love looked like. As Edward ran his fingertips across her forehead and down her cheeks, his eyes still on hers, she let herself imagine. "Amelia, I know I shouldn't be here but you are just so rare. I can't bear the thought of leaving, ever."

In the sincerity of his words, twenty years of trauma faded away and Amelia felt an inner peace she'd never experienced. Amelia unwound Edward's hands from her waist and led him to her bed.

For a week, Amelia spent her days hunting down doctors and the evenings in Edward's arms. He hadn't invited her to his home for fear of being seen by the neighbors, so they stayed in the hotel room and found ways to ignore the shabby room. Edward seemed smitten, though Amelia sensed not just by her affections. He stood taller when Amelia took his arm and other men watched with envy, and she fed his ego with compliments about his position and savvy. He in turn kept her informed about the drug initiatives and announced he'd taken the liberty of uncovering the unofficial AMA opinion for her. They were lying in her bed when Edward told her of his findings.

"I know you were having a hard time getting the docs to talk to you, so I made a few inquiries." Edward rubbed Amelia's arm and kissed her bare shoulder with a tenderness that made her shudder.

Amelia sighed. "I don't mind that you helped but I mind that you had to. I can't do this work if men won't talk to me."

"Most men just don't know how to handle you and your modern job. You approach them with your business mind and feminine body and they can't reconcile the two. Now, if you try talking to them like a woman first, maybe save some of the business for later, then I assure you they will listen."

Like Sam, Edward thought she should use her sexuality to gain advantage. Neither considered their suggestion demeaning in any way.

"And if I use my 'feminine wiles' to get their attention, will they ever listen?" Amelia had her doubts. "Listening requires respect."

"There's where you're wrong, Miss Lobbyist. Men will listen for all sorts of reasons. Greed, fear, lust. You just have to figure out what works."

Amelia wanted to change the subject. She didn't like that Edward had no qualms about her flirting with other men and wished he'd show a little jealousy. Plus, she had a more urgent and unsettling topic on her mind.

"So, how much longer before you can run for a Congressional seat?" Amelia asked as she twisted so Edward could kiss the back of her neck.

His lips lingered and then he raised his head. "Why? Are you afraid of my coming to Washington?"

Amelia rolled over on her side to face Edward and then propped herself up on her elbow. "Not at all. I could introduce you around; maybe even let you take me to dinner sometime." She hoped to sound jovial as her insides crushed in against her. Sam had sent her to Ohio for two weeks and her time was up. They never spoke about the future like those in a normal courtship, and now Amelia didn't want to leave the man she feared she loved.

"Would you even have time to entertain me? I'm sure the great Sam Ward has you busy with all sorts of *special* dinners." He kissed the tip of her nose.

She couldn't ignore his insinuation. "Do you think I'm some sort of bed-hopping tart?"

Edward slid closer so Amelia felt their thighs press together. "I like that image," he said.

"Me as a tart?" Amelia said, but her words were lost in his lips. She let him kiss her and move his hands along her body. She wanted to let the topic slip from the room like the heat through the unsealed windows, but she needed to know how he felt about her. Her heart raced.

"Edward, why are we here?" she asked, then cringed at her poor phrasing. That's not what she'd meant to say and yet felt afraid to say any more. She wanted to tell him that she loved him and ask if he felt the same way, but she couldn't leave herself so defenseless. She said nothing and her foolish question festered in the stagnant air.

Edward tucked a few strands of hair behind her ear. The gesture was soothing and gentle, and Amelia heard her own audible sigh. Then he lowered his hand and said, "We're here because you couldn't possibly invite me to a suite at someplace regal like the Willard Hotel. Here," he paused to look at the broken chair propped against the cracked window, "is perfect for this. Don't you think?"

Amelia pressed her face against his shoulder to hide her reaction and he embraced her, seemingly unaware of what he'd really just said. Sam warned of men like Edward and she hadn't listened. As much as Edward spoke of his respect, his comment told her the honest truth.

Once Edward left in the morning, Amelia sent Sam a

telegram with a simple note that she'd finished her job. She sent the same message to Edward and left for Washington on the afternoon train. When she arrived in D.C. at dusk, she went to Sam's home to give him a full report on what she'd learned at the conference.

"A bright career ahead of you," Sam said and then offered to pay her hotel expenses as reward for her good work. Amelia accepted his generous gift with a simple nod.

"Are you all right, my dear?" Sam asked. They stood in his doorway, his hand on her shoulder.

Amelia patted his hand. "I'm fine. Just tired from the trip. The work was," she paused, "a great learning experience just as you said it would be. Thank you for sending me. The whole affair was very enlightening."

Mrs. Stockett made pot roast to celebrate Amelia's return. Then, after an hour of questions about the doctors, Mrs. Stockett let her go upstairs to unpack. Everything in the room looked just as she'd left it and yet Amelia felt ashamed for the naive girl who once lived in the plain room. She hadn't lied to Sam; she'd learned a great lesson to help start her "bright career." Edward saw her only as a toy and she'd proved him right by inviting him to her bed. She'd never make that mistake again.

Just the same, the honorable state senator did her bidding because of his lust, and Edward had unwittingly proved his and Sam's point about using her assets. The men in charge would indeed get used to Amelia's knowing glances and she'd learn how to make them listen.

Almost finished unpacking her trunk, Amelia found her name tag still pinned to her dress. She unpinned the paper and held it over the trash bin just as a cat cried in the alley behind the house. Amelia shook her head against the past. The fat lady had indeed sung and tomorrow the new Miss Amelia Cooke took center stage. Amelia went to her mirror and slid her official badge into the frame. Thanks to Edward T. Stillman, Amelia knew how to succeed and no matter how much more time she needed to work with Sam, she'd prove her worth and become a great woman and even greater lobbyist, a queen to match The King.

★ ★ ★ ★ ★

PART TWO

★ ★ ★ ★ ★

CHAPTER SIX

Standing on the doorstep of the home of Senator Ivan West gave Edward Stillman chills down his spine. He didn't know the senator well and couldn't understand why the senator wanted him to rush over at such a late hour. Plus, the route past the Music Hall again reminded Stillman of Amelia and the contemptible note of dismissal she'd left him six months earlier. After Amelia left, he had a fleeting thought to give chase like some feeble ninny. He told himself that rage drove him to such drastic thoughts, when in fact he felt stupid and insulted for believing that Amelia cared about him in any way beyond how he could help her. The terse note said volumes, and Stillman refused to let a conniving, status seeker like Amelia Cooke take up any more of his time.

Noise from behind the door cleared away thoughts of Amelia. A messenger in the middle of the night usually meant someone had died, but from the shouting Stillman heard coming from inside the house, no one was dead, at least not yet. Stillman straightened and then knocked, prepared to introduce himself to a grumpy footman in a sleeping cap. When the door opened, Stillman jumped.

"Father, what in the world are you doing here?" Stillman asked.

"Get in. And close the door," Stillman's father said.

His father, the great former U.S. Representative Theodore Stillman, stood in the center of a large, circular entry hall with his arms folded across his chest. Beyond the hall, Stillman saw a dark receiving parlor and, to his left, a staircase to the upper floors. His father still wore the dark suit he'd seen him in earlier that day, but the pale-blue cravat, the one his mother bought him for special occasions, hung loose around his neck.

Movement to Stillman's right made him turn. Senator West, also with his arms folded, wore a black robe over pajamas. His feet were bare.

"Senator, Sir, I came as fast as I could. What's so urgent?" Stillman asked.

"I didn't send a note." Senator West turned to Stillman's father. "So that's why you sent for your trusted man. This is ludicrous, Ted. I want you out of my house, now, or I'll send for the police."

Stillman's father laughed. "You won't send for the police unless you want me to tell them the little story I just shared with you. So for the last time, Ivan, let's just be reasonable. I sent for Edward so you could tell him the good news yourself." The elder Stillman's eyes never left the senator's as he said, "Son, you're going to be Ohio's next congressional senator. Mr. West is stepping down."

The senator unfolded his arms and ran his hands through his thinning gray hair. At the age of 74, Stillman had heard that West had some minor health concerns but nothing to warrant retirement.

"I've already told you, I'm not going anywhere," the senator said. He walked around Stillman's father and up the first few steps of the staircase. "And go ahead and tell that story to anyone you want, Theodore. I don't care. In fact, when Margaret gets back from her sister's tomorrow, I'll tell her myself. Now get out and don't come near me again. Am I making myself clear?"

West didn't look back as he walked up the stairs in the slow, purposeful movement of a man with bad knees.

"West!" Stillman's father roared.

Stillman knew that whatever his father had lorded over West was now of no use. He also knew the affliction of his father's temper.

"Father, let's go. I'm not sure what's going on, but we'll talk in the morning." Stillman touched his father's shoulder, but he shrugged him off as he glared at the back of the senator ascending to the top of the stairs. Before Stillman could react, his father bounded up the steps after West and seized his arm.

"No one tells me what to do. No one. So let's stop playing games. You won't tell your wife that you're a cheating louse because of her heart condition. Tomorrow, you'll announce your retirement and endorse State Senator Edward Stillman as your replacement."

Senator West had served three terms and had a reputation for his unruffled, almost detached demeanor. As Stillman watched, he saw firsthand how the senator earned his reputation. Even from Stillman's vantage at the base of the stairs, he could see the senator's cold stare.

"I'm surprised you don't want the job for yourself. Couldn't get reelected could you, Ted? What do they call you one-term little House men? Not a 'lame duck.' " He snapped his fingers, the sound a hollow rattle of old bones. "Oh, yes, I remember: a 'flaccid duck.' "

Stillman cringed and waited for his father's rant of obscenities. His father never spoke about losing the reelection after one term, but he knew the loss still stung. His father thrived on a position of power and being called a flaccid anything struck at his ego. And his father always struck back.

There was no ranting. Stillman watched and did nothing; there was nothing he could do. His father grabbed the thick lapels of West's robe and yanked him forward, close enough to whisper something in his ear, but Stillman couldn't hear what he said. Then his father pushed West back and let go. West tottered and flapped his arms to stop himself from falling backward. Had he been on flat ground he wouldn't have lost his balance. Stillman's father watched, *unfortunately unable*, he later said, to help.

West fell the full length of the stairs and landed in the entryway at Stillman's feet. The crack of the senator's head against the cold white marble echoed before an unsettling silence. Stillman looked up at his father and then down at West and the red stream crawling toward his polished black boots. His father had taught him how to bandage wounds on their many hunting trips, and Stillman liked to imagine himself as the type to spring into action. But Stillman's movements were slow, dazed. He stepped over the blood, pulled up his trousers at the knees, and knelt beside West to check for a pulse.

"Is he dead?" His father's question sounded hopeful, and Stillman felt bile rise in the back of his throat. Stillman stood and nodded.

"Let's go. No one's here, but the footman will find him in the morning." His father tied his cravat as he descended the stairs.

"We have to send for the authorities and explain the accident. Father, it was an accident, right?"

"Don't question me. Of course it was an accident. I didn't push him. The old geezer fell. Nothing more to it. So why should we get involved? All that can come of this is bad publicity, which we don't need right now." His father reached the bottom of the staircase, picked up his hat and coat on the entry table, and then brushed past Stillman to the door. "Come on. We don't need any bad press right now. A Senate seat has just opened."

Two days later, Stillman arrived at his father's study still fighting the throbbing headache that had plagued him since the

94

incident. Misgivings were worse than a long night of brandy.

"Father, your messenger pulled me out of a very important meeting. What's wrong?" Stillman asked.

"Nothing is ever that important at the state legislature. Now, sit down, Edward. Look at this."

His father handed Stillman the *Cincinnati Commercial.*

SENATOR WEST'S DEATH RULED ACCIDENTAL

CINCINNATI, October 15, 1878—Today, the coroner's office released their official findings in the unexpected death of Senator West. Congruent with preliminary reports, all evidence suggests that the senator's fatal fall in his home the night of October twelfth was accidental. Failing health and diminished strength in his legs may have contributed to the senator losing his balance.

"Why do you look angry? Now it's official. Isn't this good news?" Stillman asked.

"Never mind West. Take a look at what that half-wit reporter Maclay is saying. Calling for West's nephew, District Attorney Frederick West, to fill the seat; saying a relative to the late and great is a shoo-in for the appointment. I haven't worked all these years so some sniveling nephew could take your job."

His father's tone wasn't what raised the hairs on Stillman's neck. Theodore Stillman never fidgeted. Ever. Stillman watched as his father spun his wedding band around his finger.

A shout from the hallway drew their attention. James, Stillman's brother, burst through the door.

"You'll never believe what's happened, Father," James said. He paused and raised an eyebrow at his brother. "Didn't know you'd be here, Edward. Saves me time. I have news."

Stillman's father bristled. He had little patience for glee.

"Yes, get on with it. What is it, James?"

"Frederick West, he's going to take me with him to the Hill. If he gets his uncle's seat, he's going to put me on the bench in federal court. He says I've been a good assistant D.A."

Stillman felt a flash of jealousy tighten in his gut.

"James, I have important matters to discuss with Edward right now. We can talk about this later."

"Of course, Father. I wouldn't want to interrupt your precious time with Edward." He then turned to Stillman and added, "You'll have to come visit me Edward, in Washington."

Once James left and closed the study door, Stillman's father cleared his throat. "We need to get rid of West's nephew. That reporter, Maclay, doesn't he owe you a favor? Well, now's the time to cash in. A man must capitalize on opportunity. Use your favor, Edward, and then do him another as soon as you can. You want men to owe you favors, at all costs. Alliances are for the weak. A man owed a favor has all the power."

Stillman thought of his brother. "But what about James? If I'm elected, I can't put him on the bench. How would that look?"

"What about James? Why would I want a son that's a court judge when I can have a son that's a senator? Your brother's a fine attorney. He'll land on his feet."

To end the discussion, Stillman's father claimed he had a meeting.

"Take the newspaper and study up. And don't stay too long. I don't know when your mother's coming home. If she finds you here in the middle of the day, she'll want to know what's wrong."

When his father left, Stillman crumpled the newspaper in his hands and threw it on the desk. He wanted the congressional seat, but he couldn't get rid of the image of West's crumpled body or the sound of his skull against the cold floor. Stillman rubbed his aching temples. It was an accident, a simple accident, and his father made a good point. A man needed to seize the opportunities in front of him. Stillman took a deep breath and stood. A good son never disobeyed his father.

The following week's top story led with, "Frederick West, nephew of the late Senator West, was seen leaving the Beechmont Lodging House with an unidentified man after a romantic embrace." The fallout began just as expected, and Stillman's father complimented him on his fine work. His brother called him despicable to his face and, from the rumors, far worse behind his back. One sentence ruined a man's career, then just a few days later, his life. No one suspected the quiet husband and father of two for the type to put a revolver in his mouth.

After the shock of Frederick's suicide, a large photo ran on the front page of the *Cincinnati Commercial*. Stillman stood beside the governor with his father looking on in the background. From the black and white image, few knew that Stillman's father wore his pale-blue cravat, the one he only wore for special occasions. A simple headline above the photo read, "Edward Stillman Appointed to Fill Open Senate Seat." On September 2, 1878, with the full backing of the Democratic Party, Edward Stillman packed his bags for Washington, D.C., to serve as senator, a *real one*, as Amelia Cooke had once said.

A congressional office on freshman row, the windowless interior corridor of the south wing, came with a sturdy desk with surprisingly ample drawer space; a serviceable, wooden chair; brass floor and desk lamps filled each evening with oil; two claret leather club chairs; and a thin wool area rug in a pattern that resembled rows of eyeballs. Dark mahogany panels covered the walls and suspected mold beneath, and two undersized bookshelves flanked a small brick fireplace. Furnishings were kept in good repair and replaced as deemed necessary by the building maintenance department, and all stationery and fumigation supplies were fetched by aides from a central receptacle in the basement. Pencils were in short supply. Cockroaches and ants were not.

Connected to the main office was an even smaller outer office or guard room. Congressional aides sat at plain wooden desks with a storage cabinet behind and reception chair in front. In addition to their duties as stenographer, editor, and messenger, aides provided a barrier to the noisy hallway just outside their door. Fellow committee members, enthusiasts, tourists, and vagabonds were known to wander into a congressional office without hesitation. Aides spent much of their day shooing people and flies away, both more prevalent in the spring.

Stillman spent his first week on the Hill in meetings with committee members for potential assignments. Even though he felt like a show dog dying to lift his leg on the judge's shoes, Stillman went to every scheduled appointment. His father had already briefed him on the importance of serving on the right committees.

Working late into the evenings meant leaving his new bride home alone. After the West scandal, Stillman's father arranged for him to meet Gertrude Huffington, a respectable lawyer's daughter with a fine reputation and straight teeth. She didn't ask too many questions like Amelia, and had no aspirations beyond caring for a husband and children. According to Stillman's father, a congressional senator needed a wife, so Stillman proposed to Gertrude and pushed aside any lingering thoughts of Amelia and their stirring past to embark on a bright new future. Or so he believed.

The invitation arrived during his second week in office. Stillman unfolded the thick cream paper and first noticed the special embossed lettering at the top. He read the note, set it on his desk, then stood and poured himself a glass of water from the pitcher on the bookshelf. Sam Ward had invited him to a small dinner party at his home where the company promised to be *lively and becoming.* Stillman knew the company was much more than that. Seeing Amelia again came with the new job, and he'd memorized just what he wanted to say at their reunion. With the big moment just a few days away, Stillman's voice cracked as he practiced his speech. He poured himself another glass of water.

When Stillman arrived at the home of Sam Ward, he found himself so stunned by the excess of lavish food, wine, and music that at first he didn't see Amelia standing with the speaker of the house, her hand on his shoulder. When Stillman did notice her, she had already seen him and gave him a brief nod as if at a cotillion. Stillman clenched his fists; he wanted to give the first nod. He had just one course of action left, and so he polished off a glass of wine and strode across the parlor.

"Miss Cooke, you probably don't remember me, but we met briefly at the AMA convention. How nice to see you again," Stillman said, his tone a pleasant mixture of formality and grace. Score one for the Ohio gentleman, he thought.

Amelia turned from the speaker and smiled so warmly that Stillman coughed on his own spit. "Senator Stillman, of course I remember you. Congratulations on your appointment. Have you met Speaker Rushworth? Speaker Rushworth enjoys the opera. If memory serves, I believe you have that in common."

The speaker thumped Stillman's shoulder. "Glad to meet another operaphile."

"If you boys will excuse me," Amelia said with a slight bow. She slipped away with ease. She and Sam had practiced.

Stillman felt tense as he fumbled for small talk with the speaker until Sam Ward approached with a big grin.

"Senator Stillman, I'm Sam Ward. So nice to meet you. I'd like to personally welcome you to D.C. So sorry your wife couldn't join us this evening. But how are you finding our little capital so far?" Sam Ward asked with keen interest.

"Thank you, Mr. Ward—"

"Oh, everyone just calls me Sam, Senator. Please," he motioned with his hand for Stillman to continue.

Most of the men Stillman knew did more talking than listening. Sam said little as Stillman found himself jabbering about his first two weeks in a new city. The warm gleam in Sam's eye made Stillman feel at home, as if they were old friends.

"Do you know where I can get real Ohioan sauerkraut balls in this town? I think I'm going to miss that most," Stillman added after explaining his love for his home state.

"Can't say that I do, but I'll see what I can find out. You can get just about anything in this town. Anything except clean shoes." Sam chuckled at his own joke. His genuine merriment was contagious.

"Speaking of food, I think it's about time we had our dinner. Come with me, Senator, I want to introduce you to Franz. Wonderful musician. Hoping he'll play for us later," Sam said.

Franz was no less than the famed pianist Franz Liszt, who later performed a full recital in Sam's cozy parlor.

Stillman's seat for dinner kept him as far from Amelia as possible, but every so often he glanced over at the end of the long table and once caught her doing the same. She didn't blush or act embarrassed. Amelia let her gaze linger just a bit before she turned away and smiled to the entourage perched on her every word. If he didn't know her temperament the way he did, Stillman might have imagined she looked just a bit sad before she turned away.

After dinner, Amelia kept herself engaged with various leaders and their wives, while Stillman had a profitable conversation with the new head of the war department. The evening a success, Stillman thanked Sam, noting that he found him even more charismatic than at first introduction, and made his way to the front door to wait for a hackney. He felt her presence even before he turned to find her watching him.

"So glad you could make it this evening," Amelia said. She adjusted the delicate gold pendant around her neck. "And congratulations on your marriage."

They stood alone in the foyer. Stillman tugged on his overcoat. "Is that all you have to say to me?" he asked.

"I don't know what you mean, Senator. Is there something more you want from me?" Her smile didn't waver but fury flashed in her green eyes. Seeing her indignation lit his fuse.

Stillman leaned close and smelled her French perfume. Images of their intimacy flooded his thoughts and for a moment he forgot what he'd planned to say. Amelia didn't move away like a respectable woman—like Gertrude—would do, and his anger returned. "You're nothing but a tart, an extorting vixen that will do anything for what she wants. I hope you're pleased with yourself. Your veneer may fool everyone else, but you'll never fool me again."

He expected anger or perhaps the playact of bewilderment. Amelia brushed the shoulder of Stillman's coat and stepped back. "You had a bit of lint, Senator Stillman, but I've taken care of it. Of course a man of your character knows just how to brush away what he doesn't want. Isn't that so?"

She left before he could answer, though he had nothing to say to her words or injured tone. Stillman fled in a state of confusion. Amelia wanted him to believe that he'd hurt her in some way. Ridiculous and maddening. He didn't have time for games and planned to tell her just that the next time he saw her.

Three years had passed since Stillman's first time in The Library. He could still remember when the representative from

Maryland poked his head into his office and suggested he make time for a special trip. Stillman nodded, worried because he hadn't yet been to the Library of Congress. His expression made the representative laugh. The Library was in fact an illegal gambling casino in the basement of a legitimate and popular restaurant. Both establishments were run by Mushmouth, an emancipated slave from Mississippi.

Permanently swollen lips from a beating, the details of which Mushmouth never shared, made his speech hard to understand, so he rarely spoke in full sentences. Mushmouth ran tabs, bowed, nodded, smiled, and served up the finest food, liquor, and house odds all without saying much to anyone. Unlike the tables at Pendleton's known for trading winning hands for votes, Mushmouth ran a comparatively clean game. Stillman admired Mushmouth's fortitude and decided silence the key to his success. A man remained clever until he opened his mouth and proved himself otherwise. Stillman chuckled as he checked his watch. From his seat in the corner away from the gaming tables, he had a good vantage of the entrance. With his angry father on the way, Stillman wondered who would speak first.

When the special telegrams began, his father started by making strong suggestions. *Cutting down some timber in St. Louis could really help the area sawmills,* and *a wise man would increase farming exports.* Stillman didn't mind because for the most part he agreed with his father's politics. Then the suggestions became more frequent and he made demands often with outlandish requests like endorsing a ban on firearms. His mother confirmed Stillman's suspicions. For most, luck in the stock market fluctuated, but thanks to a lackey son, Theodore Stillman only had profitable investments.

Stillman watched a corporate board trustee slip a card from his sleeve. An ace by any idiot's guess. The Library seemed apropos for the pending confrontation with his father. His father never raised his voice in public, plus the metallic smell of the money added a nice hint of irony. His father didn't like the last vote of his obedient son.

Theodore Stillman arrived in a tan cashmere overcoat and tall bowler hat. Stillman watched his father look around the room; not for him, but for anyone he knew from his days in office. Back slapping always came before family. With no one he knew, his father marched over at Stillman's wave. Stillman watched the mask of his father's broad smile crumble into a frown. If not for the noisy frolic, Stillman felt certain he would hear his father growling.

"Hello, Father. To what do I owe the pleasure?" Stillman enjoyed his own coy smile for only a moment.

"Don't screw with me, Edward. You know why I'm here. You'd better start explaining yourself before I—"

"What? Throw me over your knee like I'm eight?"

His father took off his coat and hat, tossed them on the empty chair, and sat down across from him. "Before I convince Gertrude to take the kids and stay near us in Ohio while you're in session. D.C. is no place for a lovely lady and small children. You could stay here alone, Edward. I know how much you'd like that."

As a child, Stillman once called out for his father during a storm. Troubled by the lightning, he mentioned his fear of being left alone. His father never forgot a man's weakness. But then again, his father had taught his son well, perhaps too well.

"Father, you really shouldn't have invested so much of your savings in coal. The bill for expansion lost, I'm afraid," Stillman said.

"Yes, and you still haven't explained yourself. I lost a fortune. I told you to vote in favor of the expansion. What do you think you're doing?" his father asked.

"Gathering favors, Father. Just the way you taught me."

Stillman then explained his recent dealings.

Senator Hamilton from Wisconsin approached Stillman and asked that he vote against the coal mines. Hamilton never said why, but only a fool would ask. A wide variety of confidential ventures was always at play. Stillman hadn't thought much of Hamilton's offer until an important fact surfaced.

"I'm being appointed as cabinet liaison for the White House," Hamilton had said. "You can ask the chief of staff. He'll confirm it." Stillman had every intention of confirming such a monumental announcement. "Come on, Stillman. I'll be at the White House, and I'll owe you a favor."

Hamilton had said the right words, the magic words.

"So you see, Father, the decision was quite clear. I'm sure you understand. I couldn't let something like an allegiance get in the way of a favor. A man owed a favor has all of the power."

Stillman watched his father's reaction. Mother had written to say she worried for Father's health, that he had begun taking frequent fishing trips for the sake of relaxation. Even so, Stillman so wanted out from under his father's rule that he didn't flinch when his father paled. The dutiful son who looked up to his father as a good man no longer existed. Stillman rose and felt a wave of dominance when his father remained seated.

"I think we're done here, Father. Kiss Mother for me." Stillman took a few steps and then stopped. He glanced at the stairwell that lead up to the restaurant above the hall and then looked back at his father and said, "I guess it's a good thing I'm at the bottom of the stairs and not the top."

★ ★ ★ ★ ★

1887

★ ★ ★ ★ ★

CHAPTER SEVEN

In the nation's capital, the muck slung across the senatorial floor seemed thicker than what covered the January streets. Senator Edward Stillman stamped his boots on the doormat of the Strand Gentlemen's Club, picturing the old coot who called him a dandy during the committee meeting. Stillman knew better than to challenge the obsolete senator during a session. For almost ten years he'd known that pointing out flawed logic was best left to back rooms, poker tables, and men's clubs.

Stillman stepped inside the club's foyer, straightened his waistcoat, smoothed down his slick hair, and then motioned to brush his hand through his mustache. Having just shaved off the dark hairs along with the newly graying ones, he felt foolish for his habit. A quick glance told him he was alone in the entrance hallway. Lowering his hand, he strode up the flight of steps leading to the main rooms to find Jake at his station.

The evening steward greeted Stillman with a slight bow and toothy smile, his white teeth like camellia petals against his black skin. Stillman exchanged pleasantries with Jake as he peered into the room for a quick check of the occupants. Only a select and influential few enjoyed membership in the elite club.

The arched maple wood doorway opened to a large room tinted by the haze of cigar smoke and overconfidence. Low, manly murmurs balanced the dainty ring of crystal glasses; rich leather club chairs sat in groupings of four around marble pub tables; and oversized oil paintings of gents in tailcoats whom no one knew but all claimed lineage to hung over mahogany-paneled walls.

Stillman saw two of the senators he came to meet and eyed them with a disdain he could never voice. Like himself, they claimed their role as the ambitious lot of third-termers, what the old political guard called "Damn Dogs," because they might someday be worth a damn. Though they met for drinks and went hunting, Stillman knew them as the competition. As Stillman approached with a wide smile and outstretched hand, he noticed one of the competitors was missing.

"Gentlemen," Stillman said, then shook hands before taking an open seat and signaling for a round of drinks. "Where's our other friend?"

"Gage sent his aide with a note just as I was leaving my office. The note said to go on to the club without him," George Mallory replied.

Stillman thought again that Mallory's stout frame, dark sideburns, and crooked smile made him look more like a circus barker than the senator from Virginia.

"As if we need his permission," Littlemore chimed in, refocusing Stillman's attention.

Senator Arthur Littlemore's pale complexion and fair hair served to highlight the bulging blue vein in his neck. Although on the same party ticket as Littlemore, Chandler Gage had caught the eye of the Old Guard, which meant grooming him for placement on powerful committees. Littlemore didn't hide his jealousy and often went toe to toe with Gage on the floor. Stillman liked to stoke the flames between them when it served his own purposes, but Stillman needed a united Democratic front for his new scheme. Instead of a sarcastic remark, Stillman changed the subject.

"So, how was your Christmas holiday, George? I hear Mrs. Mallory and the family decided to stay in Virginia until spring.

My Gertrude doesn't visit until then either. She and the boys stay in Ohio until the thaw. Can't say I blame the ladies. This city is a bit of a sty," Stillman said.

Before Mallory could answer, Littlemore interjected, "I was just telling George we need to go hunting before the wives get here. Never mind when the season opens."

Stillman joined in the exaggerated chuckling, then, when the forced laughter petered out, he steered the conversation toward his topic of interest. "So, George, what does your wife say about your hunting? Isn't she in some wildlife preservation group?"

Mallory sighed. "They've been caterwauling about a decline in pigeons. Pigeons, for Crockett's sake."

A tall Negro man arrived with three fresh glasses of whiskey. The men sat quietly until the attendant cleared the used glasses and walked away.

"A toast," Stillman said. "To the lovely Mrs. Mallory and her little pet projects. In fact, why don't we toast to all women. To keeping them in the bedroom and out of the voting room."

Just a few days earlier, Stillman had sat stunned alongside his colleagues as the majority leader introduced a new proposed amendment that granted women the right to vote. After the initial surprise, the Senate floor exploded in an uproar of shouting and name calling. Stillman let the others argue while he chuckled at his fortunate timing. A heated controversy could help his desire for an appointment to the Committee on Public Lands. His colleagues often underestimated the leverage of a high-profile win. Stillman hated to admit that he'd learned that valuable lesson from years of watching Amelia in action.

Over the rim of his glass, Stillman watched his colleagues react to his toast. He had invited his compatriots for drinks after a long day of sessions in the hope fatigue might loosen their tongues. Instead, Mallory drained his glass without making eye contact and Littlemore took just a sip before setting the glass down.

When Stillman asked if something was wrong with the whiskey, Littlemore shook his head. "I just don't have much to say on the subject of women having a vote."

"Not much to say?" Mallory posed. "You had plenty to say over poker. I believe you called the whole affair a—"

"I don't recall saying anything. Nothing at all," Littlemore said, the thin sound of his voice higher and faster than usual. Littlemore's eyes fluttered around the room as a drowning man searching for a buoy. When he had found his tether, Littlemore turned to Stillman and asked, "So, Edward, did you hear the public lands chairman is retiring?"

After thirty years of service, an embezzlement charge was forcing the chairman of the Committee on Public Lands to step down. Serving as committee chair came close to kingship. The coveted post even came with a special gavel shaped a little like a scepter.

Doing his best to feign ignorance, Stillman shook his head and asked Littlemore what he'd heard about public lands. Stillman reached into his breast pocket and pulled out a silver case. Slim cigars were passed around and lit while Littlemore shared how the long-time chairman came under investigation. As Littlemore boasted about how he had acquired such covert and essential information, Stillman imagined a horse with a lame leg. His fellow lawmakers were all too happy to raise the shotgun but he didn't think they had the guts to pull the trigger. Bringing about the embezzlement charge had cost Stillman three months' salary.

"You know what that appointment means," Mallory said, his words riding on a billow of cigar smoke. He rubbed his thumb and forefinger together. "Big contracts. I heard the committee approved twenty million in funds for the Yellowstone Park contract in '72. I wonder how much the honorable chairman pocketed? Have you seen his yacht?"

The conversation then turned to recapping holiday festivities. For twenty minutes, Stillman interjected comments where appropriate as he kept his focus on the comings and goings of the room. When Littlemore grumbled about the tedious, yet moldable, new senators, Stillman at last found an opening to get back on point.

"Speaking of the freshmen senators, did you see that new guy from Michigan? I thought he was going to pop a button when the majority leader announced the women's suffrage bill." Stillman paused. "I suppose if we don't want to decide, we could always stall. Anyone up for a good filibuster?"

"After the Adin Calhoun debacle," Mallory said, "I wouldn't consider starting a filibuster."

Littlemore finished his drink and snuffed his cigar. "I'd stay and hash this out, but I have dinner plans."

Stillman didn't let his curiosity get the better of him. To ask about a man's plans showed weakness. Successful statesmen kept curiosity hidden away just like the mistresses on Milk Street.

Littlemore took his leave without further comment. Mallory prattled about state water rights while he finished his drink. He then checked his watch and jumped to his feet. After a noncommittal agreement to a sparring match in the near future and Stillman's claim he was going to finish his drink and cigar before heading home, Mallory left. With the others gone, Stillman sat back down to wait for the missing Chandler Gage.

Stillman settled into his chair and signaled for the evening edition of the *Post*. A letter to the editor from Max Miller was again spouting rhetoric about government overspending and the need for increasing exports. Stillman crossed his legs, lined up the stripes on his pin-striped trousers, folded the newspaper in half, and then propped it up on his knee—the model of an engaged gentleman. The pose gave him liberty to look around as if brooding over what he read.

Because of the holiday hiatus, the Strand was at half capacity. Some of the men needed time to remove the dust from their desks and brains, and there were too many loud bars and friendly women needing immediate attention. Once the cheap whiskey had soured their stomachs, the club would resume full occupancy and proper prestige. Stillman made use of the quiet to review his plan.

After a few sleepless nights, Stillman figured out a way to use the women's amendment to not just get on the prestigious and lucrative Committee on Public Lands, but to run the whole darn show. Being appointed chairman of the committee required longevity, eminence, and substantial financial backing. As only in his third term, a babe in the eyes of the Old Guard, Stillman knew he wouldn't get another chance. The next opening could be long after his own retirement. So once he'd removed the existing chairman, Stillman used his favor to broker a deal with Hamilton, now the secretary of the interior, overseer of the committee. He'd waited ten years to call in his special favor. The final terms were clear. Swing enough support to defeat the women's voting amendment and he'd be given the committee appointment.

Stillman checked his pocket watch. He'd take a gamble on the possibility of Gage showing up. After thirty minutes of waiting, Stillman lost. Based on the ambiguity of Littlemore and Mallory, Stillman needed to talk with Gage. Gage, considered a brisk man, had the right friends, which made him knowledgeable and popular. To defeat the women's vote and capture the committee chair, Stillman needed his well-connected friends plus a nod from the almighty himself, Dexter Horton. An audience with Horton required more extensive preparation and planning.

Stillman rose and made his way toward the foyer, thinking of plausible reasons for dropping in on Gage, when he tripped on the edge of a thick rug by the steward's post.

"I'm sorry sir," Jake said. "I best check the edge of that carpet. You know, Mr. Littlemore did the exact same thing on his way out. 'Cept he was a lot less graceful and his companion saw the whole thing. Didn't know a man could blush so fast, but then he has such light skin."

Jake's eyes widened in the realization of what he'd just said. Needing to keep Jake as a pal, Stillman chuckled. "Jake, my friend, did you happen to recognize his companion? I think a good ribbing is in order."

"Sure. He went off to dinner with that pretty lobbyist," Jake said.

"Do you mean Miss Cooke?" Stillman asked.

When Jake nodded, Stillman inquired how Jake knew Miss Cooke. Jake's explanation was almost as intriguing as Littlemore's mysterious meeting. Every Monday afternoon at four o'clock Miss Cooke stopped by The Strand to demand they let her in.

"Something about discrimination and all. But she's always real polite to me when I ask her to leave."

Stillman asked if he knew where Littlemore and Miss Cooke were going, but Jake just shook his head. Stillman thanked Jake with a handsome tip.

Snow flurries were steady, so Stillman pulled down the brim of his hat, turned up the collar on his overcoat, and shoved his hands in his pockets. The evening ebb was well underway, with family men already home and interns safely tucked in bars and brothels or lingering over tedious research until the wee hours as he did himself after college. Stillman grinned, thinking of himself as a young buck. But the smile faded with a single

113

thought. Amelia had just one reason to take Littlemore to dinner.

After ten years, Amelia's success had almost outshined Sam's. She had become just what she'd set her mind to, and Stillman knew the National Women's Suffrage Association had Amelia Cooke on retainer. Who better to advocate for the proposed women's voting amendment than a female lobbyist? Adversaries once again. Though even after years of working alongside each other, keeping appearances with their polite, sometimes witty banter, and never speaking of their feud in Sam Ward's foyer, Stillman knew they'd never really been anything but.

Rounding the corner at Trenton Street, Stillman peered into the front picture window of Deville's. Every so often he spotted Amelia dining at one of the front tables like a doll on display in a shop window. He surmised she used her powers of persuasion by showing off her good table manners and cleavage. Hostile feelings he thought had long faded turned in his gut.

A round woman having dinner in a fur-trimmed shawl began flapping her thick arms and pointed at Stillman from behind the glass. Realizing he was gawking at the restaurant window, Stillman tipped his hat before continuing the few blocks to his lavish, but empty, apartment. His wife and boys stayed in Cincinnati where they had school and friends. Though Stillman knew his father had influenced his wife's decision, the arrangement kept him on an equal playing field with those unencumbered by family ties, players like Amelia.

Stillman thought of Amelia trying to gain Littlemore's vote and imagined a circling shark. To win the public lands chair appointment, Stillman must declare war on the women's cause, on Amelia. Stillman smiled at the idea of taking down the great Amelia Cooke. He'd endured years of chance meetings at restaurants, at dinners, at the . . . Stillman stopped on the sidewalk in front of his home. Why hadn't he made the connection sooner? He rushed up his front steps. Before he could go after Littlemore, Mallory, or Gage, Stillman had to consider who he needed to speak with before Amelia had her chance. If he knew Amelia as well as he trusted, she'd make a grand play at the upcoming Postmaster's Ball. Everyone who mattered went to the gala, including the delightful and attractive lobbyist in what Stillman knew was her finest element.

Chapter Eight

Amelia strode down the broad hallway toward the Willard Hotel Grand Ballroom, the lilt of orchestral music a comical backdrop to the new staffers who huddled in nervous groups and tugged at their bow ties. The gala in full swing, Amelia paused near the entrance to smooth the bodice of her emerald gown and ready herself for a proper entrance. Just as she straightened and took a step forward, someone called her name. She recognized the voice and turned with her lips pressed into a practiced smile.

"Good evening, Clancy. Always a pleasure to see the town crier. Or are you the village idiot?" Amelia asked.

Clancy Doyle had a reputation not only for his work with the *Post*, but also his excessive drinking at parties like the one where Amelia first met the lech years earlier. As a drunk, he had plausible deniability of his actions and thus didn't remember his lewd advances that set in motion Amelia being sent to Ohio, to Stillman. Since she often needed the vital information in his dubious care, Amelia put aside their past and maintained a cordial relationship. She hid her loathing beneath a well-trained, pleasant gaze.

A man Amelia didn't know stood beside Clancy. Both dressed in dull brown overcoats and bowler hats with frayed edges, Amelia could almost see the fumes from the overwhelming odor of clove aftershave.

"Amelia, I'd like you to meet Herb, our newest reporter. Just here from Indiana," Clancy said.

116

Amelia grinned, then reached in her handbag and pulled out her calling card. "I'm Amelia Cooke, political lobbyist. Perhaps we might be friends. It's always good to have friends when you're new in town."

The man glanced at the card with the reaction Amelia still despised: a mixture of repulsion and intrigue that twisted a man's face into a downturned mouth and raised eyebrows.

"I never met a girl lobbyist," Herb said, looking at Clancy. He turned to Amelia and added, "Didn't even know there was such a beast."

"Yes, well, we beasts are few I'm afraid," Amelia said, widening her grin until almost a smirk.

"Amelia's by far the prettiest lobbyist you'll meet," Clancy said. "Herb is our new restaurant reviewer."

Amelia frowned at Clancy, then plucked her card from Herb's grasp. "Why are you wasting my time, Clancy?"

Clancy touched Amelia's elbow and walked her a few steps from Herb. "I need a quote for my new piece on the vote. Could really use something divisive for my political readers. Maybe a premature claim of victory for the ladies?" Clancy asked.

"Interesting phrasing, though I'm not sure it's wise for you to use the word premature." Amelia brushed an imaginary speck from Clancy's reddening cheek. "Besides," she continued, "I thought you lords of the press were sticklers for the truth. I'd hate to ruin your upstanding reputation."

"You should know all about having a reputation." Clancy smirked and Amelia expected him to pat himself on the back. Instead, he jabbed Amelia's arm with his elbow. "Hey, how does a lobbyist sleep?" He answered his own question with: "First he lies on one side and then he lies on the other."

Amelia chuckled in the low, throaty laugh she used with drunken congressmen and attorneys. "That joke is every bit as clever as your column, Clancy," Amelia said.

Herb muttered something about leaving, so Clancy made one last effort. "No quote?" he asked.

"Well, I do have a soft spot for political reporters who wear too much cologne and seem interested in what position I sleep in."

Clancy ran a hand over his thick mustache and leaned forward to whisper in Amelia's ear.

"If you really have a soft spot for us hacks . . . don't you live in a suite right upstairs? We could pick up where we left off at dinner."

Amelia wanted to remind him they had left off at the curb after a mind-numbing evening she'd agreed to only because of a particularly difficult gun initiative.

"Perhaps some other time. You have your friend and I have . . ." Amelia motioned toward the gala.

"A rain check. I'm holding you to that, Amelia," Clancy said as he turned for the lobby.

Amelia nodded and watched him leave. When sober, Clancy kept his manners in check as well as his favors. With practice, she'd often made better use of a drunk Clancy.

With the distraction disposed of, Amelia took a moment to gather her thoughts. From the first rumblings of the potential amendment allowing women the right to vote, she'd been held on retainer by the National Women's Suffrage Association to lobby for the women's movement. Her job demanded that she remain composed, and yet Amelia had difficulty hiding her excitement at the possibility of casting a vote, of having a say. She thought of the hours she'd spent watching the boys play outside while forced to sit still in the corner. Courageous women had spent thirty-nine years giving speeches and organizing rallies and petitions to have their voice heard. A constitutional amendment meant a general victory for all women, and a special kind of victory for Amelia.

The sound of laughter turned her attention back to her work for the evening. Charming those with influence came with the job, and, though she preferred intimate gatherings, the lavish Postmaster's Ball had a fanciful elitism she enjoyed. Invitations to the ball were unnecessary. Attendance was based on protocol. However, the tradition of saying "see you at the Postmaster's" rather than circulating formal gala invitations often confused the newcomers. Unsure where to go, the junior senators showed up late, their wives with toussled chignons and wrinkled ball gowns. As Amelia stepped into the ballroom, she thought of the many Postmaster's Balls she'd attended. Even though a veteran, once again she found herself captivated by the company, and room.

The Willard Hotel ballroom featured a full row of magnificent bay windows overlooking the city. Floor to ceiling glass panes with fresh white trim framed the Capitol dome, creating a stunning tile mosaic. To eat brunch overlooking the city, tourists routinely slipped silver dollars into the palm of the eager host. For evening events, such as the Postmaster's, the windows and room itself became the showpiece.

Groupings of white taper candles were set on the windowsills, their flickering shadows mimicking the play of the room. Soaring ceilings with white columns were draped with raw silk, and French doors were left open regardless of the weather so guests could enjoy the large marble veranda trimmed with spiral box trees in planters and a railing ledge wide enough to sit upon. At many galas, Amelia made good use of the soft outdoor candle lanterns and chilled air. A man's coat slung over her evening gown was as good as a vote.

Inside, round tables draped in gold cloth and set with vibrant flower centerpieces surrounded a large wooden dance floor. A wide stone-faced fireplace added the illusion of warmth if not raising the actual temperature, and two buffet tables and a dessert pyramid flanked each end of the affair. Amelia enjoyed the sparkle of polished silver, best seen in the reflection of greedy guests eyeing piles of oysters and orange jelly candies. Amelia let herself enjoy just a brief inhale of the rich smells of roasted meats and butter before liberating a glass of champagne from a passing waiter. Although told of the delicious fare, Amelia never sampled more than a few bites; eating while working was a rookie's mistake that always ended in spillage. She would better spend her time surveying the full turnout.

The clattering dishes and mutterings sounded like a flock of gulls by the shore. Amelia watched as newly elected statesmen and energetic staffers crisscrossed the room with exaggerated smiles and empty wine glasses. The exhilaration of the new members added freshness to a room filled with the stale and pompous even as Amelia noticed her first challenge. Ladies in bright taffeta, romantic velvet, and shimmering lace were a distracting contrast to the scores of men in top hats and black tuxedos. Amelia's lobbying efforts were best received during quiet dinners in softly lit parlors where the powerful clientele were agreeably male. Wives presented an ongoing problem.

Devoid of the accessory of a wife, men loosened their waistcoats, drank an extra cocktail, and chatted with ease. At intimate gatherings, Amelia circled the room without first spending the regulatory visit with the ladies, convincing them of her harmlessness by discussing hem lengths. A jealous wife was more destructive than a federal charter with built-in loopholes. Though Amelia knew some of the ladies spread rumors about her, she needed time with the men, which meant first charming the women amassing by the dessert table.

The wives who didn't spend the cold months away from the muck of the city were a homogeneous group in their middle years. Their smooth, piled hair hid streaks of gray and overly powdered cheeks complimented expensive dresses with modest necklines. Amelia glanced at her own dress, a delicate mix of emerald velvet and satin with a neckline lower than modest but higher than indiscreet. An enviable feminine figure even at the spinster age of thirty, Amelia often drew unwanted advances and gossip. She took a few sips of her champagne, set the glass on a tray, and stepped forward with a friendly grin.

Amelia greeted the women she knew by first and last names, then allowed introductions to those new to the city. After the formalities, the ladies returned to their discussion of music appreciation in the classroom.

None of the ladies belonged to the suffragist movement, at least not officially. Political wives did not belong to a side, any side. Amelia had never seen a handbook but felt certain of at least a pamphlet on the proper appearance and temperament of a politician's wife. Even through the veiled personas, Amelia knew many of the wives were forward-thinking and quite clever.

Mrs. Rebecca Platt glanced at Amelia's formfitting bodice, then frowned. Mrs. Platt, like some, believed holding a job and living alone were unladylike.

In her usual Pecksniffian manner she asked, "Are you fulfilled by your causes, Miss Cooke?" Her sour tone mixed with the sweet-potato croquette she chewed.

"I am indeed. I'm hoping my work will change the world, or at least key parts of it," Amelia said, neglecting to mention the large paycheck, unrestricted expense account, luxury travel, and interesting company. "I certainly believe women should have a voice in the events and decisions that affect our lives. If we had the right to vote, think about how much more effectively you could look after your family. Mrs. Platt, you do want to vote? I should think you'd want to make decisions about your children's schooling and who runs our country," Amelia said.

The awkward silence saddened Amelia. She wanted women to share their thoughts and have frank discussions about the issues of the day. After a short pause filled with sipping, chewing, and adjusting hairpins, one of the ladies mentioned Henry James's new novel and the chatter resumed. Amelia had only to nod for a bit longer and then she could excuse herself. She turned her attention to the middle of the room where the posse gathered on the dance floor.

Dancing at the gala didn't start until after dinner. Until the dancing began, Amelia thought of the room as an unofficial organizational chart.

Always near the windows, perched as if prepared to jump at any moment, were the young aides and paralegals. They stood in pairs by party line nibbling their cheese and thumbnails. At the previous year's gala, Amelia approached two young foals and asked if either could help with her wrap. When Amelia touched the arm of one of the young men, he recoiled like a nervous cat.

Anchored among the dining tables were clusters of no more than eight men each. These were the mid-level congressmen who every so often glanced to the center of the room with either admiration or contempt. Amelia often wondered what Greek tragedy might play out if she ever slipped one of the middlemen a lady's dagger.

The main attraction of the evening took place at center ring where a few select men stood on the dance floor, overtly aware of the others gravitating around them. Although within reach, getting to the center of the room took more than a few long strides in polished black boots. Becoming a member of the Old Guard required reelections.

"Don't you just love the new choker necklace style from Milan?" a woman said. Amelia nodded and cooed with the others.

The Old Guard protected their coveted territory with puffed chests and eyes darting about, daring any of the younger representatives to come forward before their time. Like all of the men, they were donned in uninspired black tuxedos but several had loosened their ties and removed their top hats just to show they could. Among the brazen men uncovering his bald head and baring the tiniest tuft of white chest hair was the eighty-three-year-old congressman from Connecticut. He did whatever he pleased, including once grabbing Amelia's backside at a fundraising dinner.

Delicate giggling caught Amelia's attention and she joined in. She had no idea what the ladies found so amusing, but the wife of the representative from Oklahoma smiled at Amelia in a show of good humor and solidarity. Amelia nodded, knowing she had succeeded. The ladies were satisfied.

"Ladies, thank you for lifting my spirits. I hate to leave, but you'll have to excuse me. My work never ends, it seems. There's a gentleman over there who won't return my notes." Amelia leaned forward as if sharing a secret. "I don't think he's seen me yet, so maybe I can surprise him."

Amelia moved away from the ladies, then took a moment to again eye the men standing in the middle of the room. She wasn't surprised to see the postmaster general speaking with a few men, including the Pig Irons.

South Carolina, Georgia, and Mississippi were lost to the women's cause. They were ultra-conservative Democrats who boasted that they bathed in their drawers and didn't kiss their wives until after their first child was born. Amelia called them pig irons for their indulgence in pork and party lines. She expected to see them at the gala, but Amelia didn't like their proximity to two moderate Republicans. Pushing aside the desire to dash across the room and drag the moderates to her corner, Amelia took confident but short feminine steps and nodded greetings to those she passed. Just before she reached the men, Amelia took a moment to switch her handbag to her left wrist.

". . . then allowing not one to undress her." The postmaster had just finished a limerick when he turned and saw Amelia. "Oh, my, I didn't realize we were joined by a lovely belle. Beg pardon, Miss Cooke. No offense, I hope."

Amelia shook hands with the postmaster general and pig irons. When she then extended her hand to Senator Chandler Gage of Pennsylvania, the senator gave a curt nod but kept his hands at his sides. Amelia found his reaction interesting and returned a nod before lowering her hand. She glanced around the room and saw several of the wives watching her and whispering. Amelia took a quick breath to push away the echoes of childhood taunting.

"Why, Peter," Amelia said, pausing to tilt her head at the postmaster general, "you'll have to do better than that to offend me."

The man standing behind Gage snorted with disdain and said, "Now that's certainly true." Amelia couldn't see the speaker but she knew who belonged to the pretentious voice and was taken aback that he stood among the privileged group. Had she seen him, she might have waited to approach. Amelia steadied herself by broadening her smile and curling her toes.

Stillman stepped in front of Gage.

"Senator Stillman, always a pleasure. How are you this evening? How's your lovely wife and the boys?" Amelia asked.

"If you'll excuse me," Gage said.

Senator Gage bowed and retreated without so much as a feeble excuse. Gage rarely spoke to lobbyists; still, Amelia hoped the festive atmosphere might soften his resolve. She blamed Stillman for pushing in front of Gage. Amelia simmered. Stillman and his shenanigans were getting in her way again.

"We're all dandy. Gertrude and the boys are staying in Ohio

for the winter," Stillman said, forcing Amelia's continued attention.

Stillman certainly had enough arrogance to think he could play with big boys, but he'd taken a huge risk by leaving the sidelines with the other middle managers. Amelia wanted to make a snide comment until she noticed Stillman's benefactor. Standing beside Stillman was the reason he was able to act like one of the posse.

Stillman raised his eyebrows as if suddenly startled and turned to the man next to him. "Why, Amelia, how rude of me. I haven't introduced you."

The man awaiting introduction looked in his late fifties. He had a lithe build with deep lines on his forehead that made him look permanently disappointed.

"Bobby," Amelia said before Stillman could continue. Robert Blatchford, U.S. supreme court justice, stepped around Stillman to kiss her cheek.

"How nice to see you again," Amelia said. "We haven't chatted since the New York Historical Society dinner. Are you still collecting Chinese coins?"

Amelia enjoyed watching Stillman's conceited grin melt into a hostile glare. The fine senator from Ohio sometimes forgot that Amelia knew everyone, and, more importantly, everyone knew her. As the justice spoke, Amelia ignored Stillman and his commanding appearance. Even now, in his early forties, he had a full head of dark hair and those soft blue eyes that made him seem delighted and amazed. Amelia reminded herself that his true character lay hidden behind his good looks.

The pig iron from South Carolina cleared his throat and asked Stillman about a supreme court ruling. All of the senators turned to hear Stillman's answer to the obvious test question. Amelia put her hand to her mouth to hide her amusement. If Stillman was going to play with the big dogs, they were going to see if he could lift his leg.

"Deciding the black and white of an issue is something best left to great men like you, Chief Justice. I believe there are too many gray areas in life," Stillman answered.

First point Stillman. The noncommittal answer left nothing for the men to pick at so the Georgia pig iron asked, "So, son, what committees are you on?"

Stillman listed his affiliations and the postmaster replied, "Bunch of pansies. Those aren't committees. Those are a few boys standing around with their blue vein junket pumps in their hands." The postmaster stopped short and coughed. He turned to Amelia. "My apologies again, Miss Cooke."

"Why, Postmaster, I don't even know what you're talking about," Amelia said.

All the men, except Stillman, chuckled.

The Mississippi pig iron stopped drinking and added, "If you want to stick around, Stillman, get off buildings and grounds. Press can't wait to stir up a ruckus about some monument. Ruin a man's career." He then winked at the chief justice. "Heard there might be an opening on the Committee on Public Lands. You should give that a try." The joke wasn't lost on any of them, even Stillman, by his stricken look.

The orchestra began playing a waltz so the men shook hands and excused themselves to step outside, fill a plate of dessert, or take positions beside their wives. With dancing underway, and thus a situation for scandal, Amelia understood why the men left in haste.

Amelia moved from the dance floor and chose a spot beside the fireplace to wait. The brisk night meant everyone had at least one turn by the fire, so Amelia tucked her hands behind her back and pressed her shoulders against the cool marble mantle. Sam had warned against taking a submissive position, but Amelia knew better. A docile stance was a woman's calling card. With the message out, she didn't wait long.

"I'm impressed."

Amelia watched Stillman approach and lean against the paneled wall beside the fireplace. His body tilted slightly toward her but he continued to stare out into the room. Amelia also faced outward toward the festivities.

"That I know a supreme court justice or that I don't have to latch on to anyone to get to center stage? And did you notice the boys didn't give me any questions?" Amelia said.

Stillman ignored her comment. "I'm impressed you're wearing that flashy dress. You know what they say about gossip."

"I have no idea what you're talking about, Edward. Gossip is useful for my line of work." Amelia twisted a bit more, knowing she was giving Stillman a view of her *décolletage*. She wasn't surprised when he snuck a quick peek.

Stillman shook his head. "Nice that some things never change."

"Are you talking about my figure or your attitude?" Amelia asked.

Stillman stood close enough that Amelia smelled his cologne, the one he wore in Ohio. The scent played with her memories and for a moment she wondered why he still wore the fragrance. Then she regained herself. She wasn't going to gush because of Stillman's ploy to stir old emotions. Retreat equaled fear, and Amelia had never feared Stillman, at least not because of his political influence.

"You know you can't win," he said. Amelia turned in time to watch his face tighten. "I'm going to beat you this time, Amelia," he muttered under his breath.

Over the years they'd seen each other at various functions and had settled into an acceptable acquaintanceship of polite nods and small talk. Amelia didn't like his hostile tone and the way he glared. Something had changed.

Stillman tugged at his waistcoat and smoothed the line of hair at the base of his neck. He was exhilarated by a challenge. She'd seen his intensity and almost boyish excitement when he pursued her. As Stillman rattled the change in his pocket, Amelia wondered what he wanted this time. Before Amelia could find out, the representative from Wyoming advanced.

"You look exquisite tonight, Miss Cooke. Thank you again for a marvelous dinner last week."

Amelia unfolded her arms from behind her back and held out her hand. "It was my pleasure, Howard. Hearing about skeet shooting was so fascinating. You've made me want to give it a try."

"I'd love to show you sometime," the representative replied, taking her bait.

Amelia agreed, then watched him dash away as if he were on his way to make arrangements that very minute.

"Simpleton," Stillman said.

"I seem to recall another simpleton," Amelia said, hoping anger might shake loose his secret.

Stillman spun to face Amelia. The impulsive gesture told her that her instincts were correct. "That was a long time ago," he spat. "And you still don't have any new tricks, my dear."

Amelia's height was always her advantage. She faced him without having to crane her neck and what she saw startled her. His cheeks were flushed and his eyes darted back and forth across her face. Amelia knew in that moment that Stillman wasn't just a past opponent. He had a new passion, and she needed to find out for what.

"Edward, I heard you're against the women's amendment, but I'm curious why you're so—"

A man knocked into Stillman and they both turned toward the sound of a babbling apology. Amelia's gaze remained pleasant while Stillman huffed and brushed a few drops of wine

from his coat. In front of them stood a young man wit
hair and hazel eyes. He matched Stillman's height but l
lingering lankiness of youth. His wide smile created :
dimple on his left cheek.

"Sir, please forgive me." The young man bowed. "I'
McKenna, the new aide for Senator Horton," he said. ""
to come over and introduce myself."

Stillman tugged down the hem of his jacket, then :
his hand. "Well, of course you wanted to say hello. I un
son," Stillman said.

The young man blinked at Stillman. "Ah, no, sir, I
meet the lady." He turned his gaze on Amelia and f
dimple. Amelia introduced herself and allowed the y
to kiss her hand.

"A gentleman in our midst," Amelia said, g
Stillman. "A rare treat, I can assure you, Mr. McK
long have you been in Washington?"

Stillman cleared his throat. "I see the secretary of
I need to speak with him. If you'll excuse me . . ."

Amelia nodded and the young man said, "My ap
sir. It was nice meeting you, Mr.—"

"That's Senator," Amelia corrected.

The young man's eyes widened. He looked
stepped into the street without being mindful of w
left behind. "Senator . . . sir."

Stillman glared at the young man and was su
shoulder as he left. Amelia watched Stillman for :
disappointed by the interruption and somethin
didn't have time to think about before the you
again.

"I just bumbled that, didn't I? I've got to wo
names. Which state is he?"

Amelia told him and the boy cringed. She v

at least knew the importance and legacy of Ohio.

"It's not really that bad," Amelia said. "Senator Stillman has a short memory for mistakes if you can do him a favor."

The lad nodded then launched into talking about the festivities and his job with a relaxed, neighborly charm. After taking an assistant position just a month earlier, he already knew all of the congressman's aides, their staffers, and committees. As he rattled off draft numbers with ease, Amelia wondered if he had slighted Stillman on purpose just to get rid of him. Though Amelia thought the tactic inventive, she kept up her guard. Tricks were only commendable when used on someone else.

"I have a confession, Miss Cooke. I've been watching you all night. Green is my favorite color. And what a delight to see your eyes match your dress."

As they chatted, Mr. McKenna's poise bordered on arrogance. Amelia appreciated the rare enthusiasm he displayed at hearing her occupation, but then he touched her shoulder with his hand. Amelia glanced at his hand until he removed it, yet he didn't apologize for his forward action. Amelia found his bravado curious and a little intriguing.

Another young aide rushed up to Mr. McKenna, whispered in his ear, then scooted away without making eye contact with Amelia.

'I'm so sorry, but it seems Senator Horton is asking for me. He's in his office working on a few last minute drafts. I have to"

'Of course. Thank you for introducing yourself. I'm impressed," Amelia said.

The lad tipped his top hat. "Then are you free for dinner? There's a restaurant by my boarding house that serves passable beef stew. It's nothing fancy, I'm afraid, but I'd like you to join"

Amelia smiled. "I'm not sure poached meat is my style. But I

think you already knew that and may want to try some better cuisine."

"Too obvious?" he asked, scrunching his face. Amelia found the contrast of the boyish gesture with his handsome face and masculine ego quite attractive.

"Perhaps just a bit, but I think I'll recover." Amelia glanced up and saw Senator Gage by the exit helping his wife into her wrap. She hadn't seen Mrs. Gage eating with the other ladies.

Amelia turned back to Mr. McKenna. "Why don't you join me on Thursday? I'm having a small dinner party. Just a few select guests. I'm sure you'll find the company very engaging."

He agreed with haste and left seemingly before Amelia could change her mind. By his satisfied grin, he was already trying to deduce the guest list.

The crowd began to thin and the slurred conversations grew louder. Amelia often stayed until buttons and tongues were loosened, camping by the exit to catch a few stragglers on their way out. However, she thought again of Stillman's hostile agitation. He'd unwittingly tipped his hand about the importance of the amendment. Why he had such a personal interest perplexed her. Stillman only had strong convictions when he could see a pile of money on the table. The suffrage bill didn't offer money or prestige for the men. Amelia left the gala feeling unsettled.

She slipped from the ballroom and made her way upstairs to her suite. There were those who scoffed at her arrangements, but when Amelia reached her door, she again remarked on the efficiency of living at the Willard Hotel.

Fastened to the polished silver message clip, Amelia saw a folded note with her name in rushed scrawl. She swallowed against the nervous pull in her stomach as she seized the note, tearing the corner and leaving a small bit clasped in the metal jaw. After reading the note twice, Amelia unclenched her own jaw and stepped into her suite.

CHAPTER NINE

Amelia tightened her mantel as she rushed across 19th Street toward Maryland Avenue. She stepped over the new rail tracks after a small green rail car rattled by, then made her way down damp cobblestones forever stained from mud and too many horses. After she stepped around a tangle of carriages at the intersection, she pulled a pocket watch from her handbag. Eight o'clock in the morning. The emergency board meeting had started at seven. In the concise note left on Amelia's door the night before, Perla suggested Amelia join the meeting at Haven House but Amelia wasn't much for the inevitable hand-wringing over tea and scones.

The *Washington Evening Star* named the sweeping brick house that faced the corner of Maryland and Capitol Avenues. In a scathing editorial, a well-known satirist theorized that male chimpanzees had stronger mental acuteness for decision-making than the human females nesting like birds in their little "house haven." The name might have vanished right then if not for Preacher Ward's popular sermon "Are the Haven House Ladies Going to Heaven?" As a sign of solidarity, Perla Adams, President of the D.C. chapter of the National Women's Suffrage Association, commissioned a wooden sign and hung it right over the front door. Haven House was thus christened. Amelia thought it fitting. She always viewed Perla's role like that of a mother superior tending to her flock.

Amelia stepped onto the porch and noticed a new door

knocker on display. The knocker artistically depicted a woman's clenched fist with raised veins and pronounced knuckles. She ran her fingers along the polished brash and admired the powerful statement. The opposition felt women were too irrational and ill prepared to vote. They feared fair creatures would neglect their duties of the home and should rely upon the head of the household to make wise decisions for the family. Some women agreed, which confounded Amelia. A constitutional change at last put an exclamation point at the end of a very long sentence. After a final moment of contemplation, Amelia lowered her hand, removed her gloves, and entered Haven House without knocking.

In the foyer, Amelia untied her scarf and removed her cape. Unlike her comrades in arms, Amelia wasn't comfortable amid the cushion-filled entrance that smelled of cookies and the inevitable bouquet of flowers some do-gooder brought from home. The housewives and mothers handing out pamphlets and making signs out of millboard found the feminine touches inviting. Amelia well knew that was the point. Volunteers kept the blood pumping in a united force that had spanned generations and ethnicities since 1848. But the cat figurines and cross-stitched pillows reminded her of Sam Ward's caution. *Men won't take you seriously until you take the blasted feathers out of your hats.* Amelia saw wisdom in her mentor's words and only felt at home in one room at Haven House.

The private office of Perla Adams wasn't like the flowery public front rooms, though only a trained eye noticed the subtleties. Like many ladies' parlors there were handsome embroidered curtains of royal-blue silk, delicate gilded furniture, and a sterling tea service waiting for instruction. Yet there were no errant stitching needles left on trays or potpourri hiding in colored mason jars. In front of the demure curtains stood a handsome globe on a carved pedestal and the tall bookshelves were filled with rich leather bindings encasing an eclectic mix of authors not typically of interest to the docile lady. As Amelia stepped through the threshold into Perla's office, she heard several exaggerated sighs. The board of directors was still meeting, so Amelia had a moment to catalog the attendance.

Seated side by side on a yellow chenille settee were Nicolette and Nicole, identical twin widows supported by the war pensions of their brave, but unlucky, husbands. Nicolette served as the corporate secretary and forever held a pencil in her grasp. Nicole, often referred to as "the other one," never left Nicolette's side.

Standing by the globe, Amelia grimaced at Marion Price, heiress of the Procter & Gamble Company and the proud owner of a Rembrandt painting. Marion in fact resembled that of a Rembrandt lady with pale, round features and a forced Puritan smile. At every gathering Marion threatened to sell the painting and donate her spoils to the cause. Marion had yet to make good on her threat and Perla denied that her continued board duties, which were mainly to complain about the layout of the flyers and lecture hall chairs, were based on her financial assets. The NWSA always needed more funding.

New to the board as an assistant was Lottie Evans. She had started her work in Rochester, New York, and rose through the ranks until handpicked by Susan B. Anthony to serve as a liaison in Washington. Although young and quiet, Lottie thrived on detailed research and clerical duties. Perla had offered Lottie's services to Amelia, and now after the gala Amelia had a use for Lottie's special skills. Dressed in what some called a uniform— fitted cropped jacket, long dark skirt, and high-collared white blouse—Lottie sat taking her own notes on a small pad.

"Where were you? I'd thought you'd be here."

Amelia turned to the heiress Marion just in time to see her curt nod that added with little subtlety *where you're paid to be.*

"Ladies, I think we're finished here for now," Perla said.

Perla Adams sat behind her parson's desk with her graying hair pinned to her crown. In her late fifties, she had a broad frame and strong features that suggested her health and capability long before she exposed her clever mind. As the board members made their way toward the door, Amelia noticed Perla drumming her fingers on a stack of papers. Amelia waited until she heard the office door close before turning to Perla.

"The board is necessary and they try . . . never mind. Please, sit down. We have a lot to do," Perla said.

With contacts hidden under every rock, not much happened in the capital city without Perla's knowledge. Perla knew a great deal about the pending vote and wanted to share. Deliberations on the Senate floor were slated to start in two days.

"If the debate goes as expected, we likely have no more than three weeks until the vote is taken," Perla said.

"At least the majority chair believes voting rights are a constitutional issue and not a state farce," Amelia said.

For years, Congress relegated the battleground for women's suffrage to the state level, where lobbying state by state became time consuming and futile. For real change, women needed a national—some felt long overdue—amendment. Perla nodded as if understanding Amelia's thoughts and said, "It's about time."

"Received any telegrams from the ladies yet?" Amelia asked, twirling her index finger around the room. Lucretia Mott, Frances Willard, and Elizabeth Cady Stanton were just a few of the portraits that hung in thick, mahogany frames at Haven House. They wore their serious expressions and high-collared blouses with the same dignity and pride as debutantes wearing tiaras. As matriarchs of the women's suffrage movement, they were held in great esteem by the members of the National Women's Suffrage Association even though some of the founders were well into their seventies and a few had passed away. Amelia once met organizer Frances Willard at the Seneca Falls Annual Convention and found her more intense than a woman half her age. Amelia wasn't certain if her austere demeanor helped or hindered the cause, but Amelia kept her opinions quiet. Her position as lobbyist for the NWSA prohibited her from official membership and Amelia had overheard some of the ladies call her an outsider.

"Susan's not well and Lucy, bless her at 79, is giving a speech in Oregon," Perla said.

Even though some delegates and chapter leaders continued with lecture tours, Perla expected a full house very soon. Amelia cringed at the hallways stuffed with long black skirts and sensible bonnets cinched under thick chins. Amelia wasn't fond of the herd that once again made her feel different and alone. Amelia pulled a loose thread on her skirt and twisted the string into a knot.

"I assume you've had enough time to go through your list. What's the count?" Perla asked.

In the two days since the bill's introduction, Amelia had shored up those in her favor and had a handle on those in opposition.

"Until I'm willing to grace the bedroom of the honorable senator from Florida, I believe the vote count stands at a promising twenty-nine in our favor," Amelia said.

"Unfortunately, sacrificing your honor still wouldn't get us enough votes," Perla said.

"Unfortunately?"

An amused smile softened the lines around Perla's eyes. "You know what I mean. The point is that we need a two-thirds majority, fifty votes out of the seventy-six senators." She removed her spectacles and massaged the bridge of her nose. "We don't have much time."

Perla hired Amelia with an exclusive contract when the rumblings began. At first, Amelia had reservations about forgoing her other income since she usually lobbied for several unique projects at a time. Plus, Amelia wasn't sure the NWSA had enough momentum. Perla knew better and was insistent and generous. Amelia and Perla worked well together, so without hesitation they set out making a roll call with three columns.

The left-hand column held the names of senators who supported women in the vote because they feared the amassing power of women, quoted religious platitudes, or were up for reelection and held no opinion other than those of their constituents. The senators in the right-hand column were opposed to women's voting rights. They feared the amassing power of women, quoted religious platitudes, or were up for reelection and held no opinion other than those of their constituents. The names in the center were most interesting.

The undecided were a mix of politicians who owed favors or were sometimes scrutinized in the press for voting their conscience. A few of the senators vacillating in the center were likely to lose their seats at the end of the year and thus might have axes to grind, and several others had never made a single declaration either way about women's suffrage, at least not in public.

"Rhode Island wants to retire to a ranch in Washington State. If I can swing a good land offer, we'll have his vote. I'm also pretty confident about Powell from Michigan. He owes me a favor," Amelia said.

Perla rubbed her forehead. "Shaw from North Dakota will likely vote with Mallory. He wants Mallory's committee seat. And Dodger likes you. He'll vote in our favor just because you ask. Dodger's vote means we'll also get his cronies. He has a healthy following."

"I can get Illinois, too," Amelia said. "He'll soon be looking for a way off the ridiculous Coinage Committee. I think I can help him out."

Perla nodded, then paused to consider her next question. "What about Senator Stillman?" she asked. "Is he still undecided? Can you get the senator on our side without deep pockets?"

Amelia's stomach dropped at the mention of Edward Stillman. From his behavior at the gala, he wasn't undecided, which left the question of who had already put in a bid for his loyalty, and what, exactly, he had up his sleeve.

"Stillman's a *no*," Amelia said. "But we don't need him. I can get Dexter Horton."

Perla's deep chuckle might have seemed friendly but Amelia heard the underlying doubt. Horton stood as the Old Guard holding all the keys. As chair of the Ways and Means Committee he controlled funds like a puppet master. Everyone considered his vote essential because the ducklings followed his lead, pecking to be first in line. Gaining Horton's favor was regularly tantamount to winning, but of late he had an inconsistent voting record, and, of more interest to Amelia, he had somehow escaped major scandal during his twenty years of service. Amelia spent most of the previous evening thinking of Boyd McKenna and the luck of their meeting at the gala. Who better to find something rotting in Horton's closet, something Amelia could use to her advantage, than Horton's new impressionable young aide who liked her green eyes?

Ignoring Perla's misgivings about Dexter Horton, Amelia began the careful discussion about the undecided votes. After some respectful debate and reading through a pile of voting records that Lottie compiled at Perla's request, Amelia and Perla agreed on a strategy. Working within the time constraints and budget, the optimum course was to focus on securing votes from at least three out of five key men with enough supporters to clinch the decision. This left three men in their sights. Senators Arthur Littlemore, Chandler Gage, and Dexter Horton, especially Horton, were the linchpins.

Amelia tapped the center column with her index finger. "These are the men who need my full and pleasant attention."

The afternoon paperboy made his rounds as Perla stood and stretched her back. Embroiled in their planning, neither realized the time. Though hungry, Amelia declined Perla's offer for a late lunch and also stood. Food could wait.

"So it seems the fate of the women's vote lies with these men," Perla said as she handed Amelia the list.

Amelia bowed, savoring the determination and confidence in Perla's voice, and accepted Perla's offering as a girl taking her first holy communion. When Amelia lifted her eyes, she leaned forward and placed her hand on Perla's desk. "The fate of the vote, dear Perla, rests with me."

Perla's gaze softened like a mother watching a sleeping child. "Indeed, my dear. And I know that's just the way you like it."

Not until Amelia was safely on the front porch of Haven House did she stop to put on her scarf. The tightness in her chest made her angry, and she willed herself to cast aside Perla's unwanted mothering. Though the gesture well meaning, Amelia hadn't time for the thoughts she'd long pushed aside. She didn't like that the excitement of a place in the world had stirred memories of the time when she had no place at all. Sheer will, working with Sam, and the strength of her accomplishments helped fight her instinct to sometimes hide away and bury her head under a blanket like the once-lost child. Amelia took a moment to again run through her successive list of victories and profits. For the women to win, she couldn't let herself overreact to a few kind words.

As Amelia stepped from the Haven House porch, she spotted the afternoon newspaper lying in the walkway and speculated about the headlines written in varying flavors to appease read-ers. Amelia expected articles with drawings of herself in devil ears or a dunce cap. One of the busy bees picked up the paper and retreated inside with her find. Regardless of the reports filled with conjecture, the most sensational from Clancy Doyle, Amelia felt confident in the main picks: Littlemore, Gage, and Horton. The top three in horseracing. But, as Amelia opened the gate leading to the sidewalk, she thought of Perla's pointed mention of Stillman.

Amelia latched the gate and stepped onto the muddy sidewalk wondering if Stillman had begun making his own strategic list of names. The fleeting thought was rhetorical; she already knew the answer. Though no one knew of their past relationship, she didn't have time for interference. If all went as planned, Amelia could see the finish line ahead. Instead of a confident smile, Amelia shook her head. What seemed straight ahead inevitably had sudden and difficult turns. Hadn't she learned that the hard way? Amelia had a meager few weeks to change the course of history for all women, for herself, and she knew just what she had to do first.

CHAPTER TEN

Stillman strode from his office down the long Senate wing until he reached the Capitol rotunda, where the hollow reverberation reminded him of hiking in the Appalachian Mountains with his brother James. As teens they climbed the foothills to hear the echoing curse words they shouted, and then laughed until their sides hurt. After Stillman's election, James took a position as a wretched public defender in Cincinnati. They rarely spoke. Stillman rubbed the back of his neck with one hand while using his briefcase to push through the crowds. At noontime the Capitol was bustling.

Citizens milling around the rotunda ran the gamut from official staff to crippled veterans and drifters looking to earn money for their next meal. Most numerous were two-bit claim agents who preyed on widows who'd lost loved ones in the war. They dangled the promise of extravagant government compensation in exchange for a tidy sum. Stillman never understood why every charlatan smelled like peanuts.

Lobbyists were also in abundance, though Stillman knew Amelia disliked some of her kind. Low-class, self-proclaimed lobbyists traveled from all across the country to beg for their state causes, their shabby clothes and awkward slang making them an instant nuisance. Many were women, what the press dubbed "spider-lobbyists," who looked desperate, dragging children in tow as they rushed back and forth trying to "buttonhole" anyone who would listen. Trapping a victim by launching into the topic was commonplace. Stillman learned to glare as a means to steer clear of getting caught. As he did just that, he understood why Amelia didn't associate with her so-called colleagues.

The man Stillman arranged to meet, a portly fellow who wore thick sideburns that crawled over his fleshy face as he moved tobacco around in his mouth, stood in front of John Trumbull's painting depicting the signing of the Declaration of Independence. Stillman noted his expensive coat and polished boots.

"Mr. Zane," Stillman said.

Stillman gestured toward a bench in the center of the rotunda where two staffers ate sandwiches. "We need this bench," Stillman said to the aides.

One of the aides started to gripe, when the other seized his arm. "Whatever you need, Senator. We were just going."

When Zane sat at one end of the bench, Stillman took the other, leaving as much space between them as possible.

"I was surprised you wanted to do this here. Now. It's so busy," Zane said.

Bystanders provided shade just as leaves on a tree. Lunchtime meant everyone kept too caught up in their own affairs to notice anything.

Stillman unbuckled the leather straps of his case and pulled out a set of papers. "What do you make of these calculations?" Stillman asked as he handed Zane the papers.

Zane flipped through the stack and pretended to examine the material. Mixed in with the blank sheets was a thick envelope that he slipped into his coat breast pocket.

"They look fair." Zane handed the stack back to Stillman.

Once the papers were tucked back in the case, Stillman asked, "I trust you can deliver what you promise?"

In matters of business, legitimate and otherwise, Stillman

preferred withholding payment as motivation for quality labor. Because of the nature and superiority of Zane's work, Zane demanded an upfront cash payment. As Zane slipped his pinky finger into his ear, wiggled it about, then pulled it out to examine the bounty, Stillman thought the man repugnant. If not for Zane's impressive track record, Stillman might have offered the detective job to an intern who liked expensive cigars. With so much at stake, Stillman required the experienced, furtive methods of a man like Zane.

"I already have a few leads," Zane said. "Do you want to meet again?"

"No. Send what you find by messenger. I burn all notes."

Stillman stood and Zane lumbered to his feet. "I expect you'll have what you need in a day or so." Zane put out the hand with his soiled pinky.

Stillman paused, then shook his hand. Getting his hands dirty had rarely been as literal.

"Oh, and give my regards to your sister," Stillman said. "I hear her pies are quite tasty. Her bakery is doing so well, I'd hate for her to lose her business license."

Stillman didn't wait for Zane's response. Instead he turned and walked toward the senators' wing, wiping his hand on his trousers. Ten thousand dollars seemed reasonable in his march toward the chair appointment, especially since he'd liberated the money from excess farming subsidies. Still, leverage against Zane's sister might help ensure timely delivery. Others he knew would have used the threat and kept the money, but Stillman considered himself a reasonable man. If Zane earned his money, then they were even. By anyone's standards, Stillman felt his actions more than fair.

Phillip, a competent assistant without much ambition, which Stillman found preferable to the mouth-breathers constantly chomping at their bits, had gone to lunch. Walking past the empty desk, Stillman went to his own office, closed the door, and turned the lock.

Years of dedicated service to his country and paying homage to the powerful cronies had moved Stillman to an office with a small window facing Capitol Street. Each day he viewed a skim of a hedge below the wide boulevard and Victorian homes beyond. On bright days, beams of color streamed through a crystal prism hanging on fishing wire from the window latch. His wife gave him the prism as a special gift. Gertrude believed crystals had healing properties and nagged until Stillman promised to hang the bauble. He planned to cut it down the moment she scooted from his office. Distractions and then a sunny afternoon had left the prism in the window. Stillman never admitted how much he enjoyed the colorful display, especially when his office was filled with soothing green light. He glanced out the window and noted the dark clouds. The prism hung dormant.

Stillman turned up the gas in the oil lamp on his desk, removed his frock coat, and slung it on the back of the chair. A new stack of papers sat on the front edge of his desk. The pages, marked with tabs like tongues, meant sore hands, blurred vision, frustrating schedules, and ringing in his ears from the gibberish at endless meetings. He considered the pile with a sense of dread and wondered when the details had become drudgery. He remembered a time when he loved every bill.

A politician likened his first bill to a firstborn or first kiss. During the early days, Stillman worked late into the wee hours writing and editing, forming his revolutionary ideas into a semblance of possible laws. The creativity stirred him, and he recalled Gertrude's surprise when he'd come home wanting to make love on a weeknight. As he made time for poker games, received better committee appointments, bought a summer home on Lake Erie, and ran successful reelection campaigns, writing bills got in the way of the more exciting challenge: moving up among the ranks. Stillman smiled, then walked across the rug to the lit fireplace.

Above the stone mantel hung an oil painting of himself done by renowned local artist Geoffrey Penton. Stillman liked the rendering; his strong chin and thick dark hair shone in the oils. Penton had joked and told a bawdy tale right before beginning the first sitting. Gertrude thought the resulting sideways smirk and squinting eyes looked dastardly. Stillman thought the painting an interesting portrayal, and, more importantly, an ingenious cover for his wall safe.

Stillman pulled the lower left corner of the painting and swung it away from the wall on a hinge. Though personal safes were quite common in the homes of wealthy families, they were far from standard issue for the Capitol office. Inside the safe were bundled bills, a few loose government bonds and stock certificates, a baseball signed by the Knickerbocker club organizer, and several damning telegrams he'd never burn. Stillman had stashed upwards of two hundred thousand dollars, a nice sum from special districts, building inspectors, and the like. The public lands chair position offered ten times more.

Stillman slid his fingertips over the face of the bills and then raised the bundle to his nose. His father taught him to smell money, and the scent reminded him of losing his father from a heart attack. They hadn't spoken since the night in The Library, and Stillman sometimes blamed himself for what happened to his parents. He shook his head. He couldn't have predicted his father's outlandish reaction. Blame didn't help anyone. Hadn't his father said that? Stillman set the portrait back in place, returned to his desk, and sat with his arms folded across his chest.

He didn't like thinking about his dishonorable family, and so he focused on Zane. He needed Zane to find something damaging on Littlemore, or maybe even Mallory or Horton. If Zane could find a few devastating secrets on one or more of those powerful men, Stillman would have enough support to defeat the women's amendment regardless of Amelia's talents. Although Amelia had the power to steer men away from good judgment, all things considered, he saw tipping the scales as a game of inertia and momentum. Flirting didn't make a strong bond like men exchanging ideas and hostile words at committee meetings. Stillman narrowed his eyes, tugged at his collar, and then unbuttoned the top button. He bristled in his seat and felt the stiff wooden slats against his back. Amelia had done quite well for herself with flirting, except, Stillman thought, with Gage at the gala.

Clouds darkened and heavy rain began to fall in sheets against his office window. A crack of thunder startled Stillman and he rubbed his temples. Gage's refusal to shake hands with Amelia seemed a positive sign of solidarity, or, at the very least, a dislike of women. Meetings and sessions kept Stillman from tracking down Gage at his office, but Gage prided himself as a man of routine. Some touted his regimen as a testament to his diligent work ethic. Whatever anyone thought, Stillman knew one fact for certain. A man of routine was easy to find, and Stillman knew just where to corner Gage and put his industrious ethics to the test.

CHAPTER ELEVEN

The empty courtroom at City Hall watched in judgment as Amelia approached Senator Bradley Dodge Jenkins, Dodger to his friends. A large, good-humored man with strong hands and a wide, genuine smile, he looked out of place among the other senators with his blond hair and rugged tanned face. He often referred to himself as a lucky adventurer, which Amelia took as a humble version of the truth. Many believed Dodger made his fortune in the California gold mines; few knew his *eureka* wasn't from swinging a pick ax. He worked hard selling mining supplies and dry goods. Every new California miner and businessman alike knew Dodger, so when he ran for a congressional seat he won even without much campaigning. Unlike the men who leered and pawed, Amelia and Dodger felt the instant draw of friendship and nothing more. She appreciated him and agreed to meet with him despite the location.

"Amelia, lovely as ever. Keeping out of the muck?" Dodger embraced Amelia in a tight hug and she let his powerful arms and chest crush against her. "Thanks for meeting me here at the court. I'm testifying in a civil matter and have a little time before the proceedings begin."

They took seats in the audience facing the elevated bench where a judge would soon rule on the merits and condition of another's life. Again in a courtroom, Amelia disliked the sense of foreboding; the chamber a miniature world of good versus evil blurred by the proclamation of justice.

"So, go whole hog, my friend. I have about ten minutes," Dodger said.

Without having to bat her eyelashes or compliment his suit, Amelia needed only five.

"I want your vote, Dodger. It's that simple. The women have a real chance here. We want to decide for ourselves what's best for our family and country. Why should we suffer the indignity of having the same lack of rights as lunatics and criminals?"

Amelia glanced at the gavel balanced on the bench and felt her neck and shoulders tense with unease. She deemed her disdain for the justice system irrational, having never testified in court. Uncomfortable memories pressed in around her.

"My wife wants to vote. The little lady sometimes knows more about what's going on than I do. Did you know she belongs to a parent group that holds meetings at our house? Those ladies are as quick as powder monkeys and bright as fool's gold. I heard about the city drainage issues from one of the mothers. It's why my subcommittee started the erosion initiative. A small change, but a good one."

Amelia nodded, trying to keep focused. Dodger's plan, a practical step, gave him some much-needed positive attention. As affable as his character, his bulky size and miner's slang made him a punching bag for the press.

"It's nice to find a man who appreciates a woman's opinion," Amelia said.

"Well . . ." he grinned and his cheeks colored just a bit.

Aware of Dodger's embarrassment at her compliment, she gave him a reprieve. "So what's the case you're testifying for?"

"My neighbors are in a caterwaul about property lines. Both acting dumb as donkeys lost on the trail. Saw the whole fist-fight. Tried to stop it, but . . ."

Dodger admitted he didn't try too hard. He didn't like either neighbor and hoped they'd both move away. "Just glad this case isn't juicy enough for the papers," Dodger said as he adjusted his long legs, trying to find a comfortable position. "You of all people know I don't need more bad press. I can't take another hit."

Amelia nodded. A string of recent scandals had made sensational front-page news and hungry journalists were on the hunt to tar and feather culprits whether or not they had reliable sources. In Dodger's case, he'd suffered accusations of accepting free rail travel in exchange for his vote supporting Union Pacific. Amelia used her connections to clear him, although some damage to his reputation still remained. Few read the retraction on page ten, beside an advertisement for Beecham's Foot Powder.

"Funny when you think about it. If I were going to take a bribe, I'd claim jump for something better than a meager rail pass," he said.

Amelia wondered. "Not that you'd ever take a bribe, but what would you want?"

He didn't hesitate. "All I want is the feeling of striking gold. Took all my strength to stay back and sell Irish baby buggies and not go digging myself. The rush was a powerful draw and in a lot of ways I watched from the sidelines."

Amelia thought of Sam and his days as a forty-niner. Few knew the Sam who hiked the Sierra foothills with a pickaxe over his shoulder. Sam liked to tell stories of his escapades after he and Amelia had finished with their afternoon work. In front of the fireplace and under the afghan blanket Sam tucked around her legs with kindly attention, she'd listen with amazement to his exaggerated adventures in the Wild West. Amelia's favorite story was the time he tried to negotiate with one of the many Chinese immigrants and ended up carrying the man's mule pack for a week.

"Would you really go back to the hills, Senator?" Amelia had never seen him without a bowler and cravat. She couldn't imagine D.C. men like Dodger or Sam in muddy, rolled-up sleeves. "What about a foreign appointment, say Denmark?" Amelia asked.

Dodger raised his eyebrows. "My family's motherland? Hmm, I hadn't thought of that. Maybe in Copenhagen I could find a large enough chair."

Amelia smiled as Dodger checked his watch. She stood, aware of taking his time and Dodger seemed grateful for a reason to stand and stretch.

"Senator, thank you for seeing me. I wish you luck on your testimony today." Dodger again embraced her in a bear hug and then called her back when she turned to leave. "Don't you want to know if I'll vote in favor of the women?" he asked.

Some gestures took longer to perfect than others, and she'd fought with Sam many times in front of the mirror. "You may have one face, but I've got ten fingers," he'd say as he turned her head back to her reflection. Amelia tilted her head, her chin pointed down so her eyes were soft and welcoming. She then caressed the side of her neck before adjusting the high, stiff collar of her cream-colored shirt. "My friend, you mentioned your wife's wishes and I know how much you love and admire her. As you said, she's a bright, energetic woman like so many of us. Do I really have to ask how you'll vote?"

Dodger laughed in a deep genuine bass voice that made Amelia smile. "Okay, you have me. Actually, you had my vote before you walked in. I just always enjoy a good palaver with you, Amelia. I hope I didn't waste too much of your time."

Amelia shook her head. "Time with you is never wasted," she said, meaning every word. "And thank you."

In the noisy courthouse hallway Amelia noticed two middle-aged men glaring at each other. She passed without comment, knowing Dodger's vote also meant the support of the many disciples who followed him because of California's impressive economic growth. A quip about the infamous Hatfields and McCoys feud wasn't worth stirring up any trouble, or press, for Dodger.

Once outside, Amelia took a deep breath of the cool air to push away thoughts of trials and unfair proceedings where innocent lobbyists had to defend themselves against corporate rascals laying traps of deception. Amelia took another breath. She'd won a large contract for her client when a competitor accused her of bribery. Her employer didn't want to lose the contract, so they forced Amelia to make a hard decision. By then, Sam couldn't help. She could either defend her honor in court and lose her client and the generous retainer, or she could walk away and let her client quietly settle the matter with payoffs. She hadn't bribed anyone and often wondered if she'd made the wrong choice in taking the money, the easier road in hindsight.

Rain the previous day had turned to a light dusting of snow that created a fresh canvas for her footprints. A quick check of her pocket watch told her she had just enough time to stop at the *Post* before her lunch with Littlemore. She took his agreement to a second meal as a good sign.

The *Post* resided in the middle of Newspaper Row on Pennsylvania Avenue between 11th and 12th Streets, just a few convenient blocks from the Willard Hotel. Over the years, Amelia found the talented and ethical journalists of D.C. often helpful to Amelia's causes. Of those, she most relied on her friend Maxine Miller.

Maxine worked on the second floor, which housed the editorial and news divisions. Always in motion, the room tried to contain a labyrinth of energy so at any moment it felt like someone might jump to their feet and run screaming into the street. Amelia wound her way among the cluttered rows of desks and men without waistcoats. Telegraph machines droned and women in starched shirts and long skirts clicked on small black typewriters.

Amelia found Maxine sitting at her desk outside the office of the general editor. Her head down, she scratched out lines of text with a worn pencil. Amelia removed her gloves and tapped her index fingernail beside a vase of fresh roses on the desk.

Maxine glanced up and then back to her work. "You're late, Amelia. Can whatever you want wait until after five?"

"If it could, would I be here?" Amelia asked.

Maxine paused as if to regard the statement and then put down her pencil.

Amelia liked Maxine from the moment they met at a Haven House fundraiser. Small and lithe with a feathering of lines around her dark eyes, she reminded Amelia of a panther, with long black hair she often wore loose down her back. Maxine didn't take to her role of spinsterhood, so she made herself available to almost any man with a good paycheck and full head of hair. Maxine believed in intimate love without marriage and the right for a woman to do with her body as she pleased. What she wanted most was a front-page daily news column. Instead, her free love had earned her a few pieces in the society column, a parade of thorny roses on her desk, and a secretarial position with a man Maxine thought might have visited her boudoir. Too many glasses of wine at a company party clouded her memory. During her free time, Maxine wrote essays for the NWSA's rag, *The Revolution,* and took pride in her militia approach to suffrage.

Where the NWSA arranged lecture tours in town-hall meetings, Maxine wanted to stage grand protest rallies and march on the White House. After being jailed in England for heckling members of parliament, Maxine spoke openly about her incarceration and the torturous force-feedings. From having a tube routinely thrust down her throat, Maxine had a permanently raspy voice and the willingness to fall on the proverbial sword for the cause. Kept in check, Amelia enjoyed her enthusiasm even if she felt Maxine's tactics and lifestyle were shortsighted and ill-conceived. Though neither Amelia nor Maxine were the type of woman to routinely meet for luncheon and gossip, they sometimes shared tea and Amelia considered Maxine a friend, her only friend. Friendships took time and left marks, and Amelia had her work.

"So, what do you need, Amelia?" Maxine asked. She pushed aside a stack of papers.

Amelia leaned on Maxine's desk. "I need you to run a fluff piece about the new aide for Senator Horton. His name is Boyd McKenna, and we need something to give young Boyd a little buzz, make him the colt to watch."

Maxine rubbed her upper lip, leaving a smear of black from her pencil. Amelia chuckled, then pulled a handkerchief from her handbag and handed it to her. If a mustache would help Maxine get ahead, Amelia imagined her painting one on every morning.

After wiping her mouth, Maxine said, "I don't suppose you have any ideas."

"I'm confident you can think of something great," Amelia said, not having had time to consider plausible options.

Maxine had a degree in journalism but did secretarial duties because, according to her boss, women couldn't report hard news. Women only wrote for other women. Maxine fought to no avail, and so she gave up arguing with her boss. Soon a freelancer named Max Miller began sending insightful letters to the editor. No one had ever met Max, but her boss liked to comment that Maxine should marry the mystery man. *Max and Maxine Miller Miller.* Max's letters were routinely printed, once even on the front page. Maxine knew she succeeded with the ruse because the men at the paper deemed the idea of a woman writing compelling political arguments unimaginable.

"I'll figure something out for Boyd McKenna. Spelled like it sounds?"

Maxine made a few notes as Amelia shared what she knew about Boyd.

"When do you want the piece to run?" Maxine asked.

Amelia told her, then added, "I know I'm leaving this in capable hands."

"True indeed. One of the columnists owes me dinner. I do have very capable hands."

Amelia put on her gloves before Maxine could launch into anything more graphic. Crassness wasn't Amelia's style and she felt Maxine's manner undermined her efforts to gain the respect she so desperately wanted.

"Hey, don't get all bluenosed on me. I remember when you worked for Hell Gate Brewery. I wasn't the only one sampling the freebies," Maxine called out.

Amelia waved good-bye to Maxine and her past mistakes as she headed for the stairwell. Before she reached the first step, she heard, "Cooke, what brings you behind the curtain?" Clancy made his way toward Amelia. His hair looked tousled and the back of his shirt hung loose outside his pants. Red-rimmed eyes told Amelia he hadn't slept and he dabbed a handkerchief across his swollen, pink nose.

"Slumming, of course," Amelia replied. "You look terrible, Clancy, worse than the other night at the gala. Chasing a woman or a story?"

"Neither. Sick with a cold. Why? What do you want?" he asked.

Amelia brushed an imaginary stray hair from her forehead, drawing his eyes to hers. "Why, Clancy, you stopped me. My, do people always think I want something?" She reached in her bag and pulled out a small fold of wax paper. "Here, I have something for you. It's aspirin powder. I hate seeing you under the weather."

Clancy took the powder with a shy thank you. Amelia wanted to escape before he could infect her, but Clancy said, "Can I ask you something? Unofficially?"

Amelia paused as if considering, even though she never answered any question unofficially. She nodded and Clancy asked, "What happens if you lose, Amelia? I mean, the odds aren't great, you know that. What will the she-men do if they don't get the vote?"

The derogatory term turned her stomach and she hated that Clancy brought up what she'd avoided thinking about since she accepted Perla's retainer. Clancy watched Amelia with a look of mild anticipation, though she found him hard to read beneath the ongoing swabbing with his handkerchief. At last Amelia shrugged and asked, "What do you think will happen?"

He frowned. "Ladies are catty and can be real vicious. Back stabbers if you don't watch yourself. No offense. If you lose, I think you'd better run. They'll sharpen their claws and pin it on you. You're the easiest target."

"Get some rest," Amelia said and then left before he could ask any more questions.

Amelia searched for a cab on Pennsylvania Avenue, but the lunchtime traffic swarmed. Since senators didn't wait for lobbyists, Amelia gave up the idea of a ride and hurried on foot to Ebbitt Grill.

She reached the restaurant with just enough time to gather her thoughts and wayward hair before her engagement. The *maître d'* sat Amelia at a table near the window and brought her a cup of tea without asking.

"Thank you, Travis," Amelia said, grateful for the warm cup against her chilled fingers.

At her first dinner meeting with Arthur Littlemore, made all the more scrumptious when Littlemore mentioned he had just left Stillman at "The Club" to see her, the senator admitted his reluctance for female voters. "What's next, owning property?" he had said over the tomato salad. Over the main course of rare steaks and Amelia's delicate probing, Littlemore mentioned a pending bid for a coal mine in West Virginia. His father had worked as a miner and as a child Littlemore dreamed of owning a profitable mine. Amelia did some fast work and invited Littlemore to lunch to share good news. She could help him with his bid for the mine if he helped her by supporting the amendment. Finagling a winning bid for a coal mine required trading a racehorse for rail stock and exchanging the stock options for Texas drilling rights. Amelia often felt like a circus juggler.

Amelia looked for Littlemore, then checked her watch. Even for a busy senator, twenty minutes late bordered on bad manners. Just as Amelia thought to leave, a man stepped up to her table. She rose to greet her companion.

The chap wasn't Littlemore. A messenger handed Amelia a small note and waited until she gave him a few coins. Amelia sat back down with a fleeting glance toward the front door before she read the message. At first she thought someone had made a mistake. Who would send such a short note? Then she saw the note's author and crumpled the paper in her fist.

If the women lost their amendment, the NWSA might indeed run her out of town. But not for the petty cattiness or henpecking stereotypes created by men like Clancy. Volunteers handed out flyers in the rain and marched until blisters bled through their socks because they believed they could win. A setback so close to the finish line needed a scapegoat. If blame could be attributed to one person's incompetence, then the fight could continue; all hope wasn't lost. Amelia didn't want to think about losing her job and abandoning the life she'd worked so hard to create. She couldn't lose.

Few opponents had the pluck to brag in such a blatant manner and Amelia wanted to know what happened, what he'd done. She stuffed the note into her teacup and watched the paper sink to the bottom like a drowning victim. The message held just a few words:

Littlemore is mine.—E. Stillman

CHAPTER TWELVE

Stillman set the financial section of the newspaper on the coffee table and leaned back against his new velvet, double-ended sofa with rosewood turned legs. Outside he heard the sound of horse hooves clopping down the cobblestones of Washington Street, a prestigious address known for Italianate Victorian homes with large front rooms and arched eaves. He rested his head against the damask pillows Gertrude insisted were fashionable for the parlor and closed his eyes. Two days earlier, a Sunday, Gage had come just short of calling Stillman a no-account bum over Sunday brunch. Stillman speculated again about Chandler Gage and his baffling outrage.

Sundays in the capital were for families. Most shops closed for church and only a handful of immigrant-run restaurants opened. During pleasant spring weather, the parks were filled with strolling, lounging, and colorful toys. When the weather turned cold, residents settled into their hearth and home. The only exception was the occasional last minute draft or budget crisis, which meant the Capitol glowed all night, but even so, Stillman hated spending Sundays alone in the city. Even more, he loathed having brunch, a portmanteau word recently introduced in *Punch* magazine and now popular with the finer restaurants.

Senator Chandler Gage went to Welcher's restaurant every Sunday morning at nine o'clock. Stillman had learned of Gage's schedule from Gage's overzealous and inexperienced aide. At

158

the early hour, most of the red padded seats were tucked under bare tables waiting for place settings. Gage sat alone at a booth in the back reading the *Boston Transcript* and sipping coffee. Stillman took a deep breath and approached with what he trusted was a more casual demeanor than what he felt. He needed to speak with Gage and hadn't been able to corner him during normal business hours.

Thin, with a hawkish nose and dark circles under dark-brown eyes, most mistook Gage for much younger than fifty because he moved with the haste of a younger man, and, even with the obvious amounts of hair oil he used, his locks had a childlike, unkempt look from curls that refused to stay in place. Stillman greeted Gage with a confident smile and waited for Gage to lower his paper.

"I'm surprised to see you out so early on a Sunday morning, Edward. Not a religious man?"

Though Stillman didn't see himself as particularly religious, going to church was necessary for his position and the remark stung. He wanted to point out that Gage wasn't warming a pew either but held his tongue.

When Stillman remained standing at the table, Gage said he could join him. After ordering breakfast, Stillman started the conversation by complimenting Gage on his co-authorship of a new trade initiative and then reminding Gage of their time together on a bipartisan securities subcommittee. Gage remembered, though instead of following social protocol by praising Stillman, Gage rambled on about a tropical plants exhibit at the Smithsonian.

Stillman felt relieved when the waiter brought pancakes with fruit for Gage and a plate of eggs, ham, and potatoes for him. Stillman dug in but Gage left his fork untouched.

"Why are you here, Edward?" Gage asked.

"There's grumblings in the party, Chandler, and I need to

know where we stand on the women's amendment. The bill doesn't help any of us."

Gage took a bite of his fruit. "And why come to me?"

"Because we worked well together on your bill against animal cruelty, the one I helped you pass. A quiet Senate is good for all of us. You know the benefits of keeping a united party."

"I know no such thing." Gage put down his fork and stared at Stillman. "What I do know is that you're here talking to me on a Sunday, which means the rumors are true. You have a vested interest in the outcome of the women's bill, but any bargains you made don't concern me. I'm staying out of that. You answer to your own God . . ."—Gage paused, then added— "or maybe you don't. Either way, you and everyone else will know my decision on women's rights when I cast my official vote. We're through here."

Stillman hadn't sensed any animosity when he worked with Gage. Stunned, he left without protesting Gage's dismissal.

Stillman opened his eyes and took in his parlor. He'd made a mistake in allowing Gage to send him away. He now hoped the errand at hand would ease the sourness of the incident with Gage. Stillman sat up and reached behind one of the wall tapestries for the cord to call his footman.

Though Stillman hadn't wanted to indulge Gertrude, the parlor walls were covered with tapestries from several European vacations after she hinted that if she couldn't have tapestries, she had her eye on collecting cuckoo clocks. Stillman relented because he hated the ridiculous clock noise. At least the tapestries were quiet, and Stillman enjoyed the luxury they added to his parlor. He also treasured his authentic stone fireplace from Beardslee Castle. Importing each boulder from England cost a small fortune but he relished the opulence every time he sat by the fire.

Stillman didn't need a coach for the morning and told his

footman to fetch his warmest coat and felt, slouch hat before taking off the rest of the day. Walking through the kitchen, Stillman picked up Zane's note on the counter and left through the back entrance. When Stillman purchased the house, he had no idea he'd find the back escape route so handy.

Walking down the city street on a weekday morning made Stillman feel like a tourist. Mothers pushed babies in prams with wiggling toddlers and bags in tow. He appreciated their hard work and often wondered how Gertrude stayed so cheery after the long, sleepless nights when the boys were infants. The nanny helped, but Gertrude insisted on breast-feeding, which Stillman found a bit repugnant. Raising children was best left to women because men didn't have the stamina for the endlessness of that job. Men liked conclusions, like the suffrage debate under way and soon to close. The day's recess gave Stillman time for his outing.

The brisk air pressed against his wool shooting coat and checkered hat that he normally wore only for hunting or trotting outside to gather more firewood after his footman left for the night. For the special jaunt, Stillman turned up the tall collar and hunched his shoulders so his neck and chin slid behind the cloth. When no longer anywhere near his neighborhood, he pulled loose the tails of his shirt to look like a common laborer and stepped into a puddle of muddy water to cover his shiny shoes. Not wanting to take any chances, he walked for fifteen blocks. When Stillman reached an area where no one would recognize him, he stopped for a bottle of whiskey before hailing a hackney.

Stillman kept the torn sheet with the destination in his pocket even though he had memorized the address. In all his years of living in D.C., Stillman never stopped anywhere near the M Street bridge that led to Georgetown, a growing, affluent community reached only by crossing the iron bridge that carried M

Street across Rock Creek. Just before the riverbanks, where the Chesapeake and Ohio Canals converged, were the M Street brothels, known by all men of the city, who told stories about orgies where opium and prostitutes were passed around like a basket of dinner rolls. He never expected to see that part of town for himself nor could anyone see him making the trip.

A quick curl of the cabby's brow confirmed the driver knew the address. Stillman pulled his cap lower and purposely stumbled on the bottom step of the carriage before he slumped into the shadowed seat. Cabbies were well paid spies so Stillman took every precaution. A common drunkard going to M Street wasn't worth remembering; at least that's what Stillman hoped.

Inside the seclusion of the cab, Stillman mused that he learned the art of appearing inebriated from Amelia. A few years back when they were civil at a charity dinner, Amelia told him the key to the ruse was leaning. Thinking of Amelia made him imagine how she must have cringed and clenched her fists when she read his telegram. Sending a note may have been a bit impulsive, but he had no doubt his little excursion to M Street meant Littlemore's vote. The mere thought of taunting Amelia was too delicious.

When the hackney slowed, then stopped in front of an unpainted row house, Stillman paused at the window. After his note to Amelia, he'd spent the evening writing down, then memorizing, what he would say. In the daylight, the words felt choked in the back of his throat and as withered as the rotting boards of the houses. He coughed but the lump remained. The driver shouted something about getting out, so Stillman stepped onto the street. He paid the driver, then waited until the cab rounded the corner before he walked to the end of the block to the real address.

Snow that had melted in the city proper remained stuck to garbage and stacks of leaves that littered the sidewalks and street. The sounds of barking dogs and screaming children seemed to echo all around him even as the streets were quiet, desolate. Stillman checked behind him expecting to face a bandit, and he chastised himself for not leaving his full wallet at home. Still, seeing the peeling paint and sagging roofs reminded him that he should use the desperation of the poor in his next reelection speech.

The corner house seemed to list off the row as if it were trying to flee from the others. Peeling gray paint hinted the house might have once been black or maybe olive, but the rotted wood gave the appearance of a building covered with the pox. A ceramic blue goose sat by a bare front door without a knocker, so Stillman used the back of his hand to bang three times. He heard the creaking of floorboards just before the door opened and a frail woman with thin blond hair stood in the doorway. She wore a sheer robe over a corset and stockings. Her feet were exposed, showing red toenails.

"Come in, sir." The woman stepped aside to let him in the door.

The dim hallway smelled of mold and dust, and a bitter odor reminded Stillman of the peaches Gertrude burned while canning.

"I need to speak with Lulu," Stillman said.

Looking past the woman, Stillman saw a small sitting room with a few women in various forms of undergarments and thin robes. Two were playing cards, unaware that their robes had slipped from their shoulders. Stillman looked away, thankful there were no men. Zane's note said to visit before noon to best avoid being seen. Stillman kept himself from dollymops as a matter of principal and hygiene. Seeing the unclad bodies, dirty floors, and stained seat cushions confirmed his wise choice to stay away.

"Get me Lulu, now."

Stillman waited just a few moments, then a woman in a fitted scarlet dress descended the stairs. She wore her brown hair teased high and had painted thick black lines around her eyes. Even though he could see too much of her bust, Stillman felt relieved she wasn't as undressed as the others. He considered her role as the madam, but Zane included very specific information about her profession. Lulu did not run the house as madam nor did she work for the money. Hers was a fetish of the warped and bored.

She batted her eyelashes and nodded. "Were you referred by Martin?"

The woman held the bannister as if needing to steady herself and Stillman tightened. His scheme wouldn't work if she had taken drugs or alcohol. Stillman forgot his practiced speech and launched into his business with haste.

"You don't remember me," Stillman said.

"I remember everyone," Lulu slurred.

Stillman seized her shoulder and she jerked with surprise. He pulled her toward the doorway, away from view of the others. He shook her hard; he needed her to pay attention and do what he said.

"Lulu is your working name. Your real name is Rosaline Littlemore," Stillman said.

The woman held her place but Stillman saw the flicker of panic in her eyes. She wasn't as far gone as she pretended, or perhaps wanted to be. His strength returned and he squeezed her arm, feeling his fingertips press into her flesh.

"I'm not in the mood, Mrs. Littlemore. I don't care about your . . . whatever it is you call this," he waved his hand around the hallways and pointed to the staircase that led to the bedrooms. "What I care about is your husband, the senator, and his reputation. You know what would happen to his career should something of this magnitude get to the press."

The woman's eyes filled with tears. "Please, you can't. He doesn't know anything about this. I don't know why I . . . I mean . . . I can quit. It's just—"

"Be quiet, woman. You're an abomination to your husband. If you don't want Arthur to know about this then you'll do as I say."

Mrs. Littlemore nodded through the stream of tears as Stillman explained what he needed her to do.

"I pity your husband," Stillman said, then reached for the front door. "But be assured I will go straight to the newspapers if you don't do exactly what I told you. I hope you believe me. For Arthur's sake."

"But how . . . ?" Mrs. Littlemore asked. She was discreet and cautious; never bringing opium home and taking only referred clients.

Stillman would never ask Zane to reveal his sources. Sludge that bubbled to the surface was best left for someone else to clean up. Stillman had his own agenda, which didn't include comforting Mrs. Littlemore.

Stillman left disgusted that a wife could show so little regard for her husband and resolved that if Gertrude ever did anything so shameful, he might shoot her. As unfortunate as Arthur's poor choice of wife was, Stillman didn't care enough to lose his appointment. Stillman had his own problems to worry about.

Finding a coach meant hiking back to a more respectable area. Cabs dropped people off in the M Street district but didn't always wait or circle looking to pick up passengers. With his head low and hands dug into his pockets, he walked with purpose. The farther he got from the stench, the more he felt like celebrating. There was no doubt "Lulu" would ensure Littlemore's vote. Stillman just hoped she'd follow his instructions and not succumb to the misguided need to confess her sins. He had to trust that a woman able to hide something so appalling from her husband was shrewder than the bundle of tears he'd seen. Stillman had known many shrewd women, the least of which now fell behind in the race.

Stillman tucked in his shirt and removed his hat. As he crossed the busy intersection at Dupont Circle, he pulled out the note with Lulu's address, crunched it in his fist, and tossed the evidence and whiskey bottle in a trash barrel. He hoped Zane had more dirt soon. With Littlemore's support and Mallory's a good bet, that left Dodger for Amelia, Gage unknown, and Horton in the middle of their tug of war. With how much he paid for investigative work, if any of them had anything to hide, Zane would find out.

Returning home after his adventurous outing, Stillman tossed off his outerwear and lit a cigar. He took a long drag and let the smoke billow from his mouth and nose before setting the cigar in the bronze ashtray on the entry-hall table. Since his footman was released for the night, the day's mail still lay on the floor beneath the mail slot. He picked up the pile, noting a white paper folded over and sealed with red wax. The hand-delivery excited him; perhaps Zane already had more helpful information.

Just as Stillman broke the seal, he heard a knock on his front door. A messenger delivered an urgent telegraph. Stillman tossed the lad a few coins and slammed the door. He didn't like anything urgent. Nothing good every came in the form of urgency.

Mother dead. Scandalous circumstances.
Come home immediately or ruin your career.

He stubbed out his cigar and slumped against the hall table. His brother likely dashed to the telegraph office, unhappy about their mother's passing while at the same time delighted to stir up trouble. He had expected his mother to pass and so the news felt more like a sigh than a gasp. Though he'd miss his mother, she'd been ill for over a year. He had said his good-byes during their last visit.

Once Stillman set down the telegram, he opened the mysterious note. He read the neat script and a chill ran down his neck. Oscar Fitzwater, the stonemasons union leader, wanted a meeting. The stonemasons were strong and united by a man people called an autocratic dictator. Though never charged, police suspected Fitzwater in several irregular murders. Stillman didn't know why a man like Fitzwater wanted to see him, but a tyrant not only knew where he lived, the note was a summons, not a request. Stillman hurried to the kitchen and locked the back door. Stillman rubbed his forehead, then steadied himself on the kitchen stool. He had to decide which to do first. Leaving the city in the middle of the fight to take care of family problems seemed impossible, and yet Stillman thought of Littlemore and the ramifications of a scandal. His brother might exaggerate, but could he take a chance? Maybe he could stall Fitzwater, but he didn't know if a man like Fitzwater would accept a delay. Oscar Fitzwater, a suspected murderer and union boss, not only wanted to talk; he demanded they meet someplace private.

Chapter Thirteen

After an agonizing night eased only slightly by too much cognac, Stillman sent a telegram of delay to Fitzwater and left on the morning train to Cincinnati, before he could hear back from the marauder. Stillman decided to play the odds and act on what he knew for certain. He couldn't risk a scandal, not with the public lands position in his crosshairs.

Not wanting to let his wife know of his visit lest she insist he stay for a week, Stillman had his brother send a coach to the train station and drop him off at Denridge, the private asylum that had cared for their mother. Mrs. Theodore Stillman had had a private room on the ninth floor, the "wellness wing" as they called it. Psychiatric patients ate meals in a common room and could wonder the halls if taking their medications, but they couldn't leave the building for reasons of safety and discretion. Stillman and his brother had selected Denridge particularly for management's discretion.

Stillman entered his late mother's room and found his brother going through a box of knickknacks. James looked up. "Good to see you could make time for your mother, Edward."

"Yes, well, your telegram was dramatic. You have a flare for hysteria. Too bad you don't have a flare for clothing."

James wore a basic brown suit with stray threads at the cuffs.

"Some of us think more about the work than the perks. You wouldn't understand, Senator."

"What's the big scandal, James? Why am I here? You didn't

drag me from Washington just to claim a ceramic cat."

James put down the figurine in his tight fist and huffed. "Mother somehow did it. She killed herself, Edward. Took an overdose of pills and was found foaming at the mouth, her body swelled like a sewer rat. She even soiled herself. Awful. Disgusting. What do you think the press would make of that?"

Stillman sat down on the edge of his mother's bed. The colorful patchwork quilt from Aunt Leila remained draped over the footboard.

"All right. You're right. This isn't something we need to pass around. What is the facility doing about it?" Stillman asked.

"The director has already hushed the orderlies and nurses who saw Mother. All we have to do is pay him and he'll keep quiet. The official death certificate will list a stroke as the cause of death."

Stillman rolled his shoulders. He disliked long, unscheduled train trips. "It sounds like you have everything under control. Why in the world do you need me here?"

"Yes, I do have everything under control, as always. I don't need you. You were requested. The director said he wouldn't finalize the deal without talking with you, face to face."

"So, what does he want?"

James shrugged. "I don't know. But you're here, so let's get this over with. I'm sure you have someplace else you'd rather be. Others you're waiting to stab in the back, perhaps?"

Stillman ignored his comment. As he stood to follow James to the director's office, the bed creaked and Stillman remembered his mother lying beneath the blanket the last time he saw her. She looked puny and pale, but she had smiled and patted Stillman's hand. "Go do good things," she had said. "I'm proud of my little boy."

Stillman swallowed a lump in his throat. With both of his parents gone, he felt like an orphan and a dark pain drifted through his chest. He shook his head; the idea of a grown man as an orphan was preposterous. His parents weren't part of his daily life anymore. He had fond memories of his parents before all of the unpleasantness, and he'd miss them when he had good news or his own sons reached milestones. But he had moved on like a man should. Stillman straightened the blankets, looked about the room one last time, and left without looking back.

Facility director Dr. Reed Graham met Stillman and his brother outside of his office. He wore a white physician's coat and wire spectacles and held a clipboard to his narrow chest.

"Senator Stillman, thank you for coming. Please let's go in my office. It's been a busy morning, you know. But we can't have the patients eating each other's socks," Dr. Graham said.

James glared at his brother. "I'll be in the lobby when you're done. We need to discuss the funeral arrangements."

"Good man," the doctor said once James had left. "He visited your mother often. Took good care. Of course, he's local and you're quite far. Your mother spoke of you often. Proud as a peacock about her son the senator."

Stillman knew pandering tactics, had used them many times. The doctor wanted Stillman at ease and he aimed to find out why.

"What can I do for you, Dr. Graham? You obviously need something from me or my brother's payment would have taken care of this matter."

"Yes, I suppose that's true. You see, I'm truly more than happy to, shall we say, tuck away the details of your mother's unfortunate passing, but money is just for paying the bills, you see."

"If not money, then what do you want? Legislation? A contract? Perhaps an appointment to some honorary position?" Stillman knew the short list of requests.

"A perceptive man, Senator. Yes, we need reform that favors the ethical treatment of the mentally ill. The state-run institutions are overcrowded and quite inhumane."

Stillman shook his head. "I didn't know about the conditions, but I suppose now I have to care. Is that it?"

The doctor shifted in his seat. "In a manner of speaking. There's a bill that outlines and regulates treatment of patients. It's been circling the drain for a few years. I'm hoping that with your mother's condition and the nature of her death, you see the need for breathing life into the reform. We just need the right backing to start the ball rolling."

"I see. Yes, well, I think that can be arranged. But tell me, Doctor, why bring me here? This isn't a matter that needs a face to face meeting." Stillman didn't like the perspiration on the doctor's forehead or the way he kept rubbing his palms.

The doctor shook his head. "I'm sorry. I'm not familiar with this sort of thing. I thought matters like this needed a handshake."

Stillman watched the doctor smile and then glance out the door to his office toward someone shouting in the hallway.

"I see you're needed, Doctor," Stillman said as he stood. "I'll take care of the proposed reform if you handle my family's affairs in a confidential and respectful manner. Are we agreed then?"

"Yes, yes, very good. I'd heard you weren't averse to making deals."

Stillman felt a tingle in his chest. "And where did you hear that, sir?"

"Oh, I don't remember. This place has me running in circles. I can barely remember my own name." The doctor pulled his thin lips into a feeble smile.

Stillman didn't care for games but he'd been dragged in by someone. He paused and thought about his work. He'd been pulled away.

The doctor cleared his throat. "Yes, well, I really must go attend to matters."

"Of course. Running in circles. You're even perspiring," Stillman said as he pointed to the doctor's forehead.

"Oh, dear. Excuse me."

The doctor reached into his breast pocket and pulled out a handkerchief. As he swabbed his forehead, he turned the cloth and Stillman saw the embroidery. In bright green thread, Stillman saw the letter *A*.

"So, Edward, are we all set?" his brother asked as Stillman raced up to him. "Edward, what's wrong?"

Stillman didn't have time for a chat. Amelia had dragged him from the city on a goose chase for her own benefit and his folly. He'd seen her monogrammed handkerchief many times. He didn't know how she knew about his mother, but he had a sinking suspicion. Since her first trip to Cincinnati, Amelia had likely kept in touch with the members of the American Medical Association. She'd mentioned a doctor or two, maybe even a reform, in passing. Amelia knowing about his mother had further implications. If she knew about his family matters, Stillman couldn't help but worry about what else she knew.

"I have to get back. You can handle everything from here," Stillman said.

"You're still just like Father. Always off and running."

Stillman seized his brother's collar. Rage tickled the back of his throat. "Don't talk to me about Father. What's done is done. And, frankly, right now I don't care about what you think Father and I did to you. I have more important matters to deal with."

James removed Stillman's hands. "I'm not talking about what Father did to me. I'm talking about what he did to Mother."

"Well, I'm not talking about any of it. Is that clear? I have to get back and deal with a petty, arrogant—"

172

"What about Mother's funeral?" James asked.

Stillman buttoned his overcoat and turned to leave. "I'll have my aide send flowers."

CHAPTER FOURTEEN

Preparations for the dinner party began that morning after a messenger brought Amelia's final reply. A nice intimate number of eight were confirmed. In addition to payback for Stillman's stunt with Littlemore, getting Stillman out of town for a couple days made sure her top choices said yes without fear of pressure or reprisal. Even with the enviable guest list, Amelia's first obstacle happened at three thirty in the afternoon.

At least once a month, Amelia rented the private dining room at the Willard Hotel and made arrangements for the decorations, meal, wine, and spirits. Sam couldn't stress enough the importance and proper handling of a soiree even if elaborate gastronomy delighted Sam far more than Amelia. He could spend hours debating the choice of appetizer and if the tart salad dressing complemented the savory entree. Amelia viewed the elegance of a dinner party as part of her job, one where the planning had gone smoothly until the hotel's general manager approached with pursed lips.

Amelia stopped checking the centerpiece arrangements when the short man tapped her on the shoulder. The case of port wine en route from Virginia had an accident. When Amelia asked if the bottles were taken to the hospital, the flustered manager clarified that the carriage carrying the wine lost a wheel in a rut and flipped.

"Shall I order something else?" the manager asked.

Amelia shook her head and said she would take care of it.

Senator Mallory had an obsession with port. She already had the preferred libations for Mr. Kern of the Smithsonian and Mr. Manning, Secretary of the Treasury. The accident added a wrinkle in the evening's agenda, which left just one option.

By five o'clock, Amelia had approved the final room setup and retired to her suite to dress for the evening. A hotel attendant fussed with her hair, pinning large curls to frame her face as Amelia thought of men having a quick shave and throwing on a fresh shirt. Amelia spent two hours primping and cinching, as how she looked played a crucial part of her role for the evening. "Ridiculous," Amelia mumbled. She never expected being a lobbyist required so much powder.

Once finished dressing, Amelia checked on final arrangements for the party. At ten minutes to the hour, she decanted the burgundy and then stationed herself by the doorway to greet her guests and usher them to the second-floor dining room, an intimate space quite useful for valuable conversation.

A crystal chandelier with delicately etched glass hung over the dining area and provided a restful glow for the adjoining library alcove. Light flickered on a rectangular table set with polished silver settings and a lush arrangement of white winter jasmine. The complement of flatware suggested a rich meal with many courses and two desserts, and Amelia insisted on individual salt and pepper shakers at each place setting. She had seen political careers ruined by arguments over passing the salt. Though not her finest effort, Amelia liked the final mood that imbued festivity without drawing attention to the agenda. Unlike the butter dish, the evening's agenda was best kept hidden.

Boyd McKenna arrived promptly at seven in full evening dress of black tailcoat, white bow tie, and top hat. Amelia thought he looked surprisingly dashing in the staunch conservative fashion. Boyd addressed her with a formal greeting.

"Please call me Amelia." He agreed if she called him Boyd.

"You look," he paused to admire her and then said, "exquisite."

All of the fussing had served the first purpose of the evening. Amelia wore an off-white, beaded lace gown that draped around her waist and hips. Iridescent pearl pins were placed in her piled hair so at the right angle she appeared to glow like an angel.

Amelia thanked him with a slight bow. "And you look ready to take office."

Boyd slipped his hands around the lapels of his jacket and rocked back on his heels. "Why thank you. I kind of feel like I should make an acceptance speech."

The other guests arrived in a flurry of cloaks, handshakes, and boisterous greetings accompanied by glasses of wine. A business dinner party, meant to feed and nurture politicians without seeming too political, required a careful guest list and the elite, eleventh-hour fashion show fundraiser to occupy the wives. Amelia often invited wives to her special dinners, but tonight she needed the full attention of her company. Of course, Amelia now owed the fundraiser's organizer a favor in return.

Along with Boyd McKenna and herself, the guests included Senator Mallory; Michael Kern, curator for the Smithsonian; famed speech writer George Lyon; Secretary of the Treasury, Daniel Manning; Western Union board director, Andrew Woodin; and General Bowen Garfield. While considering party lines and positions, Amelia also matched interests, hobbies, marital status, and talents when arranging an evening. Mallory loved popular music and the general had a fine reputation for his melodious singing voice.

Two serving girls circled the room with trays of salmon croquettes and wine glasses were refilled as needed. Amelia made sure the chatter focused on the topics of weather and daily news; then, just as George Lyon mentioned the controversy over public easements, Amelia announced dinner service.

Amelia let Boyd escort her to the table. "Never forget the importance of private industry," she whispered to him.

The guests found their place cards with ease. Based on seniority, status, and the need for Mallory's vote after the loss of Littlemore, Senator Mallory and Secretary Manning were at each head of the table. Amelia and Smithsonian curator Kern sat on either side of Mallory, and Boyd and speech writer Lyon flanked Secretary Manning. In the middle seats were the general beside Amelia and Western Union director Woodin next to Boyd. Of any at a dinner table, the middle seats were the most dangerous.

A man able to hear all of the conversations around him could direct the evening. When Amelia wanted an energetic debate she need only to put the most opinionated in the middle and let the evening unfold. The men at Amelia's dinner didn't know each other well, so she expected a simple dinner of goodwill toward fellow man and, more importantly, women.

The first course of steaming lobster bisque was served. Amelia asked Mr. Kern about the Smithsonian's new tropical plant exhibit and Mallory, an amateur botanist, became intrigued and they chatted. Across the table she watched Secretary Manning joke with Boyd and Lyon, and she listened as the general explained to her and Woodin how the gramophone worked. The hot broth and warm conversation were going as planned.

As the soup bowls were cleared, Amelia signaled for the wine. She'd paired the *amuse-bouche* with Kern's favorite Rhine wine.

"An excellent choice," Curator Kern said.

Amelia explained that she'd selected a special wine for each course. "With our first dessert, you're all in for a treat," she said. "Senator Mallory, I understand you're fond of an aged port. Well, I've imported a rare Spanish port I thought you might like to try."

Mallory raised his heavy dark brows. He thanked Amelia and then turned to the general to ask about his interest level in duck hunting.

Over medium-rare filet mignon with riced potatoes and almond string beans, the conversation settled with the chewing. As full glasses of a robust burgundy were poured, Amelia introduced a topic for the entire table to discuss.

"Did you know, Senator Mallory, that originally the management of the Willard Hotel wouldn't rent me a room without a husband? Can you imagine, General, how silly that was for an independent woman like me? In fact, Andrew, I was so mad I marched down to your main office in the city and sent a telegram to the President of the United States. By the by, where do telegrams like that actually go?"

Andrew Woodin swallowed, then said, "To the Undeliverable Department for cataloging. Each quarter we submit a report of crackpots like you to the Commission of Domestic Trade. They like to keep records." He smiled, then stuffed a piece of bread roll in his mouth.

"I think Miss Cooke makes a fine crackpot," Lyon said.

"What happened with the hotel, Amelia? What changed the manager's mind?" Secretary Manning asked.

"My agreeing to help interview coiffurists for the hotel's beauty salon," Amelia said.

"Now that's hard to imagine," Lyon said.

"That Miss Cooke goes to a salon? Son, you don't see right out of your eyes," the general said.

"No, General, that Miss Cook would waste time on something so ridiculous. Tell us the truth, Amelia, did you conduct the interviews yourself or hire someone to do them for you?"

"She had help," Boyd commented. "She delegated."

Amelia turned and saw Curator Kern shaking his head. "No,

it was too important; she needed a place to live. She did the interviews herself."

"You win, Mr. Kern. Your prize is the largest slice of cake." Amelia dabbed her mouth with her napkin. "The funny part was that the most qualified applicant was a man."

General Garfield dropped his fork and nudged Amelia's shoulder. "You're a real hoot. Men doing a lady's hair. No man wants to do that."

George Lyon took a swallow of wine. "Oh, I don't know. Why not? I once helped with a speech for Queen Victoria. Jefferson often sought counsel from Mercy Otis Warren. And what about Catherine the Great or the Empress of China? If women can run a country, why can't a man fix hair?"

"Amazonian tribes have gender role reversal. We hosted an exhibit of tribal textiles last year," Kern said.

Boyd straightened. "I saw that tour at the Boston Museum."

"Fine museum," Secretary Manning said.

"One of the finest," Kern added.

Amelia enjoyed her filet and let the conversation drift at will. She had made her point, or really Lyon made the point for her. If anyone even broached a cultural reference about women, Lyon boasted about his speech for the Queen. Amelia wanted Mallory to hear that in other countries women did far more than vote.

"Did you hear about Senator Stillman from Ohio?" Curator Kern asked the group.

Amelia stiffened.

"He stopped by the plant exhibit and I overheard him talking about being appointed as chair of the Committee on Public Lands," the curator said.

Mallory bristled. "He hasn't been appointed. If anything, he's just tossed his name into the ring."

Secretary of the Treasury Manning cleared his throat. "The

rumor about Stillman is true enough. He wants the job; been courting the Secretary of the Interior like a parvenu."

Boyd then chose an inopportune moment to show his inexperience. "But can he really lobby, for lack of a better term," Boyd said, as he looked at Amelia, "for an appointed position? I should think that decision is based on merit."

The boisterous laughter added a festive lift to the party. Boyd handled the men's good-humored ribbing with a smile, staying more at ease than Amelia. She knew Stillman was digging in, and now she knew why.

With the first dessert, a chocolate cake with a tart, raspberry filling, Amelia rang for the Spanish port. In the dim lighting and after their fifth glass of wine, no one noticed the worn bottle. On a fact-finding trip to Spain, she'd saved the Spanish bottle because she liked the colorful label. Amelia never expected needing to wash out the bottle and refill it with a cheap port from the corner tavern.

"You know," Mallory began, then stopped to fork a large piece of cake into his mouth. He smacked his approval and washed it down with the port. "Chairman Palmer isn't retiring from public lands because he wants to. He was asked to step down."

"Always the last to know," Lyon muttered.

Kern chuckled. "You're not the last to know. We don't hear about anything at the Smithsonian until it's buried and dug up again."

General Garfield raised his glass and offered a toast to digging. Clinking of glasses sounded like victory.

A refreshing dollop of lemon sorbet soothed the conversation and left a fresh, sweet taste on the palate. The chatter turned to boxing, and Amelia commented on the heavyweight match between Kilrain and Smith.

"You're full of surprises," Boyd said, his grin too wide for mixed company.

Woodin elbowed Boyd in the side. "I think our lad's smitten, Amelia. You do have that effect."

Amelia shook her head. "You flatter me. I think it's just the libations. Perhaps we should take coffee in the sitting area."

Changing locations defused any further talk about Boyd and his enthusiasm for Amelia. If Boyd was embarrassed he did a fine job of hiding his emotions. As the group lumbered, full and happy, to the library alcove, Boyd laughed and slapped the general on the back.

Rounding out the evening with coffee and Belgian chocolates gave the guests time to sober and gather their wits. Wives and children were bragged about, and workloads for the upcoming weeks were compared. While the men gabbed, Amelia glanced to Mallory as he sat in a wingback chair in front of a small bookshelf. He looked relaxed as he nodded in agreement to something Secretary Manning said. Amelia knew Mallory hunted with Stillman but she wondered if they were more connected than they seemed. Having a friend with a powerful committee appointment was the next best thing to having the job—a very good reason for losing Mallory's vote.

By midnight the lethargy of food and drink had worn off enough for the satisfied to go home. Coats and hats were passed around, and Amelia escorted each guest to the parlor door and gave them small gift baskets filled with dried apricots, nuts, and wafers. She bid them safe travels and fine digestion, and then spent an extra moment inquiring about the health of Senator Mallory's wife.

As the others left, Boyd lingered by the bookshelf thumbing through a worn volume of *Oliver Twist*. When the general saluted Amelia and then kissed the back of her hand, Boyd and Amelia were left alone. Boyd set down the book and made his way to Amelia.

181

"I don't think I've ever had so much fun." Boyd was giddy from indulging in each round of wine. His cheeks were flushed and his stance listed to the right as if he were resting on a walking stick.

"I'm glad you enjoyed yourself, Boyd."

Boyd grasped Amelia's hands. "Inviting me here helped so much. Is there anything *I* can do for *you*?" he asked with a coy smile.

Amelia found his assessment of the evening amusing. Even in his drunken state, Boyd seemed to understand the Washington game of give and take and the value of the introduction. Amelia also discovered that Boyd McKenna couldn't handle his wine.

"Yes, there is something you can do for me," she said.

Boyd leaned forward and Amelia steadied him. His dimple pressed deep into his face and his eyes held her gaze with an impetuousness she hadn't seen in years, not since Stillman.

"You can travel home safely," Amelia said.

Boyd leaned forward and kissed her cheek. Amelia held her place and did not recoil from his forwardness.

"Good night, Boyd," Amelia said when he had stepped back.

"Good night, Amelia Cooke."

With the room clear, Amelia sank into her chair at the table and rang for a cup of hot tea. Amelia crossed her legs and knocked the full, silver spittoon under her seat. She never drank at her own parties. The bucket rocked and a bit of wine sloshed on the carpet. A bright red stain spread on the pale rug.

Amelia considered the dinner party a triumph in form but not necessarily function. Mallory hadn't said anything declarative about the women's vote, though Amelia did like Kern's invitation for Mallory to visit the plant exhibit. She would call on Mallory in a day or so at his office to ask about the exhibit and return Mallory's wayward glove. The box of "wayward gloves" in her bureau had a seventy-five percent success rate of

182

getting her into any office. Overall, the events of the evening had gone as planned. Her indigestion wasn't from the meal.

She now understood Stillman's motivation and his fierce attitude at the postal gala. Working a deal for the public lands appointment required extra ruthlessness, even by Stillman's standards. The figurative keys to the kingdom were his reward for squelching her amendment. Amelia swallowed against a wave of nausea. With Littlemore lost and Mallory undecided, Amelia knew Stillman would do anything to win. She considered if, like Stillman, she too had the ambition to do anything for victory, but then she pushed away her teacup and the disturbing notion. She could worry about her integrity some other time. For now, she needed Horton's vote. Amelia folded her arms across her chest; Amelia needed Boyd McKenna.

CHAPTER FIFTEEN

Amelia's boots echoed as she walked down the wide aisle of the temple that was flanked on either side by long pews facing a raised platform with a wood podium and carved, painted cabinet. High ceilings and walls were covered in dark wood, scrubbed and oiled to a pure shine, and silver wall sconces flickered beside neat rows of tiny gold wall plaques engraved with names. As an adult who regularly sat through masses, gospel meetings, revivals, bible studies, and bar mitzvahs in the name of the holy vote, she understood why the altar was missing a replica of Jesus on the cross.

"Inside the cabinet is a Torah scroll. The holy bible," a voice said from behind her. A man in a black suit and wide-brimmed hat approached with a cautious smile beneath a thick black beard and mustache. Wrinkles around his eyes gave him the judicious look of a sage even though he was younger than Amelia expected.

"You must be Rabbi Cohen. Thank you for agreeing to meet with me during your lunch time."

The man nodded slowly but his eyes betrayed the growing bewilderment of what she wanted. Amelia glanced to her left where she heard a deep rumbling of chanting. The rabbi told her a small group of men were saying prayers.

"If you're needed, Rabbi, I don't want to interrupt your *minyan*," Amelia said.

The rabbi's eyebrows shot up. "You know about a *minyan*?"

When Amelia became an adult, she thought she was freed from going to church. Instead Sam's requirements went beyond a simple Sunday morning communion cup and wafer. Being well versed in all religions meant you understood another's perspective and motivations by attending lectures and taking classes. "Religion keeps a man humble, or, at the very least, gives him a reason to fake it," Sam liked to say. From her studies, Amelia appreciated the depth of the Jewish faith and their dedication to hard work and reward for efforts done in kind.

"I've been to a few Shabbat services," Amelia said. "The Torah scrolls are beautiful."

His stare softened and he asked what he could do for her.

"I'd like to do something for you, Rabbi. If you're agreeable," she said. "Can you tell me about the new Jewish grammar school you want to build?"

Tifereth Israel Synagogue was part of a modest neighborhood where most of the residents were Jewish. To an outside observer, the wide tan stone building with arched, stained-glass windows and manicured hedges served as the focal point of the community. The houses and shops, constructed during an age of burgeoning faith, were kept near the synagogue for convenience and reverence. Continued growth pleased the community elders. Nevertheless many of the younger generation felt isolated and wanted a more secular life that meant higher wages and position in the community, even if the mainstream didn't understand their culture and beliefs.

The rabbi shifted his hat back and forth on his head. "You know about our school, Miss Cooke. I should ask how, but maybe that doesn't matter so much." He nodded as if confirming his own thoughts. "There's a passage in what you call Malachi where God is displeased with His people for their indifference and spiritual lethargy. God says, 'When you sacrifice a crippled or diseased animal, is that not wrong?' Our young today," he shook his head. "They want so much but don't realize what they're going to lose. They are a bit lazy and try to justify their actions just like sacrificing a blemished animal. That's why we need our own school, Miss Cooke. Our children must have a place to learn among those who can foster a strong Jewish way of life."

"And how are the building plans going?"

"Unfortunately we're stalled for money. Nothing new, I'm afraid. Fundraising is slow, is it not?"

As the Rabbi talked about their fundraising efforts, Amelia thought about justifying actions. As long as she did a good act, did it matter that she also benefited? Was she *sacrificing a blemished animal* because she had selfish motives?

"So, you are interested in our school. This is very pleasing. Perhaps, then, you'd like to make a donation?" Creases around the rabbi's eyes gave him a probing look.

"I had no idea that rabbis were also mind readers." Amelia explained that she, in fact, wanted to contribute five thousand dollars to the school building fund. "If this amount is satisfactory to you."

The rabbi clasped his hands together and shook them. "Thank *HaShem*. You are a blessing, my dear Miss Cooke."

Because Amelia worked with a broad range of companies, she often gave counsel on where to give donations in the name of social responsibility and tax deductions. Had the rabbi asked, she'd have told him that the sponsor of the school funding wanted to remain anonymous. Amelia always worried that an overjoyed beneficiary might demand to know whom they should thank, but she'd fretted for naught. The rabbi assumed the contribution came from her own funds and Amelia said nothing to clarify his misunderstanding. What mattered was that the funds from a recent client, Atlantic Cable Company, were legal and authorized. At least she always thought that was all that mattered.

"A courier will deliver a bank draft to you by tomorrow afternoon, if that suits you," Amelia said.

After his vigorous nodding subsided, the rabbi pursed his lips and his furry brows tilted toward each other. "You must forgive me. I don't want to offend you or seem ungrateful, but why are you doing this, Miss Cooke? I must ask how you heard about our little school. We're not exactly Trinity Church."

The wealthiest of families attended Trinity Church to show off their jewels and humanitarian efforts. There were endless stories in the newspaper about Trinity Church members running food drives or gathering alms for the poor. Whenever invited, Amelia went to Trinity as a guest. Contacts were often made over a chorus of *Amazing Grace*.

"My contacting you must feel unusual, but we are in extraordinary times, are we not? A friend mentioned your plight and was quite passionate about the needs of your community. My interest is in helping the children. Should there be a better motive?" The question stuck in Amelia's throat and she coughed.

The rabbi again expressed his pleasure and gratitude. "I would shake your hand, but our custom doesn't allow for me to do so with a woman," he said.

"A custom for many men, though yours is more official. Can you tell me why?" Amelia had always been curious. The rabbi explained simply that he reserved all physical contact with the opposite sex for his wife.

The muttering, forgotten as background noise, stopped and Amelia turned to the sound of shuffling. Ten men in dark suits and hats began filing out from a room behind the altar.

"I must go," Amelia said, then bid the rabbi a hasty good-bye. She swept back up the aisle toward the exit. Just as she reached the door, Amelia hid behind a pillar and pulled a pocket mirror from her bag. In the reflection she watched him approach the rabbi. He wore a white fringed shawl over his dark suit, and from the rabbi's grinning and flapping arms, she knew the man was hearing all about her generous, spontaneous donation.

The afternoon had turned dark with low clouds and cold air that threatened sleet. As Amelia walked in front of Ford's Theater, she thought about how she used her handy mirror for spying and yet how little she used the glass to truly see her own reflection. The rabbi's comment made her wonder if all of her deeds of late were motivated by her own gain. The sound of wind moving through the bare branches stirred her memory, and the recollection of a genuine kindness warmed her cold hands.

Several years back Amelia met a scientist working on the new field of cancer research. He'd mentioned in passing the struggles of paying high taxes on the alcohol used to preserve his specimens, so much so that the rising tax threatened to end his research. A few months later a new law exempted scientific use from the alcohol duty. She considered if she'd gained anything from promoting that bill. She hadn't and felt good in her worthwhile work even if such charitable acts were few. Arranging to provide funding for a school was constructive whether or not she benefited from the transaction. Or was it?

Amelia had done well for herself. Luxury and wealth brought comforts, but for all the bluster about her achievements she wondered if she'd lost sight of the larger goal. She remembered when she felt her unique role as a lobbyist, beyond the vanities, would help all women step out from the corner. Sam understood and cultivated her passion. But with his death, she'd lost more than her mentor. Sometimes success overshadowed the actual work and Amelia wondered if she still believed as the innocent girl who stumbled into a world not ready for her.

On the hall entry table of her suite, Amelia found a wrapped bunch of irises with a brief note. She had accepted Boyd's invitation just that morning; now work prevented him from joining her for dinner. He was available for a light supper the following night and offered to meet Amelia in the bar at her hotel.

Amelia's fury pushed aside her qualms. The presumption of meeting a woman at a hotel bar counted as one minor misstep, but Boyd McKenna taking charge in any way was inexcusable. Amelia cast his role in her play; a role that didn't include Boyd underestimating her. She shook off her coat in the entry hall and marched through the main sitting room to her desk.

The Willard Hotel's suite came decorated in soothing mauve colors throughout an ample sitting area and bedroom and bath *ensuite*. In the main area, Amelia enjoyed a marble fireplace and two small loveseats. Tall, curved windows set a regal backdrop to the cherry wood lady's writing desk she requested, and a small bookshelf beside the desk had a few tourist information books and ceramic knickknacks compliments of the Willard's decorating staff. Amelia hadn't the time or habit to add her own personal items, to collect anything that someone might steal or that she'd have to move.

At the desk, she pulled out a sheet of her custom stationery. On heavy white paper engraved with the initials AC inside a small oval, Amelia accepted Boyd's invitation but could only meet an hour later than his suggestion and wasn't able to stay too long due to other pressing plans. If he wanted to challenge her then he'd better come prepared. He was nothing more than a means to an end, Amelia told herself, doing her best to shake off the lingering doubts of the day.

Once changed out of her petticoat and dress, she let down her hair and sat in front of the fire in a dressing gown and slippers. A fresh headache pressed against her temples. Amelia didn't like that Boyd's strange combination of bold and boyish made his actions hard to predict. She slipped her fingers into her hair and twirled a section into a slip knot. Even if she felt a bit culpable for influencing Boyd, he knew the risks of Washington even before they met. She needed a cup of tea to sort out her mood and ease her pounding head, so she stood to ring for hotel service. But she didn't reach for the cord. Realization struck.

Fatigue and emotions clouded her thoughts, and yet Amelia understood that her frame of mind not just the product of Boyd's cancellation delaying forward motion for the cause. She felt guilty. Amelia untwisted her hair, smoothed the strands back into place, and walked past the hotel service cord. She poured herself a small glass of sherry from the serving cart and took a sip. The warming alcohol helped, but Amelia frowned.

The rabbi's words about blemished animals and the value of a person's motivation still rattled her. How easily a knot fell apart when tied wrong. She glanced at the flowers from Boyd, still wrapped and waiting for a vase. With the vote approaching, Amelia didn't have time for mistakes. Amelia drained the rest of her glass in one swallow. She also didn't have time to worry if winning the amendment might require sacrificing Boyd to the slaughter. When in doubt, Amelia thought back to her wise mentor and his practical solutions. *A good steak always helps.* Amelia set down her empty glass and rose to dress for dinner. She didn't feel like eating, but she knew of one important player on his way to the best steakhouse in town.

CHAPTER SIXTEEN

Even in a windowless room, the bright lights made Stillman think of a civilized bridge match as he shifted on his chair and tapped his foot. At least the felt tables and sour smell of nervous men added the proper stench for the evening's gaming. The night of festivities began by waiting thirty minutes for his companion and fun at the underground gambling hall wasn't getting any better.

When Stillman asked Floyd Palmer, retiring chair of the Committee on Public Lands, to dinner, Stillman wanted to discuss the job while steering clear of The Library. Stillman rarely went to The Library, using the excuse that he'd rather gamble on a winning stock than a losing hand. He couldn't tell anyone about the haunting memories of his father. However, Palmer insisted on the restaurant's fine chops and refused to go anywhere else. Stillman knew all about Palmer's drinking and gambling habits, and, as predicted, Palmer's desire for food waned the moment he arrived. Stillman needed the retiring chair so he ignored his growling stomach and followed Palmer into the depths.

At the poker table, Stillman folded his hand, then waited to see if Palmer would again raise the bet on a bluff. From Palmer's cavalier attitude toward his shrinking pile of chips, Stillman surmised Palmer wasn't risking his own money. Stillman thought to make a joke about coffer funds but held his tongue.

An unpredictable drunk, alcohol had started pickling Palmer's brain.

The hand finished with Palmer calling the cards. His overgrown, white eyebrows twitched against the sagging skin around his eyes and he scratched the ring of hair that clung to his head. When his two-dollar bet on a pair of eights was easily beat by a university professor with a pair of kings, Stillman hoped Palmer would quit for the night.

"Shuffle them up," Palmer called out.

"Are you sure, Floyd? I'm not sure it's your night. Perhaps some coffee," Stillman suggested.

Palmer slumped forward onto the table and propped his head up with his hands. "My good man, I have good reason to be here tonight. Did you know they're running me out of town? Unfounded!" He pounded his fist on the table, then shook his head. "I know you're eager to have a heart to heart but I'm busy right now. Run along and play with the tots in the sandbox." His voice sounded coarse and slow. Palmer hoisted his head with some effort and waved for another scotch and water.

The evening was a bust in more ways than his gambling losses, so Stillman confirmed Palmer's ability to find his way home. Palmer bragged of his knowing many fun ways and fine company who would help him. Stillman sighed and headed upstairs.

Emerging from the dark stairwell behind the bar felt like a resurrection accompanied by the smell of roasted meat and pepper. Stillman eyed a passing waiter carrying a tray of dinner plates, then looked around the restaurant for a table. Men dining alone were seated at the long wood bar in the center of the restaurant. Some were drinking their dinners while others elbowed their neighbors as they cut their steaks. Stillman found bar stools uncomfortable but he also didn't relish the idea of fending off stares for eating at a table by himself. Before he could decide where to sit, Stillman heard his name. He cringed.

Amelia sat at a table in front of the window. Behind her, snow swirled in delicate circles like the souvenir snow globes he bought his sons. Stillman wanted to slip away and pretend he hadn't heard her, but Amelia was hard to ignore. Seeing her alone gave her a vulnerability that appealed to Stillman. He also had to admit she looked inviting in a black taffeta and lace gown, her hair twisted up in the front but left long down her back. That someone with such porcelain skin had sent him on a wild-goose chase to Ohio seemed almost ridiculous. Almost. Stillman steadied himself as he approached.

"Good evening, Edward. Having a bit of fun?" Amelia asked, nodding toward the stairwell to the basement.

He relaxed his tight politician's grin when he saw the genuine humor in Amelia's eyes. "Not exactly," Stillman said.

"Perhaps you just need better company," Amelia replied. "Care to join me or have you already eaten? I was just about to order."

Stillman glanced to the bar and then back to Amelia. Eating across from a beautiful woman seemed the lesser of two evils, though he had been wrong on that account. Not wanting her to mistake his prudence for fear or retribution for her stunt, Stillman accepted with a shallow bow and sat down.

Amelia handed him her menu but he set it down. "I always order the same dinner," he said.

Stillman was amused when Amelia deferred ordering first and then agreed to have what the *gentleman was having*. Snake-oil salesmen liked to put their marks at ease. He had a notion to call her out, then thought better of revealing his cards. Best to stay a step ahead of the fair redhead.

"I'm surprised to see you dining alone," he said as he shook out his cloth napkin.

193

"My companion canceled and I was hungry. I'll tell you a little secret. I actually prefer eating alone sometimes. It's quiet. I can digest my food in peace."

"I suspect digestion is a bit pesky with a side of lies."

Amelia's light laugh gave Stillman a pleasant chill down his back. "Ah, I'm sure you understand all about that," she said.

Though he thought of a few curt quips he remained silent. The dim lighting and Amelia's tranquil expression were relaxing. He hadn't forgiven Amelia for her prank but the timing of the jaunt proved beneficial. While away, he missed a surprise financial audit. Everyone dreaded an audit, so he had her to thank. When Amelia offered him red house wine, he nodded with anticipation and took a large gulp.

"Did you see the fascinating article about Boyd McKenna in the *Post*?" she asked.

Stillman shook his head. "Maybe it came out when I was out of town."

Amelia said "perhaps" with a sly smile and then paused. "I'm very sorry to hear about your mother's passing."

"A stroke," he said. "Now what were you saying?" He didn't want to talk about his mother with Amelia or anyone.

Amelia spoke in short bursts about Boyd, the handsome young man who interrupted their conversation at the Postmaster's gala. Stillman felt an irrational tug of possessiveness; he wanted to change the subject but didn't dare.

"Ah, interesting lad," Stillman said. "At least you seemed to find him interesting. Or are you perhaps interested in his proximity to Horton?"

Amelia's smile widened. "Boyd's impressive. Daring and obviously bright. I should think he'll go far."

"Yes, Boyd will go far with a little help from you and your newspaper friends." Stillman enjoyed exposing Amelia's trick even if he considered a story on the lad one of her more savvy moves.

The waiter set a basket of bread on the table, and Stillman offered a piece to Amelia, who declined. Stillman took a slice for himself and buttered all the way to the edges. "So, have you got the boy doing your bidding yet?"

"I'm not sure I know what you're talking about, Edward. I don't know that anyone does my bidding." Her inquisitive, upturned eyes and raised shoulders seemed almost genuine.

Stillman ignored the comment and raised his wine glass. "Shall we have a toast?" he asked.

"Nice idea. Let's toast to women winning the right to vote."

"Or, we could toast to the new gun-control legislation," he said. "But then you lost that bid for your client, didn't you? Too bad, really. It's not fun to lose."

She raised one eyebrow and smirked. "Okay, how about something less controversial. We can salute the new mimeograph machine." Her smile broadened. "Or, you could make up more statistics about women."

Stillman laughed at the memory of when they met. They clinked glasses and he watched her take a quick swallow. He joined her and took pleasure in the soothing feeling. The long days and lonely weeks had taken their toll. Even if he wasn't madly in love with his wife and sometimes wondered if he'd ever felt that way about her, Stillman had settled into a comfortable arrangement with Gertrude and missed her when they were apart. Even so, Stillman couldn't help but notice the other men in the room eyeing him with envy. He relished the command in sitting across from an attractive woman. Stillman felt warmed even more by his feelings of supremacy than by the wine.

Stillman settled back against the padded booth and sighed. He knew Amelia could debate for hours but he wasn't in the mood. As if reading his thoughts, Amelia stretched her shoulders and rolled her neck in a pleasing motion.

"Truce for tonight," Amelia said.

"Agreed. And nothing said here tonight can be used against the other," Stillman added.

Amelia nodded with a slight chuckle. "You know, Edward, I sometimes think about our time together. We had some fun back before you were the great senator from Ohio."

"Another lifetime," Stillman said. "And are you having any fun now, Amelia? Do you like what you're doing? A woman with your fine . . ." he paused, not wanting to speak the compliment aloud. "I just mean you could marry a quality man, have a family, get out of this droll city."

A strange, pensive look passed across Amelia's face before she smiled. Stillman was taken aback. He had never seen her so defenseless and was stirred.

Amelia's soft gaze returned and she tipped her head slightly to the left. "I'm not sure I'm the type for a family. Some people are better on their own."

Stillman thought of a cousin who lived in the hull of a transatlantic steamer playing fiddle for tips and leftovers. "True enough for some, but I don't see how that applies to you."

"You don't?" Amelia laughed. "Let me see. You've called me a wench and a heretic. Oh, and you told the *New York Ledger* I was . . . wait, let me get this right . . . *unfit to walk Grover Cleveland's dog.* Now you think I should raise children. What's in this wine?"

Her tone held no animosity. She sounded amused. After a round of chuckles, Stillman said, "Okay, so I may have used a few more adjectives than necessary, but why shouldn't you have a family? All women should have children; it's what you're meant to do."

As soon as the words left his mouth, Stillman realized his

mistake. He steadied himself for a lecture on women's great accomplishments, but instead Amelia reached across the table and clasped both of his hands. Amelia's delicate touch felt soft and a slow prickle ran down his shoulders.

"I've come to understand that men like you are actually trying to look out for my best interests in your own misguided way, and I appreciate your concern. If I wanted a family, Edward, you know I'd have one by now."

The intensity of her stare made him uneasy in a pleasing, intense way so he was glad when the food arrived and interrupted their conversation. Stillman felt Amelia give his hands a quick squeeze before she let go.

Over braised duck they discussed the notion of collecting personal income tax and Indian claims against the government. Stillman relaxed and again enjoyed speaking to an intelligent woman. She cited facts about Lincoln's Revenue Act of 1861 and ate her dinner with the gusto of a man. He even liked that she insisted they order dessert. He wanted to keep enjoying the rare evening and took her desire for another course as a sign she also didn't want to leave. In many ways Stillman considered Amelia the ideal woman, and he thought of their passionate history. He needed to cleanse his thoughts, if not his palate.

"You know, Amelia, I've always wondered how you got Sam to mentor you. He was a generous man. Always brought sauerkraut balls to our meetings. Still, he never seemed the type to take on a protégé, especially a female one."

Amelia nodded and he could see the fondness for Sam in her eyes. She once likened Sam to a father and he suspected his death had been hard on her even if she never said a word.

"Sam said no a dozen times before I convinced him. The final straw was my showing up at one of his dinners in a man's tuxedo," Amelia said.

"You're joking."

"No. I even wore suspenders and a top hat. Sam finally believed I was serious, and frankly I think I'd just worn him down. I can be a little tenacious."

Stillman brushed his hand through his hair. "Just a little."

While women called their sordid past a charming liaison, Stillman preferred the more descriptive tryst or affair. Either way, what they shared neither could deny. As Stillman watched Amelia gaze out the window at the falling snow, he understood she was part of a time in his life he would always cherish and never forget. And even though opponents, they were also colleagues who could share a benign evening without an underlying agenda. Stillman saw their friendly dinner as a success.

Of course, Amelia had a different view of their evening.

CHAPTER SEVENTEEN

Sitting across the dinner table from Stillman reminded Amelia of how much she enjoyed influential men. The allure of status overshadowed receding hairlines and sagging bellies in a way most men didn't understand. Within a man's misguided sense of importance were his own insecurities. Since boyhood, men were trying to best their friends, their brothers, and even their fathers, and a woman who could use their self-doubt to her advantage seized the control for herself. Amelia already had a little fun by letting Stillman see through her charade of having him choose her meal. She wanted him to believe her attempt at manipulation was too weak for his prowess. Amelia found the intricate game more intoxicating than the wine.

Amelia had just refilled Stillman's glass when she mentioned Boyd McKenna. Maxine had managed a fantastic third-page story about Boyd in a piece called *The Life of a Congressional Aide*. Bringing up the article gave Amelia a way to find out if Stillman had caught Boyd's relationship to Horton. His prompt response didn't surprise her. Stillman rarely missed much, especially something as significant as the mention of Horton. Even so, she liked the way he squirmed a bit at the mention of Boyd's intelligence and charm. Someone who didn't know Stillman's calculating manner might mistake his uneasiness for jealousy. Amelia knew he was more likely hungry and anxious to finish dinner and be rid of her company. Since she wasn't yet done with him, she reminded him of the intimacy they once shared. He settled at once.

Banter with Edward was always amusing and Amelia enjoyed exercising her brain with chat about taxation and Indian rights. She appreciated Stillman's respect for a clever woman and saw his raw ambition salted with competence. Not until Stillman mentioned a husband and children did Amelia feel a prick of perspiration on her lower back. As he spoke, the stays of the corset began feeling raw against her flesh and were she alone, she would have tugged at the points pressing into her waist.

Amelia hadn't chosen a life of wifedom and children, and he knew very well her preference for being alone. Freedom to do as she pleased meant she sometimes felt lonely but even when she did consider the alternative, she'd been told she didn't possess the nurturing traits of a good mother and wife. Being alone kept life simpler, though Amelia wondered who would take care of her when she grew old. No one. Being the matriarch of an intimate circle bound together for life appealed to her ego if she let herself be truthful. And imparting wisdom and raising a proper human being seemed noble, perhaps far more so than any other job. Still, the world also needed women who weren't fit for motherhood, women who dedicated their time toward other facets of life.

When Stillman said women were supposed to have children, Amelia leaned forward and put an end to the conversation. She hadn't expected to so enjoy the feel of his warm hands in hers and she released him maybe a bit faster than she might someone else. But her tactic worked, and with the controversial topic aside, she suggested they order dessert. Stillman relaxed and she noted he appeared more than a bit tipsy.

Stillman leaned back and wound his thumbs into the pockets of his waistcoat. As compared to his contemporaries, he had only the slight distinguished arch in his stomach and the thin lines alongside his mouth gave him a friendly countenance.

Amelia found herself too aware of his bright smile and still-persuasive blue eyes. A strand of hair that escaped and curved along the crest of his forehead gave him a youthful appeal and Amelia realized she wanted to brush the strand from his face. The interest she felt faded when Stillman asked about Sam.

Sam died quietly in Italy in 1884 of heart failure. Amelia read of Sam's passing in a telegram from his good friend Henry Longfellow. Few knew that Sam died with a worn copy of Horace under his pillow, and the image made her smile. She missed him every day for a year. Then the daily grief shrank as her opportunities and responsibilities grew. She didn't like to talk about Sam and hated that bar patrons ordered a "Sam Ward," a thin peel of lemon and yellow Chartreuse over cracked ice.

The arrival of dessert distracted Amelia from somber thoughts about Sam's death. The warm apples and cream soothed them both and she found herself asking Stillman about a recent rumor.

"Edward, would you really deny funding for a home for the downtrodden just to get graft from a few contractors who want to build a hotel?"

A rare wide grin lifted his face. "Graft? I don't know what you're talking about. Projects are denied every day. Besides, you'd do the same. You like to play the innocent; it becomes a woman in your position. But money motivates all and all are attracted to money."

"It's really that simple for you, isn't it?" Amelia asked.

"Of course. As black and white as a zebra."

"Or a newspaper page," Amelia said. "But shouldn't there be some things we won't do, some measure of decency we uphold?"

Stillman loosened his tie and chuckled. Bolstered by three glasses of wine and almost two hours of sneaking glances at her bosom, his laugh sounded coarse and too loud. Amelia joined in his laughter and let him think she agreed with his jaded attitude. She never had delusions about her role and the justifications she used to ease her conscious. Still, she wanted to believe in a line she wouldn't cross.

Stillman took a large bite of his apples. "Did you know the Bureau of Statistics director eats four apples a day? Story goes that he lived in a boys' home and never had an apple until he was twenty," Stillman said. By Stillman's sudden shift in his chair, Amelia knew he understood his own slipup. Using names or titles was the calling card of an amateur given that one never knew who might be listening from the next booth. She watched Stillman push away his glass of wine.

Amelia put down her fork. "Did you know that orphans often take the last name of the city where they were raised? I suppose that would be hard if you grew up in Mooselookmeguntic, Maine," she said, glad her humor seemed to help as Stillman settled back into his seat.

Once the dessert plates were cleared, Amelia folded her napkin and placed it on the table. Even after the wine and indulging conversation, Stillman caught her signal.

"I should be going, too," Stillman said without much finesse.

"You sound a bit disappointed, Edward. Did you have another idea for this evening?" Amelia cleared her throat. She hadn't meant to sound so suggestive.

Amelia watched Stillman button his vest over his askew bowtie. His red-rimmed eyes flickered with mischief.

"Edward, do you need some help getting home?" she asked.

"Are you offering?"

"I'm offering to help you into a hackney if you'll let me."

Stillman stood and extended his hand for Amelia to join him. She accepted his arm, allowed him to lead her from the table, and waited while he retrieved their coats. As he helped her into her cloak, she felt his unyielding hand on the back of her neck.

"You don't have to stop at the hackney," he whispered in her ear.

His breath on her cheek sent a shiver down her spine. Long nights in an empty hotel room sometimes felt too steep a price to pay for her independence. Amelia closed her eyes for just a moment and when she opened her eyes, Edward stood in front of her.

"I should really get—" she began, but he grabbed the ties of her cloak and made a tight loop.

He tucked in the flaps of her collar and let his hands linger at her shoulders. Amelia couldn't stop herself from remembering flashes of their passion. She found his offer tempting, but then she watched his lips curl at the corners. He knew she was considering his advances. At once she felt revealed and removed Stillman's hands.

"Edward, we both know what a night together could be. I'm just not sure we've ever had good timing. Maybe once I win the vote we can have dinner again. If you're not back in Ohio for anything."

As she desired, his lustfulness changed course as quickly as a sailboat in a storm. He put on his own coat, having some consternation with the sleeve, then said, "I think you're right, Miss Cooke. Our timing is poor. Always was. But even with your shenanigans I'm going to win. Of course once that happens, I'm not sure anything between us will improve. In fact, you might find yourself looking for a new job."

"A threat?" Amelia asked, a thin smile pulled across her teeth.

"Fact, my dear. The hens in your pack have claws," he said.

"It's a brood," Amelia replied.

"What?"

"Hens. They're called a brood, not a pack. You're thinking of wolves. I'm sure that's a common mistake for you," she said.

Stillman bristled and muttered something about a wasted

evening before storming out the door. Amelia waited long enough for him to find a cab before heading into the cold to find her own.

Once tucked inside the cab, Amelia recapped the events and decided, though uncomfortable at times, she'd successfully stalled Stillman. While Stillman preened like a peacock, she had a nice view of Floyd Palmer dining with Karolyn, a lady of the evening. Amelia's suggestion they order dessert gave the retiring senator time to leave with his conquest without Stillman seeing them. Senator Palmer had fared much better with feminine company for the night than Stillman, and Amelia thought she might stop by the Blue Goose in the morning and have a chat with Karolyn. Amelia wasn't sure if she'd learn anything useful, but she had to try. Just as when she thought Stillman loved her, Amelia again saw his fierce desire. Only this time his lust wasn't for her.

A burst of wind shook the carriage, making the horses whinny and jerk the wheels. The driver regained control, then shouted apologies for the scare. Amelia hated rocking carriages but her alarm ran deeper than concern for her safety. She once thought she appreciated Stillman for his ambition. His being at the helm was seductive in a way she hadn't thought about since leaving him in Cincinnati. She'd protected herself then, but the situation and stakes had changed. She no longer feared a foolish girl's broken heart. Stillman didn't care whom he hurt or what imaginary lines of morality he crossed on his quest for victory. For the first time, Amelia feared not only losing but what would happen if a man like Stillman won. She dreaded what she had to do next. Then a disturbing question made her tremble and she looked out into the dark night. In order to prevail, were there moral lines she was willing to cross?

CHAPTER EIGHTEEN

In the days when Stillman held the title of student body president, rowed as team bowman, won two fencing titles, and finished top ten in his class at Harvard, he had a secret passion unbefitting his reputation. As Stillman made his way down a long corridor behind the American literature collection of the Library of Congress, Stillman thought of the hours he spent in the stockroom at the Harvard library. If anyone asked, he spent his time doing copious research on case law. In truth, the unused storeroom held scores of dime novels written by hacks who believed mailing a copy of their work meant a home on a Harvard bookshelf. The head librarian didn't have the heart to throw any book away, so boxes of cheap fiction were stacked and stowed. Stillman had stumbled across the booty while researching a paper. In a moment of inquisitiveness, he cracked open a seafaring novel and new vice.

Fitzwater insisted they meet in the old archives of the congressional library, and, as the light from Stillman's hand lamp cast long swaying shadows on the walls, Stillman considered if Mallory or Jackson were playing a prank. The scene was like something from one of the ridiculous novels until Stillman heard shuffling of either rats or his appointment, or both. Taking small, slow steps, Stillman made his way down the corridor toward the sounds, trying not to think that the narrow hallway looked like the passageway to a dungeon.

Oscar Fitzwater had numerous nicknames no one dared utter

in his presence. Though most union leaders gained notoriety and monikers for their stern conduct and forceful tactics, Oscar Fitzwater took pride in being a quiet man. He stood just five foot five with thick tufts of hair in unfortunate places and a birthmark on his right cheek that resembled a pear less one bite. Ladies described Fitzwater as cuddly because of his stubby, childlike fingers. Those who knew Fitzwater were not deceived by his spongy countenance, low voice, and distaste for making threats. He rarely threatened anyone. A man who crossed him was maimed or killed without much blustering at all. As Stillman stepped from the dank hall into an astonishing large room filled with tall bookshelves, Stillman knew that if given the choice by Fitzwater, maimed or killed, he preferred death.

Stillman found Fitzwater stooped over a round table that held an oil lamp and a large dark volume. He used his chubby index finger to run across the lines of the text.

"You can read a little faster if you tip the book," Stillman said as he stepped into the room.

Fitzwater looked up and appraised Stillman with an overt sweeping glance as if picking out the turkey for a family feast. He then placed a slip of paper inside the book and closed the leather-bound volume with an echoing thump.

A white fur cravat hung around his neck like a dead cat and his sleeves were rolled to expose squishy elbows above thick, powerful forearms. He'd slung his black frock coat over a chair as if at a family powwow. Fitzwater intimidated his way up from the humble beginnings as a stonemason on Detroit's lower east side, and after the shock of Fitzwater's note, Stillman felt a little flattered such a powerful man wanted to see him. Then, when Stillman read the dossier he had his assistant compile, he almost declined their meeting.

"Senator Stillman, it's an honor, sir," Fitzwater said in a mild voice.

They shook hands like businessmen in a boardroom before Fitzwater motioned for Stillman to sit across from him at the table.

"I've never been in these archives," Stillman said, sitting down on a dusty wooden chair.

"Ah, a treat then for a newcomer. You should plan on making more trips. There is so much to learn from these wonderful books," Fitzwater said with a sincerity Stillman found encouraging. Fitzwater then smiled, showing rather pointy canine teeth and a scattering of deep lines around his mouth. He had a smooth complexion, not the ruddy, pockmarked canvas Stillman had expected; however, his narrowing eyes were just as menacing as Stillman imagined.

"I find all kinds of useful facts down here." Fitzwater opened the book to his marker and tapped the page with his index finger. "Right here in this almanac it says Senator E. Stillman approved a bond for a levee expansion when he was on the Westchester City Council. Fascinating for a man who campaigned against using bond money. I believe you called bonds 'devil loans.' " Fitzwater closed the book. "You see, very useful. You agree, no, that knowledge is power and power is the ultimate reward?"

Stillman nodded, not sure if he should comment. Having a few facts from his aide didn't mean he knew the best way to handle Fitzwater. If knowledge was power, then by the same reasoning absence of knowledge was weakness.

"Thank you for meeting with me, Senator. I'm sure you're curious why I asked you here. I hope you're honored." Fitzwater lowered his head in a passive and vulnerable gesture. Stillman assumed he used a docile look to mislead his victims.

"Mr. Fitzwater—"

"Please call me Oscar."

"All right, if you call me Edward."

Fitzwater bowed with reverence to such a concession and absently brushed his hand across the mark on his cheek. The union boss then spoke in long sentences that wound around his point like a boa constrictor.

Stillman summarized. "So, you're saying you'd like the Committee on Public Lands to support the stonemasons. But how can I help?"

"Aren't you going to be the chair?" Fitzwater asked.

Talk of Stillman's quest had leaked and traveled. Were he lounging at the club, Stillman would dismiss Fitzwater's information with a noncommittal shrug. Among the dank archives few knew existed, denial seemed dangerous.

"The appointment isn't official yet, but I'm confident."

Fitzwater stared at Stillman. "Public lands has long supported the masons. The chair enjoys great benefits from our collaboration. Were you aware of this?"

Stillman nodded, though he didn't know much. Public lands worked with many unions but only committee members were privy to the details. Fitzwater was likely just one of the union bosses soon to come looking for him as chairman, though Stillman thought the other leaders would wait until the final selection and opt for a public location. At least that's what Stillman hoped.

"Why not wait until my appointment is official? What's the rush?" Stillman asked.

"You're an interesting man, Edward T. Stillman, and even though we haven't swum in the same pool, you've piqued my interest. I like to know who I'm dealing with and what's for sale before the bidding starts. What's for sale, Edward?"

Fitzwater laughed in a thin, high tone and Stillman imagined him with pointed horns and a pitchfork. The vision was disturbing in its believability. Stillman chuckled even though nothing was funny.

"What does your union need?" Stillman said when the tight laughter faded in around them.

A startling draft blew through the hallway and into the archive room. Stillman flinched.

"Escape tunnels from the war. Every once in a while a gust gets trapped back here." Fitzwater's passive tone did not match his glare. Stillman cursed himself for flinching and showing weakness in such a primal way.

"What I need is a larger budget for expanding our trade. The stone subsidies are pitiful. They're being cut into by the greedy steel industry. Our men can't feed their families."

What Fitzwater made sound simple was anything but. Increasing funding required a joint committee and bipartisan votes. Stillman recalled his two long years on a panel to raise farming subsidies, and that came after a push from the president. "You realize, of course, Oscar, that you're asking for something beyond my control even as chairman. I can only start a measure. Perhaps there's something more practical I can offer? What about a tax break for stone exports?"

Without remark, Fitzwater stood and walked to the bookcase where oversized volumes lay on their sides. He used the flat of his palm to sweep over the titles until he seized a book with powerful hands. Stillman watched Fitzwater flip through the pages for what seemed like several minutes. When he found what he wanted, Fitzwater set the book down, turned the large volume until the text faced Stillman, and then stepped back to give Stillman time to read. Even though the fine linen pages were marred from fingerprints and pencil marks, the image remained distinctive.

Stillman recognized the implication with a slow dread that stung like eating sour candy. Heat rushed to his neck, making the day's stubble on his chin itch. The drawing contained his family tree: his sons and wife, his parents and grandparents, all lined up like wooden ducks at a carnival shooting game. The threat was unmistakable; Stillman flinched again.

Fitzwater tied his cravat with the nimbleness of thinner fingers and slipped into his coat. His expression continued as pleasant, friendly even.

"And what happens if by some random trick of fate I'm not appointed to the chair?" Stillman asked.

Fitzwater shrugged. "Is that relevant? You said you were confident." He again smiled, displaying just the base of his sharp teeth. "Perhaps I should apologize for my brashness. I get carried away in here. So much to discover. Did you know Chief Justice Collins was once arrested for public nudity? Found that juicy morsel right over there."

With Fitzwater heading to the door, Stillman had one last chance to redeem himself and show his courage. "I thought all of the justices went nude under their robes," Stillman said. He wanted to sound jovial and unconcerned.

Fitzwater laughed in a deep burst that lasted just a moment. Then he cleared his throat. "We digress, Edward. I've given you a lot to think about so take time to consider my proposal. Contrary to the hurtful names I'm called, I'm a man of my word, Senator. My offer is genuine and if we proceed you have my absolute assurances of my reliability. I expect the same from you."

"Of course," Stillman said. "I'll consider what you've said and get back to you shortly."

"Don't take too much time, Edward. I rather like the idea of finalizing this arrangement before the appointment. I like the suspense."

Fitzwater left but Stillman stayed and waited until he was sure Fitzwater had gone. The book Fitzwater had opened still sat on the table and Stillman glanced one more time at his family tree, then closed the cover. The state seal of Ohio was embossed in the top left corner over the title *Hamilton County Public Records.* The congressional library archives were impressive, but they had no use for a common county book of records. Fitzwater hadn't stumbled upon his information. He had dug through Stillman's personal life in order to make a convincing offer.

Stillman retraced his steps and when he reached the stacks where aides and legal researchers poured over their books at lacquered desks lit by a row of bright lamps, he wanted to shout that they were all ignorant fools, including himself.

Wasn't there always another man more powerful, more cunning? Smitten with the advantages of his mission, he had ignored its inherent shortcomings. His situation felt as constricting as the wool cowl buttoned on his overcoat. He could go to the Department of Justice and report the threat. This gave him a slim chance of ending Fitzwater's career and the guarantee of ruining his own. If Stillman did as expected, Fitzwater would, in fact, pay well and honor their long-term, binding agreement; the agreement of Stillman forever hostage to Fitzwater's demands. If he declined Fitzwater's offer, Stillman imagined what horrors might befall his family.

Rain fell in thick drops as Stillman began jogging down the street, unaware of the odd stares from other pedestrians. He wanted to get home, lock himself away with a warm fire and unremarkable novel. Stillman felt pressure against his lungs. His plan to seize the chairmanship was in motion and too big to turn around. Ambition and arrogance put his family, himself, in harm's way because Stillman believed he could handle any man, even men like Fitzwater.

Water dripped down Stillman's nose and he thought of all the times he got in trouble for playing stickball in the rain. He always led the team as captain and his buddies followed him like ants until his mother called for him to come home. Then his friends scattered, afraid of Mrs. Stillman and what his friends called the "sneer of doom." Stillman thought his mother had a beautiful face, even when she sneered, and thankfully she liked most of his friends. But Stillman knew his mother wouldn't like Fitzwater. She never let him run around with the rowdy boys, the boys who played after dark.

CHAPTER NINETEEN

After living at the Willard Hotel for five years, Amelia knew all of the peculiarities of the head bartender, Mr. Frank. In his sixties, he spoke only when spoken to and wore wire-framed glasses he took off every few minutes to clean with the same rag he used on the bar. Mr. Frank was also a philatelist so as often as possible, Amelia brought him stamps from her travels abroad and in exchange he turned a blind eye when Amelia sat alone at the Willard's bar. As Mr. Frank examined her latest gift, a stamp from Belize given to her by an expatriate, Amelia wondered why a woman sitting alone enjoying a glass of wine disturbed anyone.

A woman unaccompanied in a saloon drew stares and whispers mostly from other women, their hands firmly woven around the arm of a man. Popular convention explained that a woman by herself wanted some sort of tawdry companionship. In her earlier days when Amelia feared being thrown out, she'd order two glasses of water and pretend she waited for some mystery escort. Once the folly grew tiresome, Amelia learned to ignore those around her and rarely noticed the murmurs anymore. Few, if any, stopped to consider the reasons why a woman might prefer to be out alone.

Sometimes Amelia felt stifled by the solitude of her suite in a way she never expected. As a girl, she couldn't wait for the privacy, to do as she pleased without criticism. Yet the quiet let her hear the expectations that came from within, a burden far greater than any external pressure. Being around other people freed her mind from her worst taskmaster, herself.

Amelia chose a bistro table beneath the brilliant crystal fixture Mr. Frank admitted concealed plain glass. She chose the chair facing the entrance from the hotel lobby and ordered two glasses of champagne. She'd just got back from meeting with Karolyn, Fleming's lady friend. Time wasted, though she enjoyed a nice cup of tea and local gossip with Mrs. Stockett. A few years back Mrs. Stockett's wayward husband returned only to die a week later. He'd left her just enough of a nest egg, a mystery she'd called it, that she didn't have to rent rooms anymore. "But you'll always have a room if you need it, my girl," Mrs. Stockett had said to Amelia. Amelia didn't need a room. She glanced at her pocket watch. She expected Boyd in five minutes.

That Boyd McKenna cancelled their dinner plans and asked to meet at the hotel tavern still gnawed at Amelia. She wanted to blame his attempt to take charge of their meetings on youthful arrogance, a definite misstep after Amelia's coveted introductions at her party. Boyd hadn't yet learned the delicate balance of the dance. The pendulum shifted back and forth with time and deeds, like a boat guided by the currents and winds. Paddling against the wind wasted energy, could even be dangerous in extreme circumstances. Whether Boyd fell into the camp of naive or arrogant, Amelia needed to teach him the rules and let him watch the pendulum of control shift back where it belonged.

Amelia looked up and saw Boyd standing in the doorway gazing at her. Boyd jerked at Amelia's wave, then smiled and made his way toward her. Amelia noticed he had dark circles under his eyes.

"So nice to see you again, Amelia." Boyd kissed the back of her outstretched hand. His lips were cold and dry.

Boyd sat and took a swallow of champagne. "I haven't had time for dinner. Can I order us a basket of bread?"

Amelia ordered two roast beef sandwiches and a pitcher of water.

"I'm sorry you didn't eat yet," he said. "You didn't need to wait for me."

"I know," Amelia said and smiled. She hadn't waited and wasn't hungry, but she wanted him at ease. No one liked to chew on display.

Boyd's dimple deepened to a real smile, not the boyish grin he used when he drank too much. The right elbow of his suit coat had crumpled and Amelia pictured a long day with his arm propped up to take notes. Even so, he'd freshly tied his cravat and took time to wash his face and smooth his hair.

"Now that we're at last alone, you have to tell me everything about yourself," Boyd said.

"Everything? Why in the world would you want to know everything about anyone?"

Boyd crinkled his forehead. "You can never have too much information. At least that's what Senator Horton's been saying for the past eighteen hours."

"And how are you getting along with the senator? I've heard he's not the easiest man to work for," Amelia said.

Amelia watched for downturned eyes or touching his nose or cheek as he spoke; the tells of a lie were easily read. Boyd spoke with the freedom of honesty. His post thrilled him but he admitted being somewhat unnerved by Horton's temper. Though Boyd said he wasn't one to complain about hard work and long hours, he thought the senator needed more rest.

"A few of the aides told me he's been irritable since his wife died," Boyd confessed.

Mrs. Horton died the previous year of diphtheria. Horton hadn't missed even one day of sessions.

Amelia ignored Boyd's desire to know more about her and asked Boyd about his family. Since Amelia wasn't going to share her life story, Boyd seemed content to share enough for the both of them. He spoke about his passion for cricket and interest in bird watching. He mentioned three older brothers and a younger sister whom he missed but not enough to move back home to Somerville even though his mother begged for his return. Between bites of rare roast beef, Boyd spoke of his father and the expectations of being a judge's son.

"My father worked for the county for twenty years. When I was a teenager he ran for a House seat and lost. His dream was Washington politics. That's why he pushes me so hard. I have the chance to do what he couldn't, I suppose. He just wants this so much for me. Or maybe for himself, but either way he called in the few favors he had to get me on with Senator Horton."

As Boyd continued to babble, Amelia recognized the clutches of exhaustion. Words that might find lodging behind the front teeth instead spilled in a steady, exposed waterfall that most regretted after a healthy night's sleep. Speaking was a means of self-invigoration, at least until the sentences felt heavy and the speaker lost concentration. Boyd's inexperience could lead to his peril. The inability to control the urge to ramble was a dangerous trait, one that Amelia found more intoxicating than she would ever let anyone know, especially Boyd. Stories held a special fascination for Amelia, so much so that the first Saturday of the month she went to the main library and watched enactments of beloved children's books she'd never read. Unaware of his effect, Amelia found Boyd's rambling slightly seductive.

"I apologize for going on like that. You must think me a dullard," Boyd said.

"On the contrary, Boyd. You're more interesting than I expected."

The waiter appeared and cleared Boyd's empty plate and Amelia's full one.

"It seems that the *Post* agrees with you," Boyd said after a long swallow of water chased by a sip of champagne. "I believe I have you to thank for the flattering article. No one else in this city knows my last name."

"Oh, I don't know. You made a good showing at dinner the other night. The general doesn't let too many people slap him on the back."

Boyd began to again thank Amelia for the party invitation but she stopped him by placing her hand on his. "Please stop. It was my pleasure." She left her hand for a moment, then pulled away from him. She noticed the cool air after the warmth of his skin.

Amelia nodded and smiled, as Boyd's taste of celebrity was affecting him as she had hoped. He shared that several senators noticed him in the hallway, and after just a few days he already mused if his newfound fame might help with a promotion.

"Boyd, I have to ask and please tell me if I'm being too forward. But what are you working on so hard and so late into the evenings that you don't have time for dinner? I didn't think Dexter—" she paused, "Senator Horton had any committee bills until the spring."

Boyd leaned forward and gazed at her with a raw intensity she hadn't yet seen from him. One moment he seemed the inexperienced colt and the next Amelia could see under the boyish charms a driven man not unlike Stillman. Amelia wondered if Stillman was ever as forthright as Boyd. Conversely, the thought of Boyd someday acting like Stillman made her stomach turn.

"I like that you want to know what I'm doing with my nights," Boyd said without any attempt to hide his innuendo.

Amelia thought of a cat chasing a mouse, and the question was, which part Boyd thought he played. Maybe the spirits had loosened his tongue, but whatever he was trying to do, she wasn't some sweet co-ed and time was running out. Amelia had handled men who were much more suggestive and drunk.

She crossed her legs and tilted her chin low so her eyes seem to look up at him and said, "I have a good idea of what young men do with their nights, at least when they're all alone."

Boyd's expression widened and he straightened. "Senator Horton is trying to finish Bill 142A," he said like a student giving a book report. "He wants it on the docket earlier than spring. I'm doing title research and putting together figures to buy land and real property."

Boyd swallowed the last of his water and ran his napkin across his lips and cheeks.

"I . . ." Amelia paused and looked around the room.

"Is something wrong?" Boyd asked, again the eager chap Amelia needed.

Amelia lowered her eyes. "I'm just a little worried, Boyd. I'm sure it's just rumors, but you're so . . ." She hoped she looked a bit embarrassed by her growing opinion of him. "It's just I would hate for anything to happen to you."

Even to her own ears she sounded like a smitten lass fearing for the integrity of her love. If she were kicked out of lobbying, she considered a career in the theatre.

Boyd wanted to know what she'd heard. Amelia shook her head and said it was silly and nothing to worry about. When he pressed her twice, she acquiesced.

"I'm not one for spreading rumors. I suppose I usually start them." Amelia paused but Boyd didn't enjoy her joke. His fatigue had gone and his eyes were clear and ready.

"I'm not sure Senator Horton is as honest as we think. There's talk, nothing definite really, just gossip about skeletons in his closet. Maybe using coffer funds or taking stock options in exchange for pushing through a bill. I can't even say I believe them, but, Boyd, you're so honest and working so hard. Aides are often scapegoats. I'd hate to see you take the blame for anything." As she spoke, Amelia realized how much she meant every word. The idealistic were the only ones who could save a nation spinning into the depths of corruption. Beneath Boyd's bluster of seduction, he was still fresh and shiny. She didn't want to watch him tarnish.

Boyd considered what Amelia said, then shook his head. "I can't see it. He just doesn't seem the type. He seems too . . ." Boyd thought a moment and seemed disappointed when he could only muster the word *honest.*

"Perhaps. I don't know. I've seen this so many times. News stories about other good men committing adultery or running elaborate extortion plots. When I was a girl I was told to watch out for the quiet ones. Maybe there's nothing to find. But maybe . . ."

She let the sentiment drift away like the fluffy tufts of a dandelion.

Amelia suggested they change the subject. She'd planted the seed and would add a little water before they parted. First, she needed to make sure she had fertile soil, so she propped her elbows on the table and rested her chin on her hands. "So, tell me more about your hobbies."

"You've heard enough from me. I want to know more about you and your family."

Amelia sat up and brushed a stray piece of lint from her sleeve. She felt the familiar tension in her shoulders.

"Growing up I was just like a lot of young girls who wanted to do more than embroider cushions. Don't tell anyone, but no one ever taught me how to embroider."

"Devastating. I must leave at once," Boyd said.

Amelia enjoyed this Boyd much more than the other. She just didn't enjoy the topic.

"Boyd, you know that I'm working on the women's vote.

How do you feel about giving us poor frail creatures such authority? And I should warn you I've taken a few fencing classes. My footwork is impressive."

Amelia couldn't tell if Boyd found her abrupt question unsettling. He didn't recoil or ask her to repeat herself. In a clear and solid voice he replied, "I see no reason why everyone shouldn't have a say about who governs us all."

"And does your boss share your noble view?" she asked.

"Now that's a good question. I don't know. He hasn't mentioned anything about it since I started. He's focused on this bill and nothing else."

The champagne had reddened Boyd's nose and his eyelids again looked heavy.

"This has been lovely, Boyd, but it's getting late and I should really get upstairs. I have a long day tomorrow, as I'm sure you do also."

They stood and Boyd helped Amelia with her wrap. She then let him escort her through the lobby to the foot of the main staircase.

"Thank you for being so agreeable to my changing our plans," Boyd said. "I hope you weren't put off by my suggesting we meet here. I just thought this would be easier for you. I know how busy you are right now."

Amelia liked his reasoning. "I think this worked out nicely. Don't you?"

"As my father would say, 'Better than catching a sleeping weasel.' "

She laughed in earnest. "I'm not sure you should use slang in proper company. The natives might send you back."

"Oh, I don't know. Senator Horton says 'honey-fuggled' all the time. What does that even mean?" Boyd asked.

"It means fooled or cheated, and when you've been voted into office for eight terms you can say just about anything you'd like." She paused, then added, "I suppose you can do anything you like, too."

Amelia let Boyd kiss her hand and she squeezed his palm before turning to climb the stairs. As if a last-minute thought, Amelia turned back from the first step and was encouraged when Boyd stepped up to meet her.

"Boyd, you will at least keep in mind what I heard about the senator. Maybe you should keep your eyes open for anything, I don't know . . . curious." She kissed his cheek, then brushed the imprint of lipstick with her fingers. She felt him watch her walk all the way up the stairs.

In the safety of her suite, Amelia thought of Boyd. She found his mix of intelligence, brashness, and guile appealing in a way that reminded Amelia of Stillman, but with so much on the line she wouldn't let herself become involved. She needed to stay in control so Boyd could do her bidding and find something useful on Horton. Lottie hadn't found anything, nor had Perla heard any rumblings. They didn't have much time left.

The fire in the main room was cold so Amelia stepped into her bedroom and saw the bed covers smooth and tight. She hated when the chambermaid forgot to turn down her bed. The taut edges were confining and had a sterile, untouched look. Amelia again thought of Boyd and his warm smile. When he stepped forward on the stairs, she thought he might wrap his arms around her. Bolstered within her secluded dark room, Amelia let herself, for just a moment, feel disappointed that he hadn't.

CHAPTER TWENTY

"He was a good son and fine man," Senator Gage said to Amelia, the pain of his loss heard most in the pauses between his words.

"I'm sure he was, and a brave soldier," Amelia replied.

The wind settled down to a tolerable temperature even if the location had a different sort of bite. Amelia flashed on a faint memory of a country cemetery where wood markers sat in haphazard rows. She wondered where she had been. One of the sick babies at the orphanage, perhaps? She couldn't recall an image with any color, but the sensation of grief and isolation overpowered her. Amelia turned away from Senator Gage and let her eyes drift over the scenery.

Arlington Cemetery, viewed by the nation as a symbol of respect and dignity, was especially breathtaking in the winter snow. Long rows of white-marble markers stood at attention honoring those fallen for the sake of country and honor, and, surrounded by the white hills, the markers looked to Amelia like angel's wings. Amelia stood with her back to Arlington House, once the grand estate of George Washington's adopted grandson. She considered the quiet elegance of the sweeping porticos and solid Greek columns a tribute to the soldiers until the Pacific Mail Steamship Company rented Arlington House for a celebration flowing with alcohol. Amelia saw men stumble about and deface more than their own honor that night.

Amelia turned in time to see Senator Gage place a pebble on

the gravestone of his son David C. Gage. "I wasn't thrilled about him going to West Point even though he loved it there. Top of his class. And I thought, with the war over, what was there to worry about?"

Gage stopped and shook his head, his bottom lip quivering and his gaze fixed on a horizon of dense clouds sitting heavy on the bare branches of cherry blossom trees. "I'll give you some time," Amelia said. She stepped away and moved down the wide rows of markers.

During the war, the intoxicating musk of glory drove men to choose sides and pick up rifles without thinking of the dangers, the loss. But in times of peace, patriotism ensnared the young and optimistic like a butterfly net. While extolling the merits of a military life, recruiters failed to mention the untold number of deadly training mishaps and worse. David C. Gage was one of the unlucky touted as brave for being in the wrong place at the wrong time. The official army records were sealed, but, according to what the government told the Gage family, David died in an unfortunate training accident. Thanks to Lottie and her magical powers of investigation, Amelia knew the truth and the reason why, as Senator Gage buried his son, the war department buried the incident.

Amelia read the names of soldiers, many with lives too short to have accomplished much. Did anyone miss Ruben T. Altzman or Samuel J. Walits? The stillness again reminded her of a dirt cemetery and an aching grief lodged in her side. Keeping busy and moving forward helped keep the past neatly tucked away and she didn't like when the corners started to come loose. She needed to stay focused on Gage and his loss, so Amelia turned around and saw Gage walking toward her.

Gage thanked Amelia for her consideration. "Losing a child is something . . ." he let the sentiment speak for itself and motioned for them to return to the carriage.

They had ridden five miles from the capital in a new queen-styled coach with plump padded seats and glass windows that closed well. A tray with warm coals was a nice replacement for a heavy pile of scratchy wool blankets.

Back inside the warm cabin, Gage tapped the roof and the carriage lunged forward. Amelia sat across from Gage, as he insisted she face in the direction of their travel.

"Miss Cooke, I wasn't surprised you contacted me. We all know your agenda."

Amelia bowed her head to show her comfort with his direct talk.

"But I was confused, reticent even, when you asked to accompany me here today. This is highly irregular, Miss Cooke, and I don't like irregularities. You should also know that I don't take bribes or entertain threats."

Gage believed in his own integrity, and yet honesty came in degrees. Amelia knew about the many dinners and theatre invitations Gage accepted without hesitation. Still, she had no intention of offering Gage a bribe. Information often became far more valuable than money.

"Bribes are not part of my repertoire. Nor are threats or seduction, no matter what you may have heard," she said. "Others, I assure you, are more finessed in such areas than I. My reason for contacting you is about more than the women's vote." Amelia paused to be sure she held Gage's attention. In the flickering dim light of the passing trees, Amelia couldn't see his eyes.

"Yes, very well," Gage said, impatient. "Continue."

"You know my work with NWSA, and I'm confident that you'll make your own decision on the merits of the women's vote based on fairness and justice. If I can say anything to sway you in our favor, let me remind you that God created man and woman in his image, never condemning Eve to a lesser role. But today, Senator, there's a more urgent matter that has come to my attention."

Gage leaned forward. "Wait. I need to stop you, Miss Cooke. There's something you should know. Do you have any idea why I agreed to meet with you today? Why I accepted your curious invitation to visit my son's grave?"

Amelia shook her head and waited for the answer she already knew.

"Not many know that I'm Jewish. It's not something I hide; to the contrary, people make assumptions and I leave them to their own ignorance. But I'm aware of your visit with Rabbi Cohen. If not for your generous contribution to our school, I'm not sure I would have agreed to this meeting," Gage said.

Senator Gage not wanting to shake Amelia's hand at the gala gave her her first clue. Men who declined shaking hands usually made a show of it, refusing to acknowledge a woman in the role of lobbyist. Once a duke even pinched Amelia's cheek rather than shake her hand. But at the gala Amelia suspected Gage had another reason for not touching her; the same reason why he declined appetizers that combined milk and meat. His religious beliefs were most obvious for someone paying attention.

"Sir, I wasn't aware you knew about the donation. I admit, I was hoping my contribution might remain more anonymous," Amelia said.

Gage seemed pleased by her humility and encouraged Amelia to tell him why she requested their meeting. Amelia took a quick breath and gave a fleeting glance over her shoulder toward Arlington before turning back to face him. "Senator, I have information about the death of your son."

The senator took this as an attack and turned into a man trapped by the unfairness of God's plan. Rapid and without breath, Gage fired at Amelia like the gun that had killed his son.

David was killed in a night training accident. He mishandled his weapon and wounded another young man, who lost an arm but lived. To forestall embarrassment for the family, sympathetic friends marked the incident as classified. How had she found out? He demanded to know her source. Amelia let him talk until he wore himself out.

"I know what you were told, sir, but I was recently hired for a job. The details are confidential but I assure you the source is reliable. During some research, I found a report that contained information about David. I stumbled upon the truth, Senator."

Amelia explained that David C. Gage wasn't killed by misfiring his own gun. He suffered a fatal gunshot wound during a brawl within the barracks. While eyewitness reports varied as to the reason and blame for the argument, all confirmed that David attempted to end the fight when one of the men, a staff sergeant, fired several shots from his pistol. The casualty report contained accurate information: David was killed and another young man lost an arm. Murder charges were never filed. To keep the incident quiet, the commanding officer hustled the staff sergeant off to the Eastern Lunatic Asylum for treatment of battle fatigue.

"But why wasn't the sergeant court-marshaled?" Gage's voice had a flat, hollow sound.

"Sir, court-marshals draw attention. Soldiers killing brothers-in-arms brings up all manner of questions about proper training and the strain of war. You can see why the military couldn't share the real details. The press . . ." Amelia let the obvious stand alone.

Gage nodded but kept his gaze fixed out the window. His eyes were red and tears pooled at the edges like an overfilled teacup. "That poor boy. How does he live knowing he killed his fellow serviceman?"

Gage's concern for the other soldier impressed Amelia.

"I wasn't sure if I should tell you or not, but you were lied to, sir, and I just couldn't . . ." Amelia lowered her voice. "Perhaps this whole incident is something only for God to judge."

Gage looked up and held Amelia's stare. The carriage rocked slightly and the dim light seemed to move with the rhythm. "You're a religious woman," Gage said it as a statement so Amelia didn't answer.

"Whether or not telling me about my son was the right decision, I appreciate your consideration."

Amelia nodded and let the silence fill the empty space. Lottie got lucky in finding gold; turning luck into something useful was why Amelia demanded such a fine salary.

By the time they reached Amelia's hotel, the color had returned to Gage's cheeks and he no longer tapped his fingers on the carriage door handle.

"Thank you for your time today, Senator. I hope you are even a little comforted by knowing the truth," Amelia said as she waited for the driver to open the door.

Gage narrowed his eyes. "And I suppose now you'd like me to vote for you in exchange?"

Amelia stepped from the carriage and stood in the open doorway holding the edge of the door. This allowed Gage to look down at her, his place of superiority felt if not consciously realized.

"No, Senator. I'm not the one asking for your support. I speak for all women. Our vote should stand for the equality granted not by man but by God. American women want a voice so they can help make our country great. I ask you to support women's suffrage, Senator, so that the mothers who have lost sons, like your dear wife, have a say in the welfare and happiness of our future sons and daughters. Don't they deserve that much?"

Gage nodded as he bit his bottom lip. Amelia handed him

the official documents Lottie found and then bid him good day, to which Gage nodded again and looked away. Amelia waited until the hackney rounded the corner before she broke into a wide grin. Gage also chewed his lower lip when he stood at the graveside of his dead son. She had Gage. The women had a new tally.

Gage and Dodger were on her side. Littlemore would vote with Stillman and Mallory sent a vague note about party ties, which meant he had faith in Stillman's appointment and wanted to keep a powerful friend. That left Dexter Horton. If getting Gage's vote took a dead son, using up favors with Lottie, dragging out to a cemetery in the middle of winter, and the good fortune of finding a government plot, Amelia wondered what in the world she'd need to get Horton's vote. She thought of Boyd and the invitation on her desk.

Instead of going inside the hotel, Amelia walked to the telegraph office. If she had more time, she'd make Boyd wait and worry she might decline his invitation to spend the entire day with him. According to Perla, the floor discussions were wrapping up, and Senator Horton hadn't responded to her note or basket of muffins. She needed just a few minutes of Horton's time, and Boyd now seemed like her final chance at a face-to-face meeting with the last man standing.

Amelia crowded into the telegraph office and waited for counter space to clear. Unlike those dashing off notes about the weather or need of extra cash, Amelia took her time. She composed her telegram to Boyd with extreme and feminine care.

CHAPTER TWENTY-ONE

Some compared arguing on the Senate floor to bickering spouses or kids fighting over toys. Stillman had spent the morning listening to feisty words whacked back and forth like a badminton shuttlecock until the senator from Colorado began an oration to rival Patrick Henry. Colorado held fast in favor of women voting as a matter of government and agriculture, though Stillman hadn't followed the meandering reasoning. That no one tried to shut up the Coloradan meant the natives were tired. Rather than listen to the monologue, Stillman watched Horton spin a quill on his desk. Horton appeared restless. Many of the others had already slipped out to their offices, so Stillman wasn't surprised when Horton stood. Stillman jumped to his feet and rushed to meet Horton at the chamber door. After holding the door open for Horton, Stillman asked if he could meet with Horton for a few minutes that afternoon.

Even the thinnest ray of afternoon sunlight warmed the drafty rooms and even draftier temperaments of the Capitol's coveted north side. At ten minutes till three, the agreed-upon time to meet Horton, Stillman set aside the mind-numbing details of a street-sign initiative, a mess he'd soon give Mallory as retribution for considering siding with Amelia, and glanced at the portrait of himself on the wall across from his desk.

"You're ready to take on Horton," Stillman said to his smirking self. He imagined himself winking back.

Horton rarely met with people in his office, as he preferred to hold discussions on the open Senate floor or in committee rooms where opponents stayed divided by a bulky oval table. An office implied intimacy, which is why Stillman could admit his nervousness, if just to himself. Horton was an old man of archaic principles and spirited appraisal of the ethics of others. Amid the many mishaps of congressmen, Horton had kept himself clean for over twenty years. Even so, speculation ran rampant.

There were theories that newspaper lords were on his payroll and a hidden list contained the names of those with infractions worthy of blackmail. Many believed Horton could just wave the list at a man and he would fold like a lady's hand fan. Stillman wasn't sure any of the rumors were true but with nothing proven, Stillman could proceed only using the few facts he had.

Horton preferred working alone and rarely left his office before seven. His stance on women voting was vague and his closest allies across the aisle were divided. Over the years Horton asserted his upstanding reputation like a child waving a grade card, so Stillman knew even the suggestion of a bribe or threat was too risky. Stillman also sensed the aggressive, no-nonsense tactics that Stillman preferred in committee meetings might not work with Horton. Stillman had seen Horton hurl a string of probing questions at a bold, confident man until the man himself didn't believe what he said. Stillman mopped his damp brow with the sleeve of his jacket.

If subtlety ensured a safe way to win with Horton, Stillman thought Amelia might have the advantage. Just one thought eased his mind as he stood up from behind his desk and straightened his trousers. If Amelia used her sexuality to gain his favor, Horton would see her as a tramp. Stillman might not have to win, rather just not lose.

"Phillip," he bellowed. "Bring the brush."

Phillip lunged into the room wielding a lint brush and comb.

Without prompt, he tidied the senator's coat and combed down the stray hairs just above his neck. A final yank on the base of the coat meant he looked presentable and Phillip nodded and stepped aside, giving room for Stillman to leave. Phillip didn't bow, but Stillman often wished he would, like a servant bowing to the king.

The nerves settled as Stillman arrived at Horton's office a few minutes early and Boyd McKenna greeted him. He'd forgotten about the strapping colt.

"Nice to see you again, Senator Stillman. We met at the gala," Boyd said.

"Of course," Stillman said. During their brief meeting Stillman hadn't noticed McKenna's height and confident, wide stance. "And how are you finding your new position? Do you have your own political aspirations?" Stillman asked.

The question bordered on rhetorical. All of the aides had their eye on their own inner office. The question had become protocol as a way to uncover a man's education and experience. Boyd answered properly.

"So, a political science degree from Princeton and two years at a law firm. Very sound." Stillman paused. That's when an idea leapt out with such force he swayed just a bit.

"If I remember correctly, you were quite taken by Miss Cooke at the party. You are aware of her position?" Stillman asked.

"Yes, I'm most impressed by her." Boyd kept his face pleasant, unrevealing.

"I've known Amelia for years. A wonderful woman, very bright. You'd be wise to get to know her," Stillman said, waiting to hear what he hoped. Boyd granted his wish. McKenna had arranged a meeting with Amelia the next afternoon. For a Saturday outing, the strapling was thinking of taking Amelia to Mount Vernon. Stillman thought the locale most beneficial. Amelia would be stuck with him for hours, and, more importantly, McKenna would be stuck with her.

"She's given me some very sound career advice," McKenna said, pulling Stillman from his thoughts. Stillman chuckled and said, "And she's not bad to look at either."

Boyd nodded and straightened. Stillman admired the boy's grit at trying to remain impartial. Only his tight brow and fidgeting with the flap on his jacket pocket gave away that McKenna had fallen under the influence of Amelia's charms. Stillman felt a fleeting moment of pity for the young buck.

"Son, I probably shouldn't tell you this but you seem to me a sharp man. You must know that Miss Cooke and I are on opposite sides. Still, I have the utmost respect for Amelia and wouldn't want her to embarrass herself."

Boyd asked for clarification; he'd taken the bait.

"What I mean, lad, is that Amelia wants to meet with Senator Horton and her usual tactics are, well, how shall we say, not of the type a man like Senator Horton will appreciate."

Stillman let the sentiment settle and was tickled. He sometimes forgot the raw surging power in telling the truth.

"I'm not sure I understand completely," Boyd said.

Stillman patted Boyd's shoulder. "Son, you probably haven't seen Amelia on the other side of a lobby, but I'm sure you can imagine how persuasive she is by using her femininity. Nothing too overt, of course, she's a lady. But . . ."

Watching Boyd register his message was more fun than winning a high-stakes round of billiards. The boy looked ready to vomit. "Senator Horton doesn't seem like a man who flirts. At least I've never seen him act that way."

"I would just hate to see harm come to my friend. Amelia and I go way back," Stillman mentioned again. "Still . . ." He paused and then shook his head.

Boyd persisted in wanting to know more.

Stillman pursed his lips. "It's just that I think Senator Horton is a bit in love with Miss Cooke. Since his wife died, he speaks of her in a sort of unusual, I dare say wistful, way. I can't say I'm surprised. Amelia has that effect on men and they've known each other, albeit from a distance, for years. But I shouldn't have said anything. Gossip is unbecoming. I apologize. I trust you won't mention this to the senator."

"Of course not, sir," Boyd said earnestly.

Boyd wouldn't speak to Horton, but Stillman hoped he'd relay the conversation to Amelia. Stillman wanted Boyd to believe he'd unwittingly tossed him a bone that could help Amelia. He'd have to wait and see whether or not Boyd would fetch.

Boyd escorted Stillman into Horton's office at exactly three o'clock. Suddenly unable to speak, Stillman nodded his thanks and watched as he closed the door. Stillman had made his way into the inner sanctum.

The office of the Honorable Dexter Horton from the great state of Massachusetts appeared twice the size of any office Stillman had seen. Walls were knocked down to the adjacent room, so where Stillman had his bookshelves Horton had space for a full table with four chairs, a second area rug, three bookshelves, and a plain sideboard that Stillman imagined contained a bar with spirits. Stillman swallowed down a rising wave of jealous loathing.

"Good afternoon, sir. Thank you for seeing me," Stillman said.

The men shook hands and Horton motioned for Stillman to take the club chair across from his desk. Horton's club chairs were upholstered in a lush, embroidered fabric with full and pliable stuffing.

Horton began by asking about Stillman's wife and children. Was everyone well? Were they still in Ohio? Did he have plans to visit? Stillman answered and reciprocated the questions even though he hadn't anticipated small talk. The scenarios Stillman imagined began with Horton leaning over the desk and demanding to know what he wanted and why he was wasting his time. The polite chatter had a calming effect that Stillman appreciated until he wondered if Horton's tactics involved lulling him into a fatal state of relaxation.

When Horton's wife died, every elected official and staffer turned out for the memorial. The *Evening Star* said that Beatrice Horton *was the only woman in history to halt the wheels of government.* From the notes tucked away in his pocket, Stillman knew the sixty-four-year-old Horton had two sons, both lawyers, and a daughter in college. Stillman readied himself to ask about his son's new law firm when Horton changed the tone of the meeting.

"I have a subcommittee meeting to prepare for so we should get to it. You want my vote against the women's movement. What I don't know is why you're spearheading this campaign," Horton said. Stillman noticed that he now leaned over his desk.

Even though the rumors of Stillman's desire for committee appointment were still circulating, Horton always ignored hearsay. He based his decisions solely on facts, he told Stillman, and Stillman acted happy to oblige.

"My involvement might seem a bit irregular, admittedly, but I listen to my constituents and my conscience. I represent the people of Ohio, not myself. My state is firm in its conviction. The majority believe women aren't prepared to wield the responsibility of the vote. Women will degrade politics and politics will degrade women."

Stillman had rehearsed his lines and hoped they didn't sound practiced. The wishes of residents of Ohio depended on how experts tallied the survey. Charts and graphs were wonderful tools of manipulation and fiction.

"I admit that allowing women to vote is a big step, one that

234

we can't take lightly or take back. Once women have the taste, I can only wonder what's next. Should we send mothers and wives into battle?" Horton asked. "But we're fools to talk ourselves into believing women are feeble or incapable of making important decisions. They make them every day."

"Have you heard of the Jones Bridgeworth study?" Stillman knew that he hadn't because Stillman had made it up. "The study showed that sixty-seven percent of women who want the vote also admit they are unaware of voting records, policy issues, rules of lawmaking, or how government works," he said.

Horton shook his head. "You're ignoring the fact that the same applies to sixty-seven percent of male voters, probably more. We're an ignorant country, Edward."

The use of his first name unsettled Stillman for a moment. He watched as Horton leaned back in his plush chair and waited for Stillman's rebuttal. Littlemore served on the Public Expenditures Committee with Horton and warned that Horton liked to use silence as a way to ferret out unsolicited information. A piercing gaze accompanied by calm was unnerving for most, but Stillman came prepared.

"Your daughter is away at school? Oberlin College, I believe," Stillman said, suddenly feeling like Zane. "What is she studying?" he asked

"English literature. She wants to teach at the university. We'll see," Horton said.

Stillman then asked about Horton's two sons and listened to him brag.

"If I may be so bold, Senator, you speak with great admiration for your sons. Men are expected to have worthy aspirations. But what about your daughter? You seem hesitant about her having a teaching career. Am I right?"

The wrinkles around Horton's eyes deepened. "We had children late, so I suppose I want her to hurry up and marry

235

and have my grandchildren."

Stillman nodded. "Sir, we live in a society of expectations and if women are the mothers and grandmothers and men are the lawmakers, then I see little debate on whether women should vote. For what purpose? Those who make laws must have the power to enforce them. A woman can't serve as sheriff or become a police officer. If women were forging ahead as captains of industry, I would change my opinion. But men can take care of the voting for the family and leave women at home with their home duties, wiping chins and who knows what." Stillman stood. "Senator Horton, I believe my time is up."

Horton thanked Stillman for his consideration.

"No, Senator, thank you for seeing me. I appreciate you meeting me in your office," Stillman replied.

"The committee rooms were all booked," Horton said as a matter of fact and not as an insult. As Stillman reached the door, Horton then added, "You gave me some good points to think about, Senator Stillman."

Stillman nodded and left before he could say something to undo his good work. Boyd wasn't at his desk so Stillman escaped any chance of further inquiry. Everything had gone as intended, better in fact, as his conversation with Boyd wasn't planned. In just twenty minutes he had set up Amelia and given Horton *some good points to think about.*

Though he hadn't bought any guarantees like with Littlemore, Stillman felt like celebrating his success with an early dinner and round of drinks. He had done his best and could now wait for Amelia to make her move. Stillman laughed as he stomped down the hallway toward the senator's side exit. He imagined Amelia in a dimly lit parlor wearing a tight dress as Horton cast her off like morning bedcovers. Yet for all of Horton's blustering, Stillman considered for the first time that Horton had been a widower for one long, lonely year. With his exit in sight,

Stillman stopped.

Five months after Stillman's last meeting with his father, he received an envelope addressed in his father's bold lettering. They hadn't corresponded or tried to see each other, so Stillman set aside his work. The room smelled of the sweet jasmine of spring and orange and yellow strands from Gertrude's prism danced along his bookshelf. He opened the letter carefully, wondering about the thickness, since his father was a concise man not given to the ten pages of scrawl in his grip.

At first Stillman thought his father had copied a story from a book. He wiped his reading specs on his shirt and started again from the beginning. Stillman knew of men who bet on bills passing; who rode naked down Capitol Street in the middle of the night; who kept two sets of books and never paid taxes. All the same, and even with what he knew about the death of Senator West, his father's note stunned Stillman and the shock seeped in like ground water. Theodore and Teresa Stillman, his beloved parents married forty-three years that past February, were getting divorced on the grounds of adultery.

His father never mentioned the woman's name or age, though there were hints that he'd taken a mistress much younger than his mother. From the few details his father divulged, Stillman pieced together that the liaison began right after their rift, though the meandering storyteller wasn't reliable in word or deed. His father had decided to give the house to his mother and move to Idaho with his mistress to live on a potato farm. Stillman traveled home immediately and tried to talk with his father.

"Maybe this rash decision has something to do with lingering guilty feelings . . . about . . . what happened to West . . . about the money you lost because of me," Stillman had said.

"I don't know what you're talking about, Edward. It's very simple. Men have certain needs."

237

That night, his mother attempted suicide while Stillman and his brother slept in their old rooms. In the coming weeks, Stillman committed his mother to Denridge, sold the house, and read about his father's wedding in a newspaper clipping mailed to him by the new bride.

His father died a year later and Stillman had put the incident from his mind. Now he thought of Horton and his "needs" and no longer felt like celebrating. Stillman turned around and went back to his office to figure out if he had a next plan of attack.

CHAPTER TWENTY-TWO

Though the calendar said January twenty-first, likely less than a week until the vote, a strong sun rose in the clear sky. The light dusting of snow that had covered the walks overnight melted, leaving multicolor patches in the shaded corners, and just seeing the sun made it feel warmer than the fifty degrees on the thermometer. Amelia enjoyed the sun glistening off the damp streets and saw the sunlight as a good omen for the day's outing.

She had agreed to meet Boyd at the concierge desk of her hotel, but Amelia decided to wait by the lobby window so she could warm herself like a cat pressed against the glass until Boyd arrived.

"You look lovely," Boyd said, taking Amelia's hands and kissing the backs of both.

"So, where are you taking me today? Your note was a bit mysterious," Amelia said.

Boyd grinned and Amelia wasn't oblivious to young ladies in the lobby sneaking glances at him.

When Boyd remained silent to their pending destination, Amelia said, "If you're not going to tell me, then are you going to insist I wear a blindfold? I should tell you I'm an expert at navigating this city. I can probably guess where we're going by the first turn."

"We'll see," he said.

An awaiting carriage set out southwest and looped around

the Washington National Cathedral. When they turned south on 14th Street, Boyd asked, "So, can you already guess where we're going?"

They were either going to the Smithsonian or to the docks to catch the steamer to Mount Vernon, but Amelia didn't want to ruin Boyd's fun. He looked gleeful at having a secret, so Amelia shrugged.

"I'm stumped. I guess I'm not as savvy as I thought. Or maybe that dimple of yours is distracting me." She watched his grin broaden, deepening the sweet dent in his left cheek.

Boyd chatted about his plans to go home to Somerville for a few days during the summer session break and then told a story about knocking over a stack of research material for Bill 142A. Amelia thought to tease him when Boyd seized her hand and gave it a quick squeeze. "Enough about work. Let's not give it another thought. Today is just about having a nice time and getting to know each other better. Agreed?"

Avoiding the topic of Horton wasn't part of her plan. "I suppose I could agree to that . . ." she paused. ". . . if you agree you won't be mad at me if old habits are hard to break. I rarely enjoy such a wonderful treat as a day off from work." Amelia needed to lodge the idea and wait for the opportune moment to bring up Horton.

When they passed the Smithsonian, Amelia steadied herself for the steamer. Her first time on a boat, a steamer down the Mississippi, she'd been harassed by the crew. Fearing for her safety, she spent every night awake in her cabin holding a broken bottle as a weapon. Boats were unpredictable, she couldn't swim, and Amelia didn't like the feeling of drifting back and forth with the tide.

"I know you know where we're going. Thank you for giving me a few moments of fun," Boyd said.

Beyond his freshness and the dimple, Amelia saw a great deal of astuteness and intuition. If she had learned anything from Sam Ward, she knew when to use a bit of honesty as an asset.

"I really didn't know for sure until we passed the museum. Mount Vernon is lovely, and I'm flattered by your invitation and the time you spent to prepare. Besides, what kind of a person ruins a surprise?" Amelia asked.

"My older brother. That's his trademark."

Amelia asked to know more about his brother, so as they rode along the river to the docks, Boyd told several stories of boyhood folly. She hadn't laughed as honestly in a long time.

"What about your family?" Boyd asked. "Any siblings that spit grape skins at you in the middle of the night?"

The carriage stopped. They had arrived at the docks and the driver hustled from his perch to open the door. Amelia let the question about her family carry out of the carriage and drift downriver.

Boyd took Amelia's arm and led her on to the steamer, *The Georgia*. A double-deck side-paddle boat with a white deck, red paddle, and large black smokestack, the entire upper level consisted of an open deck for warm days. Below, the lower level had rows of plain benches protected by enclosed windows. They boarded and Boyd led her up the rear staircase and to the railing.

"She seems seaworthy enough for the short ride," Boyd said in a gentle voice that made Amelia wonder if he could sense her apprehension.

To combat the building sense of dread, Amelia chuckled and thought to make a quip. Instead, she blurted, "I don't like boats, ships, canoes, schooners, dinghies. I don't care what you call them; I can't swim."

Amelia's candidness stunned her. Her amazement grew when Boyd didn't poke fun or quote safety statistics. Boyd placed his hands over hers, which she realized were gripping the railing, and kissed her forehead. "I'm an excellent swimmer. I'd never let you drown."

The whistle sounded and the lines were released. Even with the sunshine, they were cold standing outside on a moving vessel, so Boyd led them inside and they sat on a wooden bench facing a window dotted with water spots.

"I hope the sunny weather holds. My other plan was, in fact, the Smithsonian, but the sun is just too inviting. Is much of the Mount Vernon tour outside?" he asked.

Amelia assured him that along with the expansive grounds there were a variety of buildings where they could stop to warm up. Boyd nodded. "I don't want you to be uncomfortable," he said. The men she knew asked if she were cold or hot or interested in going upstairs, but she never believed they were worried if she were comfortable. The earnestness in his open eyes and genuine smile pushed away any doubt of his sincerity. Amelia was puzzled.

"Boyd, I have to ask you something and you might find this too forward. To preface, I'll remind you that you must respect your elders," Amelia said.

"You're not that much older than me, and I respect you no matter your age or position. Your intelligence and ambition demand respect on their own," Boyd said.

Amelia searched his eyes for playfulness or satire, or even an attempt at flirting. Again she found an absence of guile she hadn't seen in anyone's expression for years, not even her own.

"You really are the starting point," Amelia said.

"Is that your question?" Boyd asked but waited with a pleasant look of wonder.

"That's not really a question, I suppose. But I'm just wondering if you're real. Did we all start out like you, so trusting and naive?" The darkening of his expression caught Amelia and she continued, "Please don't misunderstand me. This isn't a criticism; just the opposite. I think our country needs more youthful ideals."

Amelia wasn't sure why she felt melancholy and wondered how Boyd would react to her going off her own script. She didn't have to wait long to find out. Before Amelia could react, Boyd leaned forward and kissed her gently on the lips. He then sat back and looked around as if just realizing there were others on the boat.

"Was that to prove you aren't as naive as I think?" Amelia asked in a playful manner. She wasn't sure what he was thinking.

"Maybe," Boyd admitted. "And because you look ravishing and I'm not the eighteen I'm sometimes mistaken for." He paused as if he needed another excuse. "And because you aren't as jaded as you think you are, Amelia. I don't think you see your own light anymore. I see it, radiating from your smile like stars on a clear night."

Amelia could recall the times she was tongue-tied as an adult. There were exactly three. One involved overhearing the confessions of a president. The second happened when propositioned by a duke known for preferring the company of men, and the third was when Sam told her she'd someday have to define her role as a woman. As Boyd sat facing her with his bright eyes filled with admiration, Amelia added a fourth to her record. She really didn't know what to say so she smiled and kept quiet.

They sat together in the calming silence watching the trees pass slowly along the Potomac. As a few intertwined couples and families with small children moved from side to side to see the views, Amelia felt reassured by having Boyd by her side and then hated that her contentment left her unsettled. Amelia had taken care of herself her whole life and the idea of leaning on anyone, even for a few moments on a ship, made her feel weak.

The boat docked at a small jetty at the base of a round hill covered in pale wild grass and patches of snow. Boyd helped Amelia from the boat, then took the lead as they marched up the narrow path toward the home Martha Washington shared with her second husband, George.

Mount Vernon embodied the spirit of idioms like "pulling one up by their bootstraps" and "forging ahead with courage." Neither completely reflected the true personality of George Washington, a wealthy landowner who never wanted the position of the presidency. The fickleness of history preferred the pageantry, and the lushness of Washington's home created a perfect backdrop for inspiration. Set among fifty acres overlooking the Potomac, the pristine gardens and gentle hills looked as if perfected in an artist's painting. George Washington himself said, "No estate in the United States is as pleasantly suited as this."

A two-story colonial square, the house stood as tall and erect as the renderings of George on horseback. Arriving at the back of the house, a large sweeping back porch divided by tall white pillars, troubled many visitors, who expected to arrive at the front door like proper guests. Docents in Revolutionary costumes beneath thick wool coats directed visitors around to the main entrance.

From the center of a circular dirt drive, the frontage of the Washington home was flat with a red roof and black shutters around every window on the first and second levels. The front door looked too small to accommodate Washington's height.

With good timing, Boyd and Amelia joined a group just beginning a tour of the house. The docent pointed out the spinet piano in the "little parlor"; described festive gatherings in the large dining room painted a stunning verdigris green; and explained that anyone who arrived at the house, even those who just wanted to meet the president, was always invited to dinner and lodging in one of the many outbuildings and barns. The tour ended upstairs in the bedroom where Washington died at the age of sixty-seven in a bed where his long legs dangled from the end of the short mattress.

"It's hard to imagine why a wealthy man kept himself so cramped and uncomfortable. You'd think he would have built a longer bed," Boyd commented as they made their way onto the back porch to stand facing the Potomac. Ice covering the crab apple branches made the trees look translucent.

Boyd had his hands in his coat pockets and kept his gaze out at the river. Amelia regarded him and noted again a newness that he wore like a scarf, visible and yet easily forgotten.

"There's safety in staying with what you know, and I think small spaces are comforting now and again. The expanse of freedom, the unknown, frightens people. I imagine President Washington sometimes wanted to curl up and lock himself away in that tiny bedroom," she said.

Boyd did not respond to her comment, and Amelia didn't dare look at him. She had no idea why she felt so introspective but she had to get control of herself. Thankfully, Boyd granted a reprieve when he asked if she'd like to walk the grounds.

The sun was higher but a breeze cooled the stirring air. Their self-guided tour led past the rustic stables and vegetable garden, and then Amelia suggested they go to Washington's tomb.

"I'm always amazed by the simplicity of the tomb," Amelia said. "It's so unlike the grandeur of Arlington."

Behind a plain brick wall and arched iron gate stood two marble sarcophagi, one for George and the other for Martha.

After being out in the cold, Amelia and Boyd were excited to find a tea shop in the old Salt House. Amelia claimed two plush armchairs side by side in front of a warm fire while Boyd brought them steaming cups of Earl Grey.

"Shall we begin where we left off?" he said. "You were going to tell me about your family. Any siblings?"

With his persistence, Amelia knew she had to say something about her family. She told him she didn't have any siblings and therefore wanted to hear more about his. But Boyd wasn't redirected. He asked about her parents.

"Both of my parents are dead," Amelia said. "They were killed in a road accident. Their carriage flipped and tumbled down an embankment."

Since moving past her upbringing, Amelia rarely spoke of her parents and she didn't know why she mentioned them to Boyd. Pity didn't make her best case and wasn't part of the script. She'd put herself in a precarious position. She also took a moment to push away the idea that sharing her personal life with Boyd felt imprudent for reasons beyond work. She needed to gather her wits.

Boyd expressed condolences about her parents. Amelia slipped her hand around his elbow and leaned her shoulder against his. "Did you hear Mr. Colt finally paid his fines for violating munitions standards? He was my client."

Boyd wanted to know how she could work for such a scandalous man. Amelia spoke of the sound gun legislation and good pay. "I've never denied that I make my living from my work," Amelia added.

"So, you don't care who writes the paycheck? Colt has a terrible reputation."

Amelia had opened the door and Boyd stepped right through. With ease she'd lifted his ban on discussing work. She felt more like herself.

"If you found out something distasteful about Senator Horton, would you quit and run back to Somerville? Or would you decide that no man is perfect and focus on the good work at hand?" Amelia asked.

Boyd took time answering the question. "I don't know. Thankfully, I haven't found anything distasteful. I think you're wrong about the senator, Amelia. Maybe his reputation is clean because he's clean. No skeleton."

Amelia chuckled and squeezed his arm more tightly. She felt him tense just a bit and then relax deeper into her shoulder.

"You're delightful. Refreshing. And, who knows, maybe you're right. Maybe I should just meet with Senator Horton and do my job." Amelia paused to let Boyd fill in what came next.

Horton didn't see lobbyists. He turned them away every day.

Amelia nodded. "But, from my point of view I think he's being unreasonable and unfair. I usually know more about the issues than the congressmen. They don't have time to read every line of a five-hundred-page bill. That's what I'm paid to do. Why not let me synthesize the highlights? Of course I'm biased, and that's why there are lobbyists for both sides. Hearing the arguments is part of the senator's job."

Suggesting that Boyd try to get Amelia a meeting wasn't going work. Boyd had to have the notion and believe he thought of the idea himself.

Boyd shifted his shoulders, causing Amelia to release his arm. She sat up and Boyd folded his arms over his chest. When Boyd turned toward Amelia, his face and eyes looked too tight, too stern for his character. She feared she'd gone too far.

"Senator Stillman came to see Senator Horton a few days ago," Boyd said.

He had Amelia's full attention.

Boyd described Stillman as friendly, almost fatherly in his manner. Though Boyd didn't confide why the senator stopped by, Amelia knew well enough.

"He gave me a warning. Well, it wasn't a warning for me as much a warning to give to you. That was his intent, though he tried to hide it."

"I can't begin to guess what in the world Senator Stillman

wants to tell me." Amelia had a dozen guesses but not one she thought Stillman would actually say aloud.

"How can I say this delicately?" Boyd muttered. "Senator Stillman has noticed that Senator Horton seems smitten with you. He believes the senator might even be in love with you." Boyd halted at the words as if he couldn't believe what he was saying. Amelia wanted to laugh at the notion but Boyd looked drained. "Senator Stillman wanted to caution you from using your . . . 'feminine wiles' on Senator Horton. I still don't know Senator Horton very well but I've only heard him speak highly of his late wife."

Boyd indeed didn't know Horton but Amelia knew Stillman far too well. Stillman was setting her up and not too cleverly at that. As a staunchly conservative man, Horton would turn away in disgust if she tried batting her eyelashes. But Stillman hinting that Horton loved her showed signs of Stillman's desperation. Amelia nodded, both at her own conclusions and Boyd's furrowed brow.

"Senator Stillman is your opposition so why should he give you helpful advice?" Boyd considered. "But you said yourself that you suspect misconduct. Maybe Senator Stillman knows something we don't. Maybe he's trying to discourage you from doing something that might actually work."

Amelia considered the notion. Possible, she supposed, but unlikely. Plus, Boyd's reasoning supported the idea of Amelia compromising herself.

"Are you suggesting I throw myself at Horton to get his vote? Boyd, I'm surprised at you. Do you think I'm capable of that? Do you think that low of me?"

Boyd's cheeks colored as he shook his head. He apologized for offending her. "I just know what the vote means to you, to society. I'm not suggesting you do anything tawdry. But could harmless flirting hurt if he's in love with you? My father always says the greater good is more important."

The greater good. How often she heard that expression when the greater good was at the expense of someone else. Amelia rose and strode out of the tea room, conscious of Boyd giving chase. He'd offended her to some degree and she wanted to use momentum created by his guilt. She also couldn't ignore her surprise at Boyd's improper suggestion and needed a moment to gather her thoughts. Perhaps all men who chose the Hill were cut of the same cloth. Ambition's lure needed a wide berth.

When Boyd caught her arm outside of the restaurant, his cheeks were pale. He cast his view on the ground and shook his head in a small tremor as if chastising himself.

Amelia kept her hands wrapped around her sides. "You know this is rather a moot discussion since your senator won't see me."

Boyd raised his head. "But what if I could schedule something? He doesn't always check the details of his schedule. I could just tell him—"

"Stop right there. I won't let you lie for me or the cause. I don't want to use you, and you know what you're suggesting isn't right. Seems to be a lot of that going on today."

The bell from the steamer dock drew their attention. A ferry returned to the city each hour and Amelia suggested it was time to leave by hurrying along the path to the dock. They boarded just in time to hear the final whistle.

Benign chatter about the scenery and weather passed the time on the steamer and then the carriage ride. Both were cordial and distracted, but Amelia feared she'd been too heavy-handed in her reprimand. She needed Boyd to get her in to see Horton; the fate of women for generations to come seemed destined to rest on the shoulders of a twenty-four-year-old boy. Amelia cringed, knowing she had to use her backup plan.

Boyd escorted Amelia to her hotel lobby. "Thank you for accompanying me today," he said.

Amelia glanced around the quiet lobby. Most of the guests were still out, the desk clerk had stepped away, and the bellman often went outside to smoke a cigarette.

"Boyd, do you mind helping me? This is a little unorthodox, though you can see the level of attendance I have here." She waved her hand toward the empty desks, then moved her eyes to the large center stairway leading to the guest rooms.

A large bureau in her room needed moving and she hoped Boyd could lend her a hand. She wouldn't keep him but a minute. Boyd hesitated, then agreed.

Amelia stepped into her suite and removed her gloves and hat, then tossed them and her handbag on the coffee table. Boyd remained by the door, so Amelia walked back and let him help her with her coat. Boyd decided to keep his coat on and asked about the bureau in a direct, businesslike manner.

"The wardrobe is in my bedroom. I hope this isn't too awkward."

Having been outside for much of the day, Amelia realized Boyd hadn't seen the full length of her fitted dress. Boyd watched her, then mumbled something and turned away. "It's warm in here," he said as he removed his coat and set it on the arm of the sofa. "Okay," he trailed as he marched into Amelia's bedroom and the task at hand.

Her boudoir held a four-poster bed covered by an ivory spread with the *WH* insignia, a wooden dresser with vanity mirror, and a large armoire with carved inlay.

"I'd like that put over there." Amelia pointed to the armoire that rested against a wall covered in flocked wallpaper.

Boyd picked up one of the ends and moved it forward. Amelia asked if she could help but he declined and "walked" the piece, changing sides to move half of the beast at a time. She stepped from the room and poured two glasses of water from a crystal decanter on the side table. When Boyd emerged a few minutes later, she handed him the glass. He drained the glass and asked for a second.

"Would you like to sit down for a minute? You look flushed."

Boyd glanced at the respectable parlor sofa and chairs. Amelia thought he might stay until he set down his glass. "I really should go. Thank you again for a lovely day."

Amelia handed Boyd his coat and watched him put it on. Then she walked him to her door and thanked him for his help. When Boyd then lingered by the door, Amelia asked if there was something else.

He paused before saying, "I noticed something in your bedroom."

Amelia raised her eyebrows.

"I mean, you don't have any photos in your bedroom." He stopped and glanced around the parlor. "Nothing in here either. I'm surprised you don't have at least one picture in a silver frame. I was just wondering why."

"And I suppose you've been in many ladies' bedrooms, then?" Amelia asked, noting his interesting and exact observation.

Boyd looked horrified. "No. I didn't mean . . . I just have a sister and my mother . . . and—"

Amelia placed her hand on his cheek and caressed his soft skin with her fingertips. "I'm glad you noticed," she whispered, and then she kissed Boyd. Unlike their earlier peck, Amelia leaned close and slipped her hands around to the back of his neck. Boyd wrapped his arms around her waist and pressed her to him.

They stayed that way for a few moments until Amelia pulled back a bit. With their arms still around each other in the narrow foyer, Boyd said he should leave without making any move to do so.

"You should," Amelia agreed, though she liked the feel of

him. She felt safe.

Boyd kissed her again, a soft, gentle kiss that lingered on her lips even after he unwrapped his arms.

"You really are an amazing woman, Miss Amelia Cooke."

"I've been called worse," she joked.

Boyd paused a moment longer, then opened the door and left, seemingly before he changed his mind.

Amelia pulled off her boots and sunk into the parlor sofa. The day included an odd muddle of drama and romance. Her candor went off script, and yet it seemed to have worked. Amelia had no doubt that Boyd would try to set up a meeting with Horton. The kiss sealed that much. What she didn't know was how to play Horton. A straight bribe wasn't going to work and Stillman had spoken the truth about Horton's distaste for lewd behavior. Still, Amelia recognized that Boyd had a point. Even conservative men were primal on some level and the innate yearning for the softer gender might be the weakness everyone had overlooked.

"Does Horton protest too much?" Amelia asked herself. She only had a few days to find out.

CHAPTER TWENTY-THREE

Sitting on the end of a long bench in the oversized kitchen of Haven House reminded Amelia of being in trouble; a stool in the corner by the wood stove often served as punishment for misbehaving. Still, the sweet smell of cinnamon and cleaning oil that Amelia normally found as oppressive as the cigar smoke in taverns brought comfort against the cold front that moved in around her. Amelia wished the company matched the perfumed scent. Teeth were bared.

"You told us we had Mallory. My friend said her maid was a friend of his maid and she overheard him talking with another man about the vote. And do you know what he said?" Though in the form of a question, Amelia recognized Marion's accusation and resisted a smart remark. Amelia already knew about Mallory from far more reliable sources.

"Ladies," Amelia addressed Marion and the group gathered around the kitchen table like hungry diners waiting for the buffet service. To Amelia, the muttering among the ladies had taken on a sort of menacing growl. Even if she could somehow get past Marion and the other board members, all of the exits were blocked.

"You have to understand that I'm not the only lobbyist on this. I don't know what changed Mallory's mind, but we have Dodger and Gage. Plus—" Amelia said.

"The fact of the matter is," the other twin said, "you still haven't got Senator Horton. Perla said we need him. Without him you won't get the others. Isn't that right? You aren't the only one who understands what's going on."

Hearing the other twin speak was refreshing even if Amelia didn't like what she had to say. Eyes were turned to Amelia and she felt their need to point fingers as a way to ease their growing anxiety. The cause meant more than life to many of the women. Amelia stood, wishing Perla would return.

"Ladies, you're premature in your panic," Amelia started.

"Premature?" a round woman called out. "The vote is any day now." The shrill fright in her voice set off the ladies like a gunshot around a flock of birds.

"Your melodramatic emotions are why men don't want us to vote in the first place!" Amelia shouted loud enough to silence the room. "Horton is going to—"

There was a loud huff from the back and then a woman with silver hair and wrinkled hands came forward. A frequent protestor Amelia knew only as Vertie, she marched toward Amelia with the same confidence as when she stared down opponents who shouted obscenities at her on the congressional steps.

"Young lady, do not pander to these women. We all know that Senator Horton is a long shot so don't pretend he's not. We're not simpletons. We may not be a grand lobbyist as yourself, but these ladies and myself are the ones toiling, shouting, toting signs, and making our plight known while you flirt and dine and who knows what. There are many rumors, you know. And we have to wonder: have we put our faith in the wrong kind of woman?" Vertie asked, bolstered by the round of knowing, disapproving nods.

Amelia waited for a few claps and more muttering to die down. She'd grown tired of the innuendo regarding her "tricks," especially from women with such venom in their eyes.

"If I may," Amelia said, "I have never said that Horton was easy nor have I guaranteed anything. If you find my methods distasteful, I encourage you to set up your own appointments and do your own bidding. I understand what's at stake, more than you know, and all I'm trying to say is that working yourselves into a frenzy isn't going to help any of us. You must let me continue as planned and trust that I'm doing what's best," Amelia said. "Aren't we all on the same side?"

"We are," a familiar voice said from the doorway. The sea parted as Perla stepped forward.

"Mrs. Walker," Perla said, "we hired Amelia because she's excellent. I understand your frustration and fear, but we need to let her finish her job without interference. A united front is critical at this point."

The ladies were quieted but not satisfied. Perla distracted the ladies with a quick accounting of the ongoing budget, then suggested the ladies get back to the tasks at hand. Within a few minutes the kitchen cleared as if Perla had waved a wand.

"Let's talk in my office," Perla said.

As Amelia following Perla down the hall, Lottie stepped into her path from the alcove under the stairwell. "I believe in you, Miss Cooke. I know you're doing your best." Before Amelia could reply, Lottie hustled out the front door. Amelia appreciated her kind words more than Lottie might ever know.

Closing the door to Perla's office, Amelia stood while Perla paced in front of her bookshelves. Amelia rarely saw Perla look like a nervous cat and asked what was wrong.

"You mind telling me what's going on? What was all that in the kitchen?" Perla asked.

Amelia had stopped by Haven House to ask Perla's advice about dealing with Horton. Not finding her in her office, Amelia had gone to the kitchen for tea. Several of the ladies were at the table.

"When I entered they stopped talking and stared at me. Maybe in hindsight I shouldn't have asked if they had something to say to me," Amelia said.

Perla continued to circle the room. "Never mind that. We're all on edge."

Perla only paced when she waited for an important telegram or needed to discuss a delicate matter. Perla wasn't watching the door for a messenger. She wanted to know about Amelia's intentions for Boyd McKenna. The question surprised Amelia more in tone than content. Perla sounded concerned for Boyd.

Amelia explained Boyd's connection to Horton and his help in facilitating a meeting. Amelia didn't share the details of their date or the kiss they shared in her hotel room because Perla wouldn't approve on many levels.

"And this young man, he understands what he's doing?" Perla asked.

Amelia tilted her head. "How do you mean?"

Perla stopped so quickly that the wide folds of her black skirt continued without her. She turned to face Amelia, her face crumpled into a tight ball. "Don't use your blushing-bride tricks with me. You know very well what I'm asking. If Horton finds out you suckered his aide, that kid won't stand a chance in this town."

Amelia gawked at Perla. She'd never heard her voice so strained or seen such fury in her eyes. She looked like a mother protecting a son, and Amelia asked if she knew Boyd. The honest question pacified Perla and she shook her head. Perla sat down on the sofa by the window and motioned for Amelia to sit next to her.

"Amelia, you're a wonderful lobbyist. You're smart and charismatic, but I worry that you get too caught up in the prize," Perla said.

"Too caught up? What does that mean?" Amelia didn't like being attacked by one of her few allies.

"Progress is rarely the result of planning. It's more often a

256

combination of circumstances that overcome man's wishes. My mother liked to say, 'We plan and God laughs.' It's true, Amelia. You must think about what you're doing, the choices you're making in the name of the grand cause. You alone have to live with your actions. I want you to think about what truly matters and what will be forgotten."

Amelia told Perla she hadn't forgotten the cause.

"That's not what I mean." Perla tugged her high collar away from her neck. "I know you're dedicated. We all are. But there's something more important at stake than just our voting. Integrity, morality . . . family. No matter what happens in a few days, you have to look at yourself and live with your choices."

Perla glanced at the empty teapot on the stand in front of them. A cup of tea might have helped wash down their discussion, but Perla didn't reach for the pot.

"Do you ever raise a glass and toast our Revolutionary foremothers who helped fight for the freedoms we enjoy?" Perla asked. "Do you even remember the names of women like Abigail Adams? The wife of the great president John Adams is my great-great-grandmother you know. It was Abigail who told her husband to 'remember the ladies' when he and Jefferson were drafting the Declaration of Independence. She knew a strong society was dependent on both sexes working together and yet we don't celebrate Abigail's bravery and vision. Don't make the mistake of thinking those women shouting in the kitchen will remember you or even think about you after all of this is over. They're human and they'll move on regardless of what you do."

Amelia kept her voice soft when she asked if Perla thought she'd done something to be ashamed of. The thought of disappointing Perla made Amelia queasy.

Perla stiffened and said she'd heard talk about the young intern. "Only you know the truth and what's going on. I just worry that you're misguided in your determination and will

. . ." She paused. "Only you know what you're willing to take with you to the grave."

Amelia chuckled to relieve her own tension. "The grave. Why so dramatic? You sound like Marion. My friend, what's going on?"

Perla looked out the window overlooking Constitution Avenue and watched a sweeper in a crisp white uniform go by before returning her gaze to Amelia. The corners of Perla's eyes drooped and the rims were pink. "I have regrets in life. We all do. And I can't stand by and watch you make a big mistake."

Amelia had never compared her life to Perla's, a woman born into privilege who viewed the world far more optimistically than Amelia.

The table holding the tea service had a lower shelf with a silver box. Perla retrieved the box and pulled out a bottle of Scotch. She turned over two porcelain tea cups and filled them with what looked like tea. Perla handed one of the cups to Amelia.

"I'm going to tell you this because I need to tell someone. I trust I have your full confidence?" Perla said, holding the tea cup by the bottom.

Amelia nodded.

"You know I took back my maiden name when my husband died years ago. But you probably don't know that I have a daughter," Perla said.

Perla didn't like her daughter's choice in a husband and said as much right before the wedding. Her daughter went into a rage and refused to speak to her. They hadn't spoken in ten years.

"Stupid, all of it. Hattie's in town and she sent a note that she wanted to see me to tell me something important. 'Important,' she wrote." Perla muttered something under her breath. "I'll say it's important."

Before walking in on the turmoil of the Haven House kitchen, Perla had found out she had a nine-year-old grandson.

Perla took a sip from her cup. She blamed herself for making a rash decision. "I've missed so much. I was a fool."

"Perla, you couldn't know what was going to happen. Now that you're speaking to Hattie again, I'm sure you can make amends."

Perla remained hopeful even if she proclaimed her daughter as stubborn as herself. "I just want you to be careful. Don't do something you'll regret for years to come. There's so much more to life than what goes on in Washington. Don't undervalue your principles or what it means to have a family. Children are joy, my dear."

"You're a wise woman, Perla, but—"

"I'm not wise, my dear; I've just lived longer and seen more than you have. And maybe I'm a bit dramatic. This was a difficult day and perhaps the ladies are rubbing off." Amelia saw the nostalgic look fade from Perla's eyes. She had let Amelia peek inside but that was as far as she was going to open the door. "Keep the real prize in mind, Amelia. The Mrs. Walkers of the world will push, but they aren't the ones in the line of fire. That said, make no mistake that if we lose the vote . . ."

Amelia knew what came next and asked if Perla would lead the mob with their torches. When she first signed on with the NWSA, Perla told her a winning cause had an army and a failed cause had a scapegoat. Perla just smiled but never answered. She raised her teacup and Amelia followed.

"Let's remember the ladies," Perla toasted, then swallowed her Scotch.

The fresh burn from the alcohol put a sharp end to their unusual conversation. Perla was needed in the receiving parlor, leaving Amelia alone in the office.

A man leading a cart piled with hay rattled by the window

and Amelia watched with a bit of envy for his simple life. The complexities she bore were not just from her job or the pending vote, and Amelia couldn't remember a time when her existence felt straightforward or normal in any way. Perla's warnings and advice were well meaning, and yet, the suggestion that Amelia consider another way of life, one that included children and the customary trappings of a family, felt too heavy to think about beneath the amassing pressure.

Others worried for her barren spinsterhood, she assumed, but Amelia felt disconnected from herself and realized she sometimes felt more of a spectator than participant. Amelia questioned if playing the games, looking for angles like a chess player hovering over a board, had removed her from her own life. But, even as a spectator, she enjoyed her lifestyle regardless if there might be another life she'd enjoy as well, or even more.

Amelia finished her "tea" and stood. Perla might have concerns for Boyd, but he was a grown man and Amelia had done nothing to harm him. If anything, she stopped Boyd from lying to his boss. The foremothers like Abigail Adams might frown upon her tactics, although Amelia sensed they, too, were shrewd and stretched the boundaries of decency in their time. Regrets were part of life and as much as Perla wanted to protect Amelia, Perla wasn't her mother, nor did she have everything to lose. Perla talked of a prize and Amelia agreed. She'd reach the prize with help from Boyd and Horton even if she had to do something the ladies, and Perla, could never know about.

CHAPTER TWENTY-FOUR

Amelia remembered once standing outside the window of Harwell's Bakery & Confectionery Store to peer in through the glass at the display of large jars filled with a rainbow of colorful cream candies, chewing gum, and hard confections pressed into tight balls. She could only imagine that the candy smelled like honey or peppermint because Mr. Harwell never let urchins inside. If she or any of the orphans moved close to the entrance, he shooed them away with a hiss. When, as an adult, Amelia finally tried black strips that looked like chocolate, she discovered they were licorice and despised the taste. As Amelia stood in front of The Strand Gentlemen's Club, again shut out behind the glass, the bitter, burnt flavor of licorice flirted across her tongue.

Amelia had agreed to meet Boyd on the sidewalk in front of the club only at his insistence. They had exchanged just brief messages and were to meet at five thirty. Boyd was late.

The streets were bustling, so Amelia stayed near the building out of the way of hurried pedestrians. Carriages rattled nearby and a man selling roasted chestnuts pushed his cart by without noticing her. When Boyd at last arrived in a flourish, he needed a moment to catch his breath. Amelia stared at him in cold silence. She didn't like waiting, especially like a vagabond in front the men's club.

"I'm sorry. But you'll like why I'm here and why I'm late . . . and why I ran six blocks." Boyd was flushed with excitement and exertion. "I spoke with Horton," he said.

Amelia had surmised as much and stood impatient to hear how it went. "And?" she asked.

Her tone didn't sound like that of the lover in her hotel room and Amelia saw his disappointment. She relaxed her gaze even though she wasn't much in the mood for games. Boyd misunderstood. He seized her shoulder and wiggled her back against the building so they were pressed in the shadow of the stairway leading up to the club's entrance. Startled, Amelia watched Boyd grin like a boy with a secret.

"First a kiss," Boyd said.

Amelia hid her seething behind tight lips. He was playing his hand too forcefully. His charms did little to overcome that they were on a public street with the vote just a few days away. Suppressing her anger, Amelia placed a playful kiss on Boyd's cheek.

Boyd chuckled. "I'm not saying a thing until I receive real compensation for my work today. Once you hear the news, you'll agree."

Amelia had little choice, which she despised even more than his demands, and she clenched her fists to squelch her frustration. After a quick glance to be sure no one was watching, Amelia leaned forward and pressed her lips against his. He responded as if they were alone in the hotel, so she stepped back and raised her hand to fan her cheeks.

"You're making me blush, sir. There are people who might see us. What will they think?"

Boyd agreed and Amelia relaxed until he leaned toward her ear and she worried he might start nibbling. He whispered just one word, *yes*.

Amelia backed up and Boyd straightened. Though genuinely excited, she didn't have time for a flirtatious dance.

"When? Where?" she asked.

Boyd sensed her urgency and answered without further

demands. Horton agreed at the last minute and Boyd expected him shortly.

"He got me in the club?" Amelia couldn't hide her astonishment.

Boyd looked confused and in that instant Amelia wanted to smack his cheek. He made grand claims of equality but couldn't fathom a woman sitting at the next table within the sacred halls.

"I don't think so," Boyd said. "He didn't say where you'd go. A restaurant I suppose."

That seemed more likely, but Amelia felt the sting. Boyd seemed unaware of her annoyance. He twitched, eager for her to say something.

"Thank you, Boyd. How did you do it?" Amelia did want to know more about the depths of Boyd McKenna.

Boyd had asked Horton about the duties and expectations of being a senator. Then he shared what Amelia had said about needing to hear both sides. Boyd did not mention Amelia's hand in his new opinion, but he did have the backbone to remind Horton that he'd given time to Stillman.

" 'If you were willing to speak with Senator Stillman, then it seems only appropriate and fair that you speak with Miss Cooke,' I said, just like that." Boyd grinned. "Said to arrange the meeting before he changed his mind and get out of his office."

Boyd's enthusiasm made him endearing enough that Amelia ran her gloved hand across his cheek and said, "I owe you a favor." This had the expected result and as Amelia began thinking of what to say to Horton, Boyd rubbed her shoulders as if she were a fighter going into the ring.

Boyd checked his watch. He had to get back to the office before Horton spotted him. "Will you be all right?"

Amelia found the question humorous but didn't dare laugh. She assured him and had just one question of logistics. Boyd wasn't sure if Horton expected to meet her outside or inside, but the cold made it difficult to wait outside much longer.

"You'd best go inside until you see Horton through the window."

Amelia thanked him for his sound advice, then watched him sprint down the street dodging pedestrians with nimble ease. She marched up the stairs to the club and opened the carved, black door. A man stood in front of the coat check with his back to the entrance as Amelia walked to the window facing the street. She had a perfect view of the steps.

"Women aren't allowed here, darling. This is a club for men only."

Amelia turned and found the man looking at her. "So then what are you doing here, Edward?" A poke at Stillman's manhood was cheap but she wasn't in the mood to play.

Stillman's broad grin paired with narrowing eyes gave the look of scrutinizing and laughing at her at the same time.

"What?" she blurted.

Amelia had never heard Stillman snicker and thought he sounded like a goat. He found something oddly funny, and she felt a gnawing panic.

"You two make such a sweet couple. He's a little youthful, but you can groom him. See, you do want to be a mother," Stillman said.

Prying eyes were the ruin of political careers, and having Stillman behind those eyes was infuriating. With Horton on the way, Amelia had no time for an argument.

"Look, I don't know what you saw or what you think, and, frankly, I don't care. If you don't mind, I'd like to use that window for business and not spying," she said. "I'll only taint your hallowed grounds for a few minutes."

Amelia didn't move, so Stillman took a step toward her.

"You can't be here, Amelia. You can't use our window for anything."

He sounded petty and Amelia took pleasure in watching him shrink a bit from the echo of his own nasal voice. Amelia explained she had precedent for standing in the foyer. "No one but you seems to care."

Stillman claimed he didn't care and sounded like a spoiled child. But instead of backing down and making a joke of the situation, he moved beside her and grabbed her elbow.

"Take your hands off me, Edward." Amelia shook off his hold.

"I can't touch your arm but you'll kiss a boy on the street corner?"

Amelia watched his nostrils flare as he balled his fists. "Are you jealous, is that what this is?" She placed her hand on his arm. "I won't deny what we had but that was a long time ago."

Stillman shrank from her touch, his eyes blazing from her assumption. "I don't want you or—" Voices from the top of the staircase drew their attention so Stillman seized Amelia's arm, dragged her into the coat-check room, and slammed the door.

Wedged against a brown overcoat that pushed her crown hat onto her forehead, Amelia sneezed from the smell of damp wool.

"You've got some nerve. Get out of my way." Amelia pushed her hat back in place, then glared at his hand still on her arm. "And let go of me." The rage in her voice surprised her.

Stillman released his grip but did not back away. He remained inches from her, and Amelia wondered if she had the strength to shove him aside. She couldn't miss Horton because of Stillman's shenanigans.

"Okay, you've had your . . . I don't know what this is, but I'm going now. It's been nice seeing you, Edward." Amelia took a step forward expecting Stillman to move. Instead he stayed

265

firm and she bumped into him; their shoulders touched and remained together.

Amelia felt her anger in a flash of emotions. Boyd had taken wild liberties on the street corner while she again waited in the cold, denied entry by arbitrary rules of birth. Now Stillman was acting like a madman. His eyes were wide and his cheeks glowed.

"I don't have the words—" she began.

Stillman grabbed Amelia's shoulders and kissed her with an abruptness that stung her bottom lip. Amelia pulled back but Stillman kept hold of her shoulders.

In his eyes Amelia saw the haunting passion of their past, a time when she wished for a life with Stillman. She thought then he had deeper feelings for her, and as she looked at him, his hair tousled and his handsome face twisted in a seething mix of pain and lust, her resolve weakened. She didn't resist when Stillman seized her neck and pulled her toward him.

Their passion became raw and frenzied. Amelia tugged at his shoulders as he groped at her waist and hips. His hands were firm and demanding, wanting to feel more than the thick fabric of her dress allowed.

Stillman moved his lips to her neck and Amelia tilted her head back. She closed her eyes as he moved his lips down her collarbone and on to her shoulder. The stubble on his chin felt rough and masculine, and for a moment Amelia thought of the first time he touched her, when her burdens melted away and she felt protected within his arms. Stillman moved his lips back to her neck and pinched the thin skin between his teeth. Amelia winced and opened her eyes. The silhouette of a man's coat watched them.

Amelia pushed Stillman back. Horton could arrive at any moment. Stillman made his choice long ago and pawing each other in the coatroom was for frivolous teenagers, not a woman about to make history.

"Get out of my way!"

Stillman's expression turned tight but he looked more himself than he had moments before. He paused, then stepped aside without protest.

Amelia rushed from the coatroom without checking for anyone in the hall, nonetheless grateful for an empty foyer. She adjusted her dress and took a handkerchief from her purse to wipe her cheeks and neck as she made her way to the window. Horton waited at the bottom of the steps. Amelia had no way of knowing how long he'd been there, but she didn't stop to think of what to say. She flung open the door and fled the men's club without looking back. Had she turned around, she would have seen Stillman again watching her from the window.

CHAPTER TWENTY-FIVE

Through the stunned eyes of his own reflection in the window, Stillman watched Amelia shake hands with Senator Horton. She greeted him with a pleasant smile and confident stance, as if nothing unusual had just transpired. The two left together heading south and Stillman thought to follow them, perhaps intercede in some way, but the missteps of the last few minutes proved his impaired judgment. He didn't know why he had embraced Amelia, only that he'd never felt so angry and desirous at the same time. Stillman wondered, with some genuine surprise, if he had acted out of jealousy for the McKenna boy. The aide had certainly finagled the meeting with Horton and Stillman witnessed Amelia's repayment in the stairwell shadows. Seeing Amelia with Boyd had sparked something he didn't want to think about.

The coat-check girl returned from some errand and Stillman gave her a curt nod. Had she been at her post he wouldn't have acted the buffoon. The girl ducked into the closet where he'd just held Amelia in his arms, and Stillman paused to lift an auburn hair from his jacket. Amelia Cooke needed to stay part of his past.

Stillman turned to look up to the top of the stairwell and bile rose in his throat. He had agreed to meet Fitzwater in just a few minutes, and he dreaded seeing him again. That Amelia would meet with Horton while he spent the evening placating a madman pressed in on him. If Amelia managed to sway Horton to her side, then Fitzwater with his threats and demands was ir-relevant. All of Stillman's toil was for naught, leaving only public humiliation. He had no other options. Without further thought, Stillman spun on one foot as he buttoned his coat. He dashed out the front door after Amelia.

Amid the rush of foot traffic, Stillman trotted in and out between clusters of businessmen and children hooked to parents. When Stillman reached Thomas Circle, he stood by the statue of the unknown horseman and considered his options. The roads jutted out like spokes on a wheel.

To the right was Horton's office, where he had never allowed lobbyists, so Stillman ruled out going right. Left he'd find Lancer's Chop House, where Horton often dined and the tim-ing worked. If he went straight he'd go to Horton's home, and the idea of Amelia in the lavish frescoed halls of Horton's residence caused more bile. Stillman had gone to Horton's home just once to pick up paperwork. He waited in the round entrance gazing at the delicate mosaic tiles on the floor while wondering if he should step into the receiving room. The deci-sion came in the form of Horton's footman, who shoved paperwork in his hands and shuffled him out like an errand boy. Stillman took comfort in the bitter memory because he saw the absurdity of Horton inviting Amelia to his home, so Stillman turned left toward the restaurant and took up his sprint.

Stillman found Lancer's already packed with the weary hunched low in their chairs. Unlike Amelia, Horton preferred dining in the back, away from prying eyes. Horton lived as a private man in all aspects of his life including the death of his wife. His wife had the courtesy of dying during the Senate hiatus so, with the mourning period over just in time, Horton returned to his desk with the same passion and tenacity as before his ordeal. Though the only sign that Horton had tended to a wife stricken and taken by diphtheria was just a few more gray hairs at the temple, Stillman considered a dead wife as good a reason as any to vote in favor of the women's cause. Stillman pushed through the front door and stormed passed the *maitre d'*.

A waiter in a serving coat approached to assist, but Stillman waved him off and continued to the back. Though a small restaurant, realization that Horton and Amelia weren't there took a while to settle with Stillman. After a few moments he felt men staring at his wild eyes and frantic expression. Stillman kept his wits even in his distress. He tapped the man sitting at a table nearest and chuckled. "Wrong restaurant. I guess I really need a break." A few men shrugged and returned to their dinners. Gossip averted. Yet Stillman still hadn't found Amelia and Horton.

Valuable time ticked away as Stillman debated what to do next. He could try to get back to the club in time to beg apologies from Fitzwater, or he could wander the streets hoping for dumb luck. Being unable to keep his appointment with Fitzwater seemed more believable and less insulting than showing up late. An emergency had kept him and he sent a messenger. Lousy bugger probably stopped at the pub and forgot his mission. Being late needed more finesse and Stillman wasn't sure he was capable after the events of the evening. His hands shook and an unpleasant longing for Amelia still pressed against his lips.

Stillman retraced his steps and stopped again at Thomas Circle. Had he been thinking like himself, someone sane, he would have known Horton wouldn't risk being seen in a restaurant with Amelia. Not in public, Stillman thought. Peering eyes lurked in the open and a savvy Horton wouldn't tip his hand. There were only ever two possibilities.

Many trysts happened after hours behind closed Capitol office doors where cleaning staff were effortlessly paid and sent away. Stillman thought again of Horton's home and imagined

Amelia standing in the receiving room, cooing and complimenting Horton on a fine library collection. Unaccustomed to the
anxious twisting in his gut and in his compromised state,
Stillman didn't know where to go. He removed his derby and
ran his hands over his damp, clammy scalp.

To lose his appointment because of the mischief of a woman
felt ironic and somehow unjust. History had given the last win
to Amelia. If the world was balanced then it was his turn for
victory, he thought, then gave a deep, bitter chuckle. If there
were truly justice in the universe then men like Fitzwater
wouldn't rule and prosper. Regardless of the location, Stillman
knew that Amelia had time alone with Horton. She had done
her best wheedling and under different circumstances Stillman
might be impressed.

A gust of wind sent a paper bag sailing down the street in the
direction of Horton's house. Stillman watched the bag float on
the current, spinning as easily as dead leaves in fall. He saw
liberation in the air, in the moving of an object without direction. Freedom wasn't in having the vote. Making choices and
forging paths were taxing, and Stillman wondered why women
wanted the burden. In their desperation for a vote, the women
hadn't realized they were already liberated and unfettered in a
way Stillman sometimes craved. He was weary from years of
making decisions, of haggling and reworking, compromising,
and adjusting. The bag fell to the ground motionless and the
night closed in around him. For a moment he thought of quit-
ting. He felt the same as he did at his father's funeral when his
brother brought up their rift.

They were standing in front of the windowseat while mourn-
ers filled buffet plates. Stillman listened to his brother rant
about his father's indiscretion. When Stillman had finally heard
enough, he told his brother to just shut up. His brother turned,
the years of hostility and jealousy raging in his glare.

"You're just like Father."

Stillman once considered nothing more noble than being like his father.

"You could have made the right choice, Edward. Instead you betrayed me. Just like Father betrayed Mother," James said.

His brother never knew that the real "right choice" had nothing to do with him. Stillman could never tell his brother about the father he didn't know because sharing the secret meant admitting his own culpability.

"I'm sorry that you feel I betrayed you. But, James, just because I couldn't take you to Washington didn't meant you couldn't go on your own. You still can."

"And become like you?"

Over the years, he thought of James when he made difficult choices. Who really wanted to be like him? Stillman didn't like self-doubt and reminded himself that having regrets made him human. If he stopped to rehash every decision, he'd never move forward.

The paper bag rose back into the air and Stillman knew what he had to do. He may long for his youth, for a time when he considered his carnal knowledge of Amelia synonymous with his optimistic views and a bright future, but those days were long gone. In the morning he would contact Fitzwater with his excuse; he had one pass. Stillman would, of course, say yes to Fitzwater's arrangement and put the issue to bed like a child with colic. Men like Fitzwater were never satisfied and his demands would deepen like tree roots searching for water.

Stillman put on his hat and tucked his hands in his pockets. He blamed stress and fatigue for his momentary lapse of judgment with Amelia and thought again of Fitzwater and what his kind of power could provide. With the vote just a day away, Stillman wasn't going to let Amelia get Horton even if he had to do something drastic. Fitzwater might be a madman but he wanted Stillman to win. If Stillman could convince Fitzwater that he needed his help to claim victory, then maybe he could turn Fitzwater into a powerful, and dangerous, ally.

CHAPTER TWENTY-SIX

The second-floor parlor of 151 Beacon Hill was smaller than Amelia expected. Two narrow stuffed chairs faced a loveseat and coffee table, and the walls were covered with a lavender trellis wallpaper, which made the space feel cozy. Trinkets and books sat neatly on bookshelves and an antique spinning wheel still threaded with gold yarn sat in the corner. When the death of Horton's wife made local front-page news, Amelia had sent flowers. Now, as she gazed at the painting of Mrs. Horton over the mantel, a reserved older woman in pearls, she wondered if Horton placed the flowers with the others in the main receiving parlor on the first floor or kept them in this room.

In front of the men's club, Amelia smiled and nodded when Horton suggested they go to his home. She was, in fact, so flabbergasted she accidentally bit the inside of her cheek. Amelia followed Horton through the front hall and paused at the main parlor. He never glanced at the room. He beckoned her forward with his confident gait and she followed. Few were invited to the Hortons' and even fewer were led beyond the larger front rooms and upstairs to the inner quarters where the family actually lived. Amelia now sat in the intimate chambers of one of the most powerful men in Washington.

"I don't drink alcohol, so if you'd like something I'll send my footman," Horton said.

"No, thank you," Amelia said, wanting to keep her tone flat until she got a feel for his disposition.

Horton motioned for her to sit on one of the stuffed chairs and he lowered himself onto the loveseat. On the coffee table she saw the second volume of *The Woodlanders* with a faded flyer for a sale on Siddalls Soap as the bookmark.

"Are you enjoying the series?" Amelia asked, looking at the volume.

His face remained unchanged. "Not really."

"Then why do you continue?" she asked, noting with some admiration the skill at which Horton kept an ambiguous tone.

"Because I began it." Horton scrunched his face, pressing his wrinkles deeper into his face. "Boyd made an impassioned speech on your behalf. I was impressed. I don't suppose you'll live up to the expectations, but I agreed to see for myself and that's why you're here."

Horton's directness showed nothing of his underlying motivation. Unsure of the best tactic, Amelia thought of Boyd's suggestion that she flirt and wondered what Boyd had said to impress Horton.

"I can't imagine what Boyd said," Amelia said.

"Can't you," Horton snapped. Amelia appreciated the reaction because any emotion gave her a peek under the veil. Horton shifted in his seat.

"I can imagine many things that are said about me, Senator, and I fear most aren't true. What is true is that I'm just grateful for your time, sir, and hope I can sway your vote toward the side of justice for women."

Horton narrowed his eyes. "Orating about justice for women? Is that what you want to do? I imagine that's what you were hired to do, Miss Cooke."

"I was hired to help prove that the women's vote is a vital step toward shaping a positive future," Amelia said.

Horton removed his glasses and poked his index finger and thumb into his eyes. He rubbed in a circle with delicate pressure before replacing his glasses and adjusting the metal frames around each ear.

She sensed that he didn't believe her; that he thought she just wanted to make some kind of deal.

"Isn't that what lobbyists do? Play games?"

"What are you suggesting, Senator?" She leaned back and waited for Horton to reply.

Horton leaned forward a bit. "You know very well what I'm saying, and you know very well why I don't like your kind. You talk in circles and make bargains. Then there's your beauty, like a siren leading men to crash on jagged cliffs. I'm not interested in games and I've never accepted money for my vote."

In the compact room stifled by the feminine touches of a dead wife, Amelia realized that, though Horton may not like games, he was a good player. Still, the thought of the senator's wife gave her an idea.

Amelia looked about the room with purpose and let her gaze linger on the spinning wheel. "This is such a charming room, Senator Horton. Your wife had a lovely eye for decor. You know, if you don't mind diverging for just a moment, I'd love to hear a little about your wife. I met her only briefly but her reputation was enviable."

The echo of Horton's wife seemed to bounce around the room like a child's wayward ball. For a moment he tensed and Amelia feared she'd brought up just the wrong topic and readied herself to be thrown to the curb. Then his gaze drifted away within some fond memory, and Amelia waited with confidence.

The senator described his wife as a saint who could do nothing evil short of read the newspaper and not fold it up properly. Amelia heard the sadness in his retelling of a funny moment when she lost her bonnet at the fair, and he repeated her name in every sentence as if summoning her from the beyond. Amelia knew well the echoing sounds and motions of loneliness. How many times had she herself clasped her hands or rubbed her shoulder without realizing how much she longed for human touch? He looked grief stricken at speaking about his wife and Amelia considered that a man like Horton likely never uttered his wife's name to anyone for fear of showing his weakness. Amelia again thought of Boyd's approach.

When Horton grew silent and lowered his head, Amelia asked if she could ring for the footman. Horton nodded and pointed to the servant's cord. When the footman arrived, she asked for two cups of strong, black tea but Horton stopped her.

"What makes you think I want black tea . . . or any tea at all?" Horton asked. He seemed embarrassed by needing her help.

Amelia sat down beside Horton on the loveseat. He didn't recoil as she might have guessed, so she placed a gentle hand on his shoulder. "While you criticize my kind, we're an observant lot. Most men don't drink tea unless nagged by their wives, and, if they agree to a cup, they take it black and strong. Since I see fresh teacup rings on the table, I suspect you've had many cups in this room since your wife's passing." Amelia paused, then lowered her hand to her lap.

When the tea arrived, Horton sat fixed with his feet planted on the floor and his eyes stationed forward. The footman began service, but Amelia dismissed him and poured the tea herself. Over many years of hiding her intelligence, flaunting her wit, persuading and cajoling, she had learned there were just two types of men. Men either fancied her company because she was a woman or needed something only her gender could give.

Horton left his tea untouched as Amelia took a few bitter sips. She preferred sugar and cream.

"Miss Cooke," Horton said as he twisted to face her. "You're the first woman in this room since Beatrice, and you have brought up my wife for a reason that I can only surmise is a way to persuade me to your cause. Beatrice was an honest and formidable woman, but she wasn't for the vote. She felt it was unladylike and unnecessary. So far, I haven't heard any real arguments to the contrary beyond the rhetoric and slogans shouted in the streets. Beatrice would also find that unladylike."

Amelia set down her teacup and told him that many women agreed and considered voting a man's job. "I mean no disrespect to your late wife, but I believe these women are more afraid than convinced. Senator, you know change is uncomfortable and most people push the newness away by telling themselves that what they have is fine and good enough. Some men may vote with care and consideration of their families, but human beings are flawed and selfish by nature. The right to vote is a human right, not a random act based on race, religion, or gender."

The senator seemed to consider this point without comment until he shifted and his hand brushed against Amelia's thigh. He made quick apologies, cleared his throat, and went silent again. Tension in the room mixed with the smell of the cooling tea and lingering sour perfume left on unwashed cushions. Amelia felt his longing for his wife in the tightness of his shoulders and the rigid posture he used to steady himself against his own thoughts. Amelia still wasn't sure what he wanted most, but she knew it was time to find out.

"Senator, you're not a man to mix sugar with medicine and I suspect you know very well the situation I'm facing. You are the crucial vote and without you, sir, we will lose. Yes, I have a bag full of tricks that may or may not work, but I'm not willing to risk the rights of women on a guess. So I must ask you in simple terms, Senator. What do you want from me? How can I get your vote?"

Amelia had never felt more exposed. She could take only a shallow breath and felt her heart beat against her chest. Horton caressed his knee as if bothered by an old injury. A clock ticked somewhere in the room and shadows from the oil lamp flickered on the walls.

"Do you know why I brought you to my private parlor?" he said at last.

Amelia shook her head, unable to utter a word.

The senator spoke for several minutes in honest, almost clinical, terms. Amelia felt dread at the base of her neck that seeped down her spine. He knew exactly what he wanted and had a specific reason for bypassing the receiving room for the intimacy of the parlor. As she listened, nodding where appropriate but not wanting to interrupt his impassioned plea, Amelia realized Sam was right yet again.

Sam had told her there would come a time when she had to define herself either as a woman or a lobbyist. He never fully believed she could be both. Amelia swallowed against a lump in her throat. In order to win the rights for all women, Amelia had to do what she told herself she'd never do to get a vote. Horton made his desire clear and left her with just one choice.

CHAPTER TWENTY-SEVEN

Amelia sighed as hot water splashed down on her shoulders and ran down her back. She slid down further into the steaming bath to let the water soak the ends of her untwisted hair.

"You can go. I can get out myself," Amelia said to the chamber girl she paid for extra duties. The girl gave a quick curtsy before placing a towel within reach of the bathtub and slipping from the room.

After leaving Horton, Amelia rushed home thinking of nothing but immersing herself in a cleansing bath. The heat and the fragrance of lilac dulled her thoughts as she closed her eyes. The steam helped soothe her thoughts, and she raised a wet hand to her forehead hoping to massage away the worry lines. Her eyes were still closed and she had started taking slow, deep breaths when she heard Boyd call out her name from the main room. Amelia jumped, banging her elbow against the hard porcelain.

Gathering her towel and senses, Amelia wrapped herself and cracked the door to her bedroom. She found Boyd pacing back and forth in front of the fireplace. At the sound of the door he turned, then he gasped and turned his back.

"Forgive the intrusion, Amelia. The maid left and I caught the door. I wasn't thinking straight. I didn't know you were . . . I shouldn't have just . . ." Boyd shook his head.

Amelia felt a surge of hostility. She wanted to tell him to

leave but she still needed him. "I'll be out in a few minutes," she said.

Ten minutes passed until Amelia emerged wearing a plain, cream-colored day dress and slippers. She'd pinned up her wet hair but loose strands stuck to the base of her neck. Boyd's gaze reminded her of a man admiring a painting. On another day, in other circumstances, his charms were pleasant, useful. At that moment, Amelia felt invaded by his uninvited and unwanted company.

"What are you doing here, Boyd?" Amelia asked, her voice tight.

Boyd rushed to her side and took her hands in his. "Your hands are so warm. And your cheeks are flushed. You look lovely."

"Yes, well, you already know what I was doing," Amelia said while worming her hands free.

Boyd looked at the ground but just long enough for convention. He then raised his head with unwavering confidence.

Amelia loathed his peacock stance. "I should throw you out," Amelia said. "Showing up uninvited to a woman's room at this hour is presumptuous to say the least. What do you think you're going to get from me, Boyd?"

Her directness affected Boyd as she'd hoped. He recoiled to the fireplace.

"I had no expectations other than to see you, Amelia. You must forgive the hour and my impetuousness. I couldn't wait until morning to see you. I haven't been able to think of anything but you since our parting." He then explained his desire to know how she fared with Horton.

"Is that why you're here?" she asked. "To find out about my dealings with Horton?"

Boyd turned to the fireplace and picked up the poker. He smashed the tip into the logs and sparks scattered and drifted up toward the chimney. "I . . ." he paused to replace the poker in the holder. Then he turned toward Amelia. "I couldn't stop thinking about my advice, my bad advice on how to handle the senator."

"Jealous of the senator or worried I won't help your career?" Amelia felt every bit as harsh as she sounded. She'd had enough.

Boyd's eyes widened. "My darling, I was thinking of your sweet face and soft lips and how I suggested you use . . . I mean . . . flaunt . . . for gain." He combed his hand through his hair.

Steam from the bath gave the room a stifling, misty quality. Heat from the fireplace and his gaze were oppressive and Amelia moved to the window. She slid the frame open, enjoying the rush of cold air, when she felt Boyd's arms cinch around her waist and he turned her from the window. Amelia gasped from the surprise.

"Darling, I'm sorry if my affection overwhelms you," Boyd said.

In a lighter mood she would have played the part of the damsel and said something about the passionate night air and his smell of manhood making her intoxicated. As it was, she was through with men grabbing her, moving her about like a doll. She felt smothered by the heat and the stench of pork on his breath. Boyd had enjoyed a nice dinner while she dealt with Horton.

Amelia removed Boyd's hands with force. "I want you to leave."

"I will. But first, you don't have to say anything but two words," Boyd blurted. He fell to one knee and pulled a gold ring from his pocket. "Miss Amelia Cooke, will you marry me?"

Surrounded by the lingering steam, the serious expression on Boyd's face, and her feet in slippers, Amelia felt like laughing. If she hadn't been so tired, she might have doubled over and laughed until her sides hurt and tears left pale lines in the rouge on her cheeks. Dealing with Stillman, then Horton, and finally Boyd McKenna on bended knee was more than she could take. Amelia used the strength she had left to keep from walking into her bedroom and locking the door.

"Please get up, Boyd. I can't give you an answer tonight."

Boyd stood and slipped the ring back into his pocket. "Then you'll think about it?" He seemed excited.

Amelia nodded. She would indeed think about it up to the point of the final vote and she no longer required further assistance from him. Until then, she needed to control her anger.

"Now really, Boyd, you should leave," Amelia said. She shifted to walk away, but Boyd hugged her. Amelia resisted, not wanting Boyd so close. But within his arms she felt kindness and the burdens of her long day overtook her. She fell against him and closed her eyes as he stroked her hair and kissed her forehead.

Boyd released her and strode to the far side of the room to retrieve his coat and hat. Amelia watched, unable to move from the window even as the frigid night air chilled her bare skin.

"Come away from the window, darling. You're shivering," Boyd said. He crossed back to Amelia and closed the window. Then he led her to the fire and rubbed her arms like a father warming a child after playing in the sea.

"Are you all right? Did I overwhelm you?" Boyd paused. "Or did something go wrong with the senator?"

A woman accustomed to candidness would sit with her hands neatly folded in her lap to share her deepest thoughts and ask for his opinion on the evening's events. Had she done what was best? Was he angry with her? Then she'd wait for his judgment like a felon before agreeing the matter best put to rest so they could press on. For Amelia, moving forward had always been a matter of putting one foot in front of the other. Boyd's question, though sincere, did not move her forward nor did she want to answer.

Amelia shook her head and said everything went well and the senator agreed to consider her points. Her strained tone was just the awkwardness of how Boyd found her and the shock of his proposal.

"You must admit I have reason to be overwhelmed." Amelia accompanied her vague response with a timid grin.

"Amelia, I don't need to know what happened with the senator. You must accept my apologies for suggesting that you do anything demeaning. If I'm a judge of character at all, then I know you both acted with integrity. Horton is a fine man and you are—" He paused and smiled. "You are magnificent."

"My dear Boyd, you really must go," Amelia said.

Boyd stopped at the door and kissed her cheek. "I'm so sorry for disrupting your bath." His expression appeared anything but apologetic. Amelia might have commented if not for his sudden move to check his watch. "Darn, I really have to leave. I have to finish some last minute revisions on 142A. That bill is going to be the death of me."

At the mention of 142A again, she asked about the bill.

"It's a land split of a national park. Senator Horton is trying to stop the Committee on Public Lands from selling off a few thousand acres for private development."

"Why? I thought your boss was in favor of growth?"

"Usually. But the project basically devastates a small community that was granted rights to the land in '72. At the time, no one cared that a few people were on the park's land. The park is huge. Now contractors want that area."

"So why not just have the developers pay to move the town?" Amelia asked.

"They've tried. The local businesses claim the final offer won't cover the relocation costs so they'll have to shut down. The senator's seen the numbers, and the town will definitely be ruined. He doesn't believe the Committee on Public Lands should take the land under these circumstances."

As a matter of precedent, the Committee on Public Lands made decisions based on personal profit rather than pity. Amelia thought of Stillman's aspirations to lead the committee. Under his rule, she knew nothing would change.

"What about help from the conservationists? They hate developers. Do they have any funds?" Amelia asked.

Boyd assured her that the conservation movement supported Bill 142A. As Boyd explained what he knew about the conservationists' point of view, Amelia understood even more than he. Deep pockets were in play.

With the topic finished, Boyd said goodnight, then put his finger under Amelia's chin and tipped her face to kiss him. Amelia again felt his tenderness and sincerity. She had done everything she could and some things she'd never imagined, and still she didn't know if she'd won the vote. Where Horton made no assurances, Boyd offered a lifelong promise. Over the years she'd been told countless times to marry because marriage made her respectable in her career choice. Boyd was a fine man with true ambition and intelligence. Some might consider him a little too young by societal standards, but soon enough he would be elected or appointed, which could only bolster her own ambition.

She watched him take a few steps, then realized the strain of the day had dulled her thoughts.

"Boyd," she called. He turned and rushed back with a smirk that made her chuckle.

"What park are we talking about?"

Boyd did little to hide his disappointment. "It's Yellowstone National Park in Montana. Might have to close a few shops, a school, and an orphanage." He moved closer. "Was that really all you wanted to ask?"

Amelia nodded and closed the door.

Moments earlier Bill 142A had meant nothing. Amelia stumbled into her parlor and stood in front of the fireplace to warm her numb body. In the face of growth, few cared if an orphanage, her orphanage, paid the price. Hadn't she herself pushed away her upbringing with great success? Amelia turned to admire her suite, the room Stillman once called too grand for a girl like her, and brushed her hand across the mantel. A box fell to the ground spilling the contents.

Amelia knelt beside the elephant-tusk trinket box Sam had left her in his will. She remembered the first time she saw the box in his parlor. How frightened she had been of Sam and wanting a new life, and yet determination carried her through. She thought of Sam and his mentorship, his true care, whenever she looked at the box. But she hadn't looked at the contents in years, perhaps too many.

The knotted rope had yellowed since Mistress Lucy presented her the gift on the day of her emancipation. Amelia ran her fingers over the bumps and curves. Other than the marks of time, the knots held firm. She picked up the rope, pressed it to her cheek, and then placed it back in the box.

As a child she'd wanted to hide away but she'd learned to tackle the world with fearless determination. Until that moment she'd never stopped to consider who taught her those grand lessons. But persistence and confidence came with a price; she'd learned that, too. Amelia took a moment to run through the characters still in play. Boyd thought he knew the markings of good character, but he was wrong. Horton, Stillman, even herself, were tainted by years of failures, losses, indiscretions, and temptations too strong to resist. Though she hadn't thought of Mistress Lucy or the matron in years, Amelia had the sudden urge to know if they were proud of her. She'd worked too hard to let anyone down.

Amelia crumpled onto her settee, lowered her head to her hands, and sobbed.

CHAPTER TWENTY-EIGHT

"Have you heard?" Maxine asked Amelia. They were seated at a table under the metal roof of the Central Market. Maxine didn't have much time and needed to meet someplace close to the newspaper even though the unending echo of the roof reminded Amelia of a train station and she found the market depressing. In the summer, the stands were filled with fresh, colorful fruits and eager shoppers. During the winter months, only a few weary farmers with wilted vegetables and a vendor selling overpriced coffee from a dirty pushcart set up shop.

"I hear lots of things," Amelia said. She sipped her coffee and added two lumps of sugar.

"Then hear this. The arguments are closed. The vote for our amendment is tomorrow morning. I like the official sound of that, 'our amendment.' Are you going to sit in the gallery?" Maxine asked.

Though Amelia had spent the morning confined to her hotel room, she'd already heard the news. Perla had sent a messenger.

"Perla doesn't want me anywhere but at Haven House," Amelia said. "Will you be at your desk with your pencil poised?"

"No. The editor only wants the political guys on this. He won't even think about a woman writing a piece. We're too biased." Maxine shrugged and said, "I don't know what he's talking about."

They both laughed, the tension and worry obvious in the short nervous bursts.

"It feels like our whole existence is hanging on this one moment," Maxine said, casting a wistful, unfocused gaze across the market. "Are you nervous?"

Amelia shrugged. She'd felt numb since learning of Bill 142A.

"Remember when we first met at Haven? I thought you were arrogant," Maxine said. When Amelia balked, Maxine added, "I mean that in a good way. Don't you remember how I followed you into the hallway?"

"To ask if I knew any good restaurants for your date that night?" Amelia had always wondered. "Why did you ask me that, anyway?"

Maxine chuckled. "I couldn't think of anything else fast enough. I just wanted to stop you and see if you were what I suspected."

"I'm afraid to ask," Amelia said.

Maxine ran her index finger around the lip of her cup. "You recommended a great Russian restaurant, said to order the *pierogi,* and then you said something that has stuck with me. It's why we're friends."

Amelia smiled. She always considered Maxine a friend and yet never knew what Maxine thought. They were too alike, too tough for their own good.

"You don't remember. I can tell by the way you're knotting your hair. Did you know you do that when you're under stress?"

"I don't." Amelia dropped the wad of hair in her grasp.

"Anyway, you said you knew how hard it was to work in a man's world. I hadn't said I wanted to be a journalist, not yet; you just knew."

Amelia knew about Maxine's goals because Perla had told her. "Well, I'm glad we're friends no matter how it happened."

Maxine raised her coffee cup. "A toast to us. Two women making history. Maybe you more than me at the moment, but I'm on your heels. First female political reporter at your service."

Amelia didn't raise her cup. She didn't like feeling responsible for Maxine's success. Perla's note also mentioned the enormity of the verdict, and yet Amelia wanted to know why women were determined to define themselves by one day, one vote.

"Aren't we more than one decision?" Amelia asked.

Maxine's eyes widened before she huffed. "You're just nervous and don't know what you're saying."

Thoughts from Amelia's sleepless night still swirled in her head. "What does all of this even mean? Do we really think that if we're granted the right to vote, men will somehow see us differently? Do you think your boss will suddenly drop to his knees and offer you a weekly political column?"

"No. Of course not," Maxine snapped, though Amelia caught the longing in her eyes. "This is just a first step. A huge first step." Maxine's eyes swept over Amelia. "Wait, what's going on? This isn't about the vote. You aren't the type to get introspective all of a sudden. What is it? Are you trying to have an excuse ready if you lose?"

Amelia felt the sting of Maxine's phrasing. *She* lost and *they* won.

The world debated the role of women as workers, as mothers, as wives. Women fought for years to prove to society and themselves that they could stand alongside men with the same rights and opportunities. But Amelia wondered if anyone, if she, had ever stopped to consider what makes a woman truly strong.

"I've labored and struggled for years under the guise that my voice, my ideas and opinions, my intellect are what give me authority in a world where men hold the reins. But what if that's not enough? What if we earn the vote and nothing changes? What if our influence rests somewhere else? Are we left with ideas and opinions and nothing more?"

Years of taking care of herself and fighting for what she wanted crushed in around her when Horton forced her to think about her role as a woman. She had defined herself by her work and now she loathed the idea that so much beyond her control created her only measure of success. In the early morning shadows haunted by the faint sounds of barking dogs and early trolleys, Amelia understood for the first time that she wanted more than what a mere vote could ever give.

"There must be something more," Amelia blurted, realizing her thoughts were trapped behind a maze of her own construction.

"What is this really about? A man? Isn't it always a man?" Maxine narrowed her eyes. "What happened between you and that Boyd kid?"

"You'll make a fine journalist. You have good instincts." Amelia chuckled at her easy out. She could blame her crisis of faith on a man, on the enemy, and put aside the bigger struggle that Maxine didn't really want to talk about. Few women did.

She told Maxine about Boyd and his proposal.

"You can't be considering marriage?" Maxine asked when she heard Amelia hadn't already said no.

"Why not?" Amelia asked. "Why shouldn't I be important to someone?"

Maxine drained her coffee, then pushed aside her cup. "So, now you're thinking about marriage and children? For Pete's sake, Amelia, you sound just like those frightened hens holding up babies, saying *what better way is there to influence the world than to raise children.* Is that what you want, to marry Boyd and have his brood?" Maxine placed her hand on Amelia's forearm. "You're just tired and worried, Amelia. I know you and this isn't the real you talking. I think you like Boyd a little more than you expected and now you feel guilty about having to turn him down. But don't. He knew who you were, and he's a grown-up. He'll learn a valuable lesson, that's all. We all have lessons to learn."

Amelia didn't reply. She let the silence pacify Maxine and listened as she launched into a monologue about Clancy. Clancy received high praise for reporting some fantastic gossip about the secretary of defense.

"Unfounded," Maxine said. "Clancy loves sensationalism and rarely checks facts."

Amelia pushed aside her cup. "I should go. Tomorrow's a big day and I still have a few loose ends to tie up."

Maxine leaned forward. "All better?" she asked. "No more silly thoughts about children or marriage, right? You don't need all of that to be important to someone. Look at me. I'm important to many." Maxine winked. "Besides, we're going to win. I know it."

Amelia fled. Her head felt heavy and she wanted to run to Haven House and talk to Perla about her doubts. With the vote less than twenty-four hours away, Haven House was pandemonium even if Perla could slip away for a minute. Amelia thought of her last conversation with Perla, about living with her choices and the regrets of life. As Maxine observed, nerves played a role in her sleepless night of second-guessing herself. But she truly wanted to believe that a bright future for womankind relied on more than one vote. Instead of braving Haven House, Amelia went back to her room. She had one last preparation to complete before the final outcome.

CHAPTER TWENTY-NINE

Even a child could interpret the importance of a bill by the activity level on the Senate floor, a rectangular room that provided light through a skylight and ventilation courtesy of steam-powered fans. The louder the motions and arguments, the more the senators cared about a bill. Stillman sat at his desk stunned by the turnout. For the vote to be called on the proposed 16th Amendment, an enormous and ground-breaking initiative, the Senate chamber wasn't even half full.

"I suggest the absence of a quorum," the lanky senator from Delaware called out.

For the third time, the swell of groans and squeaking chairs echoed up to the visitors' gallery.

After the second "quorum call" Stillman thought they were finished with stalling. Though he expected the typical stop-and-go tactic, he wasn't in the frame of mind to wait. As the clerk again began his slow methodical reading of senators' names to get an official attendance, Stillman knew he had no choice but to stay patient and look relaxed. Even Fitzwater declined helping Stillman in any way until the position became official. He would stand alone until the final tallied vote.

Without a majority turnout, there was indeed a lack of quorum needed, at least until the missing senators were forced to show up. Until the presiding officer ordered a vote, the rights of women didn't merit enough interest to cancel breakfast appointments or shooting practice. Reporters lurking in the corners muttered that the men were sending a message. Whatever the reasons—arrogance, stubbornness, or even fear— Stillman felt confident in victory and glanced to the visitors' gallery, where several women hovered. Amelia wasn't there.

The Senate visitors' gallery constituted the starting point of the women's elaborate relay. Two girls of just nineteen volunteered to take turns rushing up and down the steps from the gallery to report the votes as they were called. Then athletic women were stationed along the route from the Capitol all the way to Haven House. When the first runner arrived with reports of the stalling, her cheeks were crimson and damp. Amelia grew concerned that the dispatch might overly tax the ladies, but when the second courier arrived Amelia realized excitement, not exhaustion, caused the sweat and glow. After two hours there weren't any votes but at least Senator Stillman from Ohio stopped the third quorum delay.

The presiding officer accepted Stillman's call to rescind the quorum count and, by a unanimous floor decision, they voted to take a recess for lunch. The thought of eating made Stillman queasy and he declined offers to join a group going to McGregor's Pub for prime rib and a pint. The banality of eating seemed inappropriate and infuriating given the situation. Unable to do anything more than politely decline under the guise of work, Stillman went back to his office. His assistant, Phillip, was ill so Stillman's front reception room was empty. Knowing this didn't prevent him from jumping when there was a loud knock on the door frame.

"Come in," Perla called out over the blustering of the board and a few special invitees huddled in Perla's office. Haven House had never been as full. Ladies stood shoulder to shoulder in the hallways and common rooms, and those who had traveled from as far as Wyoming crammed the porches and spilled out onto the sidewalks. A uniformed policeman marched back and forth swinging his billy club to keep the crowd moving. As long as the women on the public street kept walking, the policeman couldn't arrest anyone for loitering.

A woman wearing a hand-knit, multicolored scarf around her neck stood in the open doorway to Perla's office. According to her report, the senators were taking a lunch break.

"What do these dad-blasted vermin think they're doing?" Marion shouted.

"Marion, please. We have to keep our wits," Perla said and then looked at Amelia.

The break was likely just because of hunger, but the continued delays were alarming and Amelia saw the desperation in Perla's eyes. She wanted Amelia to help keep the ladies calm.

Amelia hoped to add levity to the somber mood by saying, "I think the men are scared and that's why they keep stalling. Why stall if we've lost? They'd want to get that done quickly and move on. No, I believe we have a chance and the men are shaking in their muddy boots. Plus, better they're well fed and not distracted. You know a hungry man has no sense."

Perla nodded her appreciation to Amelia for the enthusiastic agreement that swept across the room. Soon Amelia's comments were shouted down the hall and out into the yard. By the time the message reached the ladies on the sidewalk outside Perla's office, the women were on the verge of victory.

"The lobbyist lady says we're going to win," Amelia heard through the window. She moved closer to the window to watch the mayhem.

Stillman had been standing by the window with his hands tucked under his arm pits when Horton knocked and startled him. Horton rarely dropped in on anyone for a visit. Stillman thought waiting for the vote created the depth of his anxiety, but seeing Horton standing in his office doorway, Stillman felt the enormity of the moment crush in around him.

"So nice to see you, Senator. Would you like to sit down?" Stillman asked, unable to move toward the door but pleased his voice didn't crack.

Horton declined. "I only stopped by to tell you that I've given this amendment a great deal of consideration. I appreciated your candor and look forward to working with you in the future," he said, then left without waiting for a reply.

Stillman turned back to the window and considered Horton's remark. Was he conceding Stillman's victory or mentioning their colleagueship as a consolation prize because he knew Stillman was going to lose? Stillman sighed and his breath fogged the window. He reached out with his index finger and drew a question mark on the frosted glass.

Maxine and Perla examined a list of possible media questions while the others in Perla's office fidgeted. Nicolette mentioned the clearing weather, which received only grunts and nods. Marion told a short story about a puppy, which got a giggle only from Marion herself. Lottie suggested they could play a card game, and a few of the ladies agreed while Amelia retreated into the dark corner. Amelia had played enough games to last a lifetime.

Stillman felt encouraged; the final game was at last getting under way. Presiding Officer John Inglass had a square body with a thin mustache twisted up on each side so that Stillman thought he looked like a cartoon villain. Along with working with the clerk to call roll and tally the votes, leading the Senate proceedings meant getting the men in their seats. Stillman watched Inglass dispatch the bellman. Once he set the bellman loose, the senators had just fifteen minutes to get to the floor for the vote.

Ringing from a passing milk cart sounded to Amelia like the official Capitol bell as she looked around the room filled with women. They were quiet for the moment, lost in their own thoughts of waiting and wishing, so she closed her eyes and imagined the scene at the Capitol. Since the Senate didn't have a majority attendance, the bellman would trot up and down the halls waving a hand bell to round up the troops. Amelia once watched the bellman followed by the stragglers shuffling toward the Senate chambers like children heading to bed. Staff managers waited by the entrance until the room filled and then closed and locked the doors. The Senate chamber doors were kept locked until the final count tallied and a decision announced.

Stillman's seat by the exit meant he heard the clack of the bolt keeping them trapped in the chamber. Amid handshaking and greetings, the men took their seats with no real urgency. Horton stood chatting with the senator from Mississippi, his foot propped up on the desk's leg like a cowboy by a railing, and Inglass laughed with the Republican from Rhode Island. Stillman wanted to shout for Inglass to hurry and start the proceedings. Instead, Stillman drummed his fingers and gnawed on his bottom lip, suddenly wondering if women around the country were doing the same. He could see gaggles huddled in small rooms, drawing energy and solace from each other in a way the men around him would never do. The posturing continued and Stillman just sat and watched. By the time the whole lot at last found their seats and the clerk called for the first senator, William Ackerman, to cast his vote, beads of perspiration ran down Stillman's back.

★　★　★　★　★

As Amelia dabbed a handkerchief across her damp forehead, one of the runners burst into Perla's office waving a piece of paper. The first few votes were cast.

"Five to three in our favor!"

Amelia kept herself separate from the cheers and hugs. It was premature to celebrate.

Stillman didn't like the jovial atmosphere even though a cheerful mood during a vote wasn't uncommon. Those on both sides of the argument seemed secure in their victory, and yet Stillman thought such an important measure deserved austerity, almost reverence. He wasn't the only one.

"A travesty, if you ask me. I don't abide by the women wanting their way, but I don't see a call for disrespect, either," Stillman's nearest neighbor said.

The old-timer from Indiana made a good point, one that Stillman openly agreed with. The women fought with bravery and deserved a fair showing or at least an acknowledgement for their hard work. Stillman was ashamed of his colleagues, even as he tallied the votes.

So far they stood at fifteen to seven on the side of appointing Stillman to his chair position. Fenton cast his vote and Stillman relaxed a bit more. The race had started as predicted even if the attitude was distasteful.

Amelia had predicted Fenton's vote but the ladies nevertheless seemed unnerved.

"Do we have enough votes left? What's the tally?" Maxine asked to no one in particular. Sour expressions replaced the early cheering.

"Amelia, did you know about Fenton? What about Gage? You said we have Gage, right?" Marion asked.

Amelia sat with a pleasant grin pasted to her ruby lips. Even beyond Perla's warning that the women might lash out, Amelia knew the ladies' questions were rhetorical to help them process the information. No one expected real answers, at least not yet.

Gage's vote in favor of the amendment wasn't much of a surprise, though Stillman still wondered what he'd done to offend him. However, he could barely hear Horton's name over the beating of his own heart. Horton stood and buttoned his jacket before casting his vote in a loud, deep voice. Stillman sunk against his chair and thought of Amelia.

The sound of the entry table crashing to the floor made everyone jump. Perla rushed to the door and was almost knocked over by a thick woman in a long black overcoat. Horton cast his vote but the runner was too nervous to look. She handed the folded square to Perla and the ladies turned. Perla held her breath as she opened the paper.

Perla kept her head down as tears slid down her cheek. She looked up with wide eyes and found Amelia.

"Yea," she said in a soft, but clear, voice. "Horton voted in our favor."

Women rushed Perla and Amelia, and Amelia felt a crush of arms around her. Ladies sobbed and applauded as the news spread inside and outside the house.

"You did it," Perla mouthed to Amelia over Marion who was squeezing Perla around the middle.

Amelia brushed tears from her eyes. The vote wasn't over and she had to remain in control, and yet she had never been more stunned. She succeeded. The shock and elation were overwhelming, and Amelia turned toward the window to wipe her eyes. Regardless of the final count, she'd done it.

"Are you okay?" Perla asked. Perla put her hand on Amelia's

shoulder and Amelia turned and nodded. Perla kissed Amelia on the cheek. "I'm very proud of you, my dear," Perla said.

Fresh tears streamed down Amelia's cheeks.

Stillman did the math while waiting for the clerk to refill the water glasses. Losing after such a public quest for glory meant a long fall, especially with Fitzwater leading the charge. Bumping down the rungs included extra subcommittee meetings in small rooms that smelled like old pickles and wasting time on meaningless initiatives that had no hope of passing. Enduring the drudgery as a young senator was easy because his career waited ahead. He had made his play, went all in, and nothing waited ahead but time served and retirement. Stillman barely heard when the voting resumed with Senator Bradley Jenkins, "Dodger" to his friends like Amelia.

If Amelia regretted anything that afternoon, it was the short time the women had to celebrate. Marion was the first to notice silence in the hallway. Louder than any of the cheering, the quiet had the feel of a fresh burial plot after the family had left. A young girl whom Amelia recognized as one of the runners at the visitors' gallery stood in the doorway. Dirt stained the hem of her dress and coal dust and mud stuck to her face.

Nicole reached out and took the young girl's hand. "Dear, you look like you've seen a ghost."

"No," the girl whispered. "Senator Jenkins voted no."

Amelia shook her head. "You must have it wrong. Dodger was a *yes*. He believed in our cause. He was a *yes* from the beginning."

The girl just stood shaking her head and Amelia thought of Dodger's many followers lined up like a set of domino tiles. The first tile was pushed over. They could do nothing now but wait for the final count.

Chapter Thirty

Disbelief and puzzlement ricocheted around the house until the type of whispering usually heard during a church sermon broke the silence. The sighs turned to sobs and then to grumbling as the realization of the situation set it. When the pitch turned hostile, Amelia steadied herself.

"What just happened, Amelia? How did you lose?" Maxine asked. Amelia cringed at the accusation coming from a friend.

Amelia didn't know what to say. No one factored in losing Dodger and his loyal disciples, who jumped like rats from a burning ship. Dodger's *no* meant their *no.*

"Look at this." A woman pushed through the door waving the afternoon newspaper. She read the front-page headline aloud: "Lobbyist Buys Jenkins."

Amelia felt their eyes bore into her flesh as they passed the newspaper around and ultimately gave it to Perla, who told everyone to settle down while she looked at the article. Perla winced as she read. When she finished, she set the newspaper on her desk and placed a protective hand over the print.

"The *Post* claims that Amelia gave Senator Jenkins stock options in Atlantic Cable in exchange for his vote. There are no details or mention of any sources."

"That's a lie," Amelia said. "I never bribed Dodger."

"Who wrote that drivel?" Maxine asked. "Wait, let me guess. Clancy Doyle. And no doubt he spoke with Dodger this morning to pressure him for a quote. Clancy loves to let his victims see the blade coming."

Perla nodded.

"Dodger was worried about bad press," Amelia said. "He told me as much when we met. With Clancy's story, he couldn't vote in our favor. If he did, he'd only confirm the rumor."

"At least we know why Dodger changed his vote, but that doesn't tell us who started the rumor," Perla said.

"I say she's the one who's lying," Vertie said. She stood and wagged her finger at Amelia. "Why did you bribe him, you wicked woman?"

Amelia glanced at Perla, who nodded. Earlier, in the empty house shadowed by the rising dawn, Amelia and Perla discussed the two possible outcomes. Losing created a volatile situation so Perla suggested Amelia prepare a speech. "Likely the one and only chance you'll get to defend yourself," Perla had said. The time had arrived, and even though a competent orator, Amelia wondered how she could say anything eloquent after all that had just transpired.

"Ladies, please, if I can have your attention for just a moment. I never offered Dodger any stock for his vote. He supported women's rights and was prepared to vote in favor of the amendment even before I spoke with him. You may not believe me, but I'm telling the absolute truth. What happened today is distressing. No less so for me, I assure you. But there was always a chance, a good chance, that we were going to lose. I tell you with all my heart that I did what I thought was best for all of us. Today we aren't the victors but the fight continues. The war isn't over unless we raise the white flag. I'm not giving up and neither should you."

The reply came as an explosion of frustrated, angry remarks about Amelia, men, the movement, and the unfairness of life in general. "This way," Perla shouted over the commotion, beckoning Amelia from the doorway. Amelia followed her into the hallway.

"Blocking the hallways is a fire hazard," Perla called out. "Please clear the corridor, ladies. We don't want the policeman outside to give us a fine."

As the women shuffled by, a petite lady stopped in front of Amelia. "Thank you, Miss Cooke, for all your hard work. I believe you. I know you did your best."

Amelia nodded. Through the front windows Amelia saw women draped on the porch and scattered around the yard and sidewalk. They were weeping and holding each other. Their pain was unnerving, and Amelia looked away.

Perla beckoned Amelia to the stairwell. "You got Horton. How did you do it?" she asked.

Amelia hadn't wanted to discuss her methods but in the wake of their loss she felt obligated. "I told him the truth, Perla. The God's honest truth. That's all he asked. He didn't want fluff or anecdotes, or me in a compromising way though I thought as much for a few moments. He actually wanted my opinion as a colleague, a professional, as a woman. At first I didn't think I could go through with it.

"I know that sounds ridiculous, but sharing my own thoughts and not the one I'm paid to have felt like giving a piece of myself away. After all these years, all my blustering, I'd never shared what I truly think with anyone. It was terrifying. Just the same, I told him everything. I confessed how I leveraged Gage's dead son and what the vote meant specifically to my career. I shared what life was like for us, Perla, as women barred from clubs and trapped by the societal rules of convention dreamed up by men. I told him about growing up hearing over and over how girls were too fragile to kick a ball and too stupid to understand math. Horton didn't say a word. He listened and when I was done, he thanked me and asked me to leave. I

303

thought . . ." Amelia just shook her head. She thought he considered her a lunatic and the epitome of why women weren't rational enough to vote.

"The truth does have some advantages," Perla mused.

"Who knew?" Amelia said and enjoyed watching Perla smile. Perla then opened the front hall closet and Amelia saw it was empty.

"I got prepared. Just in case," Perla said. She pulled a lever hidden in the corner and a panel in the back of the closet opened. "This tunnel was put in during the war. Haven House harbored slaves and a few gunrunners sympathetic to our cause. We were a good cover."

The tunnel led to the back of the house, where Amelia was to wait ten minutes to give Perla time to gather the ladies to the front porch for a pep talk. Amelia could then slip out the back without getting mobbed.

"And then what? Do you really think I need to leave the city?" Amelia asked.

Perla nodded. "At least for a few months. What happened isn't your fault, but don't we all want someone to blame when things don't go our way? Human nature, I suppose. Let's give the ladies some time. Mob mentalities are frightening, even mobs in skirts. I don't want anything unfortunate to happen. Think of this as a little vacation. You've earned it."

Amelia put on her cape. "I'm truly sorry, Perla. I'm sorry I let you down. I'm sorry everything had to turn out like this."

"I know you are. But for now, it's as you said. We're still here to press on another day. The battle isn't over; we continue to fight."

Amelia had spoken about forging on as a means to calm the crowd, and yet the true unwavering dedication and tenacity of wise and powerful women such as Perla gave her goose bumps. Amelia stood proud beside those who personified greatness with such elegance and strength. Tears burned in Amelia's eyes.

"I'm going to miss you, my dear," Perla said. "No matter what anyone tries to say, we all lost today. Not just you. Our loss today wasn't because of one person."

Perla hugged Amelia. After one last squeeze Amelia pulled away and whispered, "Wasn't it?"

Amelia ducked into the closet and Perla closed the door. The closet led to a tunnel lit only by slivers of sun through carefully placed cuts in the wood. She shuffled down the passageway searching for the light, but when Amelia bumped her head on a low beam she paused. The tightness of the space, the grief and anger left in her wake, closed in around her and she swayed, fearing she might faint. Amelia wiped her face with her sleeve and let the darkness wash over her. She wanted to stay safe in the tunnel, hidden away, but Amelia believed Perla knew best. In the morning, she'd leave the city at least for a little while, at least long enough for the fresh wounds to heal.

CHAPTER THIRTY-ONE

Amelia watched Boyd approach in long, purposeful strides. His broad shoulders and lean physique conveyed a confident strength that Amelia again admired. She knew he would go far in his career and in life.

Boyd had sent a messenger with a note to meet at the Botanic Gardens greenhouse. He thought she might enjoy the openness of the glass dome and could use the smell of fresh plants and flowers. Amelia found encouragement in the lush jungle greenery and delicate buds that lined the stone paths even as she steadied herself for talking with Boyd. She hoped the peaceful lull of sweet plants might help soften what she had to tell him.

Boyd swept Amelia into his arms. "Darling. I'm so sorry."

Since the final vote count, Amelia sent Maxine a note about her leaving D.C. for a vacation and then barricaded herself in her room to fend off interview requests and suggestive invitations to consolation dinners from those she now owed favors. The morning news reported that after the count, representatives from the NWSA had tarred and feathered the failed lobbyist, Amelia Cooke, in the recesses of Haven House and were now quietly licking their wounds. Amelia knew better.

Amelia took Boyd's arm as they strolled beside a tangle of yellow plants. She let him rant about the failed amendment for several minutes. He expressed his opinion with waving arms and condemnations for those who opposed the vote. With a gentle, but firm, hand Amelia quieted him and reminded him that using names in public wasn't a good idea.

"You never know if the 'blustering cowhide's' wife is looking at flowers in the next row," Amelia said.

"I have so much to learn," he said with a soft eagerness.

"Boyd, I can't marry you." She had rehearsed a more subtle approach that included listing his attributes and reminding him of his youth and future prospects. Among the freshness of the plants, her practiced lines felt disingenuous.

Boyd stopped walking, forcing Amelia to face him. He grasped her hands and held them to his heart. "Losing the vote makes no difference to me, to us and our future. I don't care that you lost or what that means for your career. I only care about you."

Though meant as a kind sentiment, frustration by the overall situation, more than his comment, fueled her reaction.

"Do you honestly believe that my not wanting to marry you has anything to do with the election results? You sound arrogant, Boyd, as if now that I'm a loser I don't feel worthy of your proposal. I assure you, my answer has nothing to do with the events of yesterday other than perhaps my coming to my senses."

His shoulders drooped.

"I'm sorry," Amelia said. "I didn't mean it like that. I just meant—"

"Amelia, I don't think you're a loser." He paused. "I was just hoping . . ." Boyd narrowed his eyes and shook his head. "I was hoping that after yesterday you might have changed your mind. If you had wanted to marry me, you would have said *yes* the minute I asked."

In that moment Amelia saw the real Boyd, honest and hopeful with heartfelt aspirations. She sometimes forgot that ambitious men started out with rosy cheeks. Even Stillman once had ideals and passion. The illusions of success and greed were tempting and she had witnessed too many rosy cheeks pale and wither. Amelia seized Boyd's shoulders.

"Boyd, Senator Horton is a good man. We didn't find any scandals because there aren't any. Stay with Horton. Learn from him. It's not too late for you to really make a difference. You don't have to turn into Stillman . . ." She paused. "Or me. You're a sincere person and I want you to achieve greatness because of your integrity, not despite it."

Boyd took Amelia's hands from his shoulders and held them between his own. "You're talking as if I'll never see you again. Can't we stay friends? A fine, beautiful, successful woman once told me it's always good to have friends when you're new in town," Boyd said.

"Of course we're still friends. It's just that I'm leaving D.C. for a while and don't know when I'll be back. I need a break," Amelia said.

Boyd raised her hands and kissed the insides of her wrists just above the band of her white glove. A small flutter tickled her spine and in that moment she envied the woman who would someday say *yes* to Boyd McKenna's proposal.

"Where are you going?" he asked.

"I don't know. But my travel trunk is packed and tomorrow morning I'm going to the station to get on the first train. Who knows, maybe I'll stop in Somerville, Massachusetts."

"Not a bad place to end up."

"Or start," Amelia said.

They strolled again arm in arm and she enjoyed the calmness.

"Amelia, I have to ask you something. You said Horton is a good man, but his vote. He didn't . . . I mean you and Horton . . . he didn't ask you to . . . or you didn't suggest . . ."

Amelia put his mind at ease and explained just as she had to

Perla. "I learned a valuable lesson about integrity. I hope you have, too," she said.

They reached the far end of the greenhouse and gazed out between the pristine white beams of the dome. In the distance Amelia could see the spires and the Statue of Freedom perched on top of the Capitol rotunda.

"The Capitol's magnificent," Boyd said.

"That's just a building. Nothing more than wood and stone. What's magnificent is what goes on inside." Amelia paused against the lump in her throat. She'd arrived ten years earlier with her own wide-eyed aspirations of change, of rising above her station and becoming a person of power and influence. "I guess I never thought I'd end up here. I don't like to fail."

Boyd leaned over and kissed her cheek. When he straightened, she saw the wide, bright smile he'd had the night they first met.

"Amelia Cooke, the only person who can say it's the end is you. You only fail now if you stop trying."

On the busy sidewalk in front of the Willard Hotel, Amelia wished Boyd a happy, successful life. He looked sad but hopeful and more understanding than she thought possible for his years. Amelia felt confident Boyd would keep his promise to stay on with Horton and follow Horton's path. The time had come for Amelia to go, and she had just one good-bye left.

CHAPTER THIRTY-TWO

Business travelers in black overcoats shouted at porters and dragged worn trunks to loading areas of the Baltimore & Ohio Railroad Station. Amelia arranged for her luggage at the hotel, so, unfettered but for her personal shoulder bag, she stood by a pillar between the tracks and scanned the crowd. She'd sent a note but she wasn't sure if he'd come to see her off.

"Still standing in the way, I see," Amelia heard behind her.

She turned around. "Good afternoon, Senator."

Stillman had his right arm in his pocket and left tucked behind his back like a guard at attention. The wool of his coat pulled tight across his chest.

"I like it when you call me by my title. It feels more civilized," Stillman said.

"And you're nothing if not civilized. I seem to recall . . ." They fell so easily into their old patterns but she wanted a clean slate. "Congratulations on your chairmanship, Senator. The Committee on Public Lands is a most fitting appointment," Amelia said.

"Couldn't agree more. I'm already looking at a summer house in Newport."

"Just one?"

He chuckled. "I might just miss that wit of yours. Must say I was a little surprised by your note. Are you hiking up your skirts and making a dash for it? Doesn't seem like your style, Amelia."

Amelia waited but there wasn't the smugness she expected.

310

He looked concerned. "No skirt hiking; just taking a break. But before I left I thought you'd want to follow up your note of condolence by personally pouring salt in the wound. I'm surprised you didn't come with flowers," she said.

"Who said I didn't?" He pulled his arm from behind his back and handed her a bunch of fresh carnations.

Amelia laughed. "You didn't."

He joined in her amusement and nodded. "I did, but I don't feel good about it."

They laughed together as old friends, old lovers.

"You put up a good fight, Amelia, old gal," Stillman said.

"Not good enough, it seems." Amelia took a quick sniff of the flowers, then tucked them in her bag.

Stillman shook his head. "It wasn't me, if that's what you're thinking. I didn't send that nonsense to Clancy. And, frankly I'm still baffled by Horton."

Amelia nodded. "What's done is done. The only path is forward."

"Just like that?" he asked.

Amelia held his stare and was again surprised. "Why, Senator Stillman, if I didn't know better I'd say you admire me just a little. Could it be that after all this time you actually respect me?" She grinned. "Or maybe you're just flushed from all the noise." To make her point, a sharp whistle sounded from the next track.

Stillman glanced at the ground before looking up. "I will concede, Miss Cooke, that you exceeded expectations and perhaps for a moment . . . a brief moment, it seemed I had lost. But to say I was in any way . . ." He stopped and furrowed his brows. "Why are you looking at me like that?"

Amelia tilted her head. "What do you mean? Like what?"

"Like I'm saying something funny and you're trying not to laugh." He seemed honestly confused.

311

"You can't do it, can you?"

"I resent—"

"Relax. I'm not going to force you to give me a compliment," Amelia said.

"I will give a compliment if someone has earned a compliment," he stated as if speaking to his aide.

Amelia thought of the coat-check room at the men's club. She could easily influence Stillman but she no longer wanted what he offered. She wanted more.

Stillman seemed to sense her newfound resolve. "Well, I should be on my way. I have several appointments today," he said.

Amelia glanced toward an approaching train. "I'm honored you could fit me in."

Stillman lifted his head. He looked tired but she saw the same forceful stare from so many years before. "I'm only going to say this once," he said. "If you repeat it I will deny everything. Are you listening?"

"Always." She smiled.

Stillman smiled back. "You're one of a kind, that's for sure."

"Is that what you'd deny if repeated?" Amelia asked.

He rattled his head. "No. Of course not. What I want to say is that—" he stopped and fixed his eyes on Amelia's. "You lost but you should be proud of yourself, Amelia. Very proud. You were a worthy opponent."

Amelia leaned forward and kissed Stillman on the cheek. He held her gaze for a moment longer and then said, "When you feel ready to slink back into town, look me up. Maybe I can hire you."

"As tempting as that sounds, I'm not sure when I'll be back."

Stillman sniffed. "I don't think you could stay away for long. You and I are alike, Amelia. We both do whatever it takes. It's one of our finest qualities."

"Goodbye, Senator. Take care."

Amelia watched Edward Stillman weave through the crowd until he was just another one of the black coats swaying like prairie grass. She had at last earned Stillman's respect, even if she knew they were not alike.

The train pulled to a stop and sighed before steam billowed around her. For a moment she was concealed, then the white fog cleared. Amelia let the conductor help her on to the train and she settled into her first-class seat by the window. An elderly gentleman sat down beside her and gave a quick greeting before snapping open his newspaper. Amelia thought of Sam and his true kindness as she gazed out past the tracks to where traffic bustled on Constitution Avenue. A man she met by chance had helped her more than he ever knew. Over what felt more like a lifetime than just a mere few weeks, she had answered what she'd always questioned about herself.

There was a line she wouldn't cross. There were causes and ideals more important than herself and her own success, and she'd grown beyond the young girl longing for a voice. The whistle sounded and the train lunged forward. Whatever waited ahead, Amelia conceded Stillman was right about one very important fact. She was indeed proud of herself and all that she'd accomplished, even if no one ever knew the truth or remembered her name.

CHAPTER THIRTY-THREE

In the six months since leaving D.C., Amelia had grown to appreciate the view from her kitchen window. The quiet grasslands and rise of proud trees stretched all the way up to the base of the Smoky Mountains, and she enjoyed watching the sparrows and warblers after a heavy rain. Amelia selected the one-story cottage in Morristown, Tennessee, because the white picket, storybook fence and front porch reminded her of a small Haven House. Choosing the house was far simpler than how she ended up in Morristown.

Amelia rested her elbows on her kitchen table and took a sip of hot tea as she flipped through the *Morristown Gazette*. The front page included announcements for the pig auction and town hall meeting to discuss a third schoolhouse. She had started a petition for an additional school on behalf of families in the expanding east end of town. Other local news included the obituaries of people she didn't know and crop rotation schedules, so Amelia flipped to the center section where national news was reported by columnist Mitchell Burn. She'd decided to stay in Morristown because of Mitchell Burn.

The first train out of the city went to Springfield, Illinois, where Amelia stayed a few nights. She felt restless and didn't want to settle anywhere. Part of her believed that she could return to D.C. faster if she kept moving. Weather directed her travels south and she drifted through nameless towns in Arkansas and Mississippi. When Amelia landed in Morristown, she was headed to Nashville and stayed only to wait for the morning train. In the hotel, she picked up a copy of the *Morristown Gazette.*

On the second page she found national coverage, informative and well-written, by a reporter named Mitchell Burn. The following morning, Amelia delayed her plans in order to meet the industrious, small-town reporter. Amelia and Mitchell became instant friends. She stayed for a few days and then the days turned to weeks. They enjoyed frequent dinners together discussing their lives and the world outside of Morristown. By far, Mitchell Burn's biggest story was Yellowstone National Park.

Amelia gave Mitchell the lead on the story. According to Mitchell's report, to the surprise of many in Washington, the Committee on Public Lands voted against selling any Yellowstone land. Though allegations of kickbacks were denied by the chairman, Amelia knew Stillman had earned his summer home from the well-funded conservationists.

A knock on the door startled her. She wasn't expecting anyone until evening plans with Mitchell. Amelia walked down the short hallway past mounted photos of her and Mitchell taken in front of the magic tent at the traveling carnival.

Amelia opened her front door. Maxine stood in the doorway in a pale-yellow day dress covered in soot and dust.

"Maxine. It's wonderful to see you. You got my letter. But I didn't think you'd trek all the way to Tennessee." Amelia embraced Maxine but the reception was stiff.

Maxine followed her inside to the front room. Amelia offered to take Maxine's bag and suggested she have a cup of tea.

"No to both. This won't take long," Maxine said. She sat down on the sofa, then slipped her large travel bag from her shoulder and set it on the floor. Maxine looked around the parlor and picked up a ceramic tiger from the coffee table. She examined it and set it down, grimaced, and then glared at a bookshelf filled with leather volumes and a small collection of hand-painted bud vases.

"I wouldn't believe this was your house if I wasn't seeing it for myself. Really, violet curtains? My, you've changed." Maxine glared at Amelia. "Or have you?"

Amelia sat across from Maxine on the facing sofa and asked if she was all right. "You're obviously not here for a social visit," Amelia said.

Maxine dug through her bag until she found an envelope. "This is why I'm here. As if you don't already know."

Amelia suspected what was inside as she took the envelope and pulled out a hand-written note that held just a few lines.

"I suppose you didn't have blank paper or any time to get some. Why else would you be sloppy enough to use your custom stationery," Maxine said.

"You don't understand," Amelia said, careful to keep her tone from sounding pleading. She wasn't going to ask for forgiveness.

"You're right. I don't understand. How could you do it? How could you send that note to Clancy? You knew he'd print that rubbish about bribing Dodger without checking anything. You knew Dodger would see the news, have to back out, and his cronies would go with him. You sabotaged us. Were you paid off? Is that how you bought this house?"

"No, Maxine. It's nothing like that. I can explain—"

Maxine held up her hand. "I don't want to hear anything from you. Because of you I'm still a secretary." Maxine ran her hand over her wrinkled skirt. "We should have marched and gone on hunger strikes instead of wasting our time with you. When I think of all I've been through for this cause, I could just spit at you."

"We've all been through a lot, not just you," Amelia said.

316

Maxine pursed her lips. "What a hypocrite you are. As if you ever cared about anyone or anything other than yourself. You sold us all out to the highest bidder, you mongrel."

Amelia winced at the raunchy term. "Did you come here to slander me?"

Maxine leaned forward. Her wide eyes seethed with fury. "I came here to let you know I found out about your double dealings and to tell you what I think of you."

"Will you let me explain? Will you listen?" Amelia said.

Maxine shook her head. "Why should I listen to more of your lies? Now that I'm here, looking at you and what you've become, I pity you."

Amelia suggested that if she wasn't going to listen then she should leave. Maxine rose, seized her bag, and strode to the door without hesitation. She flung open the door and stopped in front of Amelia.

"I haven't decided if I'm going to tell the others. We're already struggling to get back on our feet thanks to you. If our opponents find out about what you did, they'd just have more to laugh at. I had to pay off Clancy in more than dollars to keep him quiet. I hope you're happy. You're despicable."

Amelia shut the front door and went back to the kitchen. For months she'd worried whether Clancy was dumb enough to keep her note. Having the answer closed that chapter of her life, even if Maxine hadn't let her explain. Amelia wondered if anyone ever would.

With Stillman at the helm of public lands, Amelia knew exactly what he'd do with Bill 142A. His finest quality was his loyalty to himself and his greed. The conservationists were too well funded for Stillman to ignore. He didn't care about orphans thrown into the street, and yet the children and town were safe with him because he always sold to the highest bidder. Always. Amelia could at least rely on his greed.

If women won the vote then the Committee on Public Lands got a different chairman, one who might weigh the arguments and decide growth outweighed the needs of a few, the more obvious choice for an expanding nation. Amelia couldn't stop asking herself if a few children really matter as compared to all women gaining the right to vote. The moment she found her answer, she knew Stillman had to win the appointment. The women had to lose the vote.

Women wanted the vote to have control in the world but in their noble and righteous quest, Amelia realized that women already had the greatest influence. Maxine had even influenced her decision by her offhand comment the day before the vote. What was more important in shaping a nation than rearing the next generation? The women who raised Amelia couldn't vote and yet she owed her resilience, her confidence and voice in the world to their tutelage and care. They had given her a chance, her only chance, and in that realization Amelia knew that women already influenced the world. True lasting success came in the form of shaping generations of brave, empowered women with or without the right to cast a ballot. She thought of Abigail Adams and how far women had come in one hundred years and imagined what the next one hundred held. In the end, the orphans, not the cause, needed her more.

Amelia went back to the kitchen and warmed her tea with hot water. She sat back down in front of the newspaper article about Yellowstone. In the years ahead she'd press the news article in a decorative book alongside ticket stubs from memorable family outings, postcards addressed to Mitchell and Amelia Burn, and photos of a smiling boy with auburn hair.

By restricting the expansion of Yellowstone Park, several small businesses were spared destruction. The local grocery, a library, and a large orphanage housing 200 youths remain open in the city of Cooke, Montana.

Amelia looked at the grainy photo above the caption. She could just make out the third window from the end and thought of all the time she'd spent in the dormitory. She remembered the lost young girl who found herself, and though she didn't have an ideal upbringing, Amelia could still picture her view from that window, the place where she gazed out at the world and dreamed of someday making a difference.

CHAPTER THIRTY-FOUR

THE NEW YORK TIMES
WOMEN'S SUFFRAGE WINS BECAUSE OF
A MOTHER'S LETTER

WASHINGTON, August 18, 1920—Today Tennessee became the thirty-sixth state to ratify the Susan B. Anthony Suffrage Amendment. The win, by a margin of just one vote, makes the constitutional change effective in time for the 17,000,000 women of the country to vote in November's presidential election. Miss Alice Paul, Chairman of the Woman's Party Members, said ultimately the women's amendment hinged on "an 11th-hour declaration" by the young Tennessee state legislator Harry Burn. The 24-year-old representative from East Tennessee, who two years earlier had become the youngest member of the state legislature, voted to ratify the amendment after he received a letter from his mother.

Tennessee was the last state needed after the U.S. Senate voted by a count of 56 to 25 to adopt the constitutional amendment back in June. The amendment, having already been passed by the U.S. House of Representatives, 304 to 89, was then given to the states for ratification. "Now the question is whether the people of these states are competent to settle the question for themselves," said Senator Wadsworth from New York as to the success of state ratification.

Burn defended his last-minute decision in a speech to the assembly. For the first time he publicly expressed his personal support of universal suffrage, declaring, "I believe we had a moral and legal right to ratify." But he also made no secret of his mother's influence and her crucial role in the story of women's rights in the United States. "I know that a mother's advice is always safest for her boy to follow," he explained, "and my mother wanted me to vote for ratification."

Supporters of the movement are touting the letter, printed below, as a powerful example of the significance of motherhood.

August 15, 1920.

DEAR SON—

Father and I are fine and your hound is well enough to dig up my herb garden. I hope you're healthy and remembering to take evening air before the wretched mosquitoes claim the night for themselves. Nashville is an exciting town for a young man, but will you come home for a visit over the hiatus?

Since the days when I read you political news reports rather than bedtime stories, I never doubted you would someday serve our country. Besides, the news was far more interesting given that I knew the characters. And, yes, I may be a bit biased, but I've known lots of senators and you are by far the finest. Someday I hope to visit you in Washington if that's where your path leads. Pride aside, I must ask why you are making the nation wait for your decision. Due to the most ironic of circumstances, yours is the deciding vote. A noble position for a noble man. But you must get on with it.

Just as I lobbied for you to clean your room and do your homework, I implore you today to be a good son. Make the right decision and ratify the 19th Amendment. I tell you with all my heart, the women of this country have waited long enough.

With love,
Mother

AUTHOR'S NOTE

One of the inspirations for this book was a letter from Febb Burn, the actual mother of the real 24-year-old Tennessee state senator Harry Burn. In the unaffected, seven-page letter, the strong-willed widow writes about the weather, the family farm, and plans for Labor Day. Then she asked that her son "be a good boy" and vote for ratification. Even though the letter is fictionalized for this book, the fact of a letter and all of the details about winning women's suffrage in 1920 are true. The suffrage amendment passed by a margin of one vote due to a mother's influence. Sometimes you just can't improve on the truth.

Read the actual letter from Febb Burn at *www.GinaMulligan .com.*

ABOUT THE AUTHOR

Gina L. Mulligan began her writing career over twenty years ago as a freelance journalist for national magazines. Her short stories are in included in the anthologies *Tudor Close: A Collection of Mystery Stories* and *Not Your Mother's Book . . . on Dogs,* and were performed at Stories on Stage Sacramento. She has won awards from the Abilene Writers Guild, San Francisco Lit-Quake, and the Soul-Making Keats Literary Competition.

After her own diagnosis, Gina founded Girls Love Mail, a charity that collects handwritten letters of encouragement for women with breast cancer. She was honored for her charitable work on the nationally syndicated television talk show *The Steve Harvey Show.*

Remember the Ladies is Gina's debut novel. To learn more or request Gina as a speaker, go to *www.GinaMulligan.com.*